THE
HANGED
MAN

Also By Simon Kernick

The Business of Dying
The Murder Exchange
The Crime Trade
A Good Day to Die
Relentless
Severed
Deadline
Target
The Last 10 Seconds
The Payback
Siege
Ultimatum
Wrong Time, Wrong Place
Stay Alive
The Final Minute
The Witness
The Bone Field

Digital Shorts
Dead Man's Gift
One By One
Flytrap

Simon Kernick

THE HANGED MAN

CENTURY

1 3 5 7 9 10 8 6 4 2

Century
20 Vauxhall Bridge Road
London SW1V 2SA

Century is part of the Penguin Random House group of companies
whose addresses can be found at global.penguinrandomhouse.com.

Penguin
Random House
UK

First published in Great Britain by Century in 2017

www.penguin.co.uk

A CIP catalogue record for this book is available from the British Library.

ISBN 9781780894478 (Hardback)
ISBN 9781780894485 (Trade Paperback)

Set in 11.75/17.25 pt Times New Roman
Typeset by Jouve (UK), Milton Keynes
Printed and bound by Clays Ltd, St Ives plc

Penguin Random House is committed to a sustainable future
for our business, our readers and our planet. This book is made
from Forest Stewardship Council® certified paper.

This one's for Max, and for all the good times in Barclye and the Galloway Forest where some of this book was written.

Prologue

Hugh Manning knew he was a marked man but he'd planned for this day for a long, long time. Fifteen years ago he'd thrown in his hat with the wrong people and from that point forward he'd been preparing for a way out. In the interim he'd made a serious amount of money. Millions. Most of which the taxman had never seen.

Right now, though, sitting in the cramped spare bedroom of the cottage he'd bought through an offshore company three years earlier, he would have given up every penny just to be able to sleep properly at night. For the last two weeks he and his wife had effectively been on the run. Diana had had an idea who he'd been working for but, even so, she'd still been shocked when he'd announced one morning that they had to leave their beloved Georgian townhouse in Bayswater for ever, with just enough luggage to fit in the car.

She hadn't liked it, of course. There'd been tears, anger and recriminations. But Diana had enjoyed the money just as much as him, and anyway there was nothing she could do about it. If she'd stayed behind, they'd have come for her too.

The plan had been to take a ferry from Felixstowe to Rotterdam using the fake passports he possessed in his and Diana's names, buy a pair of airline tickets for cash in a bucket shop, then fly from Amsterdam's Schiphol Airport to Panama City. Panama was a country neither of them had ever visited, or even researched online, so no one would come looking for them there. Manning had watched a programme on it once, though, and thought it looked a nice place to live. Even the healthcare system was world class. They'd rent a property and settle in one of the quiet towns on the Pacific coast, living comfortably on the $2.2 million he kept in a numbered bank account in the Cayman Islands until they died peacefully of old age many years down the line.

As plans went it was thorough and well thought-out, but then, like most good lawyers, Manning was a thorough man. Unfortunately, what looks great in theory can fall apart very quickly in practice, and when they'd arrived at Felixstowe there'd been some sort of security alert going on. Diana had panicked, convinced that the alert was about them, and had refused to travel. In truth Manning had panicked too, but he'd still blamed Diana for their hesitation, and now, instead of basking in the tropical sunshine of Central America, they were stuck out here in the featureless flatlands of rural Lincolnshire, waiting for the police to conclude that the two of them were dead or had fled the country and lift the all-ports alert Manning was sure they had put in place.

The Hanged Man

He was sitting at the window in the spare bedroom from where he had a good vantage point over the rolling, treeless fields, watching for Diana's car. She'd left to go shopping for supplies in Horncastle – an hour's round trip at most, but she'd been gone close to an hour and a half, and he was beginning to get anxious. Diana had never been the ideal wife and he certainly hadn't been the ideal husband. They'd lived in a state of mutual tolerance for years, and he knew she'd had at least one affair (which was about ten fewer than him), and even now, years later, she still bitterly resented the fact he'd never given her children. But right now she was the only person he had in the world, and he needed her.

The cigarette in his hand was shaking, and he drew deeply on it, trying in vain to stay calm as he blew the smoke out of the open window. He was meant to smoke outside as Diana couldn't stand the smell of it – something she never tired of telling him. Just as she never tired of telling him how she couldn't understand why he'd taken up the cigarettes again at the age of thirty-nine after ten years without them – but then she hadn't known the full extent of the depravity of the men he'd been working for, or the things he'd seen. Cigarettes had been one way of coping with the stress of his work. The other was alcohol.

He looked at his watch. 4.55 p.m. Where the hell was she? She was usually pretty efficient at the shop, being just as keen to avoid being out in public as he was. The problem was, he couldn't even phone her. Although they both carried unregistered mobile phones, the reception at the cottage, and for at least a mile around, was non-existent, so he was just going to have to sit tight. So far the authorities hadn't put out photos of either of them – and it was possible they wouldn't since there was no direct evidence linking Manning (or indeed Diana) to the crimes they wanted to question him about. After all, he was just a middleman. But if they did . . . If they did, it was going to be almost impossible to stay hidden.

And in the end, it wasn't the police he was scared of. It was the men he worked for. Because they could get to him anywhere, even in police custody. If he was caught, he was a dead man. There was no question of it.

In the background, Sky News was playing on a loop on the portable TV, with the same story dominating: the aftermath of the June Brexit vote, now a month old but still the subject of endlessly rehashed and increasingly redundant arguments, both for and against, as if any of it really mattered. But at least it kept the hunt for him off the headlines.

Manning stubbed the cigarette out in the mahogany ashtray he'd once used for his Cuban cigars, and as he looked back out of the window he saw the old red Mercedes C Class saloon he'd bought for cash at auction appear from behind the hedgerow and turn on to the long dirt track that led down to the cottage. He could make out Diana in the driver's seat, nervously hunched over the wheel – she hated driving, having got used to not doing it during the years they'd lived in London – and he felt an immediate relief that she was home. They were safe for another night at least. As soon as they'd unloaded the shopping he'd open a bottle of decent red wine and pour them both a glass.

He switched off the TV and shut the window, then went downstairs to the lounge and put some Beethoven on. As the first bars of Symphony No. 9 filled the room, he walked into the hallway.

The Hanged Man

Diana was fiddling with her key in the lock, probably trying to open it with all the shopping in her hands.

As he opened the door for her a single spasm of pure shock surged through his body because in that one moment he knew that it was all over, and that all he could hope for was that death would come quickly.

Diana was standing in front of him, trembling with fear. There were two men with her, both dressed from head to foot in the same plastic overalls that police officers wear when searching murder scenes, their faces partially obscured by surgical masks but still recognizable, which Manning knew was always a bad sign. The youngest was in his early twenties, a shock of blond curly hair poking out from beneath his plastic hood. He held a large black army knife tight against the skin of Diana's throat. A grotesque, almost childlike grin spread behind the mask.

Manning had never seen him before. He would have remembered. But the young man had the look of a true sadist.

The man standing next to him *was* familiar. Manning remembered seeing him once before, on a dark and terrible night many years earlier that was etched on his memory for ever. The man was much older now, in his sixties, but with the same strangely blank face that was hard to describe, and an unforgettable air of malevolence. He held a pistol in his hand with a long silencer attached, which he pointed at Manning's chest. Strangely, though, it wasn't the pistol that terrified Manning so much as the battered-looking briefcase the man held in his other hand. Manning dreaded to think what might be inside it.

'We've been looking for you, Mr Manning,' the gunman said

quietly. His voice was a low hiss, partly muffled by the mask, with the hint of an eastern European accent, and there was an almost playful quality to his words as if he was expecting to enjoy whatever was coming.

'I'm er . . .' Manning tried to speak but he couldn't get the words out. His mouth was dry and his legs felt weak.

Diana was whimpering quietly and a tear ran down her face, but Manning couldn't worry about her. He was too busy desperately trying to think of something to say that would stop these two men from killing them both.

The gunman nodded to the blond man, who pushed Diana into the house, still holding the knife to her throat, brushing Manning aside as he came in. The gunman came in afterwards, shutting the door behind him.

'Do you have a desk in here anywhere?' he asked.

Manning looked at him, not sure if he'd heard correctly, so the gunman repeated the question, except this time he pushed the barrel of the gun against Manning's forehead.

'Yes, yes,' Manning answered urgently, wondering what on earth they wanted a desk for. 'We do. It's in the main bedroom.'

'Take us there,' said the gunman, motioning with the gun.

Manning stole a look at Diana but she was staring straight ahead, the blond man holding her tight to his body. He was grinning like a schoolyard bully. Manning forced himself to turn away and walk slowly up the stairs knowing that, in all likelihood, he wouldn't be coming down again. He wanted to run, to fight back, to do something, but the gunman was following right behind him. If this was a movie, all it would take was for Manning to turn round, deliver a hard kick to his chest, and send him tumbling down the stairs, then he could make a break for it out of the spare bedroom window, across the conservatory roof, and down into the field beyond. He'd have to leave Diana behind, but he'd be willing to do that. If it meant saving himself.

The problem was, this wasn't a movie, and Manning was no hero.

So he did as he was told, trying to stop his body from shaking, wondering what he could say that could possibly stave off the inevitable. And all the time he cursed himself for his stupidity, and for the greed that would now be the death of them both.

The bedroom was the biggest room in the house with a large double bed and a writing desk facing the window that Manning occasionally worked at. He stopped in front of it and the gunman put down his briefcase and told him to take a seat.

'You now have two choices,' he said as Manning sat down. 'You can watch your wife die very slowly, then die slowly yourself . . .' He paused as the blond manhandled Diana into the room, threw her roughly on the bed, and stood above her with the knife. 'Or she and you can both die quickly and painlessly.'

'Please don't do this,' said Diana, sitting up on the bed.

In one swift movement the blond man slapped her hard round the head with his free hand, knocking her sideways. The suddenness of the action made Manning jump in his seat. He hated seeing violence. His employers might have been thugs but theirs was a very different world to the one he liked to inhabit. Diana fell back on the bed, crying, and he instinctively leaned forward to comfort her.

'Don't move,' snapped the gunman, and Manning immediately returned to his former position.

The gunman then addressed Diana. 'The next time you speak, or even move, my friend here will cut you with the knife. Do you understand?'

Diana nodded fearfully.

The gunman looked satisfied. 'Good.'

He leaned down and opened the briefcase, pulling out a notebook and pen, which he put on the desk in front of Manning. Next, he pulled out a half bottle of cheap whisky, placing it next to the notebook.

'Do you like whisky, Mr Manning?' he asked, taking a step back.

Manning swallowed, looking down at the floor. 'No, not really.'

'That's a pity, because you're going to have to drink the contents of that bottle in the next three minutes. If you don't, your wife loses an eye.'

'Look, we don't need to—'

'Shut up.' The words cut through the hot, still air of the room. 'I'm not interested in your feeble begging. You just have to do as I say. Now.'

The fear Manning felt in those moments was worse than anything he'd ever previously experienced, because he knew now that the gunman couldn't be reasoned with. He and Diana were going to die in this room.

He stared at the whisky bottle, ignoring Diana's anguished weeping. He couldn't face her. Not now. Not in the knowledge that what was about to happen to her was his fault.

'You've already lost thirty seconds,' said the gunman.

The Hanged Man

Manning made his decision. He picked up the bottle, unscrewed the top, and drank deeply, ignoring the fiery hit of the alcohol. If he had to die, then at least this way he'd be pissed and not really knowing what was going on.

He took two more gulps, swallowed hard, felt his eyes watering. The end of the gun barrel was barely two feet from his face. Six months earlier he'd taken a week's crash course in the Israeli martial art of Krav Maga, having wanted to learn how to defend himself in dangerous situations. One of the techniques he'd been taught was how to disarm a gunman. He'd been good. The instructor had called him a natural. He knew exactly how to get the gun off this man now. But what you could never replicate in the classes, however good they were, was the sheer limb-stiffening terror that came from having a firearm pointed at you for real.

Manning took another gulp of the whisky. The bottle was now half empty and he was beginning to feel lightheaded.

'Stop,' said the gunman. 'Put down the bottle and write the following sentence on the notepad. "I am so sorry. I cannot go on." Write it now.'

Manning put down the bottle, focused on the page in front of him, then picked up the pen and did as he was told. His handwriting, never the best in the world, looked terrible but he could make out the words and, in a way, they were very apt.

The gunman examined the page and made an approving noise before nudging the bottle towards Manning.

Manning closed his eyes and took another mouthful of the whisky, preparing himself for the end in the easiest way possible.

And then he heard a yell like a battle cry coming from Diana, and a commotion behind him as she tried to scramble off the bed. It seemed she wasn't going to die quite as easily as him.

He opened his eyes and saw that the gunman had momentarily pointed his gun towards the bed.

Without even thinking about it, Manning jumped up from the desk, his mouth still full of whisky, and grabbed the man's gun arm by the wrist, yanking it so it was pointing away from him. As the gunman swung round to face him, Manning spat the whisky straight into his eyes and shoved him backwards hard enough that he fell down on his behind, still holding on to the gun while frantically rubbing his eyes.

The blond knifeman meanwhile had grabbed Diana, pulling her backwards into his grip. She looked at Manning desperately, and he looked back at her for the briefest of moments as the knife blade punched through the pink T-shirt she was wearing – and then he was running for his life, literally jumping over the gunman, his foot making contact with his head with a satisfying whack.

Manning felt a euphoria he hadn't felt in years as he sprinted the few yards across the landing and into the spare bedroom, slamming the door behind him. He crossed the room in a moment and yanked open the back window facing on to the garden, and scrambled out.

There was a drop of about four feet on to the conservatory roof and, as the door flew open behind him, Manning jumped down, hoping the glass would hold. It did, and he scrambled down the angled roof before rolling off the end and landing feet first on the patio, impressed by his agility.

The Hanged Man

When he'd been writing the suicide letter, Manning knew the gunman wouldn't want to shoot him. He'd want to make his death look as natural as possible. But now, with him making a break for it, there'd be no such hesitation.

Without looking back, Manning raced across the patio to the line of mature laurel trees that marked the property's boundary, keeping his body low.

There was a sound like a pop, followed by the ping of a bullet ricocheting off one of the flagstones a few feet away, and Manning realized with a surreal sense of surprise that he was being shot at. He angled his run, staying low, and leaped through foliage as another shot rang out. Knowing he was temporarily sheltered by the trees, he ran alongside them until they gave way to the farmer's field at the back of the property.

Here, the wheat crop was waist high but not thick enough to hide in, so he kept running across the uneven ground, knowing that the further he got from the house the harder it would be to hit him with a bullet. One of the intruders must have travelled to the house in the back of the Mercedes, which meant they'd hijacked Diana somewhere nearby. It wouldn't have been too hard to do in an isolated area like this, where traffic was almost non-existent at the busiest of times. But it meant they had the keys to the Mercedes as well as access to the car they'd travelled up here in. It wouldn't take them long to cut him off.

Manning looked back over his shoulder. The house was now fifty yards away and there was no one following him, but as if on cue he heard the engine of the Merc starting up round the front of the cottage. He kept running, increasing his pace. A stone wall with a single line of barbed wire separated the field he was in from the next field along, where a bright yellow rapeseed crop grew. Beyond that was the road. He had to get there before they did, and figured he had three minutes at most as it was about a mile by car to the point where he was going to emerge.

He vaulted the wall, catching his wrist and leg on the barbed wire, ignoring the pain as it cut into him, and kept going through the rapeseed field. On the other side of the road he could see a small wood, little more than a few rows of trees but enough to give him cover.

Manning wasn't particularly fit. He tended to use the cross-trainer and the weights in the gym but it wasn't enough to compensate for his sedentary lifestyle, and the last time he'd had such a burning in his lungs was on day one of the Krav Maga course when he'd thrown up twice. He was panting like a dog and his hamstrings seemed to be tightening with every step as he approached the end of the second field. A large, impenetrable hawthorn hedge taller than he was stood between him and the road and he felt another spasm of fear as he realized he had no idea where the gate was. He looked round wildly and his heart sank as he saw that it was a good hundred and fifty metres away in the direction his pursuers would be coming from.

Somewhere in the distance he could hear a car. He recognized the sound of the engine.

It was them. Closing in.

Manning slowed down, suddenly crippled with indecision. There was no way he'd get to the gate before they cut him off. And yet there was no other way out. He considered turning round and running back to the house, but what if one of them had stayed behind? He had to do something. Now.

He made a snap decision, and immediately accelerated, sprinting at the hedge. As he reached it, he jumped up and grabbed at the top branches, tearing his hands on the thorns as he forced his way over it through sheer willpower, the thorns shredding his clothes. He fell down the other side, landing in the road, and looked both ways. The car wasn't in sight and, as he got up and ran into the trees and the first sign of shelter, he felt the euphoria return.

He knew this area well enough. As the trees gave way to another field, this one sloping down towards another, smaller copse at the bottom, he saw the house up ahead of him. He had no idea what he was going to do when he got there, but right now it was his only hope. He glanced back over his shoulder. He could hear the car, moving slowly and still some distance away, but the road was no longer visible, which meant they couldn't see him.

The house, a rambling detached cottage with ivy strangling it on every side, was separated from the field by a single wooden rail fence. Manning clambered over it, slowing as he ran into the back garden. He needed to hide, and plan his next move. The garden was a mess, full of tangled bushes, and an old shed, but nothing that offered effective concealment.

He stopped and listened, realizing that he could no longer hear the car. The warren of back roads, tracks and country lanes round here was chaotic and, even though he was still less than a mile away from where he'd started, his pursuers wouldn't necessarily be able to find him here.

He walked round the house, looking in the windows. Nothing moved inside and there was no car in the driveway at the front, so he tried the back door and smiled with relief as it opened into a kitchen and dining area that was filled with all kinds of junk and clutter. A pile of crockery was drying on the draining board and there were drops of water in the sink so whoever lived here hadn't been gone that long.

Manning picked up a china tea cup and poured himself a drink of water, gulping it down in one go, then wiped the sweat from his forehead with a tea towel before setting it back. His breathing was slowing down, and for the first time he thought of Diana, who by now was almost certainly dead. He hoped at least they'd made it quick, and hadn't punished her for his sins.

'I'm sorry, Pootle,' he whispered, using the pet name he'd had for her back in the early days of their relationship when life had been a lot easier. He was going to miss her. He really was. Because now he was truly on his own with just the money in his pocket and a mobile phone with no signal. Even his passport was back at the cottage, and for the moment at least that was where it was going to have to stay.

He continued into the hallway and saw a landline phone on a sideboard next to the front door. He could dial 999, surrender to the police and take his chances, and for a long minute he stood there looking at the phone before finally dismissing the thought. If he cooperated with the police for a lesser sentence, he probably wouldn't even make it to trial before his employers got to him. And if he kept his mouth shut he'd carry the rap for all kinds of crimes, and probably never see the outside of a prison again. At least for the moment he was still in control of his own destiny. He had a chance of getting out of the country and making that life for himself in Panama. It wouldn't be as much fun doing it alone but it was still considerably better than the alternatives.

His breathing was coming back to normal now and he was just contemplating his next move when there was a loud knock on the front door.

Manning froze when he saw the silhouetted head at the frosted glass of the door's small round window.

It was the gunman.

He cursed. He'd been a fool to think they wouldn't be right on his trail. These people were professionals. They weren't going to let him go that easily. And he hadn't locked the back door behind him either.

The man knocked again and Manning took a step backwards into the shadows at the bottom of the staircase – which was when he heard the sound of the back door opening.

Trying to stay as calm as possible – and Jesus, it wasn't easy – he turned and began crawling up the stairs, making himself as small a figure as possible so the man at the front door wouldn't pick up movement. The stairs were thickly carpeted and didn't creak, and he was up them in a few seconds and looking around for somewhere to hide. The door in front of him led into the bathroom but there was never going to be anywhere suitable in there so he doubled back on himself and crossed the landing, darting into what looked like a junk room, before closing the door gently behind him.

He looked around. The room contained a single bed covered in boxes of junk, with more boxes littering the floor, and an old ceiling-high dressing cupboard covered in scratches. He could hear movement downstairs. They were in the house now and it wouldn't be long before they came up. He needed to think fast.

He went over to the old-fashioned sash window and stared out. It was a long drop to the ground, further than he could jump without risking injury. But what choice did he have? The first place they'd look for him was the cupboard. Unless . . .

He glanced down at one of the boxes on the floor, a large, heavy-looking wooden chest, and a thought suddenly occurred to him.

Slowly he prised open the sash window until it was fully extended and the gap wide enough to climb out of, then he opened the chest. It was full of old clothes, and what looked like a whole curtain.

He was sure he could hear someone coming up the stairs now, imagined that gun with the silencer attached. And the knife . . . the knife with the black blade he'd last seen slicing through Diana's T-shirt, and which he knew could eviscerate him in seconds.

Moving as quietly as he could, he emptied the chest of clothes, placing them on to a pile of books stacked up in one corner. There still wasn't a lot of space left but, probably for the first time in his life, Manning was thankful that he was only five feet seven, because he was small enough to squeeze inside. He pulled his knees up so high it felt like they were breaking, grabbed the chain attached to the lid and brought it down – and then cursed. The lid almost shut but not quite, leaving an inch-wide gap. But there was nothing he could do about it now because almost with his next breath he heard the soft bump of footfalls outside on the landing.

He quieted his breathing, trying without success to force himself down and allow the lid to close, until he heard the sound of the door to the junk room slowly opening.

Then he stopped breathing altogether.

Through the gap he watched as a man came into the room. He could only see his legs but recognized the jeans as belonging to the blond knifeman with the malicious smile.

Manning swallowed, the terror he was experiencing so intense it was like every bone in his body had turned to ice.

The legs stopped at the window and, as the blond man crouched down to put his head out to look, Manning saw the razor-sharp tip of the knife in his gloved hand. He heard the man curse in a London accent and turn away. Next the man opened the cupboard, before going down on his hands and knees to look under the bed.

Manning could see him clearly now. He was barely three feet away. The moment he stood back up he was going to see the not-quite-closed chest right in front of him. He'd lift the lid, see Manning inside, and drive the knife into him. Again and again.

It took all his willpower not to cry out. He could hear his heart hammering in his chest and was sure that any second now the other man was going to hear it too.

The blond man rose, and Manning could see him turning towards his hiding place, imagined him spying the chest and smiling that malicious smile . . .

He began to shake. *Please make it quick. Please make it quick.*

The legs were now right in front of the box, and Manning held his breath as the man bent his knees as he reached down to open the chest.

It was all over.

Four Days Later

One

Picture the scene. You're at an isolated farm in the middle of the Welsh countryside. You know a young woman has been taken there by men who are going to rape and kill her. You're certain you know who these men are. You're also certain that they've killed women like this before a number of times, and yet you have no real evidence against them.

In one of the farm's outhouses you discover huge vats of acid that will be used to dissolve her body when they've finished with her, just as they've dissolved the bodies of the others. You investigate further and discover a windowless cellar with occult signs on the walls that you've seen at other crime scenes associated with these men.

Like a modern-day knight in shining armour, you rescue the young woman in a blaze of glory, arrest the perpetrators, and now, thanks to your detective work and personal bravery, you have enough evidence to put them away for mass murder for the rest of their miserable lives.

End of story.

Except, of course, that wasn't how it happened.

I found the farmhouse all right, but the men I wanted were nowhere to be seen. Instead, the place was guarded by some of their associates and in the ensuing gunfight three of them were killed, as was the young woman who'd been taken there, and the whole place was burned to the ground. I managed to get out in one piece, but it might have been easier if I hadn't because I got no thanks for what I'd done, even though over the course of the next month the mostly dissolved remains of a further seven women were dug up in the grounds, with the strong likelihood of there being more victims whose remains had dissolved altogether, leaving no trace of their existence behind.

The place was dubbed 'The Bone Field' in the media, which might not have been particularly original but was certainly a fitting description. The clamour for arrests was massive, but although I might have been certain who the main perpetrators were, any physical evidence linking them to the farmhouse was destroyed when it burned down, and these were clever people with money and influence. They'd been killing for a long time and they knew how to cover their tracks.

To complicate matters further, even now, three months later, none of the people who'd died at the Bone Field had been identified, even the woman I'd tried and failed to rescue, who was an illegal immigrant I knew only as Nicole. Of the three men killed in the gunfight at the farm, two were local guys who'd clearly been paid in cash for their services, as no record of any bank payments to either of them existed, and the other was a north London thug with links to organized crime. The problem was, none of them were going to be talking any time soon.

In the end the only lead was the farm itself. It turned out the property had been bought by an offshore company based in the Cayman Islands in 1996. So, Dyfed-Powys Police, whose jurisdiction the case fell in, brought in us, the National Crime Agency, to find out who owned the shell company. But the world of offshore finance is anything but open and transparent, and of course the shell company was owned by another shell company based in the Isle of Man, which in turn was owned by another one in Liechtenstein, and so on. The trail went round the world several times because that's how it goes when people are trying to put as much distance between themselves and their transactions as possible. If you've got big money, and access to good lawyers, then there are plenty of places to hide.

The good news, though, is that there are only so many layers you can put in place, and if the people hunting you are determined enough, and have enough resources – and with a high-profile case like this, where there was the potential for government embarrassment, we definitely had the resources – then eventually they'll peel them all away until they find a real live person at the end.

And that's what we'd finally found. A real person. A London-based lawyer who was a nominee shareholder in a Bermuda-based outfit that had made a large payment into the chain in 2015. The company had now been shut down, but that didn't matter. There was a record of a payment and that's all we needed to put the pressure on him.

But Hugh Manning was no fool. He'd worked out that one day either we or his employers would come for him, and when we'd knocked down the front door of his stratospherically priced Bayswater townhouse, a week ago now, he and his wife Diana had already upped sticks and gone, leaving both their cars and their passports behind. Since then they'd gone completely off grid, and the suspicion was they'd already left the country, using fake ID. There'd been a lot of debate about whether to publish Manning's photo in the media but, because he wasn't considered a suspect in the killings themselves and the evidence against him for even indirect involvement was limited at best (plus, of course, he was a lawyer and therefore might sue), the decision had been made up top not to, which hadn't helped us much. But that's the Brass for you. Their main priority is usually covering their arses.

The thing about criminals, though, is that it doesn't matter how clever or careful they are, they will always make at least one mistake, and I can tell you from years of experience that there are no exceptions to this rule, which is why most of us stay in the job. Manning's mistake had been a very minor one, but it was enough. A few years back he'd bought a cottage in north Lincolnshire through – you've guessed it – a network of offshore shell companies, and because we had no idea the property existed, we almost certainly wouldn't have been able to find it. Unfortunately for Manning, two years ago he'd needed some emergency plumbing work done at the cottage and his wife had paid for it with one of her personal credit cards. When we'd gone back through all the statements from their various accounts, we'd found that transaction, phoned the plumbing company, and got the address.

And so here we were in the middle of the rural flatlands of the Lincolnshire Wolds, my colleague and I, looking for the cottage.

The man I was with was Dan Watts – or Dapper Dan as he was occasionally called. A short, bald and worryingly good-looking black man with the build of a welterweight boxer, which is what he'd been in his youth until he'd put an opponent in a coma from which he'd never emerged. After that, the story went that Dan had been racked with guilt, and vowed never to box again. He'd turned to the bottle first and then, when that didn't work, to God and a career in the police force.

I'd known him since my days working organized crime more than a decade back, but we'd lost touch until three months ago when our paths crossed in the Bone Field case. Now, with me exonerated of wrongdoing and back from suspension, we were working together properly for the first time, and for that I owed Dan. I've never been the easiest of cops to work with, and I've queered my pitch with plenty of bosses, but Dan had specifically requested my presence in the NCA to assist him, and clearly he had a little bit of clout because someone had stuck their neck out and said yes.

I was driving, and I slowed the car as we passed the narrow track leading down to the cottage. We could see the front of Hugh Manning's driveway.

There was a grimy red Mercedes C Class saloon parked out front.

'I think that's our car,' said Dan, 'but the plates are filthy, so I can't confirm.'

Filthy, unreadable licence plates. Always a useful tool for criminals hoping to outwit the network of ANPR cameras that cover the UK's roads.

I couldn't see anyone in the cottage's windows, but I sped up anyway, not wanting to draw attention to ourselves. I was now sure Manning, and presumably his wife too, were in residence. You see, during the search for them we'd also gained access to Manning's phone records, using them to trace his movements over the previous six months. He'd turned off the phone ten days ago and it hadn't been used since, but in the weeks before that he'd visited a south London car auction house three times, so it was clear he was in the market for a vehicle, and one that wouldn't be traced back to him. When we'd checked with the auction house, there was no record of a man with Manning's name buying a car, but I was pretty certain he had, and thankfully, like most other places in the UK, they had CCTV cameras on site. We ran through footage from the camera at the payment booth the last time Manning had been there, and sure enough there he was, blissfully unaware that he was being filmed, filling out the paperwork and handing over the cash and his fake ID – a passport in the name of Mr Simon Hearn. A quick cross-reference of purchases made at that time had established that Mr Hearn had bought an eleven-year-old Mercedes saloon, the same model sitting outside the cottage now, for eight grand. And because of its filthy plates we hadn't been able to track its movements.

I had to admit, as criminals went, Hugh Manning was one of

the better ones I'd come across in my seventeen years in law enforcement. Unfortunately, that wasn't going to be of much help to him now.

Fifty metres further along the road, and just out of sight of the cottage, was a lay-by at the entrance to a farmer's field, partially obscured by a pile of freshly dug parsnips so big you could have run a helter skelter down it. I parked there.

I stretched as I got out of the car. It had been a three-and-a-half-hour drive up here from the NCA's offices on the South Bank and we'd done it without stopping. We hadn't called ahead to alert our colleagues in the Lincolnshire force either. There were two reasons for this. First off, there was no guarantee the Mannings were here, so why worry them? Secondly, if the Mannings were indeed in residence, we didn't want them getting spooked and making a hasty exit before we arrived. I guess in the end we didn't trust our colleagues to make an effective arrest.

'This is a good place to stay anonymous,' said Dan, looking round at the fields stretching off in all directions.

It was a sunny late morning and the only sounds were the cawing of crows in the trees overhead.

'I like it here,' I said, taking in the fresh country air, only vaguely tinged with the ripe smell of manure. 'It's a good escape from the city. I could retire in a place like this.'

Dan shook his head and grinned. 'You know, for a man who's not even forty yet, you sound very old sometimes.'

I shrugged, and we walked fast in the direction of the cottage, keeping close to the hedge that ran along one side of the road so we couldn't be spied approaching. Neither of us was armed – it wasn't that kind of op – and we weren't expecting any resistance, given that Manning was a pen pusher by trade and didn't have any history of violence. I'd seen he'd recently taken a crash course in Krav Maga though, and he was going to be pretty desperate not to fall into our hands, so I was still feeling a little pumped as we rounded the corner and walked down the track towards the front door.

'I don't like this,' said Dan, who, for a Christian, had a very suspicious nature. 'It's already twenty-five degrees out here and all the windows are shut.'

'Maybe they've gone for a walk. It is a nice day.' I was hoping they hadn't. I didn't fancy a long wait. But the car was here so I was certain they weren't far away. 'Or maybe they're just very security conscious.'

As I spoke, I pulled a thin pocket knife from my jeans, leaned down and, without stopping, drove the blade into the Merc's nearside tyres, one after the other, just to make sure it wasn't going anywhere.

Dan gave me a disapproving look. He didn't always like my methods, such as vandalizing a suspect's car, but on this occasion he chose not to say anything.

We took up positions – him at the back, me at the front – and I knocked hard on the door. It wasn't a big cottage so if the Mannings were at home they would have heard me. But there was no answer.

I knocked a second time, then opened the letterbox. And that was when I caught a whiff that I recognized immediately. Human death has a peculiar and unmistakable scent, best described as a combination of rancid meat and slowly rotting apples, that's different to that of every other dead animal, except apparently pigs. You didn't have to be Sherlock Holmes to realize we were too late. But I needed to make sure, so I donned a pair of plastic gloves and got to work on the single five-lever mortise lock, which wasn't as new and state-of-the-art as I thought it would be. I'm not the best lock picker in the world but I'm competent, which was more than can be said for the lock, and I had the door open in under three minutes.

I called Dan.

'I was looking in the back window,' he said, coming round to the front of the house. 'There are a lot of flies in there and not much else.'

I told him about the smell. 'I've got a feeling the Mannings have had visitors before us. Do you want to call it in?'

He shook his head. 'No. Let's take a look inside first.'

I pushed open the door and the stench hit us both with a warm blast. Whoever was in there had been dead a while, which meant the people we were up against were operating with a lot better intelligence than we had, and that's never a good sign.

We found her in the bedroom just by following the smell. A well-built woman in her mid-forties dressed in a pink Superdry T-shirt, cut-off denim shorts and espadrilles. She was lying sprawled out face-up on the bed, her arms out to her sides in an almost religious gesture. The body was already bloated from the gases created by the bacteria burrowing away inside her, and her face and neck had turned a discoloured green like pond slime as the body steadily putrified. I'm no pathologist but I know enough about dead bodies to work out she'd been dead at least three days. Even so, as I approached the bed, disturbing the hundreds of flies on the corpse, she was still just about recognizable as Diana Manning. There were five bloodied gashes consistent with knife wounds in the T-shirt close to her heart, and a sixth wound to her belly, but not a lot of blood, which suggested she'd died quickly. My guess was that the killer had stabbed her in the belly to weaken her then, very shortly afterwards – probably in the next few seconds, judging by the absence of blood spatters anywhere else on the bed – had sat on top of her, pinning her to the bed, and finished her off with the knife blows to the heart. All of which suggested he knew what he was doing.

'There's a note here,' said Dan, who'd stopped by a desk on the other side of the room.

I turned away from Diana Manning's body, no longer wanting to look at it. It reminded me too much of my own mortality. 'What does it say?'

'It's a suicide note. It says "I am so sorry. I cannot go on." The notebook's brand new, looks like it's never been used before. No tear stains, no marks, nothing on it. And he hasn't even bothered finishing the whisky. I think if I was sitting a few feet away from my wife of fifteen years I'd just murdered, and I couldn't go on any more, I'd drain the booze so I could forget what I'd just done, and get the strength to do what I had to do next.'

'Yeah,' I said, looking round. 'And that's the problem. Where is he?'

Manning's body was nowhere in the house. We checked everywhere.

In truth, we should have called it in then and there. The rules are simple. If you discover a body, especially if you think foul play is involved, you leave the scene immediately so as not to contaminate it, call in the local CID, and let them set the murder inquiry in motion. But as members of the NCA we were here in an advisory capacity only, and I didn't want to miss anything before I handed it over to the Lincolnshire force. I've never been very good at delegating.

'So what do you think happened here?' I asked Dan once we'd done a first pass of the house and were having a last look at the main bedroom.

'It's a set-up,' he said. 'A Kalaman job.'

The Kalamans. It was a name few people had heard of, yet by any measure they were London's most successful and secretive organized crime outfit. They'd been operating for close to fifty years and had contacts everywhere, including at various levels within the police force, and both Dan and I were absolutely certain that the current head of the family, Cem Kalaman, was one of the men responsible for the murders of the girls at the farm in Wales.

'They've done this sort of thing before,' continued Dan. 'I told you about that case a few years back when a freelance investigative journalist wrote a pretty explosive piece about Cem Kalaman. His lawyers slapped an injunction on the journalist and the newspaper that was going to print the story, and three months later the journalist was found dead in the bath with his wrists slashed. His girlfriend was there too, beaten to death with an iron. No history of violence in the relationship, none of the neighbours heard anything, and the verdict was murder/suicide. That's what they're trying to do here. Deflect attention.'

I nodded. 'I'd go with that. Whoever killed Diana Manning didn't do it in a fit of passion or anger. It was quick and professional.' I looked round the bedroom. 'And this place is way too tidy. There's no sign of a struggle, and the surfaces have been freshly wiped down, unlike the rest of the house. The only problem's the obvious one. If this was meant to look like a murder/ suicide, then why the hell isn't Manning here?'

Dan didn't say anything. He was as puzzled as I was.

It was only when we were doing a final check of the house, just in case we'd missed something obvious, that we spotted it. Well, that's not quite right. It was Dan who saw the dirty marks on the conservatory roof. I missed them completely. To be fair, they were only just visible – you had to look pretty closely – and Dan was staring out of the spare bedroom window at the time.

When we opened the window we could see from the concentrations of dirt that they were partial footprints – two together facing towards the house and two more about four feet apart pointed towards the edge of the roof.

I looked at Dan. 'I can't think what the killers would be doing running along this roof away from the house, so this must be Manning. He made a break for it.'

Dan looked surprised. 'If that's the case then he's got more balls than most lawyers I've come across. The Kalamans don't usually make mistakes. I wonder if he got away.'

I stared out across the empty fields. There were no buildings in sight and, aside from a road in the distance, no sign of human habitation or activity – a welcome change from what I was used to in London but a real challenge for a forty-eight-year-old office worker like Manning who was fleeing on foot from violent killers.

'Jesus, I hope so,' was all I said, because the alternative – that the man who was our only real lead after three months of investigation was dead – didn't bear thinking about.

Two

The SIO from the Lincolnshire force was a very tall, studious-looking fellow, no more than thirty-five, with a marked stoop and a naturally morose face. He sighed loudly as he came over to introduce himself to Dan and me, as if our presence was an irritation, which to be fair it probably was. An hour had passed since we'd called in the locals and the day was getting hotter as it ran into the afternoon.

'I'm DCI Gibson,' he said. He looked at me. 'I recognize you. You're Ray Mason.'

I put out a hand and we shook. 'That's right.'

'I thought you were suspended.'

'I've been reinstated.'

'Yes,' he said, frowning. 'So I see.'

I often have this effect on people, even some of my fellow

police officers. Because I've been in the news more than once these past few years, a lot of people know who I am. At least they think they do. To them, I'm an independently wealthy cop with a shadowy past and a pretty controversial present. An air of something not being quite right has always hung over me. There have been allegations of corruption, mental health issues relating to a very public childhood trauma, even extra-judicial killings. And although no wrongdoing has ever been proven, plenty of mud seems to have stuck. And some people – and I guess I'm including DCI Gibson here – don't like that.

He looked down at Dan, who was a good eight inches shorter than him, like a headmaster addressing a pupil. 'And you are?'

Dan gave him a look that suggested they weren't going to get on. 'Officer Dan Watts. NCA.'

Gibson seemed surprised. 'So what's the National Crime Agency doing here?'

Dan and I had already agreed that, like it or not, we were going to have to come clean, so he told him about the dead woman's husband and his connection to the Bone Field case.

This perked up Gibson's interest, as it was always going to. The whole country was interested in the murders, which had been a constant feature in the media these past three months. 'But how are you so certain he wasn't involved? His wife's dead in there with stab wounds and there's a note next to her body which matches handwriting found elsewhere in the house, and which looks as if it was written by her husband.'

This was why Gibson was a DCI. He was no fool. He had a

point too. Why couldn't Manning have killed his wife? But we knew he hadn't.

'We think it's a set-up,' I said.

'Carried out by who?'

'Look, this isn't for public consumption, DCI Gibson, but we think the ultimate owner of the house in Wales is a major criminal called Cem Kalaman.'

'Never heard of him.'

'You wouldn't have done. But we believe that he, and several other men whose names we don't yet know for sure, are the ones who killed Mrs Manning.'

'So why not bring him in for questioning?'

'It doesn't work like that,' said Dan. 'The guy's surrounded by lawyers.'

Gibson let slip half a smile. 'Well, he's got one less now.'

'That's certainly true,' I told Gibson, 'but sadly there's no shortage of lawyers in the world, and it still leaves him with far too many. The problem we have – and you have too, now – is that Cem Kalaman is the head of a business empire worth several billion pounds, and he likes to use other people to do his dirty work. I bet you he's never been within a hundred miles of this place.'

'We think he sent people up here to kill Manning and his wife and make it look like a murder/suicide,' continued Dan. 'It's something they've done before. But it looks like Manning was a bit quicker on his feet than they'd been expecting and got away.' He told Gibson about the footprints on the conservatory roof.

Gibson exhaled. 'So you think he's out here somewhere?'

We both shrugged.

'More likely than not,' I said. 'We've already got tracks on his credit cards and phones so we can help you find him that way.'

'Have you got any idea who your friend Kalaman would use for a job like this?'

'No,' said Dan. 'But he's got no shortage of muscle.'

Gibson rolled his eyes. 'Great. Well, I'll get the place taken apart for forensics, and I've already got officers doing house-to-house enquiries, but' – he looked grimly round at the flat expanse of land in all directions – 'I don't think we've got much chance of finding witnesses. It feels like this one's got "unsolved" written all over it.'

I was about to comment when a female cop in plain clothes came over and interrupted us. Gibson excused himself and they stood talking in a close huddle along with another older plain-clothes guy. The DCI returned a few minutes later, looking grim-faced.

'We've found another body,' he said.

The body was at the house of the nearest neighbour, just under a mile away. Two uniformed officers had knocked on the front door, and when there'd been no answer one of them had done exactly what I'd done earlier at the cottage and peered inside the letterbox – which was when she was hit by the smell, just as I had been. She'd also seen a figure on the floor, which was enough for her to raise the alarm.

Fifteen minutes later, decked out in protective coveralls so we couldn't contaminate the scene, Dan and I, along with DCI Gibson, were directed through the back door of the property by a uniformed officer standing guard. The forensic teams weren't on site yet and we were able to walk unimpeded through the kitchen and into the hallway, again simply following the smell. I had a strong sense of foreboding, which turned to puzzlement as I approached the body.

The victim was propped up against the front door. His legs were splayed outwards on the floor and there were two large bloodstains on his shirt. A long line of dried blood ran from his mouth to his shirt collar.

I turned to Gibson, who was standing a few feet behind me and Dan, next to the body of a big black Labrador.

'This isn't Manning,' I told him. 'It's someone else.'

Three

In those few terrible seconds during which the blond man bent down and started to lift the lid of the chest in which he was hiding, Hugh Manning had been so terrified that he'd completely lost control of his bodily functions. Urine had begun streaming into his underpants, and he'd felt his bowels loosen, releasing a small, silent fart. Crouched in the foetal position, he'd reverted to being a baby.

But the blond man had stopped. Instead, Manning had heard the sound of the front door of the house opening, and a dog barking.

The killer had cursed, dropped the lid, and run from the room.

Manning had heard a man whose voice he didn't recognize say indignantly 'Who are you?' then cry out in real fear – probably as he saw the gun the second man had with him. A series of pops had followed, like champagne corks being released, and the man had cried out again, this time in pain.

After that, for a few seconds everything had been silent. Manning had exhaled, his earlier fear giving way to a sense of hope. He could hear the two men talking quietly downstairs. He hadn't been able to make out what they were saying but their tone was urgent. Their operation had obviously gone wrong, and it was unlikely they could afford to hang around much longer. Manning had thought about moving his hiding place. The blond man had already searched the cupboard so if he hid in there he was probably safe, whereas if he stayed here he was still at risk. Or maybe he should just wait?

So that's what he did. He'd never been the most patient of men so he'd forced himself to stay in the chest by counting the seconds in his head. Only when he'd got to two thousand did he lift the lid and heave himself out.

The house had been completely silent. Even so, he'd still listened for a long time before creeping to the top of the staircase and peering over the banister.

Which was when he'd seen the bodies of the man by the door and his dog at the foot of the stairs. He'd never seen a dead body before but, in that typically British way, it was the sight of the dog lying there, its head covered in blood, that had truly shocked him. It was a black Lab, like Caesar, the old family dog he'd had as a kid.

But he'd got over it fast enough because, as soon as he'd ascertained that the house was empty, he'd begun to formulate a plan.

The Hanged Man

And now, four days later, Hugh Manning was very much alive and well and sitting in the living room of a converted barn on the edge of southern Scotland's picturesque Galloway Forest, over two hundred miles across country. The barn belonged to an old university friend of his with the ridiculous but very memorable name of Harry Pheasant. Harry didn't know Manning was here, of course. No one did. But he and Harry had visited the place together with another friend of Harry's a couple of years back, ostensibly for a long weekend of walking and shooting but which had instead degenerated into a lot of drinking and not much else. However, throughout the weekend Harry had made a point of telling Manning that he could come up and use the place whenever he wanted, as long as he put money in the log kitty. He'd even shown him where the spare key was kept. So, right now, Manning was simply taking him at his word, although he had no intention of putting any money in the log kitty. He needed every penny he had.

The journey there had been long and indirect. Manning had remained in the cottage for the rest of the night along with its owner and the dog, not daring to leave in case his pursuers were still in the vicinity. He'd half expected the man's wife to turn up at some point, as there were photos of the two of them together dotted around upstairs, but she didn't. No one did, and he'd spent the night on the floor underneath the spare bed well out of sight (just in case), and slept surprisingly soundly considering his situation, location, and the fact that there were bodies beginning to go off only yards away.

The next morning he'd woken early and, feeling more

confident, had ventured downstairs. The owner's body was still by the front door. He was a long, thin man in his mid-fifties, his hair grey and beginning to thin, but who, even in death, looked like he'd spent a lot of his life outside. There was less blood than Manning had expected and he was surprised at how little it bothered him to crouch down and go through the man's pockets until he found both his wallet and car keys. His phone was in there too but Manning left that. He already had a phone.

This had been the second mistake his pursuers had made – leaving the man's car keys behind and therefore giving Manning a means of escape. He'd always thought of his employers as almost omnipotent, and he was pleased now to be proved wrong.

He'd then explored the rest of the house. It hadn't taken him long to work out that its owner, identified by his driving licence as Max Bradshaw, lived alone. All the photos of him and his wife (and there were a lot of them) were at least ten years old. There were no other photos with kids, or friends, just a couple of the dog. For some reason he wasn't able to explain, Manning had checked the dog's collar and found out that his name was Monty.

He felt sorry for Bradshaw and Monty, and also partly responsible for their deaths, but took some comfort in the fact they'd died together and without, in Bradshaw's case, having to think about it too much. If there was a God, then Bradshaw would be joining his wife, whom Manning was pretty sure had died: you didn't keep that many photos of someone who'd run off with the postman. Unfortunately he was also certain there wasn't a God, otherwise men like his employers wouldn't exist.

He'd made a cup of tea in Bradshaw's kitchen while he

contemplated his next move. Manning had spent enough time around criminals to work out how both they and the people who hunted them worked. His two pursuers would have been long gone by now. Having committed two murders in separate locations – he knew they would have killed Diana – it would be far too risky to remain in the vicinity given that they knew the police were after him as well.

The good thing was, the police wouldn't turn up here and find Bradshaw's body for a while – it didn't seem to Manning like the poor guy would be much missed – and this meant that Manning could make use of his car and credit cards for a day or two at least while he came up with a longer-term plan. This was all good of course, but he still needed cash and his passport, both of which were back at the cottage he'd fled the previous day.

The thought of going back there had scared the crap out of him, just in case he was wrong about Blondie and the gunman, and they were there waiting for him. Once again he'd actually been tempted to pick up the phone and give himself up to the police. He'd even had the mobile in his hand at one point, but he'd finally rejected the idea. He'd come this far and he had to keep going.

So it had been with a rapidly beating heart that he went back to the cottage later that morning, crossing the same fields he'd sprinted along the previous day, this time keeping close to the hedgerows to avoid detection. He'd watched the house from behind the laurel trees at the bottom of the garden until he was certain it was empty before letting himself in through the back door.

He'd let out a gasp when he saw what they'd done to Diana.

He'd thought that seeing Bradshaw's body at close quarters would have prepared him for this, but it was so much worse. His wife, the only woman he'd ever loved – or at least only one of four he'd ever loved – had been lying on the bed cut up and dead. Her last moments must have been a living hell, and Manning knew that he was responsible. He wasn't usually the type of man who felt guilt, but he'd felt it then. Guilt and sadness that he'd lost the last person who cared about him in this world.

Hurrying across the room, he'd opened the wardrobe doors and removed a panel at the back behind several pairs of Diana's shoes to reveal a small electronic safe. He'd typed in the code and pulled out his fake passport, as well as eight grand in sterling and two thousand euros, stuffing the money into his waistband, having neglected to bring a carrier bag. He'd left Diana's passport in the safe before relocking it and putting everything back in place.

As he'd walked back out of the room, he'd glanced over at the suicide note on the desk, considering whether to take it with him or not, but deciding to leave it behind, thinking it would probably confuse the police when they turned up here, which would be no bad thing.

Manning was fully aware that the full resources of the state would now be after him and that they'd also be looking for a fall guy for the Bone Field killings. He'd had absolutely nothing to do with that, and had been as shocked as anyone when the news had broken about what had happened at the isolated farm in mid-Wales. At first he hadn't even realized that a company linked to his employers (and indirectly to him) owned it. One of his jobs was to keep the properties and businesses his employers owned hidden from the view of the authorities, but there were so many of them and they were in so many places there was no way he could remember them all. It was only when it was announced on TV that the police were having difficulty establishing who owned the farm that it had dawned on him that the murders were probably something to do with his employers. He knew from experience that they were capable of some terrible things, which was why he'd been planning his exit from the business for a long time. Even so, he hadn't quite appreciated the depths they were prepared to plumb until he'd trawled back through all the paperwork and established the link between the Bone Field, his employers and, most importantly of all, himself.

Back at Max Bradshaw's house, he'd fired up the man's PC and scoured Google Maps. There were a number of large towns and cities within a hundred miles of his location where he could seek shelter. He picked Leeds. He had no ties there and it was big enough to swallow him easily. Using his untraceable mobile, he'd called a Premier Inn in the city, making a booking for that night using Bradshaw's credit card. He'd then made a second booking at the Ibis in Hull city centre, just to confuse things.

In the end he'd stayed at neither hotel but had parked Bradshaw's car in a multi-storey car park in Leeds city centre, found a back-street guesthouse half a mile away, and paid in cash for a two-night stay.

He'd only stayed for one night before remembering Harry Pheasant's place and the possibilities it offered. He'd driven up there immediately, stopping only briefly at a lay-by on the A66 near Penrith to rub dirt on both the front and back number plates of Bradshaw's old Volvo estate in an effort to make it harder to be identified by the ANPR cameras.

It would have been a real bastard if, by some unfortunate coincidence, Harry had actually been in residence, given how he'd always complained he never got to use the place, but thankfully the house had been empty when he'd turned up and the key was in the same place.

So here he was now, lying low, bloodied but unbowed, with plenty of provisions and Harry's ample stock of decent red wine to keep him going, while he pondered his next move.

The summer sun was high in the sky as he looked out of the window down towards the narrow fast-flowing river at the end of the field opposite. Beside him, leaning against the sofa, was one of the two shotguns Harry kept – a three-shot pump-action Remington. It was loaded and ready to fire, and it made Manning feel safe whenever he looked at it. He knew he couldn't stay here for ever but for now he'd shaken off both the bad guys and the good, and as he took a sip from his coffee and contemplated his first glass of wine of the evening, for this at least he was grateful.

Four

Before we left him, DCI Gibson, the Lincolnshire SIO, said that he'd appreciate our input every step of the way, before emphasizing that this was his case, not ours. He looked pleased to be heading up a double murder case, especially one with a fugitive involved, but I had no doubt he'd be calling for our help pretty quickly.

I told him that we were there in an advisory capacity only to offer what support we could. But this was bullshit. This was my case. It always had been. My whole life, not just my career, hung on bringing down Cem Kalaman and the others responsible not only for the killings of the women at the farm in Wales, but for other murders too, because I knew that Kalaman and his associates had been preying on young women for a long, long time.

Just over three months earlier the remains of two missing persons had been unearthed in the grounds of a boarding school in Buckinghamshire during excavation work. One was a thirteen-year-old girl called Dana Brennan who'd been abducted from a quiet country road near her house in the summer of 1989. I think she was their first victim.

The other remains belonged to twenty-one-year-old graduate Kitty Sinn. Kitty's case had been a cause célèbre. She'd been reported missing in Thailand in August 1990 by her boyfriend, a man called Henry Forbes, and there hadn't been a single sighting of her alive since then, even though there'd been huge media coverage both in the UK and abroad. For more than a quarter of a century her disappearance had been an enduring mystery, and the mystery had only deepened when her remains were discovered more than six thousand miles away from where she'd last been seen.

Henry Forbes told me that he knew what had happened to Kitty and who'd killed her, but he too had been killed before he'd named names, and it was my hunt for those names, and for evidence linking them to their crimes, that had led me all the way to that farm in mid-Wales.

The evidence I'd been looking for may have been destroyed in the flames that had gutted the farm and its surrounding buildings but even so I'd managed to identify the three people I believed had been directly involved in the murders.

Of the three, the key player was Cem Kalaman, a lifelong career criminal but one with a great deal of clout. He provided the protection, the muscle and the resources to keep the killings a secret. If no one knew the victims were missing, or even who they were, then no one cared.

The second player was Alastair Sheridan. A hugely successful hedge fund manager with a net worth of some fifty million pounds, he'd spent a year at the same university as Kalaman, although that was the only connection I had between them so far. Alastair was also Kitty Sinn's first cousin, and had been a direct beneficiary of her death.

The third and perhaps most interesting of the three was Alastair Sheridan's sister Lola, a reclusive artist. I say interesting because I couldn't understand her reasons for being involved. The killers liked to think of themselves as being in some kind of satanic cult, and they even had their own sign, a pentacle with an 'M' running through the middle; but, as far as I could make out, the motive for the murders (with the possible exception of Kitty's) was sexual. Now I'm aware, having been a police officer for over fifteen years, that there are women out there who get their kicks from violently sexually assaulting other women, but their numbers are very few.

The real problem we had, though, was lack of evidence. Nothing so far linked any of the three to the house in Wales, or indeed to any of the murders I suspected them of. That didn't mean I wasn't certain they were the ones responsible. I would have bet my life on it. Dan, I'm pretty sure, would have done too. We had plenty of snippets of information to back up our claims but nothing that would have a chance of standing up in court. Neither Cem Kalaman, Alastair Sheridan or Lola Sheridan was even named as a suspect in the main police inquiry.

But the point was, I knew. And I'd made a solemn promise to Dana Brennan's parents that I'd bring her killers to justice, whatever it took. And nothing had changed.

One way or another I would.

Five

The central offices of the National Crime Agency, supposedly the UK's answer to the FBI, was a dreary-looking block a few hundred metres south of London's Vauxhall Bridge. After a battle through the inevitable traffic, Dan and I finally arrived back at just after five p.m.

The boss was waiting for us and immediately convened a meeting in her office.

Sheryl Trinder was a small, wiry, severe-looking black woman who looked like she spent the bulk of her leisure time doing fifty-mile bike rides, which apparently was exactly what she did – not that she spent a great deal of time at leisure. She'd forced her way into her current position through a combination of hard work, sheer force of will, and a nose for being in the right place at the right time, and she was one of those ambitious political types who wouldn't stop until she got to the top. As such, she was very well organized, hard as nails, and someone who didn't suffer fools gladly. She wasn't an especially good detective but then she didn't necessarily need to be in her position. There were others who could do that for her. People tended to love Sheryl or hate her. Dan was in the latter camp, considering her far too interfering. Having only worked for her for barely a month, I'd yet to make up my mind. But as she glared across her outsized desk at us, a particularly severe expression on her face, I didn't think I was likely to be ending up going down the love route.

'So,' she said, drawing out the word like an accusation as Dan finished apprising her of our day so far, 'what's happened to Manning?'

Dan took a deep breath, trying and failing to keep the note of defeat out of his voice. 'We don't know, ma'am. Lincolnshire are doing a search of the whole area but so far they haven't found any trace of him. The second victim is Max Bradshaw, and his car's missing. We think the killer or killers tracked down Manning to Bradshaw's house, and Bradshaw must have come in and disturbed them. We think Manning escaped.'

Sheryl tapped the nib of her pen on the desktop with just a little bit too much force. 'He's obviously more resourceful than we thought,' she said. 'How long have the victims been dead for?'

'The doc says three to four days,' said Dan reluctantly.

This really pissed her off, as we both knew it would.

'How on earth did the people who killed his wife get to him before us?' she asked.

'It's the Kalamans,' I said. 'They've got good contacts.'

Sheryl gave me an icy glare. 'I know that. But this is hugely embarrassing to us. We're supposed to be the people with the resources and intelligence to track down anyone. We're the ones everyone comes to for our expertise, and we're being beaten at our own game by the ones we're meant to be after. You get the picture, don't you?'

We both nodded.

'You're in charge of the NCA's Kalaman team, Mr Watts. And Mr Mason here is the man you insisted you needed to help you, even though I had to move heaven and earth to get his suspension lifted. So, between the two of you, do you have any idea who Cem Kalaman might have used for this operation?'

The NCA's Kalaman team. It sounded big and important. However, in terms of NCA priorities it had traditionally been neither. Even though the Kalamans had been a criminal enter-prise for the best part of half a century they'd been largely ignored by the authorities because they tended to fly under the radar. Up until the last three months, the team had consisted of Dan Watts, another detective (who'd since taken early retirement) and two admin staff. The upshot was that we knew a lot less about their inner workings than we would have liked.

It didn't seem like a good time for guesswork or excuses, so in answer to the boss's question Dan told her that we didn't.

Sheryl didn't exactly roll her eyes but she came close. 'Then, assuming he's still alive, we need to find Hugh Manning fast, don't we?'

'We've got an alert out on Bradshaw's car at the moment, ma'am,' said Dan. 'Every ANPR camera in the country's looking for it. We've got alerts on all of Manning's and Bradshaw's credit cards too, and the Border Force have been watching out for him for the last week in case he tries to head abroad. We'll get him eventually.'

'Unless the Kalamans do first.'

'I think we should put out a photo of him,' I said, joining the conversation for the first time.

'We've already had this conversation, Mr Mason,' Sheryl responded. 'The evidence against Manning for the Bone Field killings is limited, and he's a lawyer. He could sue us for defamation of character, and he'd probably win.'

To me, this was one of the great problems of policing today. The rules got ever more detailed, the penalties for bending them ever more severe, and the rights of suspects ever more paramount. It all made bringing the bad guys to justice that much harder.

Luckily, I had a simple way round this particular problem. 'That's true,' I said, 'but we don't have to mention the Bone Field killings. We can say he's wanted for the murders of his wife and Max Bradshaw. After all, there was a suicide note in his handwriting next to Mrs Manning's body, and Manning's almost certainly driving Bradshaw's car, because the real killers won't be. A photo will flush him out. Otherwise he could lie low for a long time, especially if he knows what he's doing. And the way he's been avoiding us so far, I'd say he definitely knows what he's doing.'

Sheryl thought about it for a few moments, resuming her tapping of the pen nib on the desktop. 'OK, I'll run it by legal, and if they give the go-ahead we'll get a photo out. But that still leaves us with a huge problem. Without Manning, we have nothing. The analysis team have run into a dead end on the trail of the house's ownership. A search of the computers at Manning's law firms hasn't turned up anything useful, and everyone there is expressing complete ignorance of any wrongdoing, and putting any blame firmly on him. So I can tell you how this is going to go if he doesn't turn up very soon. He'll take the fall as the owner of that farmhouse in Wales, just as the three men you killed down there, Agent Mason, will take the fall as the Bone Field killers.'

'But that's bullshit, ma'am,' said Dan. 'We know Cem Kalaman's involved.'

Sheryl stared at him as if he was mad. 'Where's the evidence? There is none. So you'd better find Manning before the bad guys do. And in the meantime, do you have any other leads to go on? Anything that might help us at all?'

Dan and I looked at each other, then back at her.

'Yeah,' I said. 'I think we do.'

Six

One evening when Cem Kalaman was about six years old, he'd seen his father brutally beat a man. Volkan Kalaman wasn't tall, but he was powerfully built with huge forearms and the hard, rugged face of someone who'd grown up dirt poor on a farm in rural Turkey – and who'd learned that if he wanted something, he had to take it himself, because no one was ever going to give it to him.

It had been Cem's bedtime and he'd wanted to say goodnight to his father. His mother had told him no, his father was in a meeting, but Cem had pleaded with her, saying he wouldn't be able to sleep if he couldn't and, because he was her favourite, she'd relented and let him run to the office at the back of the house where he knew his father would be. But as he'd rounded the corner, the office door had opened to reveal his father standing over a man on the floor. His father was holding the man in a sitting position by his hair while repeatedly punching him in the head. The man's face was covered in blood, there was more blood on his suit – which Cem would always remember was a turd-brown colour – and he was making thin whimpering noises like an injured dog.

There'd been two other men in the room, both associates of his father. One was Cem's Uncle Faz, who was funny and liked to bounce Cem on one knee whenever he came to family social events. The other, the one who'd opened the door, was Mr Bone. Mr Bone was like a shadow, a thin, expressionless man with small hard eyes who never smiled and who always wore a hat.

Mr Bone didn't say anything when he saw Cem witnessing the beating. He just stared at him blankly, almost as if he wasn't there. It was Uncle Faz who alerted his father to Cem's presence.

When his father saw him, he immediately stopped what he was doing and let the man drop to the floor where he lay rolled up in a ball. Mr Bone was already shutting the door but his father motioned for him to stop. He then used a handkerchief to wipe the blood from his knuckles and, after telling his two associates in Turkish to get rid of the man, he came over and crouched down beside Cem.

'Let me tell you something, beautiful son of mine,' he said, stroking Cem's hair. 'Most people are weak and foolish. They are like sheep. Often you can herd them with just words but sometimes, when they turn on you, you have to take a hand to them to bring them back into line. Never be afraid to use that hand.'

Cem had nodded and said he understood. He worshipped his father and knew whatever the other man had done it had to have been bad for his father to have acted that way.

In fact, Volkan Kalaman had never wanted his son to go into the family business. He'd wanted him to be a lawyer, or an accountant, reasoning that that way he could steal people's money legally. Cem might well have followed his father's wishes too, but then his father had betrayed him in the most heinous way possible, and that had helped send Cem down the long and destructive road to where he was now.

The ticking of the grandfather clock was loud in the silence of the room as Cem sat facing the other two men. 'So what progress do we have on the matter of this lawyer, Manning?' he said. He wasn't a big man, although he'd inherited his large hands, and he looked younger than his forty-eight years, but his voice carried real authority.

The man he addressed was Mr Bone. Deep into his sixties, he'd been the organization's chief assassin for decades now, an otherwise peripheral figure whose existence very few people knew about. It had been he whom Cem had sent to deal with Hugh Manning, which in hindsight Cem realized had been a mistake. Mr Bone was a strange, cold man who gave little away, yet when his father had betrayed him it was Mr Bone who'd become his mentor. Cem knew his ruthlessness and loyalty weren't in any doubt but his age was becoming a problem, and at some point Cem was going to have to replace him.

Mr Bone met his gaze. 'Manning has disappeared completely,' he said. His voice was cold and low, and still retained vestiges of a Turkish accent. 'We are doing everything we can to track him down. We got to him first last time. There's no reason to believe we won't do so again.'

The Hanged Man

'We were lucky last time,' said Cem.

And they had been. Diana Manning had made a basic mistake. She'd called her sister's landline using a supposedly untraceable number but Cem had the advantage over the police that he wasn't constrained by the law. He'd already had one of his best security people plant bugs in the sister's house and they'd picked up the phone conversation. It had only taken a quick call to a contact in BT to find out the number, followed by a further call to a corrupt police contact to run a trace on it. Although the location wasn't exact because of the limited reception in the area, a search on the Land Registry had thrown up a single property that was owned by exactly the kind of offshore company a tax lawyer like Manning would use, and from there it had all been simple.

Except it hadn't been, and the lack of apology from Mr Bone irritated Cem. But there wasn't much he could do. Mr Bone wasn't the sort to apologize. As far as he was concerned, he and Cem were equals.

'If the police get to him he's likely to cooperate,' Cem continued, 'and we can't have that.'

He then looked at the third man in the room. He'd known Alastair Sheridan since university. They were very different people yet they were close in the way men who share long-standing dark secrets always are.

Alastair was a big, slightly overweight man with a deceptively cheery manner and an unthreatening public-school accent that made him come across as likeable and harmless. But Cem knew it was just a ruse. Alastair took after his father and, with the exception of Mr Bone, was the most black-hearted man he had ever met. This would have been almost admirable, given the way he was able to fool the outside world, except that his intense sadism had led to mistakes in the past. Not for the first time Cem wondered if he'd be better off without both these men in his life.

'Manning was your friend, Alastair,' said Cem. 'You introduced him into our fold. Can you think where he might have gone to?'

Alastair looked uncomfortable. 'We were never that close, Cem, and I haven't seen him socially for more than ten years.'

'Not since that night, eh?'

'No,' said Alastair, lowering his eyes. 'Not since that night.'

'You fucked up then.'

'It was a long time ago.'

'It could come back to haunt us. If Manning talks, and he mentions what happens, then we're in real trouble.' Which wasn't quite true. Alastair would be the one in real trouble. Even so, Cem knew that if this other secret of theirs came out, it would give the hunt for the Bone Field killers a huge push forward.

'He has no evidence,' said Alastair firmly. 'It's his word against mine.'

Cem knew it would be a lot worse than that but decided to let it go for now. He turned to Mr Bone. 'The NCA are heavily involved in this case. How far are you along trying to get an insider there?'

'We are almost there. I have identified the perfect candidate, and we're ready to move on him.'

'And he'll definitely help us?'

Mr Bone nodded slowly, his thin, bloodless lips contorting into something vaguely resembling a smile. 'He'll do absolutely anything we tell him. I guarantee that.'

'Good,' Cem said. 'I want Manning caught. I don't care what it takes. Then we can relax and hunt again.'

The hunt. It was what had brought them together all those years ago. It had been Alastair who'd coined the term back in 1988 when they were at Warwick University. At the time, he and Cem had a shared interest in the occult and devil worship, but it went deeper with Alastair. He had a fantasy. He wanted to kidnap a young woman, maybe even a teenager, and sacrifice her to the devil. Cem still remembered how he'd felt when Alastair had told him this. He had sisters. He knew it was wrong. Yet something had stirred in him too. A desire to make someone else pay for the simmering anger that was always there in him; a desire to inflict pain and wield power over others. And it was that which had won through.

He could have turned back from that path. He'd even thought about it. But he hadn't.

Dana Brennan, a thirteen-year-old girl out on her bike on a summer's afternoon, had been the first victim. An easy one to start with, Alastair had said.

Since then there had been so many others.

'We have a subject being groomed now,' said Mr Bone. 'Untraceable. She'll be ready very soon.'

The tiny part of Cem's brain where the semblance of a conscience had once been had long since disappeared. Now he was simply a hunter, those he hunted nothing more than sustenance to him. He smiled at the prospect of fresh meat, and the conversation moved on to when and where the three of them would devour it.

Seven

In July 2005, officers from the National Crime Squad, one of several forerunners to the NCA, raided a council flat in Greenford, west London, that was being rented out to a suspected Albanian people smuggler called Kristo Fisha. Fisha was wanted for the murder of another Albanian in a street brawl, but when the officers broke in they discovered Fisha's body, along with that of his girlfriend, in the bedroom. They'd both been tortured to death. During the intensive search of the flat that followed one of the investigating officers had pulled up a loose floorboard underneath the sofa in the living room and had discovered a carrier bag containing £12,000 in cash and a DVD.

It was what was on that DVD that was of interest to us now.

And, in an extremely rare example of the cogs of justice turning swiftly, less than three hours after getting Sheryl Trinder to request the long-forgotten Kristo Fisha case file from where it was being kept in secure archives at a disused RAF base in Hertfordshire, I was now holding the DVD in my hand.

It was 8.15 p.m. and Dan and I were alone in one of HQ's TV viewing rooms, nursing coffees and putting off the inevitable.

'It's eleven years since I saw what was on here,' said Dan, who'd been one of the investigating officers at the time, 'but I still remember it.'

'You don't have to watch it again.'

'Yes,' he said, sipping his coffee, 'I do.'

On the way back in the car from Lincolnshire that afternoon, Dan and I had scoured our brains for other leads to go on, and it was then that I remembered a conversation he and I had had a few months back in which he'd mentioned that DVD. I knew what was on it, which was why I was as reluctant as he was to start watching.

I looked down at the open case file. A photo of a very dead Kristo Fisha stared back at me. In the shot, he was wearing only a ragged white T-shirt and boxer shorts. His wrists had been bound with cord to each end of an old-fashioned wall radiator, while the same type of cord had been used to secure his neck to the central bar, keeping the top half of his body in place. The shape of a steam iron had been burned into several parts of his face and torso, and he was covered in deep cuts. From the amount of blood, it was clear he'd been tortured for some time before being finished off with a single stab wound to the heart. Next to the photo of Fisha was one of his girlfriend, later identified as nineteen-year-old Bulgarian illegal immigrant Milena Borisov.

She was lying naked on the floor in the foetal position with her hands tied behind her back. She'd been shot and stabbed.

'So no one was ever arrested for the killings?' I said, still holding the DVD as I skimmed through the pages. For a brutal double murder, the file was depressingly short.

'Look at the date of the raid, Ray,' said Dan. 'July the twenty-first 2005. It was two weeks after the 7/7 bombings. Three hours after we broke into that flat four other men tried to blow up the Tube all over again, and then went on the run. You remember what it was like. Every cop in Greater London was hunting down those guys, and everything else got pushed to one side. Even this. Of course we investigated, but there were no witnesses, and no obvious suspects at the time.' He sighed. 'We could have tried a lot harder, I know, but I'll be honest, Fisha was a suspected murderer himself, and Borisov was a spaced-out druggie, so no one was ever going to go the extra mile for them.'

'Yeah, I guess so,' I said.

I think there must have been something in my tone, though, because Dan said, 'Don't judge me, Ray.' His voice was calm – he wasn't the sort to raise it unnecessarily – but there was no mistaking the anger there. 'I've never shirked any case I've worked on.'

'I know you haven't,' I said.

I could understand his reasoning. It was just the way things were when resources were limited. No one liked an unsolved double murder but you could tolerate it far better when the victims were fairly low down the moral pecking order. In hindsight, though, it represented a huge missed opportunity.

Without saying anything more, I pulled down the blinds to

keep out the light from the setting sun, slipped the DVD into the player and sat back down next to Dan.

It was time to enter someone else's nightmare.

For a good minute the screen was blank. Then, just as I was about to get up and move the film forward, it burst into life without warning, revealing a girl of about twenty lying naked and spreadeagled on a bed, her wrists and ankles bound to each corner, a black ball gag in her mouth. The quality of the picture wasn't brilliant but it was good enough to see the fear in the girl's eyes as she looked around desperately. The camera filming her was fixed high up in one corner so it could take in the whole room from above. On the wall behind the bed was a large painted sign of a pentacle with a flowing letter 'M' in the middle. I recognized both it and the room immediately.

'That's the basement at the farm in Wales,' I said.

Dan looked at me. 'Are you sure?'

'Absolutely. I'm never going to forget that place.'

I'm hugely claustrophobic, a result of an extremely traumatic childhood incident, but I'd forced myself down into the basement in that house to try to rescue the girl who'd been taken there. I'd failed, and Nicole had been burned to death in the ensuing fire.

I'd been back there twice since then to see how the forensic investigation was going, but it was clear that the killers had had an emergency plan in place in case they needed to destroy any evidence quickly. Such was the intensity of the fire they'd set that it had taken firefighters more than twenty-four hours to put it out, by which time there was nothing left but ash and rubble.

On the screen, thirty seconds passed as we watched in grim

silence. There were bruises and cuts on the girl's body and, even though the footage was on the lined and grainy side, they looked fresh, as if she'd already been abused by her captors.

Suddenly the girl's eyes became fixed on something or someone in the corner of the room, and they widened perceptibly. A long moment passed before three figures dressed in long black robes and grotesque full-face hoods walked into the room in single file. All three wore gloves, too. There wasn't a single part of any of their bodies that was exposed, making any kind of identification impossible.

The men gathered round the bed, partially blocking the view of the girl. Then, from beneath his robes, one pulled out a long black knife, which he held up for the girl to see. I swallowed. This was hard enough for me to watch. I couldn't imagine what it must have been like for Dan, who had two teenage daughters only a few years younger than this girl.

The film lasted a further nine minutes as the three men tortured, taunted, beat and sexually assaulted the girl until she was semi-conscious and hardly moving, before finally the one with the knife raised it two-handed above his head and drove it into her heart, at which point the film abruptly ended. There was nothing else on the DVD.

For some time afterwards, neither of us spoke. I felt profoundly depressed. You think that as a police officer you'll get used to the depths some human beings can plumb, and then you see something that makes you realize that those depths are bottomless. This was one of those times.

'Why didn't you try to find out who these bastards were?' I said at last, my tone less accusatory than resigned.

Dan sighed. 'You know, at the time we thought it was probably fake. Like one of those snuff movies. And even now, looking at it, it's still hard to tell for sure.'

To a certain extent, I could see his point. Much of the torture of the girl was sexual in nature, and though they struck and stabbed her several times, because of the way they were positioned during the assault it was hard to see the blows actually landing. She was covered in blood at the end, but I guess it was possible – at least if you didn't know what I knew – to conclude that she was an actress, particularly as the quality of the film was poor. The ending, though, when the knife went into her chest, had looked real enough.

'But,' I continued, 'the fact that this film was found under the floorboards, along with a pile of cash, very close to the bodies of two people who'd been tortured to death might have got me thinking.'

Dan stood up and paced the room. He still moved like a boxer. His whole body was tense, the muscles of his lean frame rippling under his shirt, an expression of aggressive concentration on his face. 'Look, Ray,' he said, clearly trying hard to keep a lid on his feelings, 'we were under a lot of pressure at the time and no one thought the film had anything to do with Fisha's murder. If his killers had been after the film, the way he was tortured he would have given it up straight away. But it was still under the floorboards when we found it. And also, bear this in mind. You've seen the film. There's no way of IDing any of the three men on it. They're covered from head to toe. You never see their faces. Even the room doesn't give away anything about where it is. You can't even see the girl well enough to get a decent ID. So why bother killing Fisha and his girlfriend over it?'

'Did you ever have a workable motive for Fisha's murder?'

'From what I recall he had quite a few enemies, and not too many friends. We questioned a few people but all of them had alibis. You have a look at the case notes and see what you can come up with.'

'Look, I'm not criticizing you, Dan,' I said. 'I do know what it's like, and I know this is an old case. But Fisha got that DVD from someone. And we've got to find out who, because this was definitely filmed at the farmhouse. We also need to ID the girl. Let's see if we can get a decent still of her we can use.'

So we burned the DVD to the room's desktop PC and went back over the film, freezing and enlarging images of our victim. Strangely, watching the footage a second time didn't elicit the same emotions in me. I was already getting used to the grim content, and I suppose that's how you survive the job. If you expose yourself to the crap enough, you become numb to it.

Given the poor quality of the footage, it was almost impossible to get a decent close-up of the girl. In the end, the best we could manage were a couple of shots from the opening minute before the assault on her began. They weren't good, but someone with eagle eyes and a natural memory for faces might just be able to get an ID. Thankfully, we had such people.

The Met has a team of some two hundred officers known as

super-recognizers, who came to the fore during the 2011 London riots. They share a unique gift of being able to remember faces, even ones they haven't seen for years. If anyone was going to put a name to the girl, it would be one of them.

The door opened. It was Sheryl Trinder, who wasn't the type to knock.

'Any clues from your film?' she asked, standing in the doorway.

I told her I was absolutely certain it was filmed at the farmhouse in Wales. 'I remember the sign on the wall behind the bed. It was exactly the same.'

'The quality of the film's not good, ma'am,' said Dan, 'and it's impossible to ID the suspects. We've managed to isolate some shots of the victim and we'll get them across to the super-recognizers.'

'Let me watch the film,' she said, moving into the room.

'It's not pleasant viewing,' Dan warned her.

'I'm sure it's not, but I might be able to help. I'm one of the super-recognizers.'

I looked at her, impressed. 'Seriously, ma'am?'

She raised an eyebrow. 'Have you ever heard me joke, Mr Mason?'

'No, ma'am,' I said, 'I haven't.'

We put the film back on, but this time neither I nor Dan watched it. Perhaps I wasn't quite as numb to its effects as I thought, and I kept my gaze averted.

At least until Sheryl muttered an expletive, which wasn't like her.

'Freeze the film,' she told Dan.

He did as he was told.

'Go back a bit. There.'

On the screen we were back to the girl lying on the bed just before the assault began. Sheryl took a deep breath and turned away from the screen so she was facing me. Her icy facade had cracked a little and she looked troubled.

'I recognize her.'

'Her name was Tracey Burn. I remember her from my days in uniform in Hammersmith.'

The three of us were back in Sheryl's office now, and she was looking thoughtful. She'd insisted on watching the remainder of the film and it was clear the content had affected her, just as it had affected Dan and me.

'She lived in White City,' Sheryl continued, 'and she was in an abusive relationship with a very unpleasant piece of work. She had to call us out on several occasions when he was hitting her, and I attended two of those incidents. We arrested him both times but Tracey never pressed charges. She was terrified of him. I always remember she was a sweet little thing, but weak, with no self-esteem. When I got promoted, I lost track of her.'

'And you're sure it's her, ma'am?' I said.

'I'm almost certain. The girl in the film looks like she has a large mole just above her right eyebrow, and Tracey had one like that. I'll call my old colleagues at Hammersmith to see if they can give me full names for her and her boyfriend. Then we'll track down the next of kin and get a DNA test to see if it matches any of the DNA found at the farmhouse. If it does, this is a real break. Good work.'

She addressed me when she said this. Then, as we got up to leave the room, she gave Dan a hard look. 'I don't know what you and your colleagues were thinking when you found that DVD, Mr Watts, but it looked bloody real to me. And it should have been investigated as such.'

Eight

It was gone nine when we left NCA HQ.

I thought Dan would want to get back to his wife and kids but instead he suggested grabbing a drink and a bite to eat at the pub round the corner – a hipster's hangout where the beards and students were in plentiful supply, and where the food was good. I'd had little social contact with any of my colleagues in the force since the death of my best friend and partner Chris Leavey the previous year, so I appreciated Dan's offer. He was a good guy and I liked his company.

It was still light, but the sun had set and there was a chill in the air, so we found a table inside. I ordered the Thai curry, Dan had a burger, and we both drank lager. We didn't talk about the case. I knew he felt bad about what Sheryl had said, but there was no point going on about it. Instead we just shot the breeze about this and that, as if we hadn't just watched footage of a young woman being tortured to death. I could easily have had a second drink and carried on but I didn't want to keep Dan from his family. Having never had a real family of my own, I've always thought of it as a precious thing to be cherished.

So we called it a night after the one pint. I picked up the tab on the basis that Dan had bought the shitty service-station sandwiches on the way back from Lincolnshire, and we headed our separate ways – him back to Muswell Hill, me back to the apartment in Fulham I'd called home these past three years, but where I tended to spend as little time as possible.

When I got back, I poured myself a big glass of red wine and read through the notes on the murder of the last person who'd been in possession of the DVD: Kristo Fisha.

Fisha had been, it seemed, a grade one arsehole. Having been caught entering the country illegally in 1997, he'd successfully claimed asylum, stating that, if returned to Albania, he'd be persecuted for his homosexuality – although there was no evidence he was homosexual. Having established himself in the UK, he'd gained convictions for assault, domestic violence and drug dealing before turning his hand to smuggling in other illegal immigrants. He'd then gone into partnership with a British-born career criminal, Terry Howes, who owned an oceangoing yacht. Fisha's contacts in Albania got the immigrants – usually young women in search of a better life in the west – as far as Santander in Spain, and from there Howes sailed them across to one of the quieter south coast ports. Fisha then collected them and took them to London. There they were made to pay back the cost of their transportation, usually by working as prostitutes, either directly for Fisha himself or for another of his associates, an individual called Ugo Amelu, who was suspected of running several brothels around London.

Fisha was earning good money with his business but, because of a gambling and coke habit, he also ended up with big debts, and when one of the people he owed money to, a fellow Albanian, threatened to break his legs, Fisha confronted him outside a social club in Kensal Green. In the ensuing melee, Fisha allegedly stabbed him to death.

At the same time, Fisha and his associates Terry Howes and Ugo Amelu had been the subject of an intensive investigation by the authorities, and when Fisha was formally identified as a murder suspect, a team that included a younger Dan Watts raided his flat and discovered the bodies of him and his girlfriend. And, of course, the DVD.

Even though the investigating officers were busy with the huge manhunt for the 21 July bombers, they did manage to question a number of people regarding the murders of Fisha and his girlfriend. One line of inquiry was that it was a revenge killing, but this was quickly discounted, so the investigating team concentrated on Fisha's associates, Howes and Amelu. Both had cast-iron alibis for the time of Fisha's murder. Howes was in police custody in Spain, having been arrested for drunkenness, while Amelu was staying with family in Nigeria, having flown out on 17 July. He returned to the UK on the 26th and, when questioned under caution, claimed to know nothing about what had happened.

After that the investigation seemed to peter out. A cold case review was carried out by Surrey police in 2009, a copy of which was attached to the end of the file, but they got no further forward, and it went back in the drawer. One thing of note, though, was that Surrey police had been unable to re-interview Terry Howes, due to the fact that in September 2005, less than two months after Fisha's murder, his yacht had been discovered floating empty twenty miles off the coast of Majorca, and it was assumed by Spanish police that he'd been lost over the side, although no body was ever found.

No police officer believes in coincidence. I was pretty certain Howes had been murdered by the same people who'd murdered Kristo Fisha and his girlfriend, and that it had something to do with the DVD under Fisha's floorboards. It seemed logical to me that Fisha was using the DVD as blackmail, and that the person he was blackmailing was someone connected to the Bone Field killings, and therefore almost certainly Cem Kalaman. But this begged an obvious question. Why was the DVD still under the floorboards when the police raided the flat? And why were the killers so determined to get hold of it when no one on the film itself could be identified? We were, it seemed, still missing plenty of pieces of the puzzle.

I finished my wine and poured myself another glass. My girl-friend's a recovering alcoholic who's been sober for eight years now and I often stay with her in her cottage out of town, so con-sequently I drink a lot less these days. But when the opportunity arises, I make the most of it. I took more of a gulp than a sip of the wine, savouring the taste just a little too much as I re-read the file, just in case I'd missed something.

Nothing stood out, but someone somewhere had to know something. We could no longer talk to Fisha, or his business partner Terry Howes, but if Ugo Amelu was still alive, then maybe we could talk to him.

I logged on to the Police National Database and looked him up. The mugshots showed an angry-looking, athletically built black man with dyed blond cornrow hair and a strong jaw, the kind of guy you didn't want to get on the wrong side of – which was a useful trait for a man who was clearly a violent career criminal. Aged forty-one, he had a total of nineteen convictions and had served two prison sentences – the first, an eighteen-month stretch for GBH; the second, a four-year term for trafficking for sexual exploitation, which he served between 2006 and 2010, and which was almost certainly the result of the investigation Dan had been a part of. There'd been no further convictions since his release, which made me wonder if he too had been bumped off by the Kalamans.

I looked at my watch. It was gone eleven. I'd seen from the file that Dan had been one of the officers who'd interviewed Amelu first time round and I wanted to know what he remembered of him. I decided, though, to let him enjoy what was left of his evening at home. It could wait for tomorrow.

Instead, I called my girlfriend.

I'd been seeing Tina Boyd for three months now. I find it hard to build meaningful relationships. So does she. But somehow we'd managed. In many ways we were kindred spirits. If you were looking for truly controversial figures in the Met's recent history, only two would spring to mind. One was me. The other was Tina. She'd been shot twice, kidnapped once, held hostage, involved in at least three killings that had somehow just about held up as self-defence, suspended more times than I could remember, and was now a private detective.

It was midnight where she was, in France, but she answered immediately.

'Hey you,' she said. Her voice was warm and husky, the product of all the cigarettes she smoked. 'How's it going?'

'I've had better days.' I told her about how Hugh Manning had slipped our net, leaving two dead bodies in his wake.

'You think you're going to find him?'

'If he's still in the country we will. We should be getting his photo circulated in the media tomorrow and that'll flush him out.' I paused, finding it hard to say the words I wanted to say. But as I looked round my big, empty apartment, I said them anyway. 'I miss you.'

She laughed. 'Have you been drinking?'

'No. Well, maybe a little. It's been a long day.'

'Have one for me, eh?'

There was another pause which wasn't quite comfortable. We'd been two lonely people for a long time, and we were still not quite sure of each other.

'When are you back?' I asked.

'As soon as I've sorted out this bit of work. It's a research job. I've got a couple of interviews tomorrow and then I'll be home first thing Friday morning.'

'It'll be good to see you.' Pause. 'Anyway, I'll let you go.'

'I miss you too, Ray. I'm looking forward to seeing you. Dinner Friday night at my place?'

I smiled, much happier suddenly. 'I wouldn't miss it for anything.'

Nine

Dan Watts had been staring at the computer screen for so long he could feel his eyes drying out. The women on the screen, one after another, all in various stages of undress, stared back at him, their poses offering every kind of illicit adventure imaginable.

The PC bleeped as Gurl4fun's icon appeared in the top corner of the screen followed by a message: 'Hiya. Still wanna meet up???XXX.'

Dan sat back in the chair, shaking the stiffness out of his neck. Did he want to meet up?

Of course he did. He was addicted to these clandestine meetings. They were what had destroyed his marriage, because destroyed it was. Denise had told him that this time she wasn't taking him back. He'd gone for help after she'd caught him the first time, so when it had happened again, the sense of betrayal had been too much. Dan understood her position entirely and he was racked with guilt. He'd let down God, although in truth, his faith had taken so many knocks over the years it was now barely a shadow of what it had once been. More importantly, he'd let down Denise and the girls, the only three people in the world who truly mattered to him, and it was eating him up inside.

And yet . . . And yet even now here he was on this site looking for the same kind of meaningless meetings that had got him into this position in the first place.

'Definitely,' he wrote. 'When were you thinking?'

Her real name was Vicky, and as he waited for her reply he clicked on her profile. She had five photos as well as a very short bio stating that she was after no-strings sex, preferably on a regular basis. There'd be no regular basis for Dan. Once he'd had one meeting he never went back for a second. The women on these sites never gave him the satisfaction he was after. This girl looked pretty, though. Thirty-two. No kids. Her photos more tasteful than the norm, showing a glimpse of what was to come rather than putting everything up there on offer, like some did. They'd been chatting on here and WhatsApp for over a week now, and she seemed both friendly and sane, which wasn't always a common combination. If nothing else, she'd make him feel less empty for a short time.

'Friday nite?' came the reply.

Two nights away. Even if Hugh Manning turned up in the next forty-eight hours, Dan was still sure he'd have the time to fit in an illicit meeting. And she only lived a short Tube ride away in Crouch End.

'Sounds good to me,' he typed. 'Do you want to meet for a drink first?'

'Yup. C if we fancy each other LOL XXX.'

Her text-speak grated on him but he wasn't going to let that get in the way.

'I bet we will,' she added. 'U look hot in your fotos.'

'So do you,' he typed, feeling that first stirring of excitement. He was going to add something a little more pornographic but decided against it. He was tired, and that could wait.

He asked if she knew a pub in Crouch End called the Maynard Arms, and when she said she did, they agreed to meet there at eight.

'U can come back to mine if we like each other,' she wrote. 'Am only near. C U then.'

He wrote back that he was looking forward to it before logging off.

With a sigh he stood up, went to the window and looked down at the street below. There were still people about, including a large group outside the kebab house on the other side of the road. He hated this place. A one-bedroom flat above a pound shop, it was a far cry from the small but cosy family home two miles away in Muswell Hill they'd been in for the past seven years, but it was the only place he could get where they were willing to accept a rolling month rental. He'd been here for two months now and with each passing day he knew that the hope of any reconciliation was fading.

During that time Dan had thrown himself into his work, but even that had proved to be frustrating. For the past five years he'd been the man in charge of investigating the Kalaman organization. He'd devoted his life to it, which hadn't done much for his marriage either. And yet Cem Kalaman was still happy, free and married, and, most importantly of all, continuously one step ahead of everyone.

Who the hell said crime didn't pay?

Ten

I dreamed of death and terror, as I so often did, and somewhere in the grey before dawn my past and present collided in a nightmare more vivid than any I can remember.

When I was a boy aged seven, I lost my whole family. My father was a drunk and a philanderer. He was also a monster. One cold February evening he came home after days away from the house, and stabbed my mother to death. He then killed my two brothers and would have killed me too, but I managed to escape from him by hiding first in a cupboard while he stalked the house, calling my name, and then by jumping from a first-storey window after he'd set the house on fire.

I've had many dreams in which my father chases me through the corridors of our old family home, but over the years they've faded in their intensity. In this dream, it wasn't my father chasing me but men in long black hooded robes holding knives. As I fled from them, I kept tripping over other bodies – not those of my own long-gone family but of young dead women, their faces cold and pale, and their expressions mournful, as if they couldn't understand why they'd had to die so young. Every time I tripped and fell, the killers got closer, their knives swishing through the air. My legs felt like they had weights attached to them, but still I ran, turning corners into new corridors, completely lost now. Then a door appeared and I flung it open, just in time to see my father standing right in front of me, a huge knife raised in both hands above his head. He grinned, and the knife fell . . .

I awoke covered in sweat. The clock on the bedside table said 4.45 a.m. I knew there was no way I was going back to sleep so I got up and went for a run instead, forcing the fear back down.

London wakes early. Lights were on in the blocks of flats, and the bin lorries and delivery trucks were already out. Anyone could ambush me here, I thought. All they'd have to do was step out of the shadows, face covered, and pull the trigger. Sometimes I wondered why Cem Kalaman hadn't put out a hit on me. I knew he wanted me dead. Three months ago he'd turned up at my apartment with a bunch of goons to give me a warning beating. It hadn't worked out quite like he'd hoped though, and I wondered at what point they'd be back. I was definitely a thorn in his side, but maybe not a big enough one.

Although I was hoping that would soon change.

When I got to HQ at eight a.m., having run nine miles and had a huge breakfast at a café just down the road from my apartment block, the place was already busy and I was feeling a lot better, the terrors of the night having faded in the sunshine of a glorious July morning.

Dan was in the office we shared along with our two admin staff, and as soon as he saw me he got to his feet. 'Come on,' he said. 'Sheryl wants us in her office.'

Sheryl Trinder was standing behind her desk talking on the phone when we came in. She motioned for us to take a seat and we waited while she finished the call.

'This looks promising,' she said, putting down the phone and picking up a newspaper that had a picture of Hugh Manning on its front cover underneath the headline 'Double Killer Suspect Linked to Bone Field Murders'.

Manning was, I thought, an irritatingly good-looking guy with a round, cherubic face and an air of entitlement that seemed to spring right off the page. The good thing was his was the kind of face people would remember.

'I didn't think we were going to mention the Bone Field connection,' I said.

'Because he's wanted for two killings already, legal thought we were justified in putting it in,' said Sheryl. 'It'll be a big help too. Mentioning the Bone Field ensures front-page coverage.' She sat down. 'In the meantime, I want you both to take a look at this.' She handed an A4 photo to Dan, who looked at it then handed it to me. 'This woman is Tracey Burn's half sister, Martine Vincent, and her closest living relative. She lives in Finsbury Park and we had local officers round there late last night to take a DNA swab to see if it matches any of the remains found at the farm in Wales. We should have the results imminently.'

The photo was of a woman in her thirties with dyed blonde hair and a hard face who looked nothing like the woman in the DVD. I handed it back to Sheryl, impressed with her efficiency. I had no doubt she'd been here late last night coordinating the DNA test with the local CID to make sure it was done without delay.

'I've also spoken to one of my former colleagues at Hammersmith,' she continued. 'He confirms that they last had contact with Tracey Burn in October 2004 when they were called out to a domestic violence incident at the address she shared with her boyfriend. So she went missing at some point between then and July 2005 when the DVD was found. The boyfriend, Paul Moffatt, is still in the area. He was jailed in 2009 for child cruelty along with his partner at the time for violently abusing her three-year-old son. The child survived but his injuries were bad enough for Moffatt to serve six years for it. He's currently out on licence and back in Hammersmith.'

I felt the hackles go up on my back. Because of my own experience, I'd never been able to tolerate cruelty to kids. Though I kept my expression neutral, I think Sheryl must have spotted something in it.

'I want the two of you to interview Martine Vincent and Paul Moffatt. I know Moffatt for one will be uncooperative, but I don't want any strong-arming of him. As I've made clear to you before, Mr Mason, we do things by the book here. And believe it or not, it does get results.'

I wasn't sure I did believe it but I told her I understood.

'There's something else as well, Mr Mason,' she continued, looking down at some notes in front of her. 'You accessed the file of a Mr Ugo Amelu on the PND last night at 10.43 p.m.'

I nodded. 'That's right, ma'am. Amelu was a close business associate of Kristo Fisha, the man who had the DVD of Tracey Burn's murder. Fisha had another close associate too, a Terry Howes, but he died in mysterious circumstances a couple of months after Fisha. It's possible both men were killed over the DVD – I mean, the timing's very coincidental – so I figured that Amelu might know something, and be worth talking to.' I looked at her. 'I assume from the fact you know I looked at his record that he's already under investigation for something else.'

Sheryl nodded. 'He is. It's a very sensitive role involving another section of the NCA who were flagged as soon as you accessed his details. I got a call from the senior officer involved this morning wanting to know our interest.'

'Fair enough,' I said. 'I guess our interest is he's probably the only person who might be able to shed some light on where that DVD came from. You interviewed him at the time, Dan. Do you remember him?'

Dan didn't look too happy, and I guessed it was because I had been working on the case without discussing it with him.

'Yeah, I remember Ugo Amelu,' he said. 'He used to pimp out girls supplied to him by Fisha. I was one of the people who questioned him about the killing of Fisha and his girlfriend. He claimed to know nothing about it and had a cast-iron alibi. He was in Nigeria when the two of them were murdered.'

'So you didn't think he had anything to do with it?' Sheryl asked him.

Dan thought about it for a moment. 'I remember thinking at the time his alibi was convenient. He only flew out a few days before the bodies were discovered, and he booked his tickets at the last minute. So maybe he did know something about the murders – like who committed them. And maybe he knew something about the DVD as well. But the point was, we already had him bang to rights on trafficking for the purposes of exploitation, and we offered him the chance to cooperate on the Fisha case in return for a reduced sentence, and he still said he knew nothing. It was a complete "no comment" interview.'

'I still think he's got to be worth speaking to,' I said. 'Can you put us in touch with the team who are investigating him, ma'am?'

She looked at Dan. 'What do you think, Mr Watts?'

Dan shrugged. 'I suppose it can't do any harm. But if he wasn't talking then, I don't see why he'd start talking now.'

'It depends what the investigation is,' I said. 'And what charges he's facing.'

'I'll see what I can find out,' said Sheryl.

She was about to say something else when her desk phone rang. She motioned for us to stay, then picked up, listening while the person at the other end spoke.

When she replaced the receiver, her expression was tinged with sadness.

'That was the result of the DNA test on Tracey Burn's half sister, Martine Vincent. It's a 99.998 per cent match with remains found at the farm in Wales. That means Tracey Burn was definitely one of our victims.'

Eleven

It had been with a rather unwelcome sense of surprise that Tina Boyd realized she was falling in love with Ray Mason, which made her feel guilty that she was keeping a secret from him. But she had no choice. She'd told Ray she was out in France doing some work on a divorce case she'd taken on in her role as a private detective, but in reality she was here to see a woman who was already dead.

Three months earlier, Tina had agreed to help Ray on an inquiry and had gone to France to interview Charlotte Curtis, a British ex-pat who'd been a close friend of Kitty Sinn, the young woman who'd gone missing in Thailand in 1990. Ray was convinced Charlotte knew something about Kitty's disappearance, and it seemed that other people thought she did too – people who wanted to silence her. Tina and Charlotte had been forced to flee for their lives but Charlotte had been shot, and Tina had been informed afterwards by the French authorities that she'd died of her injuries. And that, as far as Tina could see, was still the official story.

Except a fortnight later, Charlotte had phoned Tina out of the blue to let her know that she was alive, recovering from her injuries, and now in witness protection. She swore Tina to secrecy, claiming that the French authorities had not wanted her to call but that she'd insisted.

Tina had been shocked to hear from her but was relieved to know that she was all right. She would have left it at that too. Charlotte had been targeted by Cem Kalaman because she'd been in possession of a hugely important secret: namely that the woman who'd gone to Thailand wasn't Kitty, but her cousin, Lola Sheridan. On its own, though, this was nowhere near enough to put Kitty's killers on trial so Tina had decided it was best for all concerned to leave Charlotte in peace somewhere in the anonymity of witness protection.

But then she'd received another call from Charlotte, who told her that she had new information about the case, something that she didn't want to discuss over the phone. Would she mind coming out to Brittany to discuss it in person?

Tina might have been falling in love with Ray but her PI work had been dull these past few months, and she was pleased at the chance to get out of the office. Once again she'd been sworn to secrecy and given a number to call as soon as she arrived in St Malo.

Tina had called the number an hour ago. A man had answered and in heavily accented English had told her to go to the village of La Ville Oger and park in a lay-by opposite the church.

She was sat there now, in a pretty, semi-rural area just east of the village centre, her windows open, listening to birds singing in the nearby trees as she smoked a cigarette and waited. Every time Tina travelled – especially to calm, peaceful places like rural France – she wondered why she continued to live in England, which was home to so many dark memories for her. It wasn't as if the lure of PI work kept her there. Not for the first time she entertained a fantasy of her and Ray buying their own home in a place like this, growing their own fruit and vegetables, sitting outside on the terrace at night breathing in the fresh clean air, with a couple of dogs and maybe, just maybe, kids. She was forty. There was still time if she hurried up about it. Obviously she'd never discussed it with Ray but she felt sure he'd make a good father, and it would give him a purpose that had been missing in his life, ever since his own family had been snatched away from him all those years ago. He had money too. It didn't have to be a pipe dream. They could really do it.

She closed her eyes and pictured the scene. A kitchen full of kids; laughter; music playing; an arm around her shoulders . . .

A car pulled up behind her and a middle-aged moustached man in casual clothes stepped out.

'Madame Boyd?' he said as she got out to meet him. 'Do you have any ID?'

Technically she was still very much a mademoiselle but she let it go.

'I do. Do you?'

He smiled. 'Of course.' He pulled out a Police Nationale warrant card and held it out while she looked. The face matched, and it looked genuine. It said his name was Alain Bassat.

Tina showed him her driving licence.

'Thank you. If you don't mind, we will continue the journey in my car. Yours will be safe here.'

She met his gaze. 'I'd rather not. I make it a habit not to get into cars with strange men.'

He didn't take offence but nor did he back down. 'You appreciate, Madame Boyd, what happened to Madame Curtis. I understand you were there too. The French state believes she is still in danger from those who tried to kill her, so we need to protect her current location as much as possible. We didn't actually think it was a good idea for you to come here but Madame Curtis was insistent, so we are following her wishes. However, we would like you to follow ours. That means coming with me, and I'm afraid also wearing a blindfold.'

Tina contemplated her options. She could have made a fuss but she'd come this far and didn't want a wasted journey. She also didn't think this was a trap. She'd developed a gut instinct for danger over many years, and her alarm bells weren't ringing now. If someone wanted her dead they had no need to go to such elaborate lengths. They could just as easily wait outside her cottage and put a bullet in her there.

Even so she was still wary as she got in the car next to Bassat and put on the blindfold he gave her.

They drove for about fifteen minutes through quiet, winding roads. At first Tina asked a lot of questions about why Charlotte was in witness protection and how much the French authorities knew about the people who posed a threat to her, but it soon became clear that Bassat wasn't keen on giving her meaningful answers so the journey concluded in silence.

Finally the car stopped and she was told she could take off the blindfold.

Blinking in the bright sunlight, Tina saw she was in a courtyard with a small farmhouse in front of her, and outbuildings on either side. There were no other cars and no obvious sign of people. Tree-lined fields stretched off into the distance.

As she got out of the car the front door opened and Charlotte Curtis stood there, propped up on a walking stick. She'd been quite a big woman when Tina had first met her three months earlier but she'd lost weight and her dark hair had gone grey, making her look older than her forty-seven years.

Tina stopped in front of her and smiled. 'Charlotte. It's good to see you.'

Charlotte stepped forward and embraced her. 'It's good to see you too. You saved my life. I won't forget it.'

'I did what I could, but I honestly thought I'd lost you.' Tina considered herself a self-contained woman, not used to overt displays of emotion, but she felt a wave of feeling almost overwhelm her as the memories of that brutal afternoon came flooding back.

They held each other for a long moment and it was Charlotte who pulled away first.

'Come in. Sit down. You must be thirsty. Can I get you a drink?'

Tina composed herself, said she'd love a coffee, and five minutes later they were sitting opposite each other in a cosy living room with thick wooden beams crisscrossing the ceiling. The windows were open, letting in the sounds of birds from outside.

'So,' said Tina, her eyes momentarily going to the cane resting by Charlotte's side. She'd seen how hard it was for her to walk now and knew it could so easily have been her in the same position. 'How have you been?'

Charlotte sighed. 'Bored. Tired. In pain.' She forced a smile. 'It's been hard, Tina. I've lost part of one lung so I get out of breath quickly. I'll get better but I'm never going to get back to full fitness. I miss my friends too. And my life back in Roquecor.'

'Have the French authorities told you when they're going to let you go back home?'

'Only when the threat level is considered low enough, and they don't know when that's going to be.'

'And they haven't arrested anyone involved in the shooting?'

She shook her head. 'No. They've told me that the people who attacked us were working on behalf of a British organized crime gang who are still very active. That's all I know.'

Tina sipped her coffee. 'It's true. The gang are still very active, and the British police think that their leader is one of the people who killed Kitty. They also think that he and several others are involved in the Bone Field killings. I'm assuming you've heard about those.'

Charlotte barely suppressed a shudder. 'Yes, I have. And is Kitty's cousin, Alastair, one of the others you're talking about?'

Tina nodded. 'We believe so, yes.'

'And I hear the British police haven't made any arrests yet. So how are these people ever going to be stopped?'

It was, thought Tina, a very good question, and one that frustrated many people, including herself. 'We build a case against them. It's taking time but things are happening. And that's why I'm here. You called me, Charlotte. What did you want to tell me?'

Charlotte took a deep breath. 'I've had a lot of time to think out here. To go back over old conversations I had with Kitty when we were at Brighton poly together. They were good times, and I still remember them well.'

She was silent for a moment as she thought back to a happier, more innocent past.

'Go on,' Tina prompted.

'I remember once talking to Kitty – I think we were out walking in the Seven Sisters National Park at the time, and we were chatting about how mad mothers can be sometimes, and she told me that her mum had been convinced that her sister Janet – that's Alastair and Lola's mother – had been murdered by her husband. She said that one day, when she was very young – six or seven – she remembered her mother talking to someone on the phone about it, a private detective like you, and even making an appointment to see him.'

'And did Kitty think that her aunt had been murdered?'

Charlotte shook her head. 'I don't think so. She never said anything more about it.'

There was a pause as she sipped her coffee.

Tina thought that if this was all Charlotte had then it had definitely been a wasted journey.

'So I looked into it,' continued Charlotte. 'After all, it's not like I don't have time on my hands. Kitty's aunt, Janet, died in a car crash in Italy in July 1975. She was on holiday with her husband Robert at the time. The reports said they'd left Alastair and Lola behind with relatives, but I don't know which ones. One night Janet had been drinking and she drove the car off a ravine not far from the villa, and was killed instantly.'

'I'm assuming her husband wasn't in the car.'

'No. Apparently they'd had an argument over dinner, and Janet had stormed out and got in the car. Robert had tried to stop her. He said she was very drunk. But she'd driven off anyway, and from what I've managed to find out she didn't get very far. One report said it was less than a mile. I looked up the location on Google Maps, and though I don't know exactly where the villa was, it was a mountainous area, and the roads look treacherous enough now, so God knows what they would have been like forty years ago.'

Tina thought about this. It seemed pretty extreme behaviour to jump into a car and drive off drunk when you were in the mountains in a foreign country. But drunk people aren't exactly known for their rational behaviour, as Tina could attest to from experience, and there was nothing in what Charlotte told her that suggested obvious foul play, although it was definitely something worth researching further.

But it seemed that Charlotte had already done that for her. 'I couldn't find out any more of interest about the car accident,' she continued, 'but it made me think that if Kitty's mum hired a private investigator to look into it, it was maybe an idea to try to track him down. So I did. And I came up with this.'

She opened a folder she had on her lap and flicked through a couple of sheets of paper until she came to the one she wanted, and handed it to Tina.

Tina began reading, and as she did so she realized that what Charlotte Curtis had discovered could be dynamite.

Twelve

We should have been in good cheer. The DNA test was a major breakthrough. Now we had the name of one of the Welsh farmhouse victims. Tracey Burn may have died a long time ago but it was a start, and again, I had to admit I was impressed with Sheryl Trinder. She might not have been a barrel of laughs but Jesus she got things done.

There was no good cheer in Dan, though.

'Are you trying to get me in shit?' he asked me when we were in the car en route to Tracey's half sister's place. I'd never seen him this pissed off, but then we didn't really know each other.

I glared at him. 'Of course I'm not. All I want to do is solve this case. I didn't have a chance to talk to you about Ugo Amelu before the meeting with Sheryl. Why would I bother trying to get you in shit?'

I was driving and he turned away, looking out of the window.

'Remember, I was the one who brought you on board, Ray. Because I tell you something, no one else wanted you.'

The comment stung.

'You brought me on board because you needed all the help you can get,' I countered. I thought about adding that if he and his colleagues had investigated the Kristo Fisha murder properly then he wouldn't be so irate now, but I didn't. There was no point adding more fuel to the fire.

'Don't undermine me, all right?' he said.

'Whatever you say.'

'Yeah, exactly. Remember who the senior officer is.'

'Sure, boss.'

'Fuck you,' he said, and we left it at that.

Martine Vincent lived on the ground floor of a 1980s block of Housing Association flats wedged in behind a street of neat Georgian townhouses like an unwanted relative at a family party.

The interview with her was short and chaotic. She was a large, harassed woman with four kids, one of whom, Floyd, a twelve-year-old who was as tall as me and a fair bit wider, was sprawled out on the cramped living room's only sofa watching Jeremy Kyle, while a toddler we weren't introduced to ran round in aimless circles at our feet.

Obviously we were there to give Martine bad news, so it would have been easier to have sat her down in a calm environment and gently explain that her half sister was dead, but that wasn't going to be possible, so the deed was done in the kitchen.

Martine didn't exhibit a great deal of sadness when she was told that Tracey was one of the Bone Field victims, and that her remains had been found at the farm in Wales. 'I wondered why those detectives came round for a swab last night,' she said. 'How did she get there then?'

'That's what we're trying to find out,' said Dan, stepping out of the way as the toddler came racing past as if she was on amphetamines. 'When was the last time you saw her?'

'Long time back. Years and years. We weren't close. We never lived together as kids and I only ever saw her in the street, or out in pubs.'

To a man like me who hadn't experienced a true family since the age of seven, it always surprised me when other people chose not to be close to their siblings, yet it happened all the time.

'Do you remember Tracey's boyfriend at the time?' asked Dan. 'Paul Moffatt?'

Martine pulled a face. 'Yeah. He was a real lowlife. He's still round here.'

'Do you think he had anything to do with Tracey's murder?'

'I thought you said her body was found down at that place in Wales,' Martine said. 'I doubt if Paul's ever even been outside London. He ain't exactly a criminal mastermind.'

This tallied with what we'd found out about him. Moffatt was a particularly unpleasant individual. At the age of thirteen he'd broken into a primary school with two friends and killed all the pets the children had been keeping. They'd poured bleach in the goldfish bowl, beheaded the hamsters, and drowned the rabbit. Since then he'd had a string of convictions, mainly for drugs offences and domestic violence. He liked to concentrate his ire on children, animals and defenceless women. Looking at his record, it was clear he was a coward and, in criminal terms, strictly small fry.

I looked round the cramped, untidy kitchen, then back at Martine Vincent. 'So when your sister disappeared all those years ago and didn't come back, you never thought to report her missing.'

She obviously picked up on the criticism in my voice and glared at me. 'I told you, we hardly saw each other. And anyway, she rang me once to say she'd left him. Moffatt.'

'When was this?'

'God, years ago, I don't know. She said she'd left him and moved out of London to a shelter where she was really happy, and she wasn't coming back.'

'Did she say where this shelter was?'

Martine shook her head. 'Not that I remember. It was weird really, because she never usually phoned me about anything ever.'

Dan and I exchanged looks, our earlier angry words temporarily forgotten.

'And did you see Tracey again after that?' I asked.

Martine thought about it for a moment. 'No, I don't think I did. And you know, the years just passed, and I thought she was happy somewhere. You know what it's like. You just get on with things, don't you?'

Thirteen

'Listen,' I said as we approached the shabby second-floor flat which was Paul Moffatt's last known address, 'I can't keep this up all day. I'm sorry if it seemed like I was undermining you, Dan. I appreciate you sticking your neck out to get me back on board. And you're right. No one else did want me.'

He gave me a crooked smile. 'I'm sorry, that was a bit harsh. I think I'm still feeling a little sore about the fact we never did anything with the DVD back then.'

'Forget it. You weren't to know. If anyone should feel guilty, it's the SIO.'

He nodded, though I don't think he truly believed it. Dan was a good guy and, like me, he let things affect him.

We stopped and shook hands. It was a nice gesture.

Then I knocked hard on Paul Moffatt's door.

The Hanged Man

He was definitely inside. I could hear him shouting at someone. He sounded half cut even though it was only eleven a.m. I put my ear to the door and heard the sound of rapid, stumbling footfalls, then the door flew open, revealing a dishevelled, wrinkled guy in a grey tracksuit that matched the colour of his skin. He'd clearly been expecting someone else because he continued to shout and curse for several seconds before he realized that we were officials of some kind. I'd seen Moffatt's mugshot so I knew it was him, but even so I was taken aback by his appearance. He was supposed to be forty-one, but the man in front of me looked about sixty, and not a healthy-looking sixty either. His face was round and doughy, the skin dry and flaky and covered in deep lines, and his eyes were pale and bloodshot.

'Not today,' he said quickly, trying to shut the door, 'we're just going out.'

But we weren't going to let him go that easily. Paul Moffatt was a scumbag, and though as police officers we're supposed to treat everyone, including suspects, with politeness and courtesy, in reality it isn't like that. I had no idea whether or not he had something to do with Tracey Burn's disappearance, but his involvement wouldn't have surprised me in the least. From what I could make out from his file, he would have sold his mother's kidneys for the price of a couple of grams of smack.

But it wasn't any of that which made me force the door open and barge inside. It was the sound of a young child's persistent crying. One of the conditions of Moffatt's release from prison for child cruelty was he was not allowed to live with children under the age of sixteen, or have them in his home without prior authority from social services, and this was something I was pretty certain he didn't have.

'Oi, what the fuck are you doing?' he demanded, trying to square up to me as I pushed him backwards.

I pushed him a second time and he fell back into a chair, landing on an open Domino's box containing a couple of dried-out slices of pizza. Dan came in behind me and closed the door.

'Jesus Christ,' I said, looking around. 'Don't you ever clean this place?'

We were in the living room. It was filthy, the detritus of take-away food and booze on every available surface and most of the floor. Dotted around among it all were kids' toys, dirty nappies, overflowing ashtrays, a skag pipe, even a foot-long black dildo with a piece of tissue stuck on the end. In the corner, a wide-screen TV blasted out an old football match from the 1990s. The place stank of shit, fat and stale smoke. From some other room the child's cries were loud and hysterical.

'You're not meant to have a kid here,' said Dan. 'Where is he?'

'It's my girlfriend's. She's just visiting.'

At that moment, the girlfriend came in the room, smoking a cigarette and looking stressed. I'd guess that she was probably only about thirty, but she had the skinny, unwashed look of the smack addict, and her eyes were black and sunken.

'Who are you?' she demanded.

Dan ignored her, pushing her out of the way as he went in the direction of where the cries were coming from. She followed him, shouting and yelling, so I turned my attention to Moffatt, who had clambered out of the chair and was removing a pizza slice that had got stuck to his arse, slinging it back in the box.

'I need to ask you some questions about Tracey Burn,' I said as he cleared a space on the floor for the pizza box.

'Are you the Feds? You can't come in here pushing me around. I'll have you up for assault, mate.' He seemed more confident now that he knew we were police and therefore bound by rules of conduct.

I shoved him back down in the chair. 'Shut up and listen. The quicker you answer my questions, the quicker we leave you in peace.'

At that moment there was another commotion and Dan stalked back into the room, a disgusted expression on his face, the girlfriend coming in behind him, still shouting. 'We've got to call social services,' he told me. 'There's a two-year-old in there shut in a cot with a nappy that hasn't been changed for days.'

'You fucking leave us alone!' yelled the girlfriend. 'You don't know what you're talking about! I'm his mother!'

'They're coppers,' Moffatt called out from the chair. 'They haven't got any right to come waltzing in.'

Which was when things happened fast. The girlfriend grabbed Dan by the shoulder, telling him not to ignore her. At the same time I saw a look of pure rage shoot across his face. He swung round in one movement and I thought for a split second he was going to hit her, which, given his background as a boxer, could have been a real disaster. But instead he twisted her arm round behind her back and shoved her against the wall as she yelped in pain.

'You touch me again and I will arrest you for child neglect, do you understand? Now stay there and shut up.'

I could see that Dan was exercising all his self-control to stop himself from going over the edge. This wasn't like him at all. He'd always had a reputation for being calm and collected.

The girlfriend grimaced in pain. 'All right, all right. Let go of my arm.'

'Leave her alone,' said Moffatt, but he made no move to help her.

I gave him a cold stare. 'If you want to avoid going back to prison for breaking the terms of your release, you'd better answer my questions.'

'Fuck you,' he said. 'You're not even allowed to be in here. You've got no warrant. I know my rights.'

Some people just don't get it, and Paul Moffatt was one of them, which was why after a lifetime of criminality he was still sat in a shitty little flat shooting up skag and looking like the walking dead.

'Why don't you look after the young lady in here while Mr Moffatt and I have a chat elsewhere,' I said to Dan.

He gave me a puzzled look but nodded.

'What the fuck?' said Moffatt. 'I ain't talking to you.'

'Yeah,' I said, 'you are.'

I reached over, grabbed him by his lank, greasy hair and hauled him to his feet. He yelped in pain and struggled, but years of hard living had weakened him and, like all bullies, he was no good at standing up to aggression.

Shoving his arm up behind his back, I marched him through

the living room and into the bathroom. The toilet seat was up, revealing a foul stained hole with rusty water at the bottom that probably hadn't been cleaned since I'd been in uniform, and which made it perfect for my purposes. Ignoring Moffatt's indignant shouting about police assault and how he'd have me out of my job, I kicked his legs from under him, forced him to his knees, and stuffed his head as far into the bowl as it would go, then flushed.

Moffatt bucked and thrashed, his threats turning into a desperate series of chokes as I held him in place with my knee in his back, realizing almost with surprise that I was enjoying myself. I suppose I should have been worried that he could carry out his threats and report me for assault, but the thing was, I wasn't.

I pulled his head back up by the hair, let him choke and gasp for a few seconds longer, then slammed it back again with an audible crack as it met the dirt-encrusted enamel.

'Now I'm going to ask you a set of questions, Mr Moffatt, and you're going to answer them truthfully. Otherwise things are going to get very unpleasant for you very quickly. Do you understand?'

He gripped the toilet bowl and tried to force his head back but I had all the momentum, and I just forced it back in harder.

'I said, do you understand?'

He answered with a muffled yes, so I let go of his hair and stood up, waiting as he rolled away and leaned against the wall, mouth open as he gasped for air.

'Your girlfriend, Tracey Burn, went missing over a decade ago now. What happened to her?'

He didn't answer. Instead he shot me a resentful look. So I

grabbed him by the hair again and started to drag him to his feet. 'Maybe I didn't make myself clear.'

'You did, you did,' he said desperately, so I let him go and he fell back to the floor.

I repeated the question. I felt no guilt about what I was doing. Paul Moffatt was an animal. He had no redeeming features. I was finding it hard not to lay into him some more.

'I don't know what happened to her,' he said at last, giving me the kind of imploring look that says 'I'm telling the truth'. 'Honestly. It was a long time ago.'

'What, she just walked out one day and you never heard from her again? Is that what you're trying to tell me? Because from what I heard, you wouldn't let her go anywhere without you. You're going to have to do better than that.'

'I'm telling the truth,' he said, using his shirt to dry his face. 'Honest. She went to work one day and she never came back. It wasn't like her at all. I kept trying her phone and texting, but I never got any answer. I was even going to report her missing, you know, but then she phoned from one of those withheld numbers, and said she was starting a new life out of London and she never wanted to see me again. I swore at her, told her I'd find her wherever she was . . . and she just fucking hung up on me.' He shook his head. 'And then this weird thing happened.'

I looked at him. 'Go on.'

He frowned. 'I got a visit a few days later from these two geezers. They told me not to go looking for Tracey. Said if I did, they'd break my legs. I believed them. So I stopped looking. And that was it. I never heard from her again.'

'You said walking out wasn't like her. So what made her leave in the first place?'

He thought about this for a minute. 'She used to clean for a few people, and one of them must have been putting ideas in her head telling her to dump me, because she changed. She wasn't like the normal Trace. She stopped talking to me about stuff.' He shook his head again. 'I remember thinking I couldn't understand it.'

'I know,' I said. 'You're such a catch. Do you remember the names of any of the people Tracey used to clean for?'

He laughed. 'Course I can't. It was . . . it was years ago. Another life, right? Why are you asking all these questions about her now anyway?'

There was no point holding anything back. It would be public knowledge soon enough. 'She's dead.'

He didn't say anything for a few seconds. Then he looked up at me with beaten, bloodshot eyes, and I saw there were tears in them. I almost felt sorry for him.

'What happened?' he asked.

'She was murdered. And we're pretty sure it happened not that long after she left you. Is there anything you can remember about the men who came to see you? Something they might have said?'

'Just what I told you,' he said, and I knew he was telling the truth.

I crouched down so we were face to face, close enough that I could smell his rancid breath, and when I spoke my words were calm, almost reassuring in their tone. 'If you report me for assault, or make any complaint at all, I'll come back here one night when you're asleep and I'll inject you with a lethal dose of unusually pure heroin, and hold you down while you die. Look me in the eye, Paul.'

He did, and I could see the fear.

'You know I mean it, don't you?'

He nodded. He understood. So I got to my feet and left him sitting there.

Dan was in the kitchen. He'd taken off his suit jacket, rolled up the sleeves of his expensive, perfectly ironed shirt, and cleared some space on the only worktop where he was changing the nappy of the two-year-old boy, now with a smiling face. The girlfriend was sitting quietly in a chair watching him.

'Here,' he said, handing her the child. 'That's all you need to do. Now put some clothes on him and get out of here. Go back to your flat, and if you ever have any dealings with Paul Moffatt again we'll be straight on to social services, and you'll lose him. And you don't want that.'

She took the child, holding him against her. 'But Paul . . . he'll come after me.'

'No he won't,' I said. 'We'll make sure he doesn't bother you. I promise.'

Fifteen minutes later, mother and toddler were gone, as were we, leaving a shaken Paul Moffatt to the cracked, withered bones of his life.

Fourteen

As far as Stegs Jenner was concerned undercover work was both the best and the worst job in the world. The buzz you got from playing a part, especially when walking headfirst into danger, was like nothing else on earth. It gave you a real sense of power to pull the wool over the bad guys' eyes, knowing that you were the one who was going to bring their criminal careers to a crushing, and in some cases permanent, end.

But Jesus it could scare the shit out of you too, and although you could never show it on ops, the stress could sometimes be all-encompassing. Stegs had come close to death on more than one occasion in a long and massively chequered police career. He'd watched men being tortured in front of him, knowing that he was going to be next, had been threatened with knives, guns and baseball bats – even, once, a giant leg of Parma ham by a bodybuilding money launderer with links to the Mob – and yet somehow he'd talked his way out of every corner.

Twelve years earlier that career had almost come to its own permanent end when he'd been hounded out of the Met after an undercover op went spectacularly wrong, leaving behind a dead colleague and multiple allegations of corruption. Stegs had spent nine years out in the wilderness – quite literally, as he'd been living in Friern Barnet. His missus had divorced him and married someone else, his young son had become a near stranger, and his attempt at writing a book about his exploits with the less than original title of *Undercover Cop* had foundered, not on the vagaries of the Official Secrets Act but on the fact that his writing talent was a lot closer to nil than he'd previously thought.

But the thing was, like it or not (and most of the Met's top brass didn't like it), as undercover cops go, Stegs Jenner was one of the best, and three years back he'd been recruited into the newly formed NCA after a recommendation from one of the few former colleagues who'd actually liked him.

As a general rule, the undercover ops weren't anything like as exciting as they had been in the old days when the Met wasn't so heavily scrutinized and the bosses were far more prepared to take risks, but ultimately Stegs – now forty-four, and with his best years behind him – needed the money.

And for once, the op he was on now looked like it could actually provide a decent adrenalin boost as it came towards its conclusion.

'You think he's going to be here?' said Big Tone as they walked towards the rendezvous, a rundown social club in the basement of an otherwise empty sixties building in East Acton that was simply crying out for the wrecking ball.

The 'he' in question was a Jamaican thug with the frankly amazing name of Ralvin 'Busta' Lambden, who apparently had at least ten kilos of very high-quality coke to sell, and who was currently a fugitive from the law both in the UK as well as in his native Jamaica.

Stegs turned to Big Tone. 'Let's hope so. I want to get this deal over and done with.'

He was posing as a cash-rich nightclub owner from Brighton in the market for as much coke as he could lay his hands on to sell at his club, while Big Tone, an immense black man with a head the size of a watermelon, was acting as his bodyguard.

A long-standing police informant had put Stegs in touch with Ugo Amelu, a career criminal with delusions of grandeur who'd told Stegs that he was the son of a Nigerian prince, and who was the one putting the deal together. Stegs didn't trust Ugo an inch. The bloke was as slippery as they came, but he talked a good game and came across as a lot more intelligent than your average crim – which, Stegs thought ruefully, wasn't always a good thing.

This was their first time at the club in East Acton. On the two occasions they'd met Ugo in the past it had been out in the open, where the chances of anything going wrong were small. Their first meeting had been an intro set up by the informant between Stegs and Ugo so they could check each other out, while at the second, Stegs had made a test purchase of fifty grams to sample the produce. It had come back an extremely impressive 70 per cent pure, so now it was time for the next level: a meeting with Ralvin Lambden to arrange to buy the whole ten kilos.

The club's only entrance was via an alleyway dotted with lumps of dog shit and lined with overflowing wheelie bins swarming with flies that smelled exactly as you'd imagine they would in the heat of a midday sun. They stopped outside a heavily fortified steel door with blacked-out windows on either side, and Stegs rang the buzzer on the wall and looked up at the security camera filming him and Big Tone.

A minute later, with nothing happening, he rang it again, except this time he kept his finger on the buzzer for a good ten seconds. The first rule of undercover work was never let people take advantage of you. Most criminals, Stegs knew, were predators. They could spot weakness a mile away. Stegs might only have been five feet eight and of proportionate build, but he was a master of controlled aggression.

He withdrew his finger to the sound of bolts being pulled on the other side, and the door shot open about a foot, revealing the face of an unfamiliar and very unhappy black man.

'Who the fuck are you?' he snarled.

Stegs gave him the disdainful stare he'd perfected over years of undercover work. 'We're here to see Ugo,' he said. 'We're expected.'

'Names?'

'Just tell him Mark's here,' said Stegs, using his standard undercover name.

The guy told them to wait, and shut the door.

Stegs and Big Tone waited. They didn't speak or exchange glances, knowing they were almost certainly being recorded.

This type of hassle was par for the course in the crime trade. Because of the complete lack of trust between parties, no transaction, particularly a major financial one – and a ten-kilo coke buy definitely counted as that – was ever smooth. It was like a long and complicated dance between two drunken strangers, where you're just hoping you can somehow stay on your feet to the end.

They waited for a good couple of minutes before Ugo, who'd probably been behind the door the whole time, opened up and ushered them inside, giving them both a big shit-eating grin as soon as the door was closed.

'Hey Mark, my man, good to see you.'

He fist-bumped Stegs, which seemed to be his preferred method of greeting, and nodded to Big Tone, who tended to play the strong, silent type, before leading them down a long, dimly lit corridor past a door that led to a bar with a dance floor and another one filled with gym kit and weights. There were a handful of men at the bar and two more pumping iron in the mini gym, but otherwise the place felt empty. At the end of the corridor they came to a windowless room with a table in the middle and a bank of lockers on one wall. A man the size of Big Tone was sat at the table, a baseball bat down by his side. He looked at them both with the same dead-eyed stare that Stegs liked to use himself.

'Listen, bruv,' said Ugo, 'you know the rules. Everything out of your pockets and I'm going to need to do a patdown.'

It was standard procedure, but Stegs and Big Tone still made noises of irritation as they took out their phones and wallets and chucked them on the table, just to show they didn't like being inconvenienced.

Ugo flicked open Stegs's wallet and pulled out his driving licence, grinning as he looked at the photo and then at Stegs. 'Not a good picture, bruv,' he said, but Stegs knew the real reason he'd taken it out was to check that the licence was in the right name, which of course it was. Stegs was a professional. He didn't make amateur mistakes like that.

They went through the whole process of being patted down by Ugo while the big guy ran a high-end commercial bug-finder wand up and down them, just to make sure they didn't have any-thing hidden away. As always, they came up clean. The mikes they carried were far too sophisticated to be picked up by any of the devices currently on the market. Still, Stegs couldn't help but have a tense feeling in his gut, just in case for once he was wrong.

Ugo then took the battery out of each phone to prevent them being turned on remotely, threw everything in a ziplock bag, placed it in one of the top left-hand lockers, and locked it before handing Stegs the key.

Stegs had to admit that, if nothing else, Ugo was thorough.

'Satisfied?' he asked sarcastically.

'You know what it's like, bruv, you can't take chances in this game. Come this way.'

They followed him down a flight of concrete steps towards the basement, from where harsh grime music was playing.

The tense feeling in Stegs's gut returned. Although their handler was listening in to the mikes and would call for back-up if there was any trouble, there were no reinforcements waiting nearby to help them, since this was only meant to be an introduc-tory meeting between them and Ralvin Lambden. And Stegs had a thing about basements ever since he'd been dragged down to one by a group of gangsters and made to watch while a suspected informant had been scalded repeatedly with a steam iron. The thing about hardened criminals, in Stegs's experience, was that they could go from being perfectly reasonable to full-throttle psychotic in an instant, as if a switch had been flicked.

Ugo, however, had always been perfectly reasonable. A muscular, good-looking guy of around forty, he had a wide smile and a cheery air about him. Even so, his list of convictions meant he must have exactly the same kind of switch as the rest of them.

The basement was long and narrow, and painted completely black. A dozen lamps dotted around the place gave it a dim light and there were sofas and bean bags littered around the bare floor with no real sense of order. Various posters lined the walls along with a huge Jamaican flag, and there was a strong smell of skunk, and something else that Stegs couldn't quite identify, in the air.

At the far end of the room, sitting on a high-backed chair like a throne, was a long, thin man Stegs immediately recognized as Ralvin Lambden. He was wearing a beanie hat, even though it had to be at least twenty-five degrees down there, and smoking a joint – something which Stegs knew from experience was never a promising sign.

It wasn't that which made his heart sink, though. It was the fact that there was a man dressed only in his underpants kneeling next to the chair, and chained by the neck to the wall. The man's head was bowed so Stegs couldn't see his face, but he looked worryingly like the informant who'd first introduced him and Big Tone to Ugo.

97

Ralvin pressed a button on the remote control and the music stopped abruptly. 'Stay where you are,' he said in a thick Jamaican accent, glaring at Stegs and Big Tone as he stubbed out the joint.

They did as they were told, stopping a few yards from the chair while Ugo leaned against the wall.

Ralvin then leaned over and grabbed the kneeling man's bald head with a huge spidery hand, lifting it up and confirming Stegs's worst fears. It was indeed the informant, whose name was Donny Jeeks. His face was bloodied and bruised, and frankly he looked terrified, which was no great surprise.

Out of the corner of his eye, Stegs saw Big Tone tense. They exchanged looks. Stegs's said 'Don't do anything stupid – we can sort this'.

The second rule of any undercover officer is never to admit you're a cop under any circumstances. Always deny everything. The third rule was less obvious but equally important. Never lose control of the situation, and if in doubt, attack.

Stegs attacked. 'What the fuck is this?' he demanded. 'Why have you got my friend Mr Jeeks here chained to the wall?' This last bit was for the benefit of the mike. If the handler was listening – and Stegs hoped she hadn't taken a quick tea break – she'd know that back-up might be needed at some point.

'I'm sorry to say we've got a problem, bruv,' said Ugo, whose earlier good humour seemed to have done a runner. 'Word is that this boy's a snitch. And as he was the one who put you in touch with me, we're a little bit worried that you might be Feds.'

'Why don't you ask him then?' said Stegs. 'Because I know I'm not. Are you a Fed, Tone?'

'I'm offended someone even might think that,' growled Tone, clenching and unclenching his huge fists.

'We already did ask him,' said Ugo, his voice cold.

On the floor, Jeeks was shaking. Stegs felt sorry for him. The poor guy was stuck between a rock and a hard place. Admit the truth and he'd be beaten, or even killed. But you can only stick to a story for so long under torture, and he may well already have given them up.

Stegs wasn't unduly panicked. If Ugo and Ralvin really thought they were police they'd have dropped this whole meet like a stone. There was clearly some doubt as to their identities but not enough for these guys to pull the deal just yet. And that, of course, was the Achilles heel of all drug dealers. They were greedy.

'Look, I served time with Donny in Brixton,' said Stegs, 'so he knows I'm no Fed. Isn't that right, Donny?'

Donny nodded, and started to speak, but Ralvin backhanded him hard across the face and told him to shut his mouth. 'You don't say nuttin' widout permission,' he snarled.

Ralvin then got to his feet, sizing up Stegs and Tone. He was taller than Stegs had been expecting – probably about six two. His face was pitted with acne scars, and he had narrow, cold eyes the colour of coal. Stegs hadn't seen that many stone-cold killers in his time, but Ralvin was definitely one of them.

He glared at Stegs. 'What were you in prison for, mon?'

Stegs faced up to him. 'I said all this before to Ugo.'

Ralvin came forward, until he was only inches away. 'Say it to me.'

'Possession, with intent to supply. I served two years. A year of it with him.'

Stegs waited for another question about his prison time. He knew his story would stand up under scrutiny. He knew everything you needed to know about the workings of Brixton prison from the Christmas menu to the number of running machines in the gym, and if anyone with an inside track looked up the name Mark Philpotts on the PND they'd see a photo of Stegs alongside a list of his various imaginary crimes, including details of his stint in Brixton.

But no further question was forthcoming. Instead Ralvin wandered casually back to the chair before leaning down and coming back up with a long-barrelled pistol in his hand.

Stegs's stomach did a somersault when he saw the gun. This changed everything.

Ralvin shoved it in Jeeks's face. 'Is dey Babylon?' he demanded, pointing a finger at Stegs and Tone. 'Tell me da truth and you walk. You lie, you die, mon. Right now!'

Stegs turned to Ugo, forcing himself to stay calm, pleased at least that it didn't seem that Jeeks had given them up as police yet. 'Ugo, what the fuck is this? I came here to do a deal.'

'We can't take chances, Mark.'

'Jesus. I've been dealing with you for a month now.'

'Shut yuh mouth!' Ralvin yelled at Stegs. Then, quieter, to Jeeks: 'Is dey Babylon?'

There was a silence that seemed to last a long time, and Stegs could tell that Jeeks was wavering. He wondered if the handler, hearing all this, had called for back-up. He and Tone had a code phrase. The moment either of them uttered it, reinforcements would be sent immediately. So far neither of them had, and he hoped the handler was hanging fire as well. This might be a dangerous situation, but Stegs knew as well as anyone that if the police stormed this place blind, it could well turn into a hostage situation. And with a man as violent and unpredictable as Ralvin, Stegs wasn't at all sure that they'd get out in one piece.

The silence continued.

Ralvin hit Jeeks round the head with the gun barrel. 'Speak!'

Jeeks spoke. 'No. They're not, I swear it.'

'You're lying.' Ralvin shoved the gun harder in his face.

'I'm not! I'm not. They're not Feds.'

Ralvin's finger tightened on the trigger. He was going to shoot.

'He's not lying, for fuck's sake,' yelled Stegs. 'Let him go.'

Jeeks started whimpering and shaking. Time seemed to slow right down, as it always did when Stegs was in this kind of situation, where things could go either way. He knew he had to take back control. And fast.

'Fuck this,' he said, shaking his head in disgust. 'Come on, Tone, let's go. I came up here to buy some gear, not get insulted. You don't want my money? That's fine. I'll find someone who does. We're out of here.'

He and Tone turned away together. It was a calculated risk, that Ralvin's greed would overcome his aggression.

And it did. 'OK mon, I believe you,' he said, taking the gun away from Jeeks's head. 'You ain't no Babylon.'

And just like that, all the tension in the room faded, as Ralvin and Ugo's switches shot from full-throttle psychotic back to reasonable.

'Sorry, Mark,' added Ugo with a rueful grin, as if they'd just been playing a joke, not threatening to blow a man's head off. 'We just got to be careful, you know?'

'So have we,' said Stegs. 'For all I know you don't even have any dope.'

'We got it, mon,' said Ralvin, looking worried now at the prospect of losing a big deal.

The balance of power had clearly changed, and Stegs immediately took advantage of the fact. 'No way,' he said. 'I'm not interested.'

'Come on, let's not ruin this deal,' said Ugo. 'You're still getting gear at a rock-bottom price.'

'What gear?' said Stegs. 'I don't even see any gear. I just see a lunatic with a gun.'

'The gear's here, mon,' said Ralvin, removing a picture on the wall to reveal a safe underneath. He turned his back to them and punched in a code, before pulling out a kilo bag of white powder. 'Here's a key, mon. Pure stuff. Check it if you want. Dere's another nine where dat came from. We do dis deal tonight, mon. Two hundred tousand for da lot.'

Stegs thought it was a pity that they didn't have the whole ten keys in the safe. If so they could have walked out of there and called in the bust and not have to go through with the actual deal. He was feeling a little sick having watched this drama unfold, and he found it hard to look at Jeeks, who was still kneeling on the hard stone floor, shaking with fear.

'All right, but let him go,' he said, motioning towards Jeeks.

'What do you care about him?' said Ralvin.

'He's a friend of mine, and he's not an informer. If he was, he'd have put me away years ago.'

Ralvin seemed to think about this, then nodded. 'OK mon,' he said, unchaining Jeeks and giving him a kick. 'Get your clothes and get da fuck outta here,' he snarled.

Jeeks didn't need asking twice. He was on his feet like a shot, grabbing his clothes and racing past Stegs and Tone without even looking at them. Stegs had a feeling he wouldn't be seeing him again for a while, not if he had any sense.

'So,' said Ralvin, giving them a gold-toothed grin, 'we do the deal tonight den?'

'Yeah,' said Stegs, looking forward to removing this piece of shit from the streets. 'Tonight it is.'

Fifteen

'You were a natural in there with that kid,' I said to Dan as we sat outside a back-street café eating lunch.

'I'm a father, I've done that sort of thing enough times before,' he said with a shrug. 'I just hope she stays away from a man like him. He's poison.'

'He's a coward, that's what he is.'

He looked at me carefully. 'Is that how you got him to talk? You've got to be careful, Ray. What did you do to Moffatt in there?'

There was no way I could admit what I'd done. Not to Dan. Not to anyone. 'I just asked him some questions.'

'He looked terrified, and his hair was soaking wet. You can't manhandle suspects. It'll wreck the whole inquiry, and you'll be off the case. Permanently. You heard what Sheryl said. And I need you on this right now.'

'I won't do anything that'll get back to me.'

'That's not what I meant.' He sighed. 'I've got to be honest, Ray. Sometimes I worry about you.'

'What's that meant to mean?' I asked him.

'When Moffatt was first talking back to you, you looked like you wanted to kill him. You need to keep a lid on your emotions. That's the only way you'll survive as a copper these days. You know that.'

I nodded slowly. He was right. About it all. I had felt like killing Moffatt. The black rage that's always simmering deep down inside me had come rushing to the surface when I'd been speaking to him. I could have torn him apart limb from limb in that bathroom, and I'd enjoyed flushing his head down the toilet. I'd tell you my actions worried me, except they didn't. I knew when to keep control when it mattered. But I didn't say any of this to Dan, because I could see that sometimes he had a problem staying calm too.

'Sure, I understand, Dan. But at least I got some answers.'

Dan gave a resigned shrug. 'So what do you think happened with Tracey?'

I'd been thinking about this ever since we'd left Moffatt's place half an hour before. 'The theory that fits the facts most is that someone she cleaned for encouraged her to leave Moffatt, and also put her in touch with someone else who ran a shelter outside London, because by the sound of things Tracey wasn't the kind of woman to have gone out and found the shelter herself. And it could have a perfectly innocent explanation. Except for two things.'

'The men who came to see Moffatt afterwards?'

'Yeah, that's one. Moffatt was warned off looking for her. Who by? It has to be people working for her killers making sure she'd not be reported missing. And the thing is, how did they know Moffatt had threatened to find her when he'd talked to her on the phone? Tracey must have told someone who then told the killers. The killers targeted Tracey deliberately, and they even made sure she called her half sister so that she didn't report her missing either.'

'So what are you saying?'

'The killers found her somehow. My guess is they had a connection to the shelter, which means they also had a connection to someone Tracey cleaned for.'

'Moffatt didn't give you a name?'

I shook my head. 'No. But then it was a long time ago. I wonder if one of Tracey's clients might have been Lola Sheridan. We know where Lola lives now, but we don't know where she was based back around the time Tracey went missing.'

Of our three suspected Bone Field killers, Lola Sheridan was the most enigmatic, a woman who over the years had kept herself to herself. But three months earlier an informant of Dan's had given his tracking device to the young woman we knew only as Nicole who'd ended up at the Wales farmhouse, and who en route had spent time at Lola's isolated country house in Buckinghamshire. Nicole was now dead, having been murdered in front of me as I tried to rescue her, and we'd never been able to charge Lola with anything, since Dan's informant had been acting unofficially.

'It's a bit of a stretch, isn't it?' said Dan. 'Thinking it might be Lola?'

'It's easy enough to find out,' I said.

I finished off my sandwich then put in a call to Michelle, the most able of our two admin staff, but she wasn't answering. I left a message asking her to find out Lola Sheridan's home address between October 2004 and July 2005, and get back to me with it as soon as possible.

As I put down my phone, Dan's rang.

'Sheryl,' he said, excusing himself from the table.

I sat back in the chair and drank my coffee as Dan wandered off up the road with the phone to his ear, wondering how long Paul Moffatt's latest girlfriend would last before she was back at his flat with her baby, and wondering too whether I would ever carry out my threat and give him a fatal overdose.

Dan came back, looking pleased. 'A couple of things,' he said, without sitting down. 'One, the investigation into Ugo Amelu is an undercover job, and we've got a meeting with the handler in half an hour.'

'That's good,' I said. 'And two?'

He grinned. 'We've had two confirmed sightings of Hugh Manning. Both in the same town in Scotland.'

Sixteen

Hugh Manning was sitting in Harry Pheasant's conservatory basking in the bright light of the afternoon sun and watching the river in the distance as it ran down towards the small town of Newton Stewart when he saw the police car coming down the road that ran along the front of the house.

Immediately he dived to the floor so he was out of sight, praying that the occupants of the car hadn't seen him. The double-glazed windows prevented him hearing whether they'd stopped or not so he lay sprawled out on the rug, not daring to move.

What the hell was a police car doing down here in the middle of nowhere? When he'd been up here with Harry and the others for the shooting weekend, Harry had made a point of saying that only about one car an hour ever passed this way, and that there were never any police about, which was why he never worried about driving drunk. It could have been a coincidence of course but Manning was understandably paranoid, and it didn't feel much like a coincidence to him. It felt like a net closing in on him.

Time passed. Two minutes, three, five. There was no knock on the door, so eventually he lifted his head up and looked down the front garden that sloped towards the road twenty yards away.

It was empty.

He got to his feet. The Volvo he'd been driving was parked up by the log shelter at the side of the house, well out of sight of the road. He knew the police would be looking for it by now, but thanks to the fact that he'd obscured the number plates with dirt, they wouldn't be able to trace it here.

He sighed. The police car had shaken him. He'd actually been in quite a good mood before then, having spent most of the day so far reading a book, and even managing a walk in the woodland behind the house. It was peaceful up here and he was planning on staying a week or two at least while he pondered his next move.

He realized almost with surprise that he hadn't actually checked the news since the night before. Harry didn't have a TV up here or a PC, so he was relying on his phone, but unfortunately it didn't have a signal in the house, and the wifi was proving intermittent at best, which he'd actually found quite endearing until now.

Standing in the middle of the living room he logged on to Sky News, waiting for what seemed like an age until the page opened with the headlines.

And there, staring back at him beneath the headline of the lead story, like something out of a nightmare, was his own face – a crystal-clear, near-perfect likeness. It was the publicity shot from his law firm, taken barely a month ago. It might not have shown all the lines on his face but anyone seeing it would recognize him. Manning had always prided himself on the fact he was a good-looking man, with a thick head of naturally dark hair, deep brown eyes and a permatan that actually looked real. In other words, even at the grand old age of forty-eight he still got noticed.

Late the previous evening he'd gone to the Sainsbury's in Newton Stewart to buy supplies (paying in cash of course), confident that no one up here would know his real identity. He'd even smiled and had a few words with the pretty assistant at the checkout in his English accent.

He cursed himself for his stupidity. The people in Sainsbury's might not have known who he was last night, but as soon as any of them had seen the news reports that morning they'd have been on the phone to the police like a shot – which they'd almost certainly done, hence the passing police car.

As the news report loaded, he read through it with mounting horror. It said he was wanted for questioning in connection with the murder not only of his wife Diana but also a man named as fifty-two-year-old Max Bradshaw. Mr Bradshaw's dog, Monty, featured in the article too. Manning knew that would clinch it. The British hated cruelty to animals. They weren't so fussed about human beings, but do anything to a dog and you were public enemy number one.

The cunning bastards had really got him this time. He had no doubt the police knew he hadn't killed anyone, but this was the perfect way to flush him out. The report said he was believed to be currently driving the late Mr Bradshaw's car (helpfully giving its make and registration number), and just to put the icing on the cake they were describing him as armed and dangerous.

He shook his head angrily. Dangerous? He couldn't believe the cheek of it. *He* was the one in danger.

He pocketed the phone and paced the room, trying to work out what to do. If it had been someone from Newton Stewart who'd reported him, the whole area would be crawling with police. There were only a handful of roads running off the peninsula and it wouldn't take that much manpower to set up roadblocks, so they'd catch him in no time. He was going to have to stay put.

There was also the issue of his erstwhile employers. They too would be doing everything in their power to catch him, and so far at least they'd been quicker than the police.

Manning felt the panic building in him again as the knowledge that he was trapped took hold. He picked up the Remington from where it was propped up against the sofa. It felt good in his hands. He'd fired shotguns before at clay pigeon shoots, and knew how to use pump-actions. If someone came for him, would he pull the trigger on them? Or would he instead turn the weapon on himself? Jesus, this wasn't how he'd envisaged retirement. He should have been on a gorgeous Panamanian beach sunning himself with Diana. Not out here in the Scottish wilderness contemplating suicide as the least bad option available to him.

But maybe that was, indeed, the best move. It would be quick. It would be relatively painless. And it meant that at last he could stop running.

But he didn't do it. Instead, he lay down on the bed with the shotgun beside him, and closed his eyes. In the months before he'd gone on the run he'd started doing one-to-one meditation sessions with a yoga instructor with the distinctly unyogic name of Trevor, and now he used what he'd learned to bring his breathing back under control and steadily empty his mind of all negative thoughts.

Something must have worked because ten minutes later he was asleep.

Seventeen

The location for the meeting with the handler for the undercover op against Ugo Amelu was a secure room on the top floor of a modern office block in Battersea, where the undercover team were based.

Dan and I got there just after two p.m. and were met in reception by a tall, middle-aged woman in a smart trouser suit who introduced herself as Aideen King. After the usual formalities and introductions, she led us to a room at the back of the building and shut the door.

'So, Sheryl tells me you're interested in one of our targets, Ugo Amelu,' she said, motioning for us to sit down at the long table dominating the room. 'And you think he might have information relating to the Bone Field inquiry? I have to say, he sounds a pretty horrible man, but I didn't have him down as a serial killer.'

'Years ago he worked as a pimp,' said Dan, 'and one of his close business associates was a people smuggler called Kristo Fisha, who had strong links to the people we believe are behind the killings. Fisha was murdered, almost certainly as a result of these links, and we think Amelu may have information that could help ID them. We really need to speak to him, and you know what the pressure's like on this case. It needs to be soon.'

Aideen King looked at us both in turn. 'Well, as you've no doubt been made aware, Amelu is the subject of a major undercover operation, and anything I say to you about it goes no further than this room.'

We both nodded our assent.

'Two months ago a police van was held up at gunpoint by two masked men in Shepherd's Bush. The van was carrying large quantities of illegal drugs that were on their way to be destroyed, including ten kilos of very high-quality cocaine. The robbers clearly had good intelligence because they went straight for the cocaine and left everything else. This was hugely embarrassing for Ealing CID who were in charge of the load, so there's been an effort to keep the story as quiet as possible. Then a local informant claimed that the two men responsible for the robbery were Amelu and a wanted Jamaican criminal called Ralvin Lambden, who were looking to offload the cocaine at a cheap price. Ealing called us in and we now have two undercover operatives posing as drug dealers from out of town, acting as potential buyers. The op's been ongoing for nearly a month now and is very close to fruition.'

'How close?' I asked.

'The deal's set for tonight, so your timing's very good. We're hoping to catch Amelu and Lambden with the drugs, but it's Ealing's op and they'll be the ones making the arrests and questioning the suspects. The important thing for them is finding out whether someone on the inside supplied the intel about the drugs being carried in the van, and my understanding is they think Amelu is ripe for turning. He's recently become a father for the first time, and with his record he'll be looking at a minimum fifteen-year sentence for armed robbery and possession with intent to supply, so he's probably going to want to cooperate.'

This was good news, since I was pretty sure he could shed some light on Kristo Fisha's relationship with the Kalamans.

'We need to speak to him as soon after the arrest as possible,' I said.

'You'll need to clear it with Ealing, which in your case might be a bit difficult,' Aideen King said, looking at me. 'I hear you're not too popular over there, and DCI Eddie Olafsson's running the op.'

I raised my eyebrows. I'd been working for Eddie Olafsson on Ealing's murder investigation team until three months ago when I'd been suspended after an op he was in charge of went disastrously wrong thanks, at least in part, to me. 'We've had our moments, but I'm sure he'll put that to one side for the greater good,' I responded, somewhat optimistically, remembering the last time we'd spoken, when he'd thrown a whole heap of abuse at me down the phone before hanging up.

She smiled. 'Well, we'll soon find out. He's on his way up here now.'

True to her word, two minutes later there was a rapid-fire knocking on the door and DCI Eddie Olafsson walked in.

Olaf was one of those old-school cops you don't see much these days in the Met, a short, burly bald guy who looked like a night-club bouncer. He'd passed his thirty years' service a couple of years earlier and was into his fifties, but showed no sign of wanting to retire. He was tough, volatile, swore like a trooper, and – if truth be told – I liked him, even if the feeling wasn't exactly mutual.

He gave a nod and a smile to Aideen King, then the smile died instantly as he saw Dan and me on the other side of the table.

We both stood up.

'Fuck me. Ray Mason. I didn't think I'd be seeing you for a while.'

'How's it going, boss?'

'Thankfully I'm not your boss any more,' Olaf snorted. 'But I had heard they'd let you in at the NCA. How the fuck did you manage to get out of that suspension?'

I smiled. 'As you might recall, I was exonerated of any wrong-doing. Plus, I'm a good detective with a proven track record, as well you know.'

Olaf grunted something and turned away. 'How are you doing, Dan? You all right?'

'Not bad, sir. Good to see you again.' They shook hands.

'What are you doing working with him?' He nodded his big square head in my direction. 'Don't you know the trouble he causes?'

'I'm keeping him under a tight rein,' Dan said, winking at me.

Olaf sighed and sat down. 'Aideen's told me you're both working the Bone Field case and you think one of our suspects has information.'

'That's right,' said Dan. He filled in Olaf about our suspicions, embellishing them to make it sound like we had more than we did, because in reality we didn't have much at all.

'Aideen mentioned that Amelu might be tempted to cooperate with us,' I said.

'We've got more chance with him than Lambden,' Olaf said, 'but I want both those bastards to go down for a long time, so we're not going to be doing any deals with Amelu. I'm sorry, but that's the way it is.'

'No one's suggesting that at all,' said Dan, 'but you know how big our case is, and the pressure from up top for a result. We need to speak to him, and urgently.'

Olaf's face wrinkled with annoyance. 'You'll get your chance. But this is our op.'

'All we want to do is be there when you make the arrests, so we can question Amelu,' said Dan soothingly.

'You want to come on the op? You must be joking.' Olaf pointed a fat finger at me. 'The last time I went on an op with him he dropped our suspect fifty feet from a tower block and left him as dead as a dodo, in front of about two hundred witnesses.'

'He fell,' I said. 'And like I said, I was completely exonerated.'

'You don't do as you're told, Ray. If all coppers were like you, the whole place would fall to pieces. This op is important. We need it to go smoothly.'

'Look, we'd be there just as observers,' said Dan, 'staying right back from the action. That's all. We need Ugo Amelu just as much as you do.'

'If he fucks up anything . . . *anything* . . .'

I assured Olaf I wouldn't.

He sighed and shook his head as if he was just about to make a terrible decision – which, in the light of later events, you could say he was. 'All right,' he said. 'The final briefing's at Ealing nick, 8.30. You remember the way, don't you, Ray?'

'How could I forget, sir? The best months of my life.'

'Just be there.'

And that was it. The meeting was over.

'Olaf really doesn't like you, does he?' said Dan when we were back on the street.

I laughed. 'Ah, he's got a right to dislike me. I almost got both of us killed on that last op.'

He looked at me seriously. 'Well, don't be doing the same tonight. I put my credibility on the line for you in there.'

'Don't worry,' I said, 'I won't let you down.'

I pulled my phone from my pocket and saw I had a message from Michelle. I listened to it as we walked down the street back to the car, then turned to Dan.

'See, I've got some talents as a detective. It turns out that Lola Sheridan was living at a house in Kensington from 2003 to 2006, about a mile down the road from where Tracey Burn lived, and I'd bet my life that Tracey cleaned for her.'

Dan nodded thoughtfully. 'Fair enough, but it's not exactly evidence of any wrongdoing, is it?'

'No,' I said, 'but it gives me an idea. I think it's time we paid her a visit.'

Eighteen

There are few men in the world who've killed their own father.

Cem Kalaman was one of them. He hadn't done it personally of course. It had been a professional hit carried out by two of his most trusted lieutenants, the most senior of whom was Mr Bone. The year was 1998, and Cem was twenty-nine years old.

His father had gone with his bodyguard to a café in Highgate for a meeting in a back room he liked to use. It had been a cold February night, and as they'd got out of the car thirty yards down the street, two men had approached from across the road, scarves pulled up over their faces, and opened fire with semi-automatic pistols. Caught completely by surprise, Volkan Kalaman and the bodyguard had been hit by a hail of bullets. The bodyguard had gone down immediately, but Volkan, who was a big man, had managed to stagger a further ten yards down the street before

Mr Bone caught up with him and put two more bullets in the back of his head.

Although his two sisters had never believed that Cem could have committed such a heinous crime, it was common knowledge within both criminal and police circles that he'd been the one behind the hit, sealing his reputation as an utterly ruthless operator.

But it wasn't ruthlessness that had driven Cem to murder his own father. It was rage. When Cem was twenty-one, he'd discovered that his father had a secret second family. It had been Mr Bone who'd told him about it. It would be wrong to say that he and Mr Bone had become close: Mr Bone wasn't close to anyone. But he'd taken more and more of an interest in Cem as he'd grown up, describing him as the only man who could lead the Kalaman organization into the future, because only he had the necessary strength. It had, Cem knew, been Mr Bone who'd turned him against his own father, but then his father had deserved it. Cem had seen his second family. He'd watched them. His father and mistress and their young son. He'd seen them together, and it had filled him with an anger he found hard to describe.

But he'd kept his rage on the inside, beneath a cool, calm exterior, and he'd bided his time. Only when his beloved mother had died of slow-acting throat cancer (and a broken heart, Cem was sure, for he felt certain she knew of his father's betrayal) did he take his revenge in the most brutal form possible. Because it wasn't just his father he'd killed. Within weeks of his death the mistress was found dead in her bath with her wrists slit, while the body of her eleven-year-old son was lying in his bedroom, where Cem had smothered him with his own pillow.

Cem was keeping his rage on the inside now as he stared at the giant TV screen in what his wife liked to call the drawing room. The news was featuring the hunt for Hugh Manning, which had moved to the area in and around a small town in southern Scotland on the borders of the Galloway Forest national park. The female news reporter was standing in a Sainsbury's car park where Manning had apparently been seen the night before by a customer and a checkout assistant. In the background, a group of uniformed officers were talking in front of a couple of parked squad cars. According to the reporter, police had already checked CCTV footage from the store and confirmed that it was indeed Manning, and that he was believed to be driving the car of murder victim Max Bradshaw. A photo of the model of the car appeared in the corner of the screen and she gave out its registration number.

Cem had never met Hugh Manning but he had to admit the lawyer had shown remarkable initiative to get this far. In hindsight, they should have killed him years ago, after that incident with Alastair, but it was too late to worry about that now. Everything would be rectified if they got to him before the police. Then, when Manning was found dead, Cem could use his contacts in the media to blame him for the Bone Field murders. And then finally they could put this whole saga behind them.

'Are we still playing, Papa?'

Cem turned round. His youngest child and only son, Ruslan, had come into the room through the open French windows, carrying the ball they'd been kicking around the garden a few minutes earlier.

'Sure I am,' Cem replied, beaming at his beloved boy. 'But give Papa a few minutes. I have some business to do, then I'll be out. Practise your shooting in the meantime.' He ruffled his son's thick black hair.

'I want to help you,' said Ruslan, looking up at his father.

'One day you will, boy, I promise. Now go outside.'

Cem watched his son go, hoping that one day he'd be a wealthy businessman who wouldn't have to commit murder, and who would sleep easily at night, knowing that he had no enemies. Then he turned and stalked through the house to his office suite. At the back of the main office was a fortified, soundproofed room with a biometric retinal scanner next to the door that allowed access only to him.

Inside was a single desk and chair. Cem unlocked the desk drawer, took out a satellite phone and made a call.

He was fully prepared to leave a message but the phone was picked up within two rings.

'Can you talk?' he demanded.

'I wouldn't have picked up if I couldn't,' said Alastair Sheridan.

He sounded stressed. Cem ignored his tone. Alastair was one of the only people he tolerated talking back to him.

'Have you seen the news?'

'About Scotland? Yes. It doesn't sound good.'

'If the police don't find him soon they'll have to widen the search. We need to find him first. You know him, Alastair. I want you to find any link he has to Scotland. I've looked it up on the map and the place he was seen is in the back end of nowhere. He went there for a reason. Find it.'

'I've been thinking already.'

'And?'

'I remember him talking to me years ago about a friend of his who owned a house up there. I know he used to go there sometimes for shooting weekends.'

Cem thought about this. 'How many people worked at Manning's legal practice?'

'There was only him, a researcher and a secretary.'

'He would have told them where he was going in Scotland, and might have mentioned the name of the person who owned the house. Or given them a contact number.'

'The police will be all over the researcher and the secretary by now. We can't get to them. Or his old work diaries. It's all been seized as evidence.'

Cem contemplated sending Mr Bone over to talk to the secretary but knew it would be taking too much of a risk. There had to be another way.

'You of all people know what's at stake here, Alastair,' he said. His voice was calm but cold. 'So my advice to you is to keep racking those brains until you come up with something we can use. And fast.'

Nineteen

Lola Sheridan lived in the middle of woodland about fifteen miles north-west of London, not far from the Buckinghamshire village of Little Chalfont.

The security gates were open and, after dropping Dan out of sight of the house, I pulled into the driveway and parked next to a white Mercedes SLC convertible with the top down.

The house itself was a large yet tasteful mock Tudor, with latticed windows set among snaking vines of wisteria. The lawn was neat and lined with mature shrubs and colourful flowers, and blooming hanging baskets hung down on either side of the front door. It didn't feel like the home of a monster.

I knocked on the door and waited. I hadn't called ahead, not wanting to alert Lola to my visit, and there was no answer. I looked at my watch. It was just after five p.m. As far as I knew

Lola didn't work, being independently wealthy, and her car was here, but it was possible she was out somewhere. It didn't matter. We weren't expected at Ealing until 8.30 so I could easily wait.

I was about to knock a second time when the door opened.

Lola Sheridan was a tall, overly thin woman with long, dead straight jet-black hair running down her back, and a narrow face that would have been attractive if it wasn't quite so bony. She'd definitely had work done to her face, but it didn't cover up the fact that she looked older than her forty-seven years – something that could probably be remedied if she put on a bit of weight. She was dressed casually in a black top and tight-fitting jeans and her feet were bare.

She looked at me with dark, suspicious eyes. 'Yes?'

I gave her my best smile and produced my warrant card. 'Good afternoon, Miss Sheridan. I'm Officer Ray Mason from the National Crime Agency. I wanted to ask you some questions about Tracey Burn.'

She looked puzzled, and slightly irritated. 'Who?'

'She cleaned for you back around 2004, 2005. At your house in Kensington.' I didn't know this, of course, but I was letting her know we'd been looking into her background in the hope that it might throw her off her guard a little.

It didn't seem to work. 'I've got a very vague recollection of someone of that name. She may have done, yes. But I don't think I can help you much. What do you want to know about her?'

'Do you mind if I come inside? It's also connected to the ongoing inquiry into the murder of your cousin, Kitty Sinn.'

'I thought you people worked in pairs,' she said, making no move to let me in.

'This is a major inquiry using up a lot of resources and since I'm only here to ask a few friendly questions, it seemed prudent to come alone.'

Seeing as I wasn't budging, she reluctantly moved aside, and I followed her into a large country kitchen. She didn't offer me a seat but leaned back against one of the worktops, still eyeing me carefully as I stood a few feet away facing her.

'You're the same Ray Mason who was behind the discovery of the bodies in the Bone Field?'

'That's right.'

'I thought you were suspended. Didn't you kill someone during that riot in Hackney?'

'It was an accident. I was exonerated.'

'So what has my cleaner got to do with poor Kitty?'

'She *was* your cleaner then?'

Lola smiled, as if my attempts to put her on the back foot were too amateur to bother with. 'As far as I can recall, a woman by that name did clean for me many years ago. But I've had quite a lot of cleaners over the years, so I remember very little about her. I can't even recall what she looks like.'

'Don't worry,' I said. 'You'll be seeing Tracey's photo a lot in the coming days. She's the first victim to be identified from the Bone Field. We've also recovered a recording of her murder that we believe was filmed at the farmhouse there.'

Lola gave me a shocked look. 'A murder video? How awful. The things human beings do for kicks never ceases to depress me.'

'Nor me. Even though I've seen a lot of it in my time.'

'I know. I heard what happened to you as a child. I'm sorry you've had to suffer so much. It must be hard to keep going sometimes.'

'You know a lot about me, Miss Sheridan.'

'You have a high profile for a police officer. I'm not sure that's always a good thing.'

As we talked, Lola never took her eyes off me. Her voice was deep and sultry, almost hypnotic, and she had a confidence and poise that even the best cop in the world would have trouble breaking down. I'll be honest, she unnerved me. But there was no way I was going to let her know it.

'Tracey was last seen alive in autumn 2004, about the time she was cleaning for you.'

'Can I ask you something, Officer Mason? How do you know she was cleaning for me at that time?'

I saw no reason to protect Paul Moffatt. 'Tracey's boyfriend at the time told us. He also said you encouraged her to leave him.'

She laughed. 'That sounds like a bitter ex-boyfriend to me. I don't remember any of that.'

'He also said Tracey told him she'd started a new life in a shelter outside London. Did you recommend it to her?'

'No. As I told you, I can hardly remember her at all, and I certainly didn't encourage her to leave her boyfriend. I've never had that sort of relationship with any of my cleaners. So you said this was connected to Kitty's killing. How so?'

Officially, there was still no link between Kitty and Dana Brennan's murders and those that had taken place at the Bone

Field. Obviously, though, as one of those responsible Lola knew there was a link. But I wasn't sure if she knew I knew it. I decided it was time to tell her.

'We believe that the Bone Field killers also murdered Kitty, which is something of a coincidence, given that they also murdered your cleaner, Tracey.'

'Yes it is,' she said. 'It seems they've murdered a lot of people. Well, I hope you find them soon. But if you don't mind, I've got nothing else to add.'

'Oh don't worry, we'll definitely find them now,' I said. 'We're putting out a huge appeal across the media to track Tracey's movements after she left her boyfriend. It was a long time ago, but it'll jog people's memories, and that way we'll find her trail to the farm in Wales. And when we find that, we find the killers, and your cousin finally gets to rest in peace.'

There was a knock at the front door, and we both turned round.

'Are you expecting visitors?' I asked her.

'As a matter of fact I am,' she replied. 'So if you don't mind, I'll say goodbye now.'

She escorted me back to the front door and opened it.

Standing on the doorstep was a tall, slightly overweight man in his late forties with a fine head of blondish hair and a wide, disarming smile.

'Hello,' he said, seeing me, 'I'm Alastair Sheridan, Lola's brother.' He was already putting out a hand and I smiled back, shaking it and introducing myself, even though we both knew exactly who the other was. Alastair had a firm, dry grip, and the same confidence as his sister.

'Officer Mason was just leaving,' said Lola, not quite pushing me out of the door but standing close enough to give me a good shove if she felt so inclined.

'I was just letting your sister know that we may have a lead connected to the murder of your cousin, Kitty Sinn.' I briefly explained about Tracey Burn and the DVD while Alastair listened with a polite smile on his face, showing absolutely no sign of nerves whatsoever. I have to say, if I was looking to invest a few million quid, he'd be the type of man I'd automatically want to trust. Which just confirms the old adage: never judge a book by its cover.

'That's excellent news,' said Alastair when I'd finished, as if I'd just told him he'd won top prize in a raffle. 'Please keep us posted of progress. I have very fond memories of Kitty.'

'I have no doubt,' I said, smiling back.

I'd driven about fifty yards down the road from Lola's house when Dan appeared out of the trees. As I slowed down, he jumped inside, and I accelerated away.

'Well, did Tracey clean for her?' he asked me.

I smiled. 'She certainly did. And did you get the tracker on Lola's car?'

He nodded. 'Yeah, but I almost got caught when Alastair showed up. I wasn't expecting that. What do you think he was doing there?'

'Who knows? Maybe the progress we're making is rattling them. Not that I'd have guessed it with Lola. I don't think much is going to rattle her.'

'That was the whole idea of visiting her, wasn't it? To panic her a bit.'

'Maybe. But if what we've heard is right, Tracey Burn went to stay with someone outside London after she left Paul Moffatt. For all I know it might have been the house I was just in, or somewhere else belonging to one of the killers. If that's the case, Lola's going to want to warn them now, so let's see where she goes.'

'She may go nowhere.'

I shrugged. 'Then we haven't lost anything. Either way she's going to start to feel the pressure. And that's when they all make mistakes.'

Twenty

Lola Sheridan was far more concerned about events than she'd let on to Ray Mason.

All her life she'd lived by the philosophy instilled into her from earliest childhood: survival of the fittest. The strong must, and will, always overcome the weak in order to continue the survival and, indeed, improvement of the human species. It was the direct opposite of the feebleness inspired by Christianity. Lola considered herself a warrior, and a hunter. She made sacrifices to the spirits who represented Mother Nature and considered herself a higher being than so many of those around her.

And yet, she knew that this enlightenment and strength wouldn't always protect her. The whole point of nature was its careless cruelty. No one, even the best, was exempt from destruction, and the only way hunters survived was by continually adapting to the situations they found themselves in.

So far, Lola had sat tight and waited, knowing there was no real evidence to tie her in with any of the murders. She was sure that neither her brother nor Cem (who was also like a brother to her) would ever betray her. But it was possible that events would spiral out of their control too.

This morning she'd read the cards for the first time in weeks, looking for signs of what the future might bring. She'd drawn the hanged man and the six of swords together. For her, the meaning was obvious. Her life as she knew it was coming to an end. It was time to make sacrifices and to move on to pastures and people new. Mason's visit had been a warning. She must go soon and not delay.

She and Alastair stood by the front window and watched Mason drive away, then Alastair took her by the hand and led her into the back garden.

'How long was he here for?' asked Alastair as they stood together in the shade of a weeping willow.

'Only a few minutes. I got rid of him easily enough.'

'And he came alone?'

'Yes.'

'He's trying to scare you.'

'Did you know that they'd identified Tracey Burn?' said Lola. She remembered Tracey well enough. Weak, soft and stupid – easy prey. Lola felt no guilt over her death. Her life had been dull and meaningless. In the wild she wouldn't have lasted a minute. All they'd done was put her out of her misery, strengthening themselves in the process.

'I've only just found out about it,' said Alastair. 'The police held a press conference an hour ago. That's why I came here, to reassure you that everything's under control. I've just heard from Cem and he says none of this makes any difference. They'll never be able to get enough evidence even to question us.'

'But they've already identified me as someone who knew her.'

'She cleaned for you.' Alastair shrugged his shoulders. 'So what? That's hardly a crime.'

'You know I'd never say a word, don't you?'

'Of course I do. You're my sister. You're made of sterner stuff.'

He came close and touched her cheek gently.

'We need to warn Aunty,' she said.

'I know. You need to call her. But not from here. Just in case the police are listening in. Give it an hour or two then call her from a public phone box. Tell her to stick to the script.'

Lola looked up at him, feeling safe in his presence, as she always had. 'OK, but I don't trust Mason.'

'I know. He's a problem. I've been pushing Cem to get rid of him permanently.'

'I think you may need to push harder, darling,' she said, putting an arm round her brother's waist.

'Don't worry. I will.' He ran a hand through her hair, smiling now, his eyes giving off their telltale twinkle. 'Now I've come all this way, pretty sister, and we've both got some free time. How do you think we should spend it?'

He leaned down, his breath warm on her face, and she closed her eyes.

Twenty-one

I had to hand it to Sheryl Trinder. She could do a brilliant press conference.

It was half past six and Dan and I were back in the office watching a rerun of her performance as she gave the news to the world that the first victim from the Bone Field had now been positively identified. The photo of Tracey Burn we'd seen earlier had been blown up on the wall behind her, and was also being shown in the bottom corner of the screen as she spoke. Sheryl's expression remained stoic, but there was no mistaking the emotion in it as she explained how many years ago, when she'd been a young PC, she'd met Tracey on several occasions, and found her sweet and vulnerable. She went on to say that Tracey had last been seen in October 2004 and that she'd died at some point before July 2005. She concluded by appealing to anyone who'd seen her during that period to come forward urgently.

There was the usual barrage of questions, mainly centred around how we, the police, could be so certain that Tracey had died before July 2005, and why she'd never been reported missing, but Sheryl gave very little away, and left the podium soon afterwards, her job done.

And now, as with the Hugh Manning case, it was just a matter of waiting.

Dan sipped his coffee and turned to me. 'What do you think? Will anyone come forward?'

I sighed. 'I honestly don't know. It was a long time ago, so it's not going to be like the Manning sightings. But she did call Paul Moffatt and her half sister after she'd left, so she was staying somewhere, and that means someone might have seen her. We could definitely do with a bit of luck. I'm assuming we've got no movement from Lola Sheridan?'

'Nothing yet,' he said, checking the screen on his PC. 'Her car's still at home, although she may have gone somewhere with Alastair.'

I had to admit, our plan with the tracker was a long shot, as was the press conference. In the end, Tracey Burn was a pretty average-looking woman, and she'd been dead at least eleven years. It wasn't a good combination when you were looking to give people's memories a nudge.

The phone rang in my pocket. It was Tina. I immediately perked up.

'How's France?' I asked her. 'Have you sorted out your business over there?'

'All done,' she said. 'I'm on my way back now. I've also been doing some digging into Alastair and Lola Sheridan's past, and I've found out something that might give us more background on why the Sheridans and Cem Kalaman are so closely intertwined.'

'OK. I'm in the office with Dan. He ought to hear this too. I'm going to put you on speaker.'

I got up and closed the door.

'Sure,' she said. 'Hey Dan.'

'Hey Tina,' said Dan, 'nice to hear your voice. I've heard a lot about you over the years.'

'Most of it bad, I should think.'

'No. Quite a lot of it good. The Met should never have let you go.'

'I think they think I'm a troublemaker. Like Ray.'

Dan laughed. 'He's *definitely* a troublemaker.'

'So what have you got for us, Tina?' I asked, thinking it would be nice if we could get Dan and Denise over to Tina's place one night for a dinner party. Maybe when we had something to celebrate, like putting the Bone Field killers behind bars.

'In 1976, Kitty Sinn's mother Mary hired a private detective in Northampton, a man called Brian Foxley, to investigate her sister Janet's death. As you know, Janet was married to Robert Sheridan and was the mother of Alastair and Lola. She died in a road accident in Italy in 1975 where she was holidaying with Robert, without the kids.'

I thought about that. Alastair and Lola had been very young when they lost their mum. Just like me when I lost my family.

'The circumstances of the accident look suspicious,' continued Tina. 'But it's what happened to Foxley, the private detective, that makes it interesting. He stabbed his wife to death and then hanged himself that same year, 1976. I don't know how long after taking the case this was but he never had any history of violence towards her, and from what I've read they had a very stable marriage.'

'That's a proper Kalaman MO,' said Dan, 'making a double murder look like a murder/suicide.'

'Well, it worked,' said Tina. 'The case was closed straight away with no suspicion that there was anyone else involved.'

'So what do you think really happened?' I asked Tina. 'Could Robert Sheridan have murdered his wife, the private detective found out, and Sheridan approached someone from the Kalaman organization to have him killed?'

'It seems logical.'

'Cem would have just been a kid then, no more than eight years old,' Dan said. 'His father was running the family business at the time. Volkan Kalaman was a pretty nasty character, and we're almost certain he'd personally killed two men by the mid-seventies, but he was more of an old-fashioned gangster than his son. He only killed when he absolutely had to. This looks like a bigger, more complicated job than I'd associate with him. It can't be a coincidence though.'

'No,' said Tina, 'it's definitely not a coincidence.'

'Where did you get the information from?' I asked her.

'You know I've been looking into the background of the Kitty Sinn case for a while now – I just came across it. Can you do me a favour, Ray? Find out who the investigating officer was on the Brian Foxley case, and whether he's still alive. If he is, I'd like to talk to him. I don't know if it'll come to anything, but I want to dig a bit deeper.'

I told her to leave it with me then stood up with the phone, switching it off speaker, and turned away from Dan.

'Is dinner tomorrow night still on?' I asked quietly.

'It is,' she said, equally softly. 'And I'm really looking forward to it.'

When the call was over, Dan grinned at me. 'Am I seeing the new, softer Ray Mason? I'm jealous.'

'Why? You've got Denise and the girls. You've got a fantastic life.'

'I know. But it's a great feeling when you're falling in love.'

'Who says I'm in love?'

'It's obvious, brother. And do you know what? I'm pleased for you. It might calm you down a bit.'

'We'll see,' I said, sitting back down and thinking about this new information from Tina.

I'd always thought the link between the Sheridan and Kalaman families had begun with Alastair and Cem meeting at university in the late eighties, but it seemed now that it had started a long way back from that. But what had brought them together? And what had turned the three children – Alastair, Lola and Cem – into such monsters?

I took the photo of Dana Brennan, the girl I'd always believed to be the first victim they'd abducted, from its place in my wallet, and examined it. A pretty young girl with blonde hair looked back at me with a huge gap-toothed smile. This little girl would have been forty now, a year older than me, but she'd been snatched from her bike barely half a mile from home before disappearing into thin air, only for her bones to emerge, along with Kitty Sinn's, back in April.

I stared at her photo. Dana had been their first victim; then it had been Kitty, killed by her cousins in an elaborate murder that had fooled the police for more than two decades, and had served to enrich both of them. And since then they'd carried on killing with impunity.

But it was the case of Dana, their youngest victim, that had always affected me the most. I'd seen at first hand the destruction to her family, the terrible cost of not knowing what had happened to her.

'Hey, we've got something here,' said Dan, interrupting my thoughts. 'It looks like Lola Sheridan's on the move.'

I replaced the photo in my wallet and went over to where he was staring at a map on the PC screen. He zoomed in on the flashing red dot of the tracker and we watched in silence for a few minutes as Lola's car drove through the winding Buckinghamshire back roads for several miles before stopping in a small village.

Dan switched the map to satellite and zoomed in further, then moved to Google street view. Quaint cottages appeared on either side of the road, as well as a pub slightly further down. But it wasn't them that grabbed our attention. It was the red phone box in the foreground.

Dan switched back to the satellite map where the red flashing dot remained stationary about thirty metres south of the pub. In other words, right next to the phone box.

Like I said, criminals always make mistakes, however good they are.

Three minutes later, at 6.46 p.m., Lola's car was moving again, going back the way she'd come, and we watched as she drove directly home.

'So your idea paid off,' said Dan, looking up at me. 'She's called someone. Now we just need to pull up the records from that phone box and we'll find out who. Well done, Ray. I'm impressed.'

'I'm not just a pretty face,' I said, finally feeling like we were getting somewhere.

Twenty-two

Tina was sad to leave Charlotte Curtis behind.

They'd spent the afternoon in the garden after a leisurely lunch of cold meats and fresh bread from the local bakery. Charlotte had drunk two glasses of rosé. Tina hadn't had a drink in eight years and usually seeing someone else drink didn't bother her (if it had she'd never have lasted five minutes with Ray), but today, relaxing in the sunshine in the near silence of the French countryside, she'd experienced a powerful urge for just one glass, and it had taken an awful lot of willpower to stop herself.

She and Charlotte had never had much of a chance to talk before. The last time they'd met they'd been fleeing on foot across country, being chased by French associates of the Kalamans. But this time they'd had a chance to talk about Kitty Sinn, the woman who'd started it all, and Tina had let Charlotte reminisce about their time together at university. Kitty had sounded like a lovely young woman, and it seemed a terrible injustice that she'd lost her life in the way she did.

When it was time for Tina to leave, she and Charlotte had shared a long hug, and Charlotte had looked her in the eyes. 'Do you know, Tina, I've spent so much of my life sheltered from all the darkness of the world – even Kitty's disappearance didn't affect me as much as it should have done – but now I feel like I've seen the very worst it has to offer. I have nightmares. How on earth do you cope?'

In truth, Tina had found it incredibly difficult to cope over the years. 'Because I've got no choice,' she'd said. 'It's either that or be defeated. And I'm not going to be defeated. Neither are you.'

And with that, she'd driven away, hoping that Charlotte would be able to return home again soon. Whether that happened or not depended at least in part on whether Cem Kalaman could be brought to justice, and Tina had a good feeling about the lead that Charlotte had provided. A double murder forty years ago might not look like much on the surface, but if Tina could establish a link between the Kalamans and the Sheridans, she could build a picture of how they'd murdered Dana Brennan and Kitty Sinn as well as the numerous women who'd died since. And somewhere in that picture she hoped would be the evidence to help bring them down.

While trawling the internet in Charlotte's garden that after-noon Tina had managed to track down the only surviving sibling of Brian Foxley, an unmarried sister two years his junior, and had even found a landline number for her. The sister's name was

Pauline and she was seventy-five and still living in Northampton, the same town in which her brother had run his private detective business.

Tina was tired. It had been a long day. But she decided to call Pauline anyway.

The phone rang for a long time before it was answered by a woman with an uncertain 'Hello?'

'Miss Foxley?'

'Yes. Who is this? Look, if you're trying to sell me something—'

Tina thought she sounded pretty sprightly for seventy-five, with a healthy dose of suspicion. 'I'm not. I'm ringing about your brother, Brian. My name's Tina Boyd. I'm a private detective as well.'

'Brian's dead,' Pauline Foxley said coldly. 'He's been dead a long time.'

'I know. I've been hired by the estate of one of his last clients to look into what happened to him.' Tina had rehearsed this conversation, and she kept to her script. 'Their belief, and mine too, is that your brother and his wife were murdered, and it was made to look like a murder/suicide. I hate to bring up the past like this, Miss Foxley, but I'd like to ask you some questions.'

There was a pause, as if Pauline was gathering herself. 'Look, I don't know you . . .' she managed eventually.

Tina gave her name again, as well as her website address and licence number. 'Would you like to check them out and I can call you back?'

There was another pause as Pauline wrote everything down. Tina hoped that she would be as thorough with her memories as she was with her attention to detail.

'Hold on,' she said, and Tina heard the phone being put down on a surface.

It was a good three minutes before Pauline came back on the phone. 'All right,' she said. 'What do you want to know?'

'The first question's quite a direct one, but it's important I get an honest answer. Is it possible your brother did actually kill his wife?'

'No,' she answered emphatically.

Tina had been prepared for that. Most people aren't going to think their siblings are capable of murder. 'Why not?'

'Lots of bloody reasons,' said Pauline, her voice suddenly full of righteous anger. 'Brian was a good man. He was a police officer for ten years before he became a private detective, and he never had any trouble with anyone. He didn't have a temper. He didn't drink much. They said he was full up with whisky when they found him. He didn't even drink whisky. And most of all, he had no reason to hurt Glenda. They had their ups and downs, of course, who doesn't? But he never raised his hand to her, so when the police said they thought Brian had stabbed Glenda to death, and then hanged himself, I knew he couldn't have done it, and I told them so.'

'Forgive me, Miss Foxley, but I was also in the police force a long time and I investigated a number of murders, and relatives of suspects often say that.'

'Well then, let me tell you something else. Brian was scared of the sight of blood, right from when he was a child. John, his brother – God rest his soul – used to tease him about it because he had to have a blood test once and he fainted. He'd never have done what they said he did to Glenda, stabbed her all those times. He didn't have it in him.'

'And you told all this to the police?'

'Everyone told them. John, Mum, his friends.'

Tina suppressed a sigh. This wasn't exactly evidence.

'Were the two of you close?'

'Yes we were.' Again Pauline was emphatic. 'We only lived a couple of miles apart. There's not a day goes by when I don't think about him.'

'Did he ever talk to you about a case he was working on not long before he died involving a woman who died in a car accident in Italy?'

'No. He didn't talk about his work. He was professional like that.'

'Miss Foxley, I think Brian must have found something out about this particular case that got him killed. Is there anyone he would have confided in?'

'Glenda. He would definitely have told her.'

'Anyone who might be alive now?'

'It's such a long time ago.' There was frustration in her voice.

'Can you try and think?' Tina persevered. 'Anyone he was friendly with who might be able to help?'

'You could talk to Ken, I suppose. Not that I've seen him for a long time.'

'Who's Ken?'

'Ken Wignall. He was a policeman friend of Brian's. He promised to talk to the officer in charge of the case and tell him that Brian wouldn't have killed his wife. He might know something.'

Tina pulled up at the side of the road and made a note of the name.

'And do you know where I might find him?' she asked.

'The last I heard he'd moved out to Brackley to live with his daughter and her husband. He hasn't been that well. I can probably get a number for him if you want.'

'Yes please, that would be great.' Tina didn't like the fact that he hadn't been well. 'And one last question, if you don't mind. Do you remember the name of the police officer who ran the case?'

'No, but I remember he was a big fat lazy bastard and a bloody awful detective.'

Tina burst out laughing. 'Why don't you say it like it is, Miss Foxley?'

The older woman chuckled. 'Well he was. And please, call me Pauline.'

'OK, Pauline. Don't worry, I'll find out his name. Thank you for your help.'

'You do believe me about Brian, don't you?' she said, serious now. 'That he wouldn't have done it?'

'I need to look at the case further,' Tina replied, 'but yes I do. And I'll do what I can to prove it.'

'Thank you,' Pauline said. 'That means a lot to me.'

Tina gave Pauline her mobile number, asked her if she could find a number for Ken Wignall as soon as possible, then apologized for bringing up the past.

'No, I'm glad you did,' said Pauline. 'When you get to my age, the past is all there is.'

When Tina ended the call she saw that Ray had sent her a message saying that the SIO on the Foxley case, DCI Melvyn Rogers, had died of a heart attack in 2002.

She sighed. Finding answers after all this time wasn't going to be easy.

Twenty-three

It was just gone ten p.m. and Dan and I were sat in our pool car on a back street in Acton, waiting for the undercover op to get going.

The briefing at Ealing nick had been pretty straightforward, although it had been strange for me going back there after three months away. The two NCA undercover operators (who'd not been there, so there was no chance of them being compromised) had arranged to be in a pub on the Uxbridge Road at 9.30, from where they were to await further instructions from Ugo Amelu on when and where the deal was to take place. Two armed tactical support teams in unmarked vans, as well as two cars containing Eddie Olafsson and other detectives from Ealing, plus our own car, were in different positions within a hundred-metre radius of the pub. Although Dan and I were strictly observers, we'd found a good spot on the Uxbridge Road with a view straight up it. Both undercover ops were wired for sound and wearing miniature GPS devices, with their mobiles automatically connected to Olaf's, so we had their exact location at all times. The plan was that when they received their instructions, either by phone or face to face, the back-up team would know about it and would follow them to the rendezvous at a safe distance. As soon as they confirmed the presence of the contraband, one of them would give the code phrase 'great stuff – it's all there', and then, once they were safely out of the area, armed units would move in and make the arrests. If, on the other hand, things went wrong and they needed to be extracted immediately, the code phrase was 'No way, we're leaving right this second'.

I'd just finished eating an Italian BMT from Subway – my sustenance for the evening – and it had tasted exactly like the processed crap it was. Dan had ordered a twelve-inch steak and cheese melt and was still finishing his, along with a huge vat of Diet Coke.

'You know,' he said between mouthfuls, 'I did undercover work for a little while back in my early twenties.'

'You never told me that.'

'I don't tell you everything.'

'What kind of cases were you on?'

'Same as this one but on a much smaller scale.'

He took another bite of his sandwich, getting some sauce on his face. It made me wonder how he stayed in shape, because that was the thing about him. He always looked lean and svelte, with plenty of muscle and no fat. It was very unfair.

'Did you do it for long?'

'For a while. Most of the time it was easy. You turned up, pretended to be a buyer. The seller pulled out the drugs. You nicked him. It didn't do any good, of course. You nick one, someone else just comes in and takes his place.' He found a napkin, wiped his face, and took a drink from the Coke. 'Then one day me and another undercover guy turned up on this estate in Brixton acting as small-time dealers from Harlesden wanting to buy some crack. We were still knocking on the door when these boys appeared out of nowhere and surrounded us. There were about six or seven of them – kids really, but a couple of them had knives. That's when you realize how vulnerable you are. Back-up was a quarter of a mile away.'

'What did you do?'

'They were nervous, but there was one you could tell was the leader. All it would have taken was for me to give him one quick left hook and he'd have gone down just like that, and the others would have bolted. I thought about doing it too. The kid might have been holding a knife but his guard was wide open.' He shook his head slowly, looking out of the window. 'But I couldn't. When you've killed a man with your fists, it makes you much more careful about using them again. Just the thought of it makes me nauseous. So we gave them the money. We were carrying five hundred quid and we gave them the lot. They called us pussies and ran. Back-up arrived two minutes later but never caught them. It was a set-up, must have been, and the thing was, it put me off undercover work. I didn't want to be thrown in that situation again, which was why I applied for detective. But I'll tell you something. I admire those two in there. You've got to have real balls to do that job.'

'Yeah, I know,' I said, remembering the intensity of an undercover op I'd been involved in years ago in the military, one that had ended in disaster, and whose ramifications were still being felt years later.

Which was when I saw a car pull up opposite the pub and a tall black man get out and look around. I took out a pair of binoculars and focused in on him.

I recognized Ugo Amelu straight away. He was looking down the street towards us, but too far away to see me. I could see him though, and sense his body language. He looked pumped up and ready for this deal, and I wondered as I watched him take a mobile from his pocket what we'd need to do to convince him to talk.

The next second the radio crackled into life. It was Olaf.

'Target 2 is here and phoning UC1. All units stand by. It looks like we're live.'

Twenty-four

Stegs and Big Tone were sat at a corner table of the pub, facing the door and nursing drinks. Tone was drinking Coke but Stegs was deliberately breaking the rules and drinking Stella. He needed the drink to keep calm. The conversation between the two of them was sparse. Stegs had worked with Tone on several jobs, and he liked him, but the mood tonight was tense, and anyway, they had to be very careful what they said in case someone working for Ugo was listening in. The supposed African prince was a grade A prick, but he was also cunning, and in these sort of ops, where trust between the parties was non-existent, you could never be too careful.

The pub was busy with a sizeable crowd of white metrosexual twenty- and thirty-somethings that contained a hefty beard quotient. It was the type of place Stegs hated, inhabited by exactly the kind of people he also hated, and he had no idea why Ugo had chosen this pub as a meeting point, since all three of them would stand out a mile. But Stegs had long ago ceased to be surprised by the criminal classes whose behaviour was always erratic and often completely irrational.

He sat back in his chair and looked around, wanting to see if anyone was paying them undue attention. No one was. They might as well have been invisible, which for some reason irritated Stegs. He didn't like the way all these people were sitting there gawking at their phones, or talking about their crap jobs in media, without a care in the world, while he and Big Tone were risking their lives on their behalf. Frankly, they didn't deserve it.

He looked at his watch. Five past ten, and his pint glass was almost empty. He wanted another one but knew that would be the kind of move that could potentially cost him his job, and he couldn't afford that, not with his outgoings.

His undercover phone began vibrating in his pocket. The number was withheld, but Stegs knew who it would be. He put the phone to his ear and leaned forward so he was out of the worst of the pub's background noise.

'Yeah?'

'What's up, bruv,' said Ugo. 'You in the pub?'

'Course I'm in the pub,' said Stegs, feigning righteous irritation at being messed about. 'We've been sitting here waiting for you for the last half hour.'

'Sorry bruv, I got held up. Come on out. I'm over the other side of the road.'

'Right,' said Stegs with an exaggerated sigh. 'We'll be out in a minute. Come on,' he said to Tone. 'He's outside.'

Ugo was standing next to a Porsche Cayenne parked slap bang in the middle of a bus lane, which was typical criminal behaviour. Stegs bet he owed thousands in parking fines that would never get paid.

'How you doin', bruv?' said Ugo, flashing a pearly white smile. 'Your taxi's here. You got the money?'

'Yeah, I got the money,' said Stegs.

'Where is it? You ain't hidin' two hundred on you, are you?'

He was still smiling, and that was the thing about Ugo. He smiled a lot which, given the business he was in, always unnerved Stegs.

'It's nearby.'

'Nearby ain't no good to me, bruv. You're going to need to bring the money with you. Otherwise there ain't no deal.'

'Where are we going?'

Ugo looked round. 'Well, we ain't doin' it here, are we? We've got the stuff about a mile away. You jump in here and we can go and sort it out. But you need to bring the money.'

Stegs stepped right up close to Ugo, who was a good six inches taller, and glared up at him. 'You want us to get in a car with you and go some place we don't know with two hundred grand? I may come from the provinces but I'm not a complete fucking idiot. We're parked round the corner so we'll follow you to where the gear is. But I've got a friend, and the money's going to stay with him until I've seen the goods. If I like what I see, and I know I'm not being ripped off, I'll phone him and he'll come with the money.'

Ugo's smile immediately did a runner, but Stegs didn't give a shit about that. It was essential he set out his stall early as a man not to be messed with. If Ugo and Ralvin Lambden thought they could get away with it, he knew they'd try to rob them, especially on a one-off deal like this.

'Then I'm going to need to see the money first,' said Ugo. 'So I know you ain't Feds. Otherwise it's a no-go.'

Stegs and Tone exchanged looks.

'All right,' said Stegs. 'Follow us.'

The three of them walked two hundred metres round the block, passing a large white van with blacked-out windows with the name of a local plumber on the side that Stegs knew contained at least six heavily armed cops, whose presence he was very glad of. Every so often both he and Tone glanced over their shoulders, just to make sure no one else was following and it wasn't a trap.

The car Stegs and Tone were using for their undercover role was a BMW X5 – a classic bad boy car – that had been borrowed from Counter Terrorism Command. It was completely wired for sound, and sitting in the driver's seat was the third member of their undercover team, a middle-aged guy in a cheap suit who looked not unlike a young Keith Richards but who in reality was a decorated firearms officer. His name was Ron and Stegs hadn't worked with him before, but he looked the part, and Stegs liked the fact he was carrying a Glock 17 that he knew how to use.

Stegs nodded to him now and opened the rear passenger door. There was a holdall on the back seat. They'd both been expecting Ugo to want to see the money up close so the holdall had been packed to make it appear as if it was stuffed with wads of cash.

Each wad was supposedly five grand in twenties, but only the top and bottom few notes of each wad were real money, the rest a mix of varying qualities of counterfeit notes borrowed from the NCA evidence room, and paper. There were also ten separate tracking devices among the money, and two in the material of the holdall itself, so even if they were robbed there was no way the bad guys were going to get very far with it.

Yes, tonight the bad guys were doomed. The important thing was that they didn't take any of the good guys down with them.

Stegs leaned in and unzipped the bag, switching on his mobile phone torch to illuminate the contents. Ugo leaned in beside him, and took a sharp intake of breath. Stegs could almost smell his greed, along with the job lot of expensive aftershave he'd doused himself in. He pulled out a wad that had more real money in it than the others and handed it to Ugo, knowing that out here in a public place he wouldn't have time to give it anything more than a cursory examination.

'Satisfied?' he demanded as Ugo quickly flicked through it. 'And don't try anything. Ron here's armed.'

Ron turned round in the seat and eyeballed Ugo but didn't reveal the gun.

Ugo threw the wad back in the holdall, flicked a couple of notes on the one next to it, then nodded at Stegs, the grin firmly back on his face now. 'Yeah, bruv, I'm satisfied. Stay here. I'll come round with the car. Then you follow me.'

They watched him go before jumping in the X5 – Big Tone in the front, Stegs in the back.

'Looking good so far, but we're going to have to watch him,' said Stegs. 'UC1 to Tango 1. Did you get all that?'

'Loud and clear, UC1,' said Eddie Olafsson.

'Keep us nice and close, all right? I don't trust Ugo, and I trust that loon Ralvin even less.'

'We've got full back-up here, UC1. You're in safe hands.'

Stegs had heard that one before. In these days of increased health and safety, ops were a lot more tightly run. There'd been a risk assessment of this one and, because of the value of the targets, it had been given the all-clear. Even so, Stegs knew it could go tits up in a moment. Still, he felt a thrill go through him at the prospect of some real excitement. Not many things were exciting in his life. His ex-wife had remarried, his teenage son hardly spoke to him, he had no money, and his last girlfriend had left him for an accountant. But he still had this. The adrenalin shot of danger, mixed with that most potent of fantasies: the illusion of power.

The Porsche Cayenne appeared at the end of the road and Ugo waved for them to follow him.

Stegs grinned from the back seat. 'UC1 to Tango 1. OK, we're live.'

Twenty-five

It had begun to rain, and the city streets were slick and gleaming with reflected light as we pulled off the Uxbridge Road and headed into a winding warren of back streets in the direction of Hammersmith.

The back-up team travelled in a very loose convoy, keeping a long way back from the undercover vehicle, and sometimes taking different roads, so as not to arouse suspicion. An armed surveillance car containing three officers was at the front, just in case there was an ambush, and then a further minute behind them were the support vehicles and Ealing, with us bringing up the rear, a long way from any of the action.

I doubt we'd gone a mile and were listening to the radio traffic between the various vehicles when the armed surveillance team came on the line.

'Tango 2 to all units. UC1 and target vehicle have turned into the west entrance of the Cray's Pond Estate from Webber Avenue. There are two IC3s loitering at the entrance who may be lookouts. We are continuing southbound on Webber Avenue. Traffic is sparse, so advise all other cars not to follow us but to take an alternative road and suggest rendezvous on Cray's Pond Road out of sight of the west entrance.'

'Tango 1 to all cars,' said Olaf, sounding uncharacteristically nervous, 'affirmative. Rendezvous on Cray's Pond Road unless advised otherwise by Tango 2. The Cray's Pond Estate is scheduled for demolition. There are very few people still living there, and a lot of places to hide. We may have to abort. It could be too dangerous.'

In the car, Dan and I exchanged glances. It would be a nightmare for us if the op was aborted, but as we turned into Cray's Pond Road, I could see Olaf's point.

The estate loomed up on our left, silhouetted among the sodium glow of the streetlamps: a brooding, dark fortress of brutalist 1960s concrete blocks, many visibly crumbling, linked by a series of covered walkways, and providing a multitude of ambush points and escape routes. It was in fact very similar to the estate in Hackney I'd gone into on my last op with Olaf. That one had gone disastrously wrong, ending in the death of our suspect and a full-scale riot. None of us could afford a repeat performance.

Tango 2 was right. Traffic was sparse and the street largely empty, meaning we'd stand out if we weren't careful. Up ahead I saw the white van containing one of the armed response teams park up directly in front of Olaf's vehicle so I kept going, sneaking into a parking space next to an off licence a hundred metres up the road, which afforded us a view of an empty walkway running between two of the buildings. In my rear-view mirror I saw a couple of grimy-looking drunks stumble out of the off licence, cans in hand, and cross the road, disappearing into the darkness of the estate.

It was, I thought, either a very good or a very bad place to do a major drug deal, depending on where you were in the equation, and the undercover cops going in there weren't at the good end.

Twenty-six

'Where the hell's he taking us?' said Stegs, looking out of the X5's window at the buildings looming around them. The place had an abandoned feel. On the way in, Stegs had seen a sign saying that demolition work was due to begin here soon and a brand-new urban village was being built in its place, and if anyone still lived here, they weren't showing themselves tonight.

They drove past a row of ground-floor flats with caved-in windows, missing doors, and walls covered in graffiti, following Ugo's Porsche as it drove deeper into the estate.

'See those two,' said Big Tone, motioning towards the shadows of one of the buildings where a couple of kids in hoodies loitered, watching them pass. 'They're look-outs.'

'Did you hear that, Tango 1?' said Stegs to Eddie Olafsson.

'We've got kids watching us next to the third building in on the right-hand side.'

'I hear you, UC1. No problem. We're going to allow the targets to drive out of the estate with the money and take them on the street, well away from you. Just make sure you record the transaction then get out of there.'

'Roger that,' said Stegs, sitting forward in his seat and feeling the adrenalin surge through him. On jobs like this, Stegs was the king. He had real power. He was essential to the op's success. Without him it was nothing, and for just these few minutes, all the other mundane shit of his life faded into nothingness.

Twenty yards ahead of them, Ugo's Porsche Cayenne indicated and made a turn in front of one of the buildings. The X5 followed, turning on to an entrance ramp that led down into an underground car park – a cavernous space lit by overhead strip lights, several of which had ceased working. Up ahead, Ugo stopped his car next to a BMW saloon, the only other car in the place.

'Stop here,' said Stegs to Ron as they came to the bottom of the ramp. 'Can the camera on this thing film the whole deal from here?'

Ron stopped the X5. 'Of course it can. It's state of the art.'

'OK,' said Stegs, taking a deep breath and opening the door. 'Stay here and wait for us.'

He and Big Tone walked across the empty car park as the X5 ticked over behind them. The plan was simple. As soon as he and Tone saw the drugs, Stegs would wave Ron over. They'd make the exchange, with the camera on the X5 filming everything – and giving the back-up teams a few minutes to get fully in position – then give the code phrase, jump back in the car and get the hell out of there. As soon as Ugo and his buddies followed suit, they'd be nicked by the waiting cops. Job done.

The car park smelled of piss. The ceilings were low, and because it was dimly lit, shadows formed in the corners among the supporting pillars running down either side, giving the place a menacing air.

Ahead of them, Ralvin Lambden and a large Rastafarian with an angry-looking pitbull on a lead got out of the saloon and joined Ugo next to the boot. Ralvin and Ugo were both grinning at Stegs and Tone as they approached.

'Keep your wits about you,' Stegs whispered out of the corner of his mouth. 'I never like it when crims smile this much.'

'Don't worry, I'm on it,' Big Tone whispered back.

They stopped when they were a couple of yards away from the others.

'How you doin', mon?' asked Ralvin, seemingly a lot happier now than he had been when they'd met earlier. 'You got the money?'

Stegs nodded. 'Yup. It's in the car. Ugo's seen it.'

'It looks like it's all there, bruv,' Ugo told Ralvin.

'We need to count it,' said Ralvin.

'As long as you don't take too long,' said Stegs, knowing that only a brief examination would reveal that most of the money was counterfeit. 'I don't want to hang round here any longer than I have to. Have you got the gear?'

Ralvin nodded. 'Course I got the stuff, mon. It's in here.' He tapped the car boot.

'I'll need to test it before we hand over the cash,' said Stegs.

'Yeah, but don't take too long, mon. I don't want to hang round here any longer than I have to.' He gave Stegs a big gold-toothed grin to show he was joking, then flicked open the boot.

Stegs walked over, giving the snarling pitbull as wide a berth as possible, and peered inside, while Big Tone stood behind him watching his back.

There it was in a holdall: ten clear packets of white powder sealed with duct tape. Stegs felt a surge of relief as he realized this wasn't a rip-off. He would have happily turned round right now and headed straight back to the X5 but behaviour like that would have immediately raised suspicion. He needed to act the part, so he reached inside and picked up one of the packets, pulling back a piece of the duct tape to reveal its contents.

At the same time someone's phone started ringing. The noise was loud in the empty car park, and Stegs looked round and saw Ugo pull his phone out and answer the call. Ugo turned away and walked round the other side of the Cayenne as he talked quietly.

Stegs stiffened. He really didn't like the timing of this call but knew it was essential he continue to act natural, as if it didn't bother him in the least.

He licked the tip of his forefinger, put a small amount of the coke on it, and put it in his mouth.

Straight away he felt the tingling sensation on his tongue. It was good stuff.

He looked down. The pitbull was sniffing round his ankle. 'Get that fucking thing away from me,' he snapped at the Rastafarian, who glared back at him, but gave the dog's lead a quick yank.

Which was the moment when Stegs heard Ron lean on the X5

horn behind them. Before he could react, there was a loud crack and Big Tone pitched forward with a barely audible grunt, smacking his forehead on the edge of the boot. Directly behind him stood Ugo, holding a baseball bat close to his chest. He snarled at Stegs and lifted the bat again.

The whole thing happened so fast Stegs was momentarily rooted to the spot, knowing there was no way he could get out of the way of the bat before it came down on his head. This was the thing about violence. However much you expected it, or had experienced it – and Stegs had seen violence too many times – the suddenness and brutality of it never ceased to shock. Out of the corner of his eye he saw Big Tone land in a heap on the concrete floor, the back of his head bleeding, already unconscious and no help at all.

'It's a fuckin' set-up!' yelled Ugo. 'There are Feds all over the street out there!'

Pure fear shot through Stegs and he bolted. But he'd gone barely a yard when he was yanked backwards and pulled into a headlock, the strength of the grip so strong that he knew it must be Ralvin. Stegs felt himself being swung round, just as Ron screeched towards them across the car park. Ron was no longer blasting away on the horn. Instead Stegs could clearly see him reaching into his jacket pocket for the gun. He was talking as well, no doubt into the X5's mike, telling back-up that everything had gone tits up.

Out of the corner of his eye, Stegs saw Ralvin lift a gun with his free hand and the next second he let off five shots in rapid succession, the noise from them deafening in the confines of the car park. It was difficult to know whether he was shooting to kill or just trying to blow out the tyres, but either way the front driver's side wheel blew and a bullet slammed into the windscreen.

Ron ducked down out of sight and the X5 stalled, leaving it stationary in the middle of the car park about fifteen yards away.

'Ugo, get da fuckin' money!' yelled Ralvin in Stegs's ear as the pitbull barked wildly.

Stegs couldn't believe it. In the confusion of the moment, Ralvin still thought that the money they'd brought with them was real.

So, it seemed, did Ugo who sprinted over to the X5, still holding the bat he'd used to attack Big Tone, and tried to open the rear passenger door. It was locked, so he dropped the bat and was reaching in the back of his jeans for something when he suddenly yelped in fear and jumped back.

'He's got a gun!' cried Ugo as Ron fired two shots from inside the X5, shattering one of the windows.

Ugo fell over on his arse trying to get out of the way but a moment later he was on his feet again.

'I can hear the Feds!' he shouted, running back towards them. 'They're coming!'

As if on cue, the white van Stegs had seen earlier near the pub drove slowly down the ramp, with armed CO19 officers coming down behind it on foot.

The Rasta let go of the pitbull which immediately started sprinting towards the van, still barking wildly, while Ugo ran past Stegs and Ralvin and kept on going. The Rasta immediately turned and ran in the same direction.

'Where you boys goin'?' cried Ralvin in surprise, as if the question wasn't completely obvious, and for a moment his grip on Stegs loosened a little, allowing him to speak.

'Go while you still can,' Stegs hissed, hoping Ralvin's sense of self-preservation would kick in.

Unfortunately it didn't. His grip on Stegs's throat tightened as two shots rang out from the other side of the car park and the pitbull went down.

It was hard for Stegs to imagine how things could go any more wrong, but then – and this was the story of his life – they did as Ralvin shoved the still-smoking barrel of his gun against his temple, the hotness of the metal making him gasp in pain, before dragging him towards the driver's side of the BMW saloon.

At least six armed CO19 officers appeared from round the back of the white van and began fanning out, their weapons pointed at Ralvin – and, unfortunately for Stegs, at him too.

'Armed police! Drop your weapon now!' barked one of them as the officers slowly approached. 'Drop it or we will shoot!'

'Come any closer and I kill him!' yelled Ralvin. 'I'm driving out of here wid him and you ain't gonna stop me, unnerstand? Him my hostage.'

Ralvin had clearly been watching too many movies if he thought he was just going to leave with Stegs and no one was going to stop him. Maybe that kind of thing worked in Jamaica but they couldn't have it happening round here. It would be too embarrassing.

Ralvin's breathing was getting shallower and faster as the cops kept coming, moving into a semi-circle, and Stegs could tell he was coming to the same conclusion.

'You are surrounded,' shouted an armed cop. 'This is not helping. Let him go.'

'Come any closer and I shoot dis wasteman. Den I shoot you. Unnerstand?' Ralvin stopped moving, and Stegs felt the gun being removed from his temple as he pointed it in the general direction of the cops, holding Stegs in front of him like a human shield. 'I told you. Get back!'

Stegs had never been so scared in all his life. But in the midst of the fear he remembered a martial arts move he'd been taught in an introductory self-defence course he'd done the previous year in the esteemed surroundings of Hendon Town Hall, about how to deal with someone who grabs you by the throat from behind. Stegs wasn't at all sure it was designed to stop wild-eyed gunmen as strong as oxen, but this was life or death, and rather than mull over all that could go wrong, he just did it.

Grabbing the arm holding him with both hands to ease the grip on his throat, he dropped down in a lunge, putting all his weight into his feet and catching Ralvin completely by surprise. The speed and force of the movement pulled Ralvin forward with him and, before he could right himself, Stegs slammed his head backwards into his face, enjoying the sensation of hitting soft tissue, and did a wild backwards karate chop aimed at Ralvin's nuts. Unfortunately, in his panic he missed completely and caught him on the thigh instead. But Stegs knew better than to stop there and, still keeping all his weight in his feet, used his elbow instead, this time striking lucky.

Ralvin grunted in pain and made the cardinal error of letting go of Stegs, who then dived to the floor. He'd barely hit it when he heard the sound of Ralvin's pistol being fired one more time, and then shots rang out seemingly from every direction and Ralvin fell heavily to the ground, making Stegs think that all these bullets were going to generate an awful lot of paperwork.

He waited a good five seconds before lifting his head, watching as the first CO19 ran over to where Ralvin lay on his back in a sprawled heap, the gun still in his hand, and attempted to administer first aid.

It's a bit late for that, thought Stegs, slowly getting to his feet.

The car park was now crawling with heavily armed police, while a few feet away Big Tone had woken up and was propped up against the BMW, rubbing his head and looking dazed.

The problem was there was no sign of the Rasta or Ugo Amelu.

Twenty-seven

Dan and I had heard everything over the radio as a frantic Olaf ordered CO19 in to save UCs 1 and 2, one of whom had been hurt.

It's hard when all the action's going on around you and you're there as an observer only, especially when you can't actually observe anything. I was getting tired of sitting in the car and now that there was no need to stay hidden I got out and breathed in the less-than-fresh London night air, which was when I heard a single shot from a high-calibre weapon I didn't immediately recognize and didn't think was police-issue being fired from inside the estate. Then came another burst of fire – at least a dozen shots this time, coming from MP5s.

Dan was out of the car now too. 'Shit,' he said. 'That doesn't sound promising. I hope to God they didn't take out Ugo.'

I was just opening my mouth to answer when two figures

crossed my vision as they sprinted past on a walkway just inside the estate. I only caught the briefest glimpse of them, but that was enough to recognize the lead runner as Ugo Amelu. The man behind him, running equally fast, was a shorter, older man in a bomber jacket and jeans.

Dan saw them too and, since we couldn't hear any obvious signs of pursuit, we exchanged a quick glance and made a collective decision not to be observers any more.

'Well he's not dead yet,' I said as we jumped back into the car and pulled out while Dan grabbed the radio and called in what we'd just seen and our location.

When we'd spotted them, Ugo and the other guy had been running parallel to the road we were on so I drove in the same direction, as Olaf shouted down the radio telling us to keep the suspects under surveillance but not to attempt arrests as they were likely to be armed. 'Back-up is on the way!' he yelled, knowing that he'd be the one in trouble if either of us got shot. And just in case we hadn't heard him properly, he shouted it again.

He sounded stressed. No one wants shots fired on one of their ops – it's a mountain of paperwork – and by the sound of it CO19 had fired at least a dozen, which meant someone was dead. Olaf couldn't afford any more drama.

But, as I looked in the rear-view mirror and didn't see any immediate sign of reinforcements, I decided I had no choice but to add to Olaf's stress levels. I swung a sharp right at the end of the estate, and saw a road leading into it up ahead. I turned into it, drove between two buildings, and came out in a large square with a vandalized children's play area in the middle. On the other side, running in front of a line of boarded-up ground-floor flats, were Ugo and the other guy. They turned our way as I drove towards them but didn't slow down and I could see they were aiming for a flight of steps leading up to the flats on the upper floors.

I accelerated hard, then yanked the wheel round in a screech of tyres, bringing the car to a halt just in front of them. Dan was closest to the pavement and he already had his door open before I'd fully stopped. He was out of the car fast, but credit to Ugo, he was even faster. He accelerated, dodging Dan's outstretched arm, and carried on running, so Dan hit the other guy instead with a waist-high rugby tackle that saw them both go crashing into a wall, with the suspect getting by far the worst of it.

I could hear the sound of a siren approaching from somewhere out on the main road, but it was still a good thirty seconds away and Ugo was already bounding up the staircase, moving fast. If he disappeared into the bowels of the estate it wasn't going to be easy to find him. And there was something else. As he'd passed us, I'd seen a gun handle poking out of the back of his jeans.

So he was armed. And I wasn't.

The thing is, in the heat of a pursuit, you don't tend to think about the extreme danger you're putting yourself in. You get swept up in the excitement, the adrenalin courses through your veins, and it's almost as if you're invincible. Plus if you really want to catch your quarry you're going to take some big risks. And I really wanted Ugo Amelu.

As I ran up the steps after him, I saw him disappear down a

first-floor walkway that connected to the next building. I didn't know how fit he was but he had to be tiring the pace he was going at, and I was still pretty fresh.

As I got to the walkway I just had time to see him reach the end then turn a corner and disappear. I redoubled my pace, my footsteps clattering on the hard concrete, and turned the way he'd gone. I ran past another bleak row of empty boarded-up flats then rounded another corner where a second flight of steps led back down to the ground floor.

I descended them two and three steps at a time and, as I reached the bottom, saw an open door to my left leading into the darkness of an abandoned flat.

Rubbish, including used syringes, littered the floor inside. Ahead of me was a more open area with a line of overflowing wheelie bins on one side, flats on the other, and beyond that a patch of sparse grass and a wooden fence that marked the border of the estate.

I stopped, panting from the exertion. Ugo was nowhere to be seen. I turned towards the open door, realizing that I was about to put myself in a very vulnerable position.

Which was when I heard the sound of heavy breathing behind me.

I swung round fast as a fist flew out of nowhere and connected with the side of my head, sending me bouncing off the doorframe and crashing to the ground.

Through my momentarily blurred vision I saw Ugo coming towards me out of the gloom, aiming a kick at my face. I was dazed, but my training kicked in. Instinctively I sat up and wrapped both arms round his foot while it was still in mid-air, knocking him off balance. He slipped and fell, rolling over on the concrete as I jumped up. Trying to shake the pain out of my head, I lurched towards him.

But he was quick. He rolled on to his back and pulled out his gun, pointing it straight at my chest.

I froze, knowing that there was no way I could knock it out of his hand, and he got to his feet, keeping the gun trained on me. He was panting heavily, but there was something in his expression that unnerved me. A sense of triumph.

'You're Ray Mason,' he said.

'That's right,' I answered, wanting to keep him talking. I could hear sirens coming from different directions but they still seemed to be a long way away. At that moment, I was on my own. 'Why don't you just put the weapon down, Ugo? You're in enough trouble as it is.'

He looked surprised that I knew his name but quickly regained his composure. Grinning, he wiped the sweat from his face with the sleeve of his jacket.

'Do you know there's a fifty grand bonus on your head?' he asked.

'I didn't. But thanks for keeping me posted.'

His finger tightened on the trigger. The gun was pointing right between my eyes. I thought of Tina and realized just how much I had to lose.

'Fifty grand's not worth a life sentence, Ugo,' I said, keeping my voice calm, 'which is what you'd get if you pull the trigger now.'

He seemed to think about that for a moment but his gun hand

remained worryingly steady. 'No, bruv. It's well worth it. I'd do you for free.'

Somewhere in the distance I could hear shouted instructions. Reinforcements were finally coming.

Ugo momentarily took his eyes off me as he tried to work out their location, and I lunged for the gun.

He pulled the trigger, but I'd already knocked his gun hand to one side and the bullet ricocheted wildly off the wall. I tried to strike him flat-handed on the nose, while simultaneously grabbing the wrist of his gun hand and twisting, but I slipped, and as he moved, matador-like, to one side, I crashed into one of the wheelie bins.

This time I managed to stay upright, but as I swung round to face him I saw that I was too late. He'd taken a couple of steps backwards so he was out of range and was pointing the gun at me again. Except this time, something in his face had changed. He looked excited and determined, as if he'd just made a decision that pleased him, and I knew then that he was going to shoot me dead.

There was a roar from the steps above us and, as we both looked up, I saw Dan come charging down and leap the last five steps. Ugo swung the gun round and pulled the trigger a second time as Dan crashed into him, and for a moment I thought Dan was hit, but then he let loose a two-punch combination to Ugo's face that was so rapid it was almost a blur. Ugo's legs literally went from under him and he fell to the floor with Dan on top of him. The gun flew out of his hand and clattered along the ground. Ugo tried to lift his head, blood seeping on to his chin from a split lip, but couldn't quite manage it. He looked dazed as Dan shook him angrily.

'You see this?' he demanded, pointing to a tiny camera on his jacket collar that I knew he liked to wear. 'Open your eyes. Look.'

Ugo just about managed to open his eyes and looked to where Dan was pointing.

'It's footage showing you trying to kill me. That's attempted murder. You want that played in court? Because if you don't, you'd better start talking, brother. You need to tell us about Kristo Fisha.'

'Who?'

Dan leaned forward and grabbed his face hard with one hand. I hoped he'd turned off the camera. 'Kristo Fisha. Your old buddy. Remember him?'

'What about him?' asked Ugo, looking confused.

'You're going to tell us why he and his girlfriend were tortured to death.'

'I don't know what you're talking about.'

'You know exactly what I'm talking about,' hissed Dan, tightening the grip on Ugo's face.

But he never got a chance to continue. We both heard the sound of racing footsteps coming from above and, as I stood behind Dan to shield him from their view, three CO19 officers appeared at the top of the steps, weapons outstretched. At the same time three more appeared on the waste ground up ahead, coming towards us. Seeing that we'd secured the suspect, they lowered their weapons.

Dan let go of Ugo's face and glared down at him. 'Ugo Amelu, I'm arresting you for possession of an offensive weapon with intent to endanger life. You do not have to say anything—'

'I know the fucking drill,' groaned Ugo, who was bleeding badly from his mouth wound.

Dan slowly got to his feet, subtly tapping the camera. 'OK, we've got him, gents,' he said, picking up Ugo, and together we led him up the steps.

We both knew we needed to get him alone where we could talk to him in private. Dan had only arrested him for possession of a firearm with intent, but his lapel camera had recorded evidence of him trying to kill us both, so we had something on him. Something that would get him to talk. We only had a few minutes before he was taken into custody, but if we worked fast this would be enough.

Except we never got the chance because before we were even halfway up the steps, we were met by DI Glenda Gardner, my nemesis at Ealing nick, coming down with another female detective I didn't recognize. She looked angry.

'You were meant to be observers,' she snapped, grabbing a still-dazed Ugo by the arm and pulling him away from us. 'Not charging around getting involved.'

'It's a good thing we did,' I said, 'otherwise you wouldn't have got him.'

But she was no longer listening as, surrounded by CO19, she and the other detective marched Ugo Amelu back up the steps, across the walkway and away from us.

Twenty-eight

Dan and I now had a serious quandary.

British law clearly states that a police officer who's the victim of a crime must not continue to investigate that crime because he's now directly involved, and therefore his presence on the investigating team would be prejudicial to proceedings. So if we wanted to continue our conversation with Ugo in an interview room we were both going to have to forget the fact that he'd tried to kill us, which meant he was going to wriggle his way out of two attempted murder charges. The problem was, these attempted murder charges were probably the best reason for him to cooperate with us, but by then we'd be off the case and relying on other officers to do the questioning for us.

It wasn't a position either of us wanted to be in.

'What are we going to do?' Dan asked as we walked back

through the estate in the direction of the flashing lights. A few civilians moved about in the shadows of the buildings, staying well back as emergency vehicles continued to stream into the estate. 'We almost got killed nicking that arsehole, and now he's off limits.'

'We need to think about this,' I said, looking round to check we were on our own. 'Did your camera record?'

'It should have done. I switched it on when we left the car. The footage goes straight to my mobile.'

He fished the phone out of his pocket and flicked through files until he came to the one he wanted. He switched it to mute and pressed play as I stood next to him. It was high-quality footage showing a slightly shaky view of the route we'd taken in pursuit of Ugo. Dan moved it forward until it showed him rounding the corner on the first-floor walkway just at the moment when Ugo was taking two steps backwards and pointing the gun directly to my head, while I stood in front of him, my hands held up in a defensive gesture. Ugo then turned round rapidly in the direction of the camera, still holding the gun, as Dan rushed towards him. The gun went off with a muzzle flash a split second before Dan hit him head on. The footage was then a blur as the two men crashed to the ground, before showing a bleeding and dazed Ugo.

Dan pressed stop, and pocketed the phone.

'Jesus,' I said, 'how did he miss you? Any jury seeing that's going to convict him of at least one count of attempted murder.' I took a deep breath. Watching the footage had brought home to me how close we'd both come to death. 'You saved my life, mate,' I said, wondering whether I should give him a hug or something. In the end, I settled for a simple thank you.

'I'd expect the same from you,' he said.

'And you'd get it. Even so, charging him like that when you knew he was going to pull the trigger was a brave thing to do.'

'You know what it's like. You don't stop to think.' He looked at me. 'I can't believe I was just telling you that I haven't punched someone since, you know, that night, and then half an hour later I hit Ugo.'

'I'm glad you did, otherwise we'd probably both be dead. And now we've got something we can use as leverage against him. Ugo knows we've got it, so there must be a way we can make a deal with him. And there are no other witnesses. We can even skew our statements so that it sounds like his gun went off in the struggle and there was a lack of intent to kill. He'll still go down a long time, but it'll be a lot less than it would be if we release the film.'

'But, Ray, how are we going to make a deal with Ugo if we can't talk to him?'

I took a deep breath and wiped the last of the sweat off my brow with my sleeve, thinking fast. We were back out in the estate's parking area, close to our car. The exit was currently jammed with a line of squad cars and ambulances and I could see Ugo being led in handcuffs by a group of three CO19 officers towards one of the ambulances.

'He's going to hospital for a check-up,' I said. 'We can get to him there.'

'How, Ray? We can't just stroll in. And it's too risky to do it any other way.'

'Too risky for both of us, but I've got a lot less to lose than you. Drop me off at the hospital. I'll make out I need to get treatment for shock. You go back to Ealing, and delay giving your statement until you hear from me. That way, if Ugo doesn't talk we can still get the bastard for trying to kill us.'

'But how are you going to get to him?'

'Let me worry about that.'

Dan still hesitated. 'I need you on this case, Ray. If you get caught interfering with a suspect, especially one who's taken a shot at you, you could get suspended.'

He was right. What I was suggesting was highly illegal. But Dan also looked like he didn't have the energy to argue. Like me, he had to know this was our best method of progress.

'Can you send me the film on WhatsApp so I can show it to him?'

Dan shook his head wearily. 'I'll give you this, Ray. Working with you definitely isn't boring.'

'I'll take that as a compliment, but don't do anything yet. We've got company.'

Olaf was coming towards us, not looking best happy. 'Has someone read him his rights?' he demanded, motioning to where Ugo was disappearing into the back of the ambulance.

'I did,' said Dan. 'And Ray's not feeling too good.'

'I think I banged my head during the struggle,' I said, rubbing the back of my scalp, and trying to look suitably dazed.

Olaf didn't appear sympathetic. 'What did I tell you about interfering, Ray?'

'If we hadn't, they'd have got away,' I said, my voice an exaggerated croak.

'You need to get checked out. Then I want you both down the station to make statements. I heard Ugo was armed and he fired two shots at you. Is that right?'

We both nodded. Even the most cursory glance at Ugo's gun would show that it had been fired and the two rounds would have been audible.

'There was a struggle for his gun,' I said, trying to sound non-committal. 'He pulled the trigger.'

Olaf gave me a disdainful look. 'Another of your nine lives eh, Ray? You know how much shit I'd have been in if you'd got killed? Heaps. But at least we can do him for attempted murder now as well as everything else.'

'What else have you got on him?' asked Dan.

'Well, aside from possession of class A with intent to supply and possession of a firearm, he's on film smacking one of the UCs on the back of the head with a baseball bat. So GBH at least. Plus we've probably got a case for armed robbery.'

'How's the UC?'

'He's awake and en route to hospital. He's a big bugger so if anyone's going to survive a crack on the nut, it's him. That prick Ugo could be looking at twenty years. Obviously you two can't speak to him any more. Are you going to send anyone else across from the NCA to interview him?'

Dan nodded. 'Yeah, we'll sort it out. How did the rest of the op go? We heard shots.'

'The shots were Ralvin Lambden. He decided to go down fighting. Obviously the death of any human being diminishes me, even an utter lump of shit like him, but he fired first so not even the IPCC can pin that one on us. And at least we've made two arrests, so it wasn't a total disaster. Now, take Action Man here to get his head looked at. Then get back down the station. We need those statements.'

'Oh, and one other thing,' added Olaf as we walked towards our car. 'If either of you even thinks of trying to interview Ugo off the record, I'll have your arses, you understand? I know what you're like, Ray.' He stared me down. He was a long-serving cop. Back in the days when the prospect of retiring on a decent pension wasn't looming quite so large he was the type of guy who'd bend the rules if the circumstances required it. Now, though, he was as much a prisoner of them as everyone else.

I was about to reply when I saw a small guy with thinning sandy hair and a very purposeful expression approaching Olaf from behind.

The guy called out Olaf's name.

Olaf turned round. 'Hello Stegs, good work in there,' he said. 'I owe you a drink.'

'No problem,' said the man called Stegs with a big smile. 'And this is for almost getting me killed.' He launched a knee into Olaf's balls before Olaf had time to react and then, as he went down on both knees making a noise like a rapidly deflating balloon, Stegs carried on walking, giving Dan and me a wink as he passed. 'Well done on getting Ugo,' he said.

'A pleasure,' I said in return. I looked down at Olaf, doubled up in pain, then back at Dan. 'And on that note, I think it's time to go.'

Twenty-nine

We followed the ambulance and escort car taking Ugo to hospital, and as they turned into the A&E entrance, Dan pulled up at the kerb.

'Have you got your reading glasses on you?' I asked him.

He gave me an odd look. 'Yeah. Why?'

'I need to borrow them.'

'What for?'

'Just give me them.'

He reached inside his jacket pocket and handed them over, and I put them on. They were a tight fit but thankfully the lenses were weak enough that my vision wasn't blurred too much.

'Is that the extent of your disguise, Ray? Because I've got to tell you, it's not going to fool many people.'

I took off the glasses and slipped them into my suit pocket. 'They're just a prop,' I said, getting out of the car.

'Seriously, Ray, this has got disaster written all over it.'

'Look, if it fails, I'll take the fall. Stay here. I'll be back soon.'

I shut the door before Dan could say anything else and walked towards where they were unloading Ugo from the ambulance, brushing myself down and straightening my tie so it didn't look like I'd just been in a fight. Ugo already had a bandage on his head and he was accompanied by two paramedics and three armed CO19 officers I didn't recognize, who were gathered tightly around him as they led him through a rear door into the hospital. So far there wasn't anyone here from Ealing, but it wouldn't be long before someone was, and if they saw me there was going to be trouble.

I'm reckless. I always have been. Perhaps it's because I was orphaned so young. After what happened that terrible night it's been deeply ingrained in me that life could end suddenly at any time. Ultimately I could have gone one of two ways: retreated into my shell to escape the terrors of the world, or gone out there and tried to defeat them. I chose the second route. I like to think there's a method to my madness – that I only take risks when I'm sure the return's going to be worth it. But my weakness is that I don't consider the downsides enough. And there was a big down-side to this. Dan was right. If it came out that I was interfering with a suspect it would be the end of my career, and potentially the end of the case against Ugo. I've had some good results in my time, and that's what's kept me in the job, but I knew that this time round I was definitely in the last chance saloon.

Still, you know what they say. Who dares wins.

The door Ugo and his escort had gone through locked

automatically so I gave it a minute, then pressed the buzzer. When it was answered, I told the person on the other end that I was here to see the prisoner who'd just been brought in, and was promptly told to go through the main A&E entrance next door and I'd be met there.

Given it was past eleven at night, A&E was the usual bedlam, with the drunks, the walking wounded, the mentally ill and the hypochondriacs all packed together in one place. Tonight the main entertainment was a full-on wrestling match featuring a very large screaming drunk in a T-shirt that was way too tight for him and jeans that hung down over his arse, and three security guards and a police officer. The drunk was on the floor with the rest of them on top of him but, even so, he was still refusing to give up.

I went round them and was met at a side door by a harassed-looking nurse who let me inside. She gave my ID a cursory check and told me that the prisoner was in a treatment room at the end of the next corridor.

As I walked in the direction she'd pointed me, I saw that the treatment bays on both sides were full of people waiting for attention. One man was fast asleep in a chair. A woman in one of the bays up ahead was screaming while other people tried to calm her down. The whole place seemed to be operating at breaking point, and I had nothing but admiration for the staff who had to work here and administer treatment night after night. But at the moment the chaos suited me fine.

As I passed one of the bays I saw that a patient lying on a bed was being treated by a doctor behind a curtain. On a metal tray table next to the bed were a number of bits and pieces of para-phernalia, including a stethoscope. I stepped inside the bay, picked up the stethoscope and carried on going, putting it round my neck and shoving on Dan's reading glasses.

As I rounded the corner, I saw two of the CO19 officers outside a door. I didn't know where the third was. If he was inside the room I was in trouble, but I'd cross that bridge when I came to it.

As you've probably gathered by now, I'm one of the most recognizable police officers in the Met, but one thing I've learned is it's amazing how easy it is to dupe people if you act confi-dently enough, especially if they've already made assumptions, and I was hoping the stethoscope round my neck would help with that. So I walked straight up to the officers, looked them both in the eye, and said that I was here to examine the prisoner, and could I have some privacy.

And, amazingly, they said yes, and moved out of my way to let me inside.

I don't know where the third CO19 was, but he wasn't in the room. Only Ugo was there, sitting in one corner, looking pissed off.

He looked up when I shut the door.

'Hey, what the fuck's going on?' he demanded as I took off my glasses. 'You're a Fed. I ain't talking to you. You're not meant to be here. I'm calling my lawyer.'

I leaned in close and flat-palmed him on his injured nose.

He gasped in pain and pushed a bloodied handkerchief to his face, eyes watering, clearly shocked that he'd just been so casually assaulted by a police officer, and one posing as a doctor as well.

'Make any more noise and I'll kill you,' I hissed, pulling up a chair opposite him. 'Now, let's start again, shall we? I'm here to make you an offer, and it's one I think you'd better listen to. We haven't got much time so if you want to avoid two attempted murder charges, you're going to have to start talking fast. Take a look at this.'

I took out my phone, found Dan's camera footage and pressed play, thrusting it in his face.

Ugo stopped groaning and looked.

'See this,' I said, leaning in close and keeping my voice quiet. 'That's you shooting straight at a police officer. I'd say that's twenty years in itself. Luckily this footage hasn't been shown to the senior investigating officer yet, and it doesn't have to be. But you've got to help me. Now.'

'How?' he said suspiciously.

'Kristo Fisha. You remember him, don't you?'

He blinked. 'He's dead, bruv.'

'I know that, Ugo. I want to know why he died, and where he got the DVD of a woman being gang-raped and murdered from. And I know you know the answers to all those questions.'

'No way,' he said, moving away from me. 'I don't know what you're talking about. Go on, get out. I ain't talking.'

I smiled at him. 'Ugo, if you're done for the drug and gun possession and GBH on an undercover police officer, even with your record, you'll probably only get fifteen years and serve half of it. That's a bit of a stretch, but it's manageable. If you help me, my colleague and I will say your gun went off during your struggle with me, and we weren't sure if you were trying to hurt us or not. That means there won't be two attempted murder charges. But if I walk out of here now, this footage goes on record, we back it up with witness statements, and you'll serve twenty minimum.'

He shook his head. 'Nah, forget it. I'll take my chances.'

'Really? OK.' I got up. 'Let me tell you something else. I'm going to spread the word to the Kalamans that you're a snitch, and that you did help us. Let's see how long you last behind bars then.'

That got his attention. He stared at me, trying to gauge if I was serious about this. My expression told him I was. I would have done too. I'd have made this piece of shit pay with his life without it even flagging up on my conscience.

'You've got ten seconds to make up your mind, Ugo.'

'You promise you won't fuck me?'

'Yeah,' I said. 'I promise.'

He took a deep breath. 'This is off the record, right? Because I'm not testifying in court.'

'It's definitely off the record.'

'What do you want to know?'

'Why was Fisha murdered? And if you tell me you don't know, I walk and you'd better start counting the days till your sixtieth birthday because that's when you'll be coming out of prison.'

Ugo was silent for a moment. And that confirmed everything for me. He knew why Fisha had died.

'He pissed off the wrong people,' Ugo muttered.

'How?'

'It's a long story.'

'Make it a short one.'

'You know he was a people smuggler, right? He used to sell me bitches. I'd put them to work with clients I had. But there was one girl he brought in who he really fell for. He didn't want her to do any work. He wanted to set her up in a flat somewhere, spoil her. Problem was he never had any money, so he couldn't afford to. And anyway she was up for earning some cash. So I got her earning, you know, although I didn't tell Fisha. He was well dodgy, not someone you want to get in a beef with.' He paused. 'I had a client, right. He lived in a nice pad in Mayfair and he paid well because, you know, he liked to be a little rough with them. I paid the bitches extra to go see him, otherwise they complained. Anyway, one time I take Fisha's girl to see him in this big pad he's got out in the country, because she doesn't drive, you know, and I arrange to pick her up from there the following morning. But then I get a call later that night – two, three o'clock, something like that – from the client, and he says they've got a problem. When I get to the house, the client's there with a friend of his – you know, they're both rich suits, and they're both looking shit scared. But there's also another couple of people there, and I recognize one of them as being connected to the Kalamans.'

'Do you have a name?'

'No, but he was wearing a hat, so I knew straight away he was the old guy they call Mr Bone. He was cold, man. Real cold. And

I don't ever want to see him again. Anyway, this guy puts a gun to my head and asks me who else knew the girl was there. I say no one, and he says that's good. He's very calm. He tells me to forget I ever saw her and if the Feds ever come asking about her, I tell them I haven't seen her. Then he gives me a number to call if anyone else comes asking questions.'

'So you reckon they killed the girl?'

'Yeah. I think the client, and the friend who was with him, got a bit rough with her and went too far. Obviously they must have had some seriously good connections so they call this guy Mr Bone to get rid of the evidence. That's what I think. Cos I never saw the girl again.'

'And I don't suppose you remember her name?'

He shrugged his shoulders. 'Nah, bruv. Come on, it was a long time ago.'

'But you still remember the client's name, don't you?'

He nodded. 'His name was Alastair something.'

'Sheridan.'

'Yeah, that's right. But that ain't all.' Ugo suddenly looked pleased with himself. 'This Sheridan man's friend, the one who was there with him that night, I know who he is too.'

'Who?'

'He's the one you people are looking for. The one whose face is all over the news for that double murder.'

It must have been a long day because it took me a couple of seconds to work out who he was talking about. I frowned. 'Hugh Manning?'

'Yeah, bruv, that's him. I remember his face from that night.'

It was strange. In all the evening's drama I'd forgotten about Manning and the sighting of him in Scotland, although I'd have heard if he'd been arrested. Now it was even more important that we talked to him.

'So what's all this got to do with Kristo Fisha?'

'I told you, Fisha was obsessed with this girl. When he hadn't heard from her for a few days he started asking questions. He must have found out that she'd ended up at the client's house – you know, Sheridan – because the next thing I hear from one of my bitches is that Fisha and his business partner had broken into his house looking for her, and when they didn't find her they robbed the place and got away with some real sick shit. Snuff movies, you know. Where people get killed on film.'

'Then what happened?'

He looked away.

'Did you tell Mr Bone about it?' I asked.

Ugo looked back at me, deflated. 'Yeah, I told him. Then I got on a plane and left the country.'

I had a lot more questions but I knew I was running out of time. 'Thank you, Ugo. You've been a great help.'

He grabbed my arm. 'And you're not going to use that film you took of me?'

'Get your hand off me.'

Seeing my face, he did what he was told.

'No,' I told him. 'We won't.'

I put Dan's glasses back on and walked out of there, thanking the officers and telling them I'd be right back.

My timing was lucky. A man looking much more like a doctor

than I did was walking towards me, a puzzled expression on his face. He raised an eyebrow as we passed each other and looked like he was about to say something, but I just kept going.

I had what I needed. And now more than ever, we needed to get hold of Hugh Manning.

Thirty

Hugh Manning was a light sleeper. He always had been, and these days, thanks either to his expanding prostate or his shrinking bladder, he had to get up at least once a night to take a leak.

As his eyes opened in the darkness, he yawned and turned over, checking the time on the phone. 11.56 p.m.

He was surprised. He'd only gone to bed an hour ago and there were no telltale pangs telling him it was time to piss. He'd drunk a bottle of Pomerol earlier that he'd pinched from Harry's steadily diminishing collection of reds. Maybe that was what was disturbing his sleep.

He closed his eyes, felt sleep begin to envelop him again.

And then he heard it, standing out in the heavy silence of the night. The low rumble of a car engine close by. As he listened, the engine cut out.

Manning felt his heart start to beat faster as the fear took hold. He'd been getting better at controlling it, and drinking always helped, but freshly woken and groggy, he was unable to stop its advance.

'I can't go on like this,' he whispered to himself, reaching down beside the bed and picking up the shotgun.

And then he heard slow, gentle footfalls on the gravel outside, as if someone was trying to be quiet.

Had the police located him? Worse, had the Kalamans?

He propped himself up on the pillows, pointing the shotgun towards the open door, wondering what he'd do if someone actually came in. Did he have the balls to pull the trigger? And what would happen then? He'd have to go on the run again, but where? He'd seen on the news websites that they'd set up roadblocks around the area so there really was no escape.

He could no longer hear the footfalls on the gravel. He listened. There was just silence. Somewhere off in the forest an owl hooted, and slowly, very slowly, Manning felt himself begin to relax a little.

And then he heard the sound of someone fiddling with the front door lock. Again the movement was deliberately quiet, as if they were trying not to be heard.

The door slowly opened. Manning's whole body went rigid as he heard someone creeping through the hall.

If it was the police, and they knew he was here, why didn't they call out and identify themselves? And how could they have found him anyway?

But someone had found him, and if it wasn't the police, it

was those two animals who'd come for him and Diana in Lincolnshire.

A shadow fell across the doorway. Manning inhaled audibly and his finger tensed on the shotgun's trigger. He'd checked it was cocked and loaded before he'd got into bed. He was going to fire.

'Who's there?' came a voice from the corridor outside.

It was a voice Manning recognized immediately.

'Is it you, Hugh?'

'Jesus,' said Manning, letting all the breath out of his body as the relief flooded through him. 'Harry?'

Harry Pheasant appeared in the door, dressed in a check shirt and what, even in the dim light, looked suspiciously like red trousers.

'Bloody hell, Hugh. Glad to see you've made yourself at home, but can you put that thing down now?'

Manning carefully placed the shotgun on the bed and stared at his old friend. 'What are you doing here? It's the middle of the night.'

'Why do you think? Because I saw the news and guessed you'd come here. Come on, get out of bed. It's been a long drive. I need a drink. And we need to talk.'

Five minutes later they were sitting in the living room with a bottle of decent Margaux that Harry had brought with him. Manning, who'd been forced to flee Lincolnshire without most of his clothes, was wearing a pair of pyjama bottoms belonging to Harry that he'd found in one of the cupboards and which were way too big for him.

The Hanged Man

Everything about Harry was big. His legs; his shoulders; his belly these days; and definitely his personality. He had a kindly face, though, with ruddy cheeks, and the scattering of broken veins that was a testimony to good living. He was, thought Manning, a prime candidate for gout. But he'd always been a loyal friend and Manning was glad he was here now.

Harry took a drink and eyed him closely. 'What the bloody hell's happened, Hugh? Tell me you didn't kill Diana and that other chap.'

Manning laughed hollowly. 'Of course I didn't.'

'So who did?'

'I'd rather not say.'

'Look, you've always been a good mate of mine, which was why when I saw you were on the run and had been spotted just down the road in Newton Stewart, I didn't call the police. I wanted to talk to you myself. But you've got to tell me the truth.'

Manning sighed. 'A long time ago I started doing legal work for a client. I became friendly with him and he introduced me to other people he knew, and I started doing work for them – helping to move money offshore out of the taxman's reach, that sort of thing. But it turned out that these people my friend introduced me to were all working for the same criminal gang. And it's that criminal gang I've been working for for most of the past fifteen years. The thing is, I didn't really know what I was getting involved in until it was too late. I know that's not a good excuse.' And it wasn't. It wasn't entirely true either. Manning had had plenty of chances to walk away, at least in the early days, before the Kalamans had got a real hold on him – and yet he hadn't.

Harry looked at him from behind his outsized wine glass, and

197

Manning thought he saw disapproval in his friend's expression. 'You obviously made a lot of money doing it,' he said.

Manning nodded. There was no point denying it. 'I did. But Christ it's come at a cost.' He thought back to the house in Lincolnshire, and how he'd been forced to write a suicide note while Diana was being held on their marital bed. 'I found out something I shouldn't have so Diana and I went to hide out in Lincolnshire. But they caught up with us.' He paused and took a deep breath. 'I got out. Diana didn't.'

Harry took another gulp of his wine.

'You believe me, don't you, Harry? I could never kill anyone. I promise.'

'You've certainly made a pig's ear of things, that's for sure. So, what did you find out?'

Manning shook his head. 'Harry, the less you know about any of this the better. And I'm sorry that you're involved now.'

'That's what friends are for. You did me a big service once, so I'll help if I can. Talking of friends, who was the bastard who introduced you to this gangster in the first place?'

'Again, you don't want to know.'

'Why? It's not going to make any difference.'

'Because you've met him before, that's why. I introduced you to him a long time back.'

'It's not Alastair Sheridan, is it?'

Manning stared at him, and suddenly his heart was beating hard again. 'How did you know?'

'He left me a voicemail message today, asking if I still had this place.'

Thirty-one

Manning put down his wine and got to his feet. He felt like he was going to be sick and paced the room trying to calm himself.

'What did you tell him?' he asked eventually.

'I haven't called him back yet,' said Harry. 'Why are you looking so scared? Is he still involved with this gangster?'

'Very much so. How does he know about this place anyway?'

Harry shrugged his massive shoulders. 'After you introduced me to Alastair, we kept in touch. I thought he might be useful in business. I've had money invested in some of his funds for a while and occasionally I see him at client days. I think I must have mentioned this place to him and said he should come up here and stay some time.'

'But he's never been?'

'No.'

Manning stopped pacing. 'Thank God for that.'

'He doesn't know where this place is, and remember, you made me put it in the name of an offshore company, so Alastair and his gangster friends have no way of finding it.'

Manning couldn't believe Harry's naivety. Like so many people, he had no idea how powerful the Kalamans were. 'It doesn't work like that, Harry,' he said. 'They'll narrow down the search to somewhere round here and they'll be looking for places owned by offshore companies.'

'I'll tell you what I can do,' said Harry, looking pleased with himself. 'I can phone Alastair back, or send him a text, telling him my house is up in Inverness. That'll throw them off the scent.'

Manning shook his head. 'It might give us a bit of breathing space, but at some point they'll look into your background and find out where this place really is. Then they'll also realize you were protecting me, and that'll put you in real danger. I appreciate you thinking of ways to help, Harry, but I can't do that to you.'

'Can't you talk to Alastair? Get him to call the dogs off?'

'No. He's as much involved as anyone. He wants me dead, Harry.'

Harry looked confused. 'To be honest, that's not the Alastair I know. He's always seemed a pretty decent chap to me.'

Manning picked up the wine, and took a long gulp to steady his nerves. 'Alastair Sheridan's a monster. I've seen him do things that you can't imagine.'

'Like what?'

Manning remembered the night at Alastair's house all those years ago and the young Moldovan woman lying with her head bashed in. Alastair had been naked above her, the bronze sculpture in his hand, dripping blood. But it had been the wanton excitement on his face that had been truly shocking.

'Seriously Harry,' he said, 'stop asking questions. Suffice it to say, Alastair and this gangster friend of his are involved in some really dark stuff.'

'All right. Point taken. Just tell me one final thing though, and be honest with me: have you been involved in any of this dark stuff?'

Manning shook his head emphatically. 'No. I did wrong, I'll admit that. I broke the law to help some bad people. But I've never been involved in anything else.' He didn't like the distasteful look on Harry's face. 'I'm telling the truth, Harry,' he said, putting on the most sincere expression he could muster. 'I promise.'

'Then what on earth are you going to do?'

Manning sat back down. 'I don't know.'

'The way I see it, you have two choices. You can either keep running, and if you want to do that I'll drive you out of here in the boot of my car, drop you off somewhere, and then you're on your own.' He leaned over and poured himself some more wine, offering the bottle to Manning, who decided he had little to lose and topped himself up close to the rim of the glass. 'Or I drive you into the police station at Newton Stewart first thing tomorrow morning and you give yourself up.'

Neither choice suited Manning. The first would almost certainly result in capture at some point soon, and so lead to the second one anyway. But giving up was something he desperately wanted to avoid. He was genuinely touched by how Harry was trying to help, though. Manning didn't have many real friends. Like so many wealthy professionals, he'd cultivated associates, people who were of use to him in some way. And all that had done was get him to where he was now: on the very edge of the precipice looking straight down.

'If you know so much about Alastair and his friends and their, er, dark stuff, you might be able to do some sort of deal with the police,' Harry pointed out.

'I know. But this gangster I'm talking about has some very good contacts. He'll have me killed, even in protective custody.'

The two of them were silent while they pondered the very limited options available.

It was Harry who broke the silence. 'Would it work if you handed yourself in to someone high up in the police, someone who's incorruptible and who can do what it takes to make sure you stay safe?'

Manning thought about this. He didn't think anyone could help him against Cem Kalaman, but right now anything was worth considering. 'Possibly. Do you have someone in mind?'

Harry nodded. 'I think I might.'

Thirty-two

'Did your cunning disguise work?' Dan asked me as I got back into the car.

'Believe it or not, it did,' I said, handing him back his glasses. 'Drive, and I'll tell you all about it. We don't want to keep Olaf waiting too long.'

Dan turned the car round, and as we took off in the direction of Ealing nick I started talking.

'Ugo pimped some girl Kristo Fisha liked to one of his clients, who happened to be Alastair Sheridan. From what I can work out, Sheridan got too rough and killed her, then brought in Cem's people to make the problem go away. Ugo was told to forget the girl ever existed, which he says he did, but then apparently Fisha found out what happened and broke into Alastair's house and ended up finding the DVD of Tracey Burn's murder and taking it with him. Ugo admitted that when he found out what Fisha had done he told the Kalamans, and they got rid of Fisha and the woman he lived with. I don't know why the killers didn't find the DVD under the floorboards. Maybe there were a lot of DVDs. Maybe he made copies, and he forgot about this particular one when they were torturing him.' I shrugged. 'But now at least we know where the DVD came from.'

'Do you have an ID on the girl Sheridan murdered?'

I shook my head. 'Ugo doesn't remember her name.'

'He pimped her out and sent her to her death and he can't even remember her name? He really is a classy guy.'

'But that's not all. According to Ugo, Alastair had a friend with him the night he killed the girl. None other than Hugh Manning.'

'Shit, you're joking.' Dan shook his head. 'That's gold dust. No wonder they want Manning dead so bad.' He blew out a long breath. 'By the way, I've just been on the phone to Sheryl.'

'She's still in the office?'

'Of course she is. She says there's still no word on Manning.'

'What about Tracey Burn? Has anyone come up with any sightings of her from when she went missing?'

'Nothing useful yet. HQ have set up a dedicated twenty-four-hour hotline to take calls from the public because the Welsh police haven't got the resources. They're going to collate the info, and if any decent leads come through they'll get in touch directly with me or you.'

I looked out of the window at the night-time streets, wondering how many other people had disappeared since Tracey had gone in search of a better life all those years ago. And how many of them had been preyed upon by Alastair Sheridan and Cem Kalaman.

'Have you ever come across someone called Mr Bone?' I asked Dan.

'I've heard the name mentioned a few times over the years, yeah,' he replied. 'Mainly by very minor associates of the Kalamans, people right out on the fringes. Supposedly he's one of Cem's top hitmen, been part of the outfit since the early days. Someone told me once they reckoned he'd killed thirty people.'

'So why haven't I heard about him?'

'Because there's never been any proof that he even exists. Certainly no one using that name's ever been ID'd, and during the one time Cem was under twenty-four-hour surveillance back in the early 2000s there was no mention made of him.'

'Ugo said that it was a Mr Bone who was at Alastair Sheridan's house that night getting rid of the girl and clearing up the mess.'

'Did he describe him?'

'He said he was an old guy wearing a hat.'

Dan grunted. 'That narrows it down.'

'The man who escaped from me at the farm in Wales, the one who set the place alight? He was an old guy in a fedora. And Tina reckoned it was an old guy in a hat who shot Charlotte Curtis in France. It sounds to me like he exists.'

Dan sighed. 'Then we'd better start looking for him. Is Ugo prepared to testify?'

'No. I recorded the conversation but it's inadmissible.'

'So, what do you want to do about the attempted murder charges, Ray?'

'Ugo's a piece of shit, and my first instinct is to make him suffer, but I gave him my word. And if a man can't keep his word, he's nothing. Also, he's the one person we have who's got concrete information. He might not want to testify in court now but it's still possible we could use him again at a later date.'

'I think you're being too kind to him, Ray. Plus he tried to kill both of us.'

'I agree, but I'm going to let the fact that he tried to kill me slide because he's given us a load of information that we didn't have. And I told you, I made him a promise.'

Dan didn't look too convinced. 'Well, in the spirit of generosity, I'll let it go too. So we lose the film and make out that the gun went off by accident, yes? Olaf's not going to be pleased.'

'No,' I said. 'It'll be the second kick in the balls he's had tonight.'

Thirty-three

It had just turned nine a.m. when Tina walked through the front door of her cottage. The overnight ferry crossing from St Malo had been smooth and quick and she'd slept well, so as soon as she'd made a coffee she sat down in her back garden with her laptop and lit a cigarette, enjoying the morning sunshine and the view up to the hill in the distance where she sometimes liked to walk with Ray.

She was intrigued by what she'd learned yesterday on her trip to France and wrote down what she'd got so far.

In July 1975, Janet Sheridan, the mother of suspected serial killers Alastair and Lola Sheridan, dies in a car accident in Italy. Her sister Mary Sinn suspects that Janet was murdered by her husband. Even though the Italian police have ruled it an accident, at some point in 1976 Mary hires a private detective to find out whether her suspicions are true. The private detective, Brian Foxley, takes the case, but if he discovers anything suspicious it's not made public, and then in that same year he allegedly stabs his wife to death and hangs himself afterwards. The police conclude that it's a murder/suicide and close the case.

Tina stopped typing. So what did Mary Sinn do next? The deaths of Brian Foxley and his wife would surely have made her even more suspicious that her sister's death was no accident. Unfortunately, Tina couldn't ask her. Mary had died in 1992, having never recovered from the disappearance of her only child Kitty in 1990, and her husband had died in 1988, having divorced his wife some years earlier.

Tina shook her head slowly. A whole family – mother, father, daughter – all gone. If Robert Sheridan had killed his wife and got away with it, then he was a very cruel man, and that cruelty had extended to his children, Alastair and Lola.

The problem with a case like this was that most of the people involved in it were now dead, and any survivors were unlikely to remember enough to help. And even if she did find out what had really happened to Janet Sheridan, or the Foxleys, it wasn't going to do much to bring Kitty Sinn's killers to justice.

But Tina prided herself on one thing more than any other. She wasn't the type to give up.

Pauline Foxley, Brian's sister, had sent her a text message last night saying she couldn't find a number for Brian's old friend Ken Wignall, who'd been a police officer at the time, but apparently he was still alive and, in Pauline's words, 'living up round Brackley somewhere'.

So that was her first task. Find Ken Wignall.

It's not hard to find anyone if you know their name. People can't hide very easily any more, and if you have access to the number of databases Tina did in her role as a private detective it's only a matter of time before you track someone down. In Ken Wignall's case, it took Tina just over twenty minutes to find an address and a landline phone number for him.

She actually crossed her fingers before she made the call. If Wignall didn't answer then she was pretty much back to square one.

He didn't. The phone rang and rang until eventually it went to voicemail. An electronic message asked her to leave a message, so she did, giving all the relevant details, so that Wignall, or whoever picked up the message, could check her out. Then she went off to make another coffee, wondering whether she should call Ray or not. They hadn't spoken since the previous evening, and he'd texted later to say he and Dan were working late.

The coffee was still brewing and she was halfway through sending him a text to say she was back home safely and looking forward to seeing him for supper when the phone rang.

It was Ken Wignall.

'You're not *the* Tina Boyd, are you?' he asked.

'I am,' she said. 'Are you *the* Ken Wignall?'

'That I am,' he chuckled.

He sounded, Tina thought, like a nice guy. He would be in his seventies now but he seemed lively and cheerful. She just hoped his memory was on the ball.

'I wanted to ask you some questions about the death of Brian

Foxley,' she said, giving him the same cover story she'd used with Pauline, claiming she'd been hired by a former client of his to look into the case.

'He took his time, didn't he?' said Wignall. 'It happened forty years ago.'

'Some new evidence has come to light which I'm not at liberty to disclose.'

'Why aren't the police involved then?' asked Wignall, and Tina realized he wasn't going to be fobbed off very easily.

'Well, I'm hoping they will be, but I just wanted to get your own thoughts on what happened. As you know, the police concluded it was a murder/suicide.'

'That never rang true for me,' Wignall said immediately. 'I remember Brian was working for Mary Sinn – you know, the mum of that poor girl Kitty whose remains were dug up a few months back. This isn't anything to do with that, is it?'

'No,' said Tina.

'Brian asked me to check out Robert Sheridan, Mary Sinn's brother-in-law,' continued Wignall. 'He thought Sheridan had killed his wife. I was a PC but there wasn't much I could do. Sheridan didn't have a criminal record. He didn't have a proper job either, the lazy sod. He preferred to live off his wife who, as you probably know, came from wealthy stock. He was a sponge, but that was about all you could say about him.'

'What did Brian think of him?'

'Brian was very suspicious. He told me he'd found out that Sheridan knew some very dangerous people – gangster types – and they were involved in all sorts: devil worship, orgies, that kind of malarkey. He told me Sheridan certainly didn't seem like a man in mourning, and he'd got some young live-in nanny as well for the kids who Brian was sure he was having an affair with.'

Tina frowned. She knew from the Bone Field case that the killers had an interest in the occult. Perhaps Alastair had got his from his father. 'But did he have any evidence at all that Sheridan had murdered his wife?'

'Nothing that I ever heard about.'

Tina sighed louder than she'd intended. 'I'm afraid I'm going to need more than this before I can persuade the police to reopen the case.'

Wignall was silent for a few seconds. 'Brian was scared, I remember that. He thought he'd stumbled on to something pretty bad, but when the investigating team searched his office after his death, they didn't find a file on the case. I remember thinking that was strange because I know Brian had been working on Janet Sheridan's death for at least three months, and I know Mary Sinn paid for him to fly out to wherever it was where Mrs Sheridan had her car accident. So it was a pretty big case for him.'

'But didn't Mary go to the police after Brian's death and tell them her suspicions if she thought her sister's death was murder?'

'No. I told the investigating team about Brian's investigation, and a couple of them went and questioned Mary, but as far as I know she either didn't want to cooperate or whatever she said wasn't enough to reopen the case.'

Tina thought about this. The only reason Mary Sinn would have clammed up so suddenly was if she'd been afraid, either for her own life or that of her daughter. Kitty would only have been about seven at the time, and the killings of Brian Foxley and his wife would have scared her. Perhaps Mary had been told she and Kitty would be next if she didn't keep quiet. It stood to reason, given the ruthlessness of the people involved.

But it also gave Tina an idea. 'Was Brian the sort of private detective who would have given his clients regular progress reports?' she asked.

'Oh yes,' said Wignall, without hesitation, 'definitely. He was a very diligent bloke.'

'What do you think happened to those progress reports?'

'I honestly don't know. It was all such a long time ago. I still think of him, you know.'

Tina knew she wasn't going to get much more from him. 'Look, thanks for your help, Mr Wignall, I appreciate it.'

'If he was murdered, will you find out who was responsible?'

'I'll do everything I can,' Tina assured him.

'I know you will. I know your reputation. You get stuff done.'

Tina ended the call and sat back, feeling deflated. Where once she'd been a high-ranking murder squad detective with a string of scalps under her belt, now she toiled alone out on the periphery, away from all the action. Which was probably why she was putting so much effort into a forty-year-old case that was paying her nothing on a day when she could have been out walking in the sunshine. Because she still wanted to prove herself to a world that had passed her by.

She lit a cigarette and thought about the progress reports Brian Foxley would have sent to Mary Sinn. It was possible they'd never existed, but Tina thought this unlikely. If Foxley had been working the case for anything close to the three months Ken Wignall had estimated, and had flown to Italy as part of the job, he'd have had to give Mary something in writing to show her what he was doing for the money she was paying him.

So what would Mary have done with those documents? If she'd been threatened by someone, she wouldn't have given them to the police. She might possibly have handed them over to whoever was threatening her. But if Tina had been Mary, she would have kept any evidence against her sister's killers somewhere secure just in case she ever got the opportunity to use it. It would have been too unsafe at home. So she'd have given them to someone for safe-keeping. Someone she could trust.

Like a solicitor.

Tina didn't know if Mary Sinn had had a family solicitor but her own parents had used the same solicitor for more than thirty years on those few occasions they'd needed one. Tina also knew there would have been plenty of news stories centring on the Sinn family around the time Kitty disappeared in 1990, so she went on the National Archives website and trawled through all the available articles until she found one from the *Northamptonshire Telegraph*, dated 12 August, in which a man identified as Mary Sinn's solicitor – a Mr John Howard of ACB Howard and Co. – appealed for her to be left in peace after a number of incidents involving reporters camping outside the family home.

A quick search on the Law Society database revealed that the firm was still active and based in Market Harborough.

It was a huge long shot, and Tina had no doubt that John Howard had long since retired. Even so, she called the switchboard number, introduced herself to the youngish-sounding man at the other end, and explained as briefly as possible why she was phoning.

'Let me put you through to the senior partner,' he said.

After a minute or so a woman came on the line. 'I understand you want to talk to John Howard.'

'That's right. I'm a private detective. My name's Tina Boyd.' Tina started to explain what it was about but the woman cut her off.

'Yes, I recognized your name,' she said. 'I'm afraid John died eight years ago. But perhaps I can help. I'm his daughter, Barbara Howard. We worked together for a number of years.'

Tina relaxed a little. Barbara sounded friendly, interested even. 'I'm doing some work on the Kitty Sinn murder case, and I know your father was Mary Sinn's solicitor.'

'Yes, that's right. For almost twenty years. Right up until her death in fact.'

Tina decided to come clean. 'Well, forty years ago Mary hired a private detective to find out whether or not her sister was murdered. A few months after taking the case, the private detective allegedly stabbed his wife to death then hanged himself. Both cases were closed, one as an accident, the other as a murder/suicide. I wondered if Mary ever talked about either case to your father, or gave him any documents relating to them.'

There was a long silence at the other end. Tina was wondering if she'd moved away from the phone when Barbara spoke again.

'I think I can help you,' she said.

Thirty-four

'DCI Olafsson tells me that the two of you, while acting as observers, apprehended and arrested Ugo Amelu, during which two shots were fired. But apparently, according to your statements, both discharges were accidental.'

Dan and I were back in Sheryl Trinder's office, nursing strong coffees and feeling the effects of a long night. It didn't seem to be affecting her though. She was as alert and bullish as ever on this Friday morning, watching each of us carefully as she spoke, and her words were laced with scepticism.

'That's right, ma'am,' said Dan, and we both nodded.

'I got there first,' I said. 'We were wrestling and the gun went off twice. It fell out of Ugo's hand and we arrested him.'

'I'm surprised,' said Sheryl, leaning forward and steepling her hands as if in prayer, 'that neither of you even pushed for an attempted murder charge. Especially as Mr Amelu isn't cooperating at all with the arresting officers. He's answered "no comment" to every question that's been put to him, and DCI Olafsson's furious.'

'But the op was a success, ma'am,' I said. 'One of the chief suspects is dead and Ugo's in custody so there was no point in either of us lying about him trying to shoot us.'

'I'm not suggesting you're lying, Mr Mason, but I do wonder if there's something you're not telling me. Because there you were yesterday telling me how important it was you spoke to Mr Amelu, yet today neither of you seem especially worried that he's not cooperating.'

There was no way of course that we could come clean. We'd made our statements at Ealing, pissing off Olaf hugely in the process, and it was far too late to change our stories now. This didn't mean that we couldn't give Sheryl something, however, and we'd both agreed the previous night what that something should be.

'We had a few minutes with Ugo before he was taken away,' said Dan, 'and he gave us a snippet of information off the record. He told us that Kristo Fisha stole the DVD of Tracey Burn's murder from Alastair Sheridan's house.'

Sheryl's eyes widened, but she looked more annoyed than pleased. 'Are you serious?'

'Yes, ma'am. Apparently, Fisha broke in and stole it. He had some dispute with Sheridan about a woman. That's all he was prepared to say.'

'But he won't testify,' I added. 'Well, unless we offer him immunity, of course. Then he might.'

'That's not going to happen.' She glared at me. 'And I hope you didn't offer Mr Amelu your own deal. Because if you did, you'll both be up for gross misconduct.'

I shook my head. 'No one offered him anything. We didn't have time.'

'So why did he cooperate with you? And now, suddenly, he won't.'

'Because it was off the record.'

'I was sat on top of him at the time, ma'am,' said Dan. 'I'd just disarmed him. He was scared. He seemed to want to talk.'

Which wasn't entirely true, but seemed plausible enough. I was sorely tempted to tell her about Manning too but I knew that would really give us away. Instead I asked if there was any news on him.

'Nothing yet, Mr Mason,' Sheryl answered, 'and don't change the subject. If I find out you've bent the rules in any way, you're gone. I appreciate the efforts you've put in so far, and the fact that both of you put yourselves in the line of fire last night, but I'm not having either of you ruin this investigation by ignoring the law. Do I make myself clear?'

'Crystal, ma'am.'

She seemed about to say something else but at that moment there was a knock on the door, and an officer I didn't recognize put his head into the room. 'Ma'am, I'm sorry, but we've got a call from a woman who has information about Tracey Burn. She sounds authentic.'

This got everyone's attention. Because Tracey Burn had now been confirmed as the first Bone Field victim to be positively identified, her disappearance was getting round-the-clock media attention, which meant the twenty-four-hour hotline was being inundated with calls from the public, even though she'd been dead at least eleven years. The calls were being sifted by the hotline staff so only those considered of real interest were put through to Dan and me.

This was the first.

Sheryl nodded brusquely. 'Thank you. Patch it through to my phone. Mr Mason, you take it.'

As the call came through, I picked it up and introduced myself.

'Hello,' said the voice at the other end. 'My name's Martha Harvey. Mrs. I think I might have some information about that poor girl, the one they found at the farmhouse in Wales.'

'Thanks for calling, Mrs Harvey,' I said, trying to put her at ease. 'You're talking about Tracey Burn?'

'Yes, that's her. The woman on the news. I live in a village called Pittonslow in Hampshire, between Salisbury and Winchester. A long time ago I saw her there. She was staying with Anthea Delbarto.'

'And who's Anthea Delbarto?'

'She's a lady who lives in the village. She has a big house and she occasionally takes girls in – you know, vulnerable ones who've run away from boyfriends. That kind of thing. She's been doing it for years. Anyway, I saw Tracey Burn once when I was out walking the dog. She was out on her own and she told me that she was from London and she was staying with Anthea for a while to get back on her feet. She seemed very nice.'

'And did you see her again?'

'No, that was the only time. The girls who stay at Mrs Delbarto's tend to keep themselves to themselves. But one of the women in the village, Ingrid Riley, she remembers seeing Tracey as well.'

'Do you know how long she was there for?'

'I don't, but the girls usually stay with Anthea for a bit.'

'And it was definitely Tracey Burn you saw?'

'Yes,' she said emphatically.

But even if she hadn't been certain it wouldn't have mattered. It had to be her. We'd released certain information to the public, including the approximate date she'd gone missing, and the fact that she lived in London, but there'd been no mention of the fact that she might have been living in a shelter for victims of domestic abuse.

Tracey Burn had definitely been at this shelter, I was sure of it.

Thirty-five

Hugh Manning rued the day he met Alastair Sheridan.

At the time he'd been an up-and-coming corporate lawyer working for a well-established firm in the City and, even though he was not yet thirty, he'd already developed a reputation as a financial whizzkid, and was being compensated accordingly with a generous six-figure salary and plenty of benefits. The future had looked bright.

The meeting had happened one night at a networking evening run by a lawyer friend of his. Manning didn't usually bother attending such events. He didn't need to network. People came to him. But this particular one was in a private room at the Mandarin Oriental in Hyde Park, and promised to be lavish, as befitted probably the most luxurious hotel in London. And Manning was never one to turn down free champagne and food. However, he hadn't been enjoying it particularly and had just been about to make his excuses and leave when he was confronted by a tall, avuncular-looking chap in a top-end suit. He had a shock of boyish blond hair and a broad smile. They say the devil wears the best disguises, and with Alastair Sheridan it was absolutely true. Manning had liked him on sight, and they'd quickly got talking.

Alastair had told him about his newly set-up investment fund that was expanding rapidly, and making returns of 25 per cent per annum. Manning had been intrigued, but not enough to leave his current firm. They'd stayed in touch and become good friends. They played golf together, even went out on double dates with their respective partners.

But it had soon become clear that Alastair had an edge to him. He liked to be unfaithful and enjoyed the company of hookers. And Manning found himself all too willing to get involved. One night the two of them had hired a hooker and had sex with her together. Manning wasn't yet with Diana so he hadn't felt too guilty, and in truth, he'd found it one of the most exciting experiences of his life. He and Alastair began to make a habit of it. Hire a whore, fuck her. Sometimes humiliate her too. Make her do things for extra money. Manning knew this was bad, but if a man like Alastair – friendly, affable, charming – could do it then somehow it didn't feel too wrong.

In the end it had seemed like a natural progression for Manning to come and work with Alastair, whose fund continued to do well and had somehow managed to avoid the downturn in equities post 2000.

It was, of course, the single worst decision he'd ever made.

But credit to him, Harry Pheasant had at least come up with a plan that could offer Manning a way out. It meant cooperating with the police. It meant testifying against his former employer and one-time friend in a court of law. But if things worked out the way he hoped, he might just avoid jail time and live long enough to get into witness protection.

Which was why Manning was currently lying down in the back of Harry Pheasant's Lexus, travelling east towards Gretna Green on the A75. He'd spent the first hour of the journey in the boot. Harry had been stopped at a police roadblock and for several terrifying minutes Manning had had to lie there helpless as he listened to the officers questioning his friend. He'd been convinced they were going to search the car and find him, but Harry had answered their questions with cheerfulness and confidence, and they'd let him go.

Now Manning was putting the second part of the plan into action. Having set up a hotmail account on his burner phone, he re-read the email message he'd been working on for the last half hour for about the tenth time. It said everything it needed to say and contained enough relevant information to convince the recipient that it did indeed come from Manning himself.

But Manning was no fool. He knew that the recipient might want to trace his location using his phone, but he'd planned for that. He'd set up a private virtual network on the phone when he'd taken possession of it, which meant that the message would go via an encrypted virtual tunnel, thereby hiding the IP number.

He sat up a little so he could see out of the window. An empty lay-by was coming up a few hundred metres on the left. Manning pressed Send, made sure the message had gone, and switched off the phone.

He asked Harry to pull over, and as the car turned into the lay-by and slowed down, he opened the back door slightly and threw the phone into the long grass.

Ten minutes later they were on the M6 heading south.

Thirty-six

'Anthea Delbarto, née Redbridge. Aged sixty-four, no criminal record. Owns Wycombe House in Pittonslow.'

Dan handed me an A4 photo fresh off the office printer. It showed an attractive, well-dressed woman with silver hair who'd clearly had a fair bit of work done to her face but who just about managed to carry it off. In the photo she was at some outdoor summer event and had a drink in her hand. She was smiling at the camera, showing a very healthy set of white teeth, and looked worryingly normal.

I looked up at him from my desk. 'So this is the owner of the house where Tracey Burn stayed. What else have we got on her?'

Dan shrugged. 'Not a lot. She was married to James Delbarto, a retired businessman fourteen years her senior, who died of a heart attack in 1998. According to his obituary, they were married ten years. No children. I've scanned the net and I can't find anything about her running a shelter for victims of domestic abuse, so it must have been something she did privately.'

'It probably was,' I said. 'The witness I spoke to on the phone, Martha Harvey, said a good few young women had stayed over the years, but that they and Mrs Delbarto kept themselves to themselves, and didn't socialize in the village. If Lola recommended that Tracey go there, then she must know Mrs Delbarto somehow.'

'We still don't know she did recommend that Tracey go there. It's all still very vague, Ray.'

I raised my eyebrows. 'Tracey cleaning for Lola is not a coincidence. There's a connection somewhere. Did you find out who Lola was calling yesterday evening?'

'No, good point. I'm waiting for the BT rep to call me back. It got a bit lost in all the drama of last night.'

Which was a fair enough point. We'd both been shot at less than twelve hours earlier and however tough you think you are it still leaves you with a sense of real shock. A few inches either side and Ugo's bullets would have killed us. It was something best not to think about, so I didn't. Instead, while Dan chased his contact over at BT for the records from the phone box Lola had been at, I looked up the village of Pittonslow on Google Maps. It was twenty miles west of Winchester and about the same distance north of Southampton. It was also at least two hundred miles from the Bone Field farm where Tracey's remains had been discovered, and a good seventy miles from where she'd been living with her boyfriend in London.

I was looking a second time at the smiling photo of Anthea Delbarto and wondering how a respectable-looking woman in her sixties could possibly be connected to the Bone Field killers when Dan came off the phone.

He looked at me with an inscrutable expression.

I looked back at him. 'Well?'

'At 6.43 p.m. yesterday, a call was made from that phone box to a landline number in Hampshire.' A big grin spread across his face. 'The number's registered to Anthea Delbarto.'

Thirty-seven

It had just turned midday when Tina pulled up at a house in the village of Heddingworth. It was a large, bland-looking new-build that looked out of place between two pretty cottages. A white Audi convertible with the top down was parked outside and Tina parked her own car next to it.

Barbara Howard, the daughter of Mary Sinn's solicitor, had asked Tina to meet her at her home and not the firm's offices in Market Harborough, so Tina knew whatever she wanted to talk about was going to be something worth hearing.

Tina had already checked Barbara out. Fifty-two years old with a degree in Law from Brunel, she'd worked as a solicitor in London for ten years before returning home and taking over the family business from her father when he retired in 1999. She'd been married for five years in the early 2000s, but it had ended in divorce. There were no children.

Barbara had already opened the door before Tina had a chance to knock on it. She was a tall, thin woman with dark hair and unflattering glasses, dressed in a trouser suit. She gave Tina a surprisingly awkward smile. 'Thank you for coming here,' she said in a soft voice. 'What I have to say isn't for public consumption.'

'I guessed that,' said Tina as they shook hands.

Barbara offered her a drink but Tina declined. She'd already had three coffees today. Any more and she'd be flying.

They went through to a large study at the back of the house that faced on to a paved garden with a view to the back of another big new-build house beyond. It made Tina yearn for France with its open spaces, and opportunities for solitude. Even here, in the English countryside, there were people everywhere, and the journey up on the M1 had been a nightmare.

There was a sleeping cat on one of the chairs and Barbara shooed it away before sitting down. Tina took a seat a few feet away.

'I think this is what you're after,' said Barbara, tapping a hard plastic file on the desk next to her. It looked old and slightly warped. 'Mary Sinn brought this to my father in 1976, shortly after Brian Foxley's death. It's a copy of his report on his investigation into whether her sister Janet's death was murder, and whether Janet's husband, Robert Sheridan, was responsible. There are also some photographs. Mrs Sinn had a number of specific instructions regarding the report. Firstly, my father was not to view the contents or tell anyone else about it. Secondly, he was to store it somewhere very safe, not in his office or house. Apparently, she didn't consider either secure enough. Thirdly, if anything happened to her – or if she died suddenly, in suspicious circumstances – then he was to take the file to the most senior ranking police officer he could find and remain with him or her while they reviewed its contents. As you probably know, Mrs Sinn died of an overdose in 1992, and my father believed there were no suspicious circumstances, therefore the contents shouldn't be made public.'

Tina was surprised that Mary's suicide hadn't constituted suspicious circumstances in John Howard's eyes, but she let it go.

'But your father didn't follow the instructions to the letter, did he?' she asked. 'He told you about it.'

Barbara nodded. 'That's right. In 1991, over a year after Kitty Sinn went missing, Mary came to see my father. She was certain by then that her daughter was dead, and that she'd been murdered. She was also convinced that her former brother-in-law, Robert Sheridan, and his children, Alastair and Lola, were somehow involved in the killing, although she was unable to give any evidence to support this theory. Given that Kitty had gone missing in Thailand, my father was convinced she was wrong.

'Mary wanted to release this file to the press – mostly, my father thought, to ruin her brother-in-law and drive a wedge between him and his children. That was when my father read its contents for the first time. When he'd finished, he advised Mary not to publicize it.'

'Why?' asked Tina.

'Because nothing in there was evidence, either that Janet's death was murder or that Robert was responsible. It wouldn't have stood up for one minute in a court of law and Mary risked being sued for slander if she repeated any of the allegations made in the report. My father was also concerned for Mary's safety. He too believed that Brian Foxley had been murdered and didn't want the same to happen to her.'

'So what did Mary do?'

'I never met her, but apparently she was not an easy woman. However, my father could be persuasive and he had some influence, having been her solicitor for almost twenty years. He convinced her to let him continue to keep the report under lock and key, and if the situation ever changed and the information in it became relevant to an investigation into Robert Sheridan, it could be released then.

'As you know, Mary died the next year but my father kept the report even after she was gone. To be honest, I didn't know anything about it until he was just about to retire. He told me the whole story, gave me the report to read, and let me decide what I wanted to do with it. Frankly, I agreed with his assessment of it. There's nowhere near enough to bring a case against Robert Sheridan, even if he were still alive. It certainly seems like he was a very unpleasant man, but that's not actually a crime.'

'So why have you still got it?'

'I was intrigued by the disappearance of Kitty Sinn. I wondered what had happened to her and whether it had something to do with what's here in the file. When her remains were found, I dug it out and re-read everything. I didn't do anything with it because I wasn't sure who to show it to, or what relevance it had.' She looked at Tina carefully from behind the glasses, like a headmistress. 'And what's your interest, Miss Boyd? I have to admit, I've read about you and your, er, adventures. Obviously you're a private detective now. So you must be working on behalf of someone.'

'I've been helping the police in a freelance capacity, looking into the background of the Sheridan family,' Tina replied carefully.

Barbara raised an eyebrow. 'I didn't know the police subcontracted work these days. Austerity must be really biting.'

'I'm doing it on behalf of one of the detectives.'

'So they are looking for a family connection behind Kitty's murder? That sounds like Mary was on the right track after all.'

'We don't know that for sure, and the fact that I'm the one here tells you it's not high on the police agenda.'

'But they're not getting any closer to establishing how Kitty's remains ended up in a school in Buckinghamshire, are they?'

'Not as far as I know,' Tina lied. She and Ray had solved the mystery with the help of Charlotte Curtis. Unfortunately, they didn't have a shred of proof to back it up.

'I know that Alastair and Lola Sheridan inherited a lot of money when their grandmother died,' Barbara continued, 'a good part of which would have been Kitty's, so they definitely had the motive for murder. And Alastair's definitely done very well for himself since, which is actually quite impressive after the upbringing he and his sister had.'

'Do you think Robert Sheridan killed his wife?'

Barbara allowed herself a small smile. 'Speaking with my non-legal hat on, yes.'

Tina nodded slowly. 'Do you mind me looking at Brian Foxley's file?'

'There's no point preventing you. Mary's dead now.'

And that was the sad thing, thought Tina. All of these people – Mary, Kitty, even Robert – were dead, yet their actions, and the fates that had befallen them, were still having a major impact on the lives of so many others.

She took the file that Barbara handed her and started reading.

Thirty-eight

The file that Brian Foxley had prepared for Mary Sinn contained three typed progress reports, each dated approximately a month apart, between June and August 1976. The last one had been compiled only eight days before he'd been found dead.

The paper was yellowing and faded with age but everything was still legible.

The first report summarized Mary's suspicions, as told to Foxley. She believed her sister had been murdered by her husband for her money. Each sister had inherited a £200,000 cash payment on her twenty-first birthday, paid out from a family trust set up by her father's estate. In 1960, when Janet had received hers, this was a huge sum of money, making her a very wealthy young woman. Mary and Janet were also paid a further £10,000 per annum for life starting on their twenty-fifth birthdays, so whichever way you chose to look at it, they were both very good catches. Mary had married an insurance broker called John Sinn, and in 1966 Janet had married Robert Sheridan, a self-proclaimed artist who was also involved in the antiques trade. Sheridan, it seemed, had no money of his own and was seen as something of an idle charmer by members of Janet's family. However, the marriage lasted nine years, until Janet's death in 1975, and they'd had two children, Alastair and Lola.

As mentioned by Ken Wignall, Foxley had travelled to the spot where Janet had died in the car accident in Italy, and had spoken to investigating police officers and locals. According to his report, they believed that her death had been an accident, although one local woman claimed to have seen a stranger driving in the area around the time she'd died.

The tone of that first report didn't make encouraging reading for anyone thinking Janet's death was murder, and it was clear that Foxley was just covering the bases.

The tone changed in the second report as Foxley dug deeper into Robert Sheridan's background. It appeared that not only was Sheridan an inveterate gambler who'd been bailed out by his wife at least twice in the year before her death, but in the months after the accident he'd travelled to London regularly to stay in hotels and gamble in casinos, leaving his children with the new nanny he'd hired. He seemed to have a group of London friends he spent time with. Foxley identified several of them, but the one that caught Tina's eye was Volkan Kalaman, a man Foxley described as 'a senior figure in the London underworld with interests in gambling, prostitution and the importation of illegal drugs'. An attached photo showed the two men laughing together in the street. Volkan was hard-faced and broad-shouldered, and a good six inches shorter than Robert who, Tina had to admit, was a remarkably handsome man with a lean, angular face and a full head of wavy dark hair worn long. In the photo, Sheridan was wearing a shirt and tie covered by a long coat which, unusually for the mid-seventies, seemed to fit him perfectly, and he had the look of a real charmer. He didn't look much like a grieving husband, and Foxley's tone in the report was both disapproving and concerned, but there was still nothing that suggested Sheridan might be a killer.

It was the third report in which things became interesting. Foxley was convinced that Sheridan and the nanny were having an affair, and felt that if he could get photos of them together then it might be enough to get the British police to look more closely at Janet Sheridan's death. So, on the night of Saturday, 14 August 1976, he'd taken up surveillance on the family home, knowing that Sheridan had dropped his children off with their grandmother earlier in the day.

What he witnessed that night changed everything.

I arrived at eight p.m. and concealed myself in woodland, next to the house. I knew both RS and AR were in residence because I saw both of them at various times inside the house, but not together. I then logged three cars arriving at 20.37, 20.49 and 20.58. The first contained an unidentified couple; as did the second. The third contained an unidentified male, who brought with him two cages, each containing a cat. When all the visitors

235

were inside, the curtains were drawn in every room in the house and the windows closed which I thought was odd as it was a very warm night. I took all the registration numbers on the cars and also ventured close to the house to see if there was any way I could see or hear what was going on inside. Then at 22.50, all the lights were extinguished.

I was curious as to what was going on so I remained on site. At 00.15, lights started coming on in the house again, and then at 00.20 I heard laughter in the back garden. I made my way round to that side of the house, keeping hidden in the undergrowth, and witnessed Robert Sheridan with a female from one of the unidentified couples. The female was naked but appeared to have dirt stains on her face and body. She and Sheridan then had sexual intercourse on the outside patio while drinking from a glass that I thought at the time contained wine. They then went back inside. A few minutes later, the unidentified man who had brought the cats came outside. He was fully dressed and carrying a large plastic bag which he placed in a corner of the patio very close to where I was hiding. After a further thirty minutes of waiting, during which time no one else came outside, I came out of my hiding place and inspected the contents of the bag. Inside were the mutilated remains of the two cats, which I photographed but did not include with this report for fear you would find them too offensive.

I remained on site for a further two hours, during which time none of the guests left, and all the lights were again extinguished. Assuming they were staying the night, I went home but returned at 06.30 in order to photograph them when they did finally leave.

The Hanged Man

This I succeeded in doing and I have enclosed the photographs on page 4 along with the names of those I have so far managed to identify. I have not identified the man who brought the cats as the car he was driving was a rental. However, I feel certain I have seen him before in the company of both RS and Volkan Kalaman in London and I will endeavour to find out who he is with the utmost urgency.

In conclusion, I believe there are some very unpleasant things going on in RS's house and it would definitely not be considered a safe environment to bring up children. I will telephone you this week to arrange a meeting at which we can discuss the options available.

BF

August 20th

Tina finished reading and checked her notebook. Brian Foxley had been found dead on 28 August, just over a week later. She was puzzled. What Foxley had discovered didn't look at all good for Robert Sheridan who was clearly involved in some kind of occult activity with a like-minded group of people, but it hardly seemed worth committing murder for. Yet Tina was certain that was what had happened.

She turned the page on the file and saw a set of five black and white photographs mounted on black card. These were the five guests Foxley had caught on camera the following morning. Three men and two women. They were good close-ups, obviously taken with a long lens, and she examined each one closely, stopping when she got to number three.

The man was standing by a car with a hat in his hand, squinting against the sunlight, dressed almost formally in a shirt and tie. He was young, mid-twenties, with a bland, almost nondescript face. But it was the shape of the head that gave him away – an almost perfect square. And the eyes ... Even though he was squinting, they still resembled small dark holes with nothing behind them.

Barbara Howard had left Tina in the study to view the file in peace but now she came back into the room.

'You look like you've seen a ghost,' she said.

Tina nodded slowly. 'I think I have.'

But it wasn't a ghost she'd seen. It was a cold-blooded murderer. Half a lifetime might have passed but Tina still recognized the man who'd tried to kill her and Charlotte Curtis in France three months earlier, and then, barely a few days later, had come close to killing her and Ray at the farmhouse in Wales.

She stood up. 'Can I borrow this file? I promise I'll return it but I want to show it to a contact of mine in the force.'

Barbara looked thoughtful. 'Keep it,' she said eventually. 'But please don't say where you got it from. I think it's time I left this case to the professionals.'

So, with the file under her arm, Tina walked back out into the warm sunshine of a July day, knowing that she'd found another of the Bone Field killers.

Thirty-nine

Anthea Delbarto, the woman who, it seemed, took in female victims of domestic violence, and who'd taken in Tracey Burn nearly twelve years ago, lived just outside the village of Pittonslow.

Her address wasn't easy to find and we missed the turning twice before making our way up the winding single-lane track that led to a pair of high oak gates topped with a curved row of supposedly decorative wrought-iron spikes that would keep out all but the most determined of burglars.

'Good security,' I said as I stopped the car in front of them.

'You know what the rich are like,' said Dan. 'Paranoid.'

And Anthea Delbarto was definitely a rich woman. Her husband had had a successful career when he was alive and had left her an estate in excess of £8 million on his death, so she could easily afford to take vulnerable young women in. We'd just visited Martha Harvey, the woman who'd met Tracey Burn briefly in the village all those years ago, and she'd told us that Mrs Delbarto seemed a very nice, polite woman who, though she kept herself to herself, was popular in Pittonslow, especially after she'd provided half the funds to completely refit the village hall three years earlier. And it was still, of course, possible that Mrs Delbarto's connection to Lola Sheridan was entirely innocent. After all, she'd called the hotline at ten o'clock that morning to say that Tracey had stayed with her many years earlier.

Which was what Dan had reiterated to me several times on the way here. 'So Delbarto could be an unwitting dupe in all this which means we need to treat her with kid gloves,' he told me. 'And we can't let on that we know about Lola's phone call to her. The tracking device was completely illegal so it's got to stay out of this conversation.'

'Don't worry, Dan,' I told him as the gates opened and we drove inside. 'I can do kid gloves.'

The house itself was a large art deco dwelling – visually striking, even if it was beginning to look a little bit tired, built over three floors, and with a grand wrap-around balcony, surrounded by what an estate agent would call a mature, well-stocked garden but which in reality was beginning to get overgrown. There were a couple of chicken coops in one corner with chickens running free, and several scuttled out of the way as we pulled up in front of the house. I liked the place immediately. It reminded me of the rambling old house I'd spent my first seven years in.

The door was opened before we had a chance to reach it by an attractive woman with thick, fashionably cut grey hair and the kind of flawless skin you see on adverts for expensive anti-ageing moisturizers. She was dressed in jeans, ballet pumps and a white cheesecloth blouse. Only the hefty diamond on her ring finger gave any hint of her wealth.

She greeted us with a good afternoon and an expansive smile, not looking at all like a woman who had something to hide.

Dan thanked her for seeing us at such short notice as she invited us in. She led us through a huge hallway with a staircase in the centre. There was a real air of faded glamour about the place, which somehow made it feel even more like a home. A large photo portrait adorned one wall showing a younger Anthea with her husband – a balding, jowly man a lot older than her. She was smiling at the camera, he wasn't. Looking at him I'd have thought it would be the other way round since he was so clearly batting above his average.

Anthea stopped by the door to a kitchen that was the size of my apartment where a woman was chopping vegetables, and asked if we wanted something to drink.

I asked for coffee. Dan plumped for tea.

'Katy, would you mind making the drinks for us? I'll have mint tea, please.'

The woman stopped what she was doing and turned round. She was younger than I'd been expecting – mid-twenties, with a petite build and elfin features. I gave her a smile and she gave us all an even bigger one back. It reminded me of the smile you might get from a Disneyland employee – all dimples and no depth.

'Sure,' she said. 'It'll be a pleasure.'

'So, you're here about Tracey,' said Anthea as she led us

through a pair of open French windows to an outside terrace, motioning for us to sit down at a table sheltered from the early afternoon sun by a trellis covered in winding grapevine. 'I can't believe what happened to her,' she continued, visibly shuddering. 'I felt so awful when I read about those poor women at that place . . . the Bone Field, or whatever the media are calling it. It's appalling to think there are people out there – human beings – who could systematically plan the murder of young women like that. And then I saw on the news that Tracey, someone I knew so well, was one of their victims. I was shocked. And that's when I called the hotline you'd set up.'

'Do you remember Tracey well then?' I asked.

Anthea smiled. 'I grew close to her. I've grown close to many of the girls here, but I remember Tracey as peculiarly vulnerable. She was a sweet girl – perhaps not the brightest I've come across, but she had a kind heart and a real deep-down strength too. I thought we'd finally got her to the point where she didn't need her abusive boyfriend any more.'

I frowned. 'What do you mean?'

'Well, when Tracey left here she told me she was going home to London. She didn't explicitly say that she was going back to him – the boyfriend – but because she had nowhere else to go, and I know she still had feelings for him, I assumed they'd ended up together.'

I shook my head. 'Tracey's boyfriend told us that after she left him he only ever heard from her once, and that was by phone, when she told him she was severing all contact with him. He never saw her again.'

'I know. I was there providing moral support to her when she made that call.'

'How long did she stay with you for, Mrs Delbarto?' asked Dan.

She appeared to think about this. 'I honestly can't remember. About two or three months?'

Dan nodded slowly. 'Let me get this right. So she left here one day and went back to London, but didn't tell you where she was planning on going?'

'That's not unusual, detective. I provide a safe space for women and girls in need of shelter and help, but when they want to leave, I don't try to stop them.'

'And you never heard from her again?'

'No.'

'Is that usual?' I asked. 'You look after these women for quite long periods of time. Clearly you bond with them. You'd assume they'd keep in touch after they leave.'

'And they usually do. I'm still in touch with a number of my girls.'

'So weren't you worried when you heard nothing from Tracey? I mean, enough to report her missing.'

Anthea shook her head. 'No. I assumed she'd gone back to her boyfriend, which does I'm afraid happen, and was simply too ashamed to admit it. I had no reason to think that anything untoward had happened to her.'

'So there was nothing she said or did here, or anyone she spoke to, that might offer a clue about how she met the men who killed her?' asked Dan.

'No. I'm sorry I can't help more.'

There was a pause in the conversation as Katy brought the drinks in, still smiling widely as she put them down on the table.

I thanked her and asked how long she'd been staying here, noticing immediately that she shot a look at Anthea before answering.

'Quite a while now,' Katy said. 'Months.'

'About six, I think it is,' said Anthea.

'God, is it that long?'

'And sadly Katy's leaving us soon,' Anthea continued. 'Off to start a new life in France.'

'That'll be nice,' I said. 'Adventure's good for the soul.'

Katy smiled. 'I'm looking forward to it. But I'm a bit nervous too.'

'Thank you, Katy,' said Anthea, cutting short the conversation.

Katy nodded and left the room without another word.

'Six months is a long time to be staying, isn't it?' I said when she'd left the room.

Anthea leaned forward in her seat, and her voice dropped to a whisper. 'Katy's had a very traumatic time. Five years ago her parents were killed in a car accident, and she ended up in a very abusive relationship with a violent boyfriend who got her involved in drugs and shoplifting, and who ended up putting her in hospital. It's taken a long time to build her back up into the woman she should be.'

'I understand that,' I said, because I did, and I immediately felt a pang of sorrow for what had happened to her.

'How many women have you had staying here over the years?' asked Dan.

Anthea furrowed her brow in thought. 'Do you know, I'm not sure. I don't keep records as such. I started taking in young women and the occasional older foster child after my husband died in 1998. I found spending time with them helped to soften my bereavement. I don't usually have more than one girl at a time, and there have been gaps. Perhaps a dozen or so altogether?'

'And how do they all find you? Do you advertise?'

She sipped her tea before replacing it on the table. 'Not as such. It's more word of mouth. People in the area have heard of me and know what I do, and I have some contacts among social workers and therapists.'

'Were there any other women staying here at the same time as Tracey?' I asked.

'I don't believe so, no.'

So far the questioning had all been very civilized, and there was nothing in Anthea Delbarto's demeanour to suggest she had anything to hide, but her answers had all been conveniently vague, and there was something else too. I'm a very good judge of character. I get strong, almost physical first impressions of people, and my first impression of Anthea Delbarto was that there was a coldness in her that didn't sit comfortably with the words coming out of her mouth.

'Can you remember who put Tracey in touch with you?' I asked, watching closely for her reaction.

She turned slightly from my gaze, appearing to think about it. 'Not off the top of my head. It was a—'

'Long time ago,' I finished. 'Yes, I know. It wouldn't be Lola Sheridan, would it?'

This was the moment of truth. Would Anthea deny knowing Lola?

But she didn't. Instead, she looked thoughtful. 'Lola?' She shook her head. 'No, I don't think so.'

That caught me out. 'Do you know Lola then?' I asked.

'Not really any more, but I certainly did.' She smiled. 'I was her and her brother's nanny while they were growing up. Why would you think it might have been Lola who'd put Tracey in touch with me?'

'Tracey used to clean for Lola at about the time she left her boyfriend,' said Dan.

Anthea looked surprised. 'Oh, well, I suppose it might have been. I can't honestly recall. My memory's not as good as it used to be. I'm sorry I can't be of more help.'

She was playing us. I knew it. By being vague about Lola's involvement rather than denying it, and using the length of time that had passed as an excuse, Anthea was making sure she didn't say anything incriminating – and the problem was, like Lola, she was confident and wouldn't fluster easily.

We were hitting a brick wall, and the worst of it was I felt sure she was involved in the Bone Field killings. It was something in her eyes. A glint of triumph, as if she knew we suspected some-thing but could do nothing about it. That and a complete lack of shock about what had happened to Tracey. She talked like she cared but I could see she didn't. It was a show.

It struck me then that she groomed the vulnerable young women who stayed with her – women like Tracey who ended up at the Bone Field – and I wondered if she was doing the same with Katy, a girl with no family who'd been staying with her six months.

'Is there anything else I can help you with?' asked Anthea.

'I think that's probably everything,' said Dan, who'd clearly decided we weren't going to get any further with Anthea. 'Unless you've got another question, Officer Mason?'

I considered asking her about Lola's phone call to her home number yesterday evening, but I felt sure she'd have a smooth enough answer to that and, since it involved an illegal tracking device, it was best to heed Dan's advice and keep it back for now.

'I have got one question,' I said. 'You mentioned that Katy's parents are dead. Does she have any brothers or sisters?'

Out of the corner of my eye I saw Dan give me a puzzled look.

'Why on earth are you asking me about Katy?' Anthea countered. 'You're here about Tracey Burn.'

'It's a simple question.'

She gave me a cold look. 'No, she hasn't.'

'Do you remember who put Katy in touch with you?'

'Yes. A counsellor from Salisbury.'

I took out my notebook, and I saw her flash a look at it. 'Can you give me his or her name?'

'I really don't see where this is going.'

I held her gaze. 'Again, it's a perfectly innocent question. You don't have to answer it if you don't want to.'

'I don't want to. In fact I don't want to say anything else to either of you. I'm not going to be talked to like a criminal in my home when all I've done is try to help people.'

'I'm sorry, Mrs Delbarto,' said Dan, looking across at me. 'I'm sure Officer Mason didn't mean to sound accusing.'

'It's too late for that,' she said, standing up. 'Now, I'd like both of you to please leave.'

'I think you're being a little unreasonable, Mrs Delbarto,' I said, getting to my feet. 'I'm just trying to get to the bottom of a murder case.'

'Well I don't care what you think,' Anthea said. 'And you're not going to get to the bottom of it by accusing me of lying.'

She walked round the table as if preparing to shoo us out, so we walked ahead of her back through the house. I didn't look at Dan. I could see he wasn't happy.

But I wasn't finished yet.

As we passed the kitchen, I paused. Katy was still there, chopping vegetables.

'Excuse me, Katy, can you tell me who first put you in touch with Mrs Delbarto?' I asked with a smile.

Katy turned round, momentarily confused, her eyes immediately seeking out Anthea's.

'Don't answer him, Katy. You're under no obligation. I've told these men to leave.' Anthea stood between Katy and me, her eyes blazing. I thought she might even strike me. 'Now please go,' she said quietly, her voice bristling with anger. 'Now.'

I looked back at Katy, but she'd already turned away, and I knew that she wasn't going to say anything.

Dan grabbed my arm. 'All right, Ray, let's go.'

For a moment, Anthea and I stared at each other, and I felt the darkness in her like it was a physical presence. Then I turned and walked away.

It was only when we were back in the car and driving out of the gates that Dan finally spoke.

'What the hell were you doing in there, Ray?'

'Rattling Anthea Delbarto's cage. She's involved, Dan.'

'Even if she is – and let's face it, with the paltry evidence we've got, it's still a very big if – that's not the way to get her to talk. This is your problem, Ray. You want to solve everything in one day. I'd have thought you'd been a cop long enough to realize that it just doesn't work like that, but obviously I'm wrong. I've been chasing the Kalamans for years and I still haven't managed to nail them. But I keep chipping away and I know eventually I'll get there.'

I didn't think it was wise to tell him he was taking his time about it. He was too pissed off for that.

'This woman was Lola and Alastair Sheridan's nanny, she was the last person to see Tracey Burn alive, and we know she's still talking to at least one of the Bone Field killers. So what do you think the plan of action should be?'

'We'll look into her background, her connections to these people. We'll talk to people who know her. And if there's anything dodgy there, we'll find it. But it'll take time. And I don't know if you're going to be around to see it, because I'm betting that Mrs Delbarto's on the phone to HQ right now complaining about you. Jesus Ray, you're hanging by a thin enough thread as it is.'

Dan took a deep breath and pushed his foot down on the accelerator. I didn't know what to say. He was right. I was letting my instincts get the better of me. I hadn't always been like this. For a long time I'd been good at sealing myself off from the stresses of the job. It had never been easy, but I'd managed it. But not now. Because right from the moment I'd told Dana Brennan's parents I'd find her killers, I'd become emotionally involved in this case. And it was ruining my whole perspective.

My phone vibrated in my jacket pocket. It had vibrated during our meeting with Anthea Delbarto as well. I fished it out now and checked the screen. I'd had a missed call, a voicemail, and now a text message.

I read the text and frowned.

'What is it?' asked Dan, seeing my expression.

I looked at him carefully and wondered how well I really knew him.

'Can I trust you, Dan?'

'I might be pissed off with you,' he replied, 'but that doesn't mean you can't trust me.'

'And do you trust me to do the right thing?'

'Where's this going, Ray?'

'I need you to trust me on something, otherwise I can't tell you about it.'

He stared at me for a long moment. 'OK, I do.'

'It's Tina,' I said, deciding I did know him well enough. 'She's heard from Hugh Manning.'

Forty

It was when Tina was stuck on the M1 round Luton on the way back from her meeting with Barbara Howard that, more out of boredom than anything else, she'd checked the emails on the website she used to promote her private detective work, and seen the message.

The title of the email said URGENT, and as soon as she'd seen who it was from, and the level of detail in it, Tina had been certain of who the sender was.

Her phone rang. It was Ray, no doubt responding to the text she'd just sent him.

'I got your text,' he said. 'I've told Dan but no one else. So, what does Manning want?'

'He wants to give himself up. But he's scared that if he just walks into any old police station then the Kalamans will get wind

251

of it and he won't survive more than a few days. He wants to put himself under the protection of someone he trusts, and who he's certain hasn't been bought by the Kalamans. In other words, you.'

'How certain are you that it's him?'

'You'll have to check the actual email yourself but the sender knows you're not after him for the murders of his wife and neighbour. He knows that you're interested in his Bone Field links and, incidentally, he says he's entirely innocent of anything do with the killings there.'

'It could be a trap,' said Ray. 'The Kalamans have all those details. And I know they want me out of the way.'

'That's true, but this person wants to speak to you before any meeting. Do you want me to send him your number?'

There was a pause for a couple of seconds before he spoke again. 'Yes. Please. But tell him he's only got until tomorrow morning to make contact. I don't want him dictating things.'

'Sure,' said Tina. 'I'll send you his email now. I've got more to tell you too, about the Sheridans. But it can wait until tonight.'

'I'll see you then,' he said, and rang off.

Tina stared at the phone for a moment. It wasn't like Ray to be so brusque, and she was almost surprised to realize it upset her.

Falling in love, it seemed, was hard work.

Forty-one

I re-read the email purporting to be from Hugh Manning, and Tina was right, it seemed genuine enough. It provided plenty of detail and could only have come either from Manning himself or someone from the Kalamans looking to set me up. Apparently, the sender had approached Tina because he'd read a newspaper article about her, which also mentioned that she was in a relationship with me. I remembered that article. It had pissed me off. Both of us could have done without the publicity.

The sender also said that he was no longer in Scotland, which stretched credulity a little. I knew the Scottish police had had the area where Manning had last been seen in lockdown, which would make it very hard for him to get out. Unless he'd had some kind of help.

Still, it had to be worth pursuing.

We stopped at traffic lights in the village centre and I showed the email to Dan.

'If this is genuine, then we need to tell Sheryl,' he said when he'd finished reading it, 'and use it to track down Manning's location.'

I shook my head. 'No way. You've seen how careful he's been. I bet you he'll have encrypted that message so we won't be able to use it to get his location. And if he's telling the truth and he's got out of Scotland, if we spook him now it might be the last we ever hear from him.'

Dan sighed in exasperation. 'Shit, Ray. Do you know what you're asking me to do? Get involved in another of your short-cuts to justice? I've got a wife and family to support. I've got to start doing things by the book.'

'Look, I'll be the one to meet Manning and I'll take full responsibility. It'll be nothing to do with you. But I can't risk other people getting involved and it all going wrong.'

Dan tapped his fingers on the steering wheel. He looked torn, and I felt bad for putting him in this position.

'OK,' he said at last as the lights turned green and we pulled away, 'we'll do it your way. I won't say anything to Sheryl. But you've got twenty-four hours to get hold of him, and if it doesn't work, then we go by the book. I need to call Sheryl and tell her how it went with Anthea Delbarto. She's taking a personal interest in Tracey Burn's disappearance. I'll skip the bit where you got us chucked out of the house.'

'That's probably a good idea,' I said.

Ten seconds later Sheryl came on the line. 'Are you on hands-free, Mr Watts?' she demanded.

'I am, ma'am.'

'And is Mr Mason with you?'

'He is, ma'am.'

I didn't like the underlying tone of her voice. She sounded angry.

And it turned out she was.

'I want you both back here right away. Do not go anywhere else first. And when you do, come straight to my office.'

Dan and I exchanged puzzled glances.

'Can we ask what it's about, ma'am?' he said.

'No. Just get back here.'

'We're down in Hampshire at the moment so it's going to take us a while.'

'Get back as fast as you can. And don't break any more laws in the process.'

Ninety minutes later, at just short of four p.m., we walked into Sheryl Trinder's office.

'Don't bother sitting down,' she said, which meant it was going to be bad news. 'I've been reliably informed that someone impersonating a doctor at Ealing hospital last night spent ten minutes alone with Ugo Amelu. Under questioning, Amelu simply answered with "no comment" when pressed about it. I'm also told that there is CCTV footage available from cameras in the hospital that will help to identify the person involved. But before I request it, I'm going to ask you both straight up: was it either of you two?'

I was surprised that the incident had been reported, and wondered by whom. But there was no point in denying it. It was, I suppose, the story of so much of my work in the last couple of years. Dan was right. I just couldn't stop cutting corners. I should have known I'd be found out – and maybe deep down I did – but I'd gone ahead with it anyway.

'It was me,' I said. 'I got Dan to drop me off at the hospital for treatment, but rather than getting it I blagged my way in to speak to Ugo Amelu off the record. Dan knew nothing about it.'

Sheryl sighed wearily. 'I've been asking myself why you would risk talking to Mr Amelu off the record when your colleagues could easily have questioned him at Ealing. And the only reason I could come up with was that you wanted to do a deal with him which was that in exchange for information, you and Mr Watts wouldn't press the attempted murder charges against him. Which means that the two of you would both have had to collude on it.'

'It didn't happen like that,' I said. 'I didn't make any deal. I put pressure on him.'

She eyed me carefully. 'What kind of pressure?'

There was no point sugar-coating things any longer. I already knew I was finished but I had to protect Dan. 'I suggested that the Kalamans might hear that he was an informant.'

'You threatened him?'

I paused. 'Yes. In a roundabout way. But I also found out something about Hugh Manning. Something I didn't mention this morning.' I told her about how Amelu suspected that one of his escort girls had been murdered at Alastair Sheridan's house, and that Hugh Manning had allegedly been present.

She looked dubious. 'It sounds like a fairly outlandish claim.'

'Ugo Amelu had no reason to lie.'

'He did if you were putting pressure on him. It seems very coincidental, with Manning's photo all over the news.'

'It's why he remembered.'

'But will he testify to that on the record?' Sheryl's look told me she didn't think he would.

'We might be able to persuade him to.'

She shook her head. 'Bullshit. He's not cooperating on any level at the moment, and no one sees that changing.' She turned to Dan. 'Did you have anything to do with this?'

'No,' he said.

'Good.' She turned back to me. 'Mr Mason, your actions are incompetent as well as being completely unprofessional. If any future defence lawyer gets hold of what you've been up to – and it's not going to be that hard to do – the whole case against Ugo Amelu could collapse.' She was no longer looking at me angrily. It was disappointment I could see in her expression now, which somehow seemed a lot worse. 'One of the truly upsetting things about all this is that you're actually a good detective, but I can't have you on the team. You don't follow rules. You might think you're the Lone Ranger, but I can't have a team full of Lone Rangers. The whole enterprise would go under. You're a liability.'

Her words cut right through me. I could feel the rejection in them, and for a couple of seconds I was back on my first day at the new school I'd had to attend after the death of my family. The boy from the burning house. Seven years old and all alone.

Then Sheryl told me I was suspended and that she'd be recommending my dismissal from the force.

I could have told her about Hugh Manning contacting me. But I didn't. If necessary, I'd bring him in as a civilian. They weren't going to get rid of my influence that easily.

Instead I removed my ID and placed it on the desk in front of her. 'I'll save you the trouble,' I said. 'I resign.'

And with that, I turned and walked out of there, with just the briefest nod to Dan, who stood staring at me like he'd been punched.

Forty-two

The man who only a handful of people knew as Mr Bone had been born sixty-five years earlier in Turkey, and given the birth name Mergim Nushi.

As a child growing up in a small town on the south-west coast, his mother had taken against him, singling him out for far worse treatment than his four siblings, as if she was ashamed of the child to whom she'd given birth. His brothers and sisters had followed suit. He'd never known exactly why, nor had he asked, but as he'd grown up he'd become angry and withdrawn, a friendless loner who'd learned to hate those around him. He dreamed of death and destruction, of creating a virus that wiped out all of humanity except him, where he alone walked the world, proud and victorious.

It had always seemed like fate to Mergim Nushi that he would become a killer, and so indeed he did. At the age of twelve.

There was a boy in the town called Taavi who sometimes worked alone in his father's hardware shop. He was the same age as Mergim and they were known to each other. It was interesting because Taavi was one of the few people who'd never knowingly upset him, yet one cold winter's evening when the streets were quiet, and night had fallen, Mergim had visited the shop pretending to need some water. Taavi was just closing up and Mergim had seen his father a few minutes earlier in a nearby coffee shop, so he knew that he was alone in the shop.

Taavi had been reluctant to pour him water and had asked him why he didn't just wait until he got home, barely a ten-minute walk away. But Mergim had begged, explaining that his mother was refusing to let him back in the house until dinnertime, which wasn't for another hour, and eventually Taavi had relented.

Mergim had always been proud of how he'd carried out that first kill. No one had seen him go into the shop. In fact, no one had even noticed him on the way over there. He'd always been like that. Someone who blended into his surroundings. And if anyone had come in while he and Taavi were talking then he would have just taken the drink and that would have been it. Unfortunately for Taavi, no one had come in, so when he'd gone into the back of the shop to get the water, Mergim had followed him round the counter, and then, as Taavi stood at the water barrel with his back to him, he'd produced a pocket knife he'd sharpened especially and, as quick as a flash, stabbed him in the neck with it, jumping back to avoid the squirting blood.

Taavi had managed to turn round and stagger towards him, a look of total shock on his face, and for a few seconds Mergim thought he was going to have to stab him again and risk getting covered in blood, which he knew would be a problem and might lead to him getting caught for what he'd done. But then Taavi had collapsed to the floor and Mergim had watched, with the kind of excitement he still found hard to put into words, as the boy's life ebbed steadily away in front of him. The power he'd felt had been incredible, and for several minutes he'd simply stood there, looking down at the unmoving Taavi, surrounded by a pool of his own blood, knowing that he, the child they all hated, had taken a life. And he'd known that he would never experience anything as pure and joyful as murder.

And then, forcing himself back to reality, he'd wiped the blade of the knife on Taavi's shirt, slipped it back into his pocket, and exited the shop through the back door, disappearing into the shadows as he made his way home, warmed and comforted by his dark secret.

Since then he'd become Mr Bone and had killed many times, both as part of his job within the Kalaman organization but also, alongside Cem and the others, for the pleasure it still brought to end a life. Young women had always been their victims – trophies, as Mr Bone liked to think of them – but he would have happily killed anyone, young, old, male, female. It was the snuffing out of a life he found so fulfilling. But since the discovery of their killing ground, the place the media called the Bone Field, three months earlier, they'd avoided taking any more trophies. It had been too risky. Now, just as they were thinking the time was right, and a new trophy was being groomed, more complications had arisen. The hunt for them was getting too close. Mistakes had been made, both by himself and by others. And they were running out of opportunities to rectify them.

Mr Bone put down the secure phone he'd been talking on and booted up the laptop in front of him. He was sitting in a strong-room in his apartment, the only place where he could talk and work freely. Protected by state-of-the-art locks, the room was like a cell, with bare, soundproofed walls made of reinforced concrete. There were no electricity sockets, and nowhere to hide a listening device, making it as secure a space as a private citizen could create.

When the laptop was fully booted, he logged into an anony-mous, password-protected hotmail account and wrote a simple message, which he saved to the otherwise empty Drafts section. The message read 'Contact now. Line Red. Urgency Red.' Then he logged out, having not sent the message across the web, thereby making it impossible for the security services to pick up. Only one other person had access to the email address, and at the moment he was checking it frequently for the updates left in the Drafts section.

Now it was just a matter of waiting – something Mr Bone was well used to, having so little else in his life to keep him occupied.

An hour later he got the call he was expecting.

'What is it?' said Cem Kalaman.

'We have a problem. The police have been asking questions close to home. They've found out about the sanctuary.'

'How much do they know?'

'One of the officers asking questions is Mason. He suspects

something but he has no proof. The problem is he's going to keep digging until he finds something.'

'I agree,' said Cem. 'I'll leave that to you. How are things moving on your plan to secure an insider in the NCA? We need that even more than we need Mason gone.'

'We're almost there, but it takes time.'

'We haven't got time, my friend. Manning will be caught soon. Accelerate your plans. I need someone now.'

The line went dead and Mr Bone put the phone down on the desk and sat back in his chair, thinking. Cem Kalaman was a good businessman but he wanted everything done immediately, and didn't understand the importance of planning and patience. A spider has to spin a whole web in order to set its trap, and that was what he'd been doing these past weeks. Spinning his web.

Now all he had to do was tempt his victim in.

Forty-three

I got to Tina's at just after seven on one of those beautiful summer evenings that should have made me glad to be alive, but tonight just didn't.

It was the first time I'd seen her all week but I wasn't feeling much like celebrating. I'd been escorted out of the building without even a goodbye to Dan, and told in no uncertain terms not to contact anyone from the NCA in either an official or an unofficial capacity. I was definitely off the case this time.

As soon as she answered the door, Tina could see there was something wrong. I guess I wasn't making much of an effort to hide it. The full reality of what had happened was only just beginning to sink in and, in the end, I only had myself to blame. Dan and Sheryl were both right. I was a liability, incapable of stopping my emotions from getting the better of me, and I'd let myself and them down. And the parents of Dana Brennan.

On the way to Tina's I'd stopped at the pub just down the road from her cottage. They knew me to say hello to in there as Tina and I occasionally popped in for a quick drink and a Sunday roast, and I think the landlord had been surprised when I sank two pints in quick succession.

'Bad day?' he'd asked.

'Terrible,' I'd replied.

'That means tomorrow will be better,' he'd told me with confidence, but that wasn't going to be the case. Even if I brought in Hugh Manning, unscathed and ready to cooperate, it wasn't going to get me my job back.

But it felt good to see Tina, and as soon as we were behind closed doors we kissed for a long time. I think we would have gone further but she asked me why I'd turned up with such a long face, and that pretty much killed the moment.

I gave her a rundown of what had happened since I'd seen her last while she made coffee and I poured myself a glass of red from a bottle I'd picked up at home. As I've said before, I didn't make a habit of drinking in front of Tina, but I made an exception tonight.

We sat down at the kitchen table, and she put her hand in mine.

She really was a beautiful woman, I thought as I looked at her, with thick black hair that fell down to her shoulders, high cheekbones, and perfectly defined features. Considering she was forty, and the kind of life she'd led, there were very few lines on her face, and when she smiled, which she did much more these days, it created two small dimples on either side of her mouth. Even the hardness in her dark eyes, built up during a career in which she'd suffered some of the worst things life had to offer, had softened of late. I hoped this had something to do with me.

'So you're still waiting to hear from Manning?' she asked.

I nodded. 'If I haven't heard by nine tomorrow morning, I'll hand it over to NCA, and they'll have to deal with it.'

'Do you think it's a good idea anyway, you dealing with it now? You're not a part of the investigation any more, so there's nothing you can do to protect him.' Her expression was sympathetic but there was an underlying edge to it. 'Tell me this isn't putting your own ego above the greater good.'

I sipped the wine, thought about it. 'It isn't. According to the email you got, Manning will only give himself up to me, and the NCA will never let me meet him alone. They'll want to micromanage it, which means having dozens of other people involved to make sure he doesn't escape. If Manning gets wind of that, he'll run, and it's possible we won't see him again.' I paused. 'I don't know what to do, Tina, frankly. But I'm going to wait for his call and see what happens. Then I'll make a judgement.'

I took another sip of the wine. Jesus, it tasted good. But I knew it was best to make it my last glass. I didn't want to be drunk if Manning did call.

'So what have you found out?' I asked her.

She tapped a folder on the kitchen table. 'This is the report made by Brian Foxley, the private detective I was telling you about, hired by Kitty Sinn's mother Mary to investigate whether or not her sister's death was an accident, and who ended up dying for his troubles along with his wife.'

'And you managed to find the report after all this time?' I was impressed.

'You're not the only decent detective out there, you know.' She smiled, showing her dimples. 'It's not the original document. Apparently that went missing after Foxley's death.'

'And did the detective find out anything conclusive?'

'No, there was nothing conclusive in it at all, at least regarding Janet Sheridan's death. But I think Foxley saw things – and people – he shouldn't have seen. Robert Sheridan was a pretty unpleasant individual who probably did kill his wife. It seemed he was a friend of Volkan Kalaman's so if he'd needed help he would have known where to get it. Either way, he certainly didn't mourn her passing. Within a few months he had a young live-in nanny to bring up the children, with whom he was having an affair. He was also into sex parties and occult stuff, just like the Bone Field killers.'

'Jesus. No wonder Alastair and Lola grew up like they did. Did you know that Anthea Delbarto, the woman we saw today who takes in vulnerable young women, including Tracey Burn, was the Sheridans' nanny?'

Tina frowned. 'I was wondering what had happened to her. According to the report she was involved in the occult parties, so if she took in Tracey Burn, she's probably involved in the killings now.'

'That's what I thought.'

'The question is, what do you do about it? By the sound of things, you've already let her know she's under suspicion.'

And it was true. I'd messed up. I should have been there to help build a case against her piece by piece. Instead I'd put Delbarto on her guard.

'There was someone else who attended an occult party at Robert Sheridan's house who caught my eye.' Tina reached over and opened the folder, flicking through it until she came to the page containing the photos of the house guests. 'Have a look at this one,' she said, tapping the one at the top.

I leaned forward and inspected it. The colour had faded over the years but it was still a clear enough shot of an olive-skinned man in his twenties holding a hat in his hand. Beneath it in type were the words 'Not yet identified'.

'That was the man who tried to kill me in France,' said Tina. 'I'm ninety per cent sure of it. Is he the man you saw at the farmhouse in Wales? I never got a proper look at him there, but I remember him speaking, and he had an eastern European accent.'

I looked carefully at the picture, searching for signs of familiarity. The shape of the man's face was right, as was the hat, but three months had passed since that day at the farmhouse and I knew the tricks memory can play on a person. And four decades had passed since this photo had been taken.

'It could be him,' I said. 'I'm not sure.'

'Brian Foxley never did ID him. He died a week after this report was produced.'

'Ugo Amelu talked about a Kalaman operative he saw at Alastair Sheridan's house on the night the prostitute died, an older man in a hat. He called him Mr Bone. Is there any mention of a Mr Bone in there?'

Tina shook her head. 'No.'

'Someone somewhere must be able to tell us who he really is.' I got up from the table. 'I need to speak to Dan.'

I knew I was forbidden from having any contact with him but he needed to know about Anthea Delbarto's involvement in the occult parties at the Sheridan family home, and he was probably going to be the best person to find out who Mr Bone actually was. I'd been forced to hand back my work phone but I had a second with all my numbers on it and I used it to call him now.

It went straight to voicemail so I left a message saying there was some urgent information I needed to share with him, and requesting he ring back as soon as possible. I remembered him telling me in the car earlier that his youngest daughter had friends coming over, so he was having to deal with a houseful of teenagers. On almost any other occasion I would have left him to his family time, but not tonight. Maybe it was just another sign of my impatience but I called his home phone, and for a long time afterwards I wished I hadn't.

His wife Denise answered on about the tenth ring. I could hear kids shouting in the background. It sounded like they were having a good time.

'Hey Denise, it's Ray Mason, Dan's partner. I'm sorry to bother you on a Friday night, but is Dan there? I need to speak to him urgently.'

There was a long silence. 'He obviously hasn't told you, has he? We split up a while back. He doesn't live here any more.'

The news hit me like a hammer blow. I don't know why. It was no more shocking than anything else I'd seen or discovered these past few days. And yet it felt like some kind of betrayal. Dan and I had worked well together these past few weeks, and I'd grown close to him.

But obviously not close enough.

'I'm sorry to hear that,' I said at last. 'Do you know where he's living?'

'I'm sorry, I don't,' she said.

I wanted to ask her what had happened between the two of them, but knew it was nothing to do with me. Instead I apologized for intruding and ended the call.

'What's wrong?' asked Tina when I came back into the kitchen.

I slumped down in my seat, feeling utterly deflated, and took a bigger drink from the wine than I should have done.

'He never said a word to me about it,' I said after I'd told her about Dan and Denise. 'Nothing. I thought we were good buddies. Not like Chris and me were good buddies, but close.'

'He probably just didn't want to talk about it.' Tina got up, came round the table, and gave me a hug.

I put my arm round her waist and drew her to me, kissing her through the material of her shirt.

On the table, the folder was still open at the page showing the photos, with the man I now thought of as Mr Bone at the top. I hadn't looked at the others, but now one of them grabbed my attention.

I kissed Tina again then moved out of her embrace, pulling the file towards me.

'Did you say the other people on this page attended one of Robert Sheridan's occult parties?'

'That's right. Apparently it was one where they made animal sacrifices.'

I looked at the photo that had grabbed my attention. It was of the top half of a well-built man with thick, dark hair, flecked with grey, and the type of full-face beard that was all the rage these days. The caption beneath it stated that, like Mr Bone, he too hadn't been identified.

But that didn't matter.

Even after all these years, I'd recognize my father anywhere.

Forty-four

Dan Watts rolled out of bed, grabbed his jeans from the floor, and checked his phone. He had a missed call and voicemail from Ray. He looked at his watch. It was almost eleven and the message had been left over three hours ago. Dan wasn't bothered. Right then he had no desire to speak to Ray, and anyway, he was busy.

Behind him on the bed lay the woman he'd been chatting to online for more than a week now, Gurl4fun, aka Vicky Smith. So far it had been a fun date. In the end they'd had a quick phone conversation early that morning before he'd gone into HQ in which she'd suggested they skip the pub altogether and just meet at her flat in Crouch End. Dan had had enough of these encounters before to know that there was nothing suspicious about that. It was simply the way things worked. Cut out all the fat and get straight down to the business of fast, furious, uncomplicated sex.

The Hanged Man

Even so, when he'd been on his way over here, he hadn't been able to shake the empty feeling that somehow this tryst wasn't going to make him feel any better. It would just be like the others. Short, hollow, unfulfilling. It made him realize quite how much he missed Denise and the kids. He knew that if he'd been able to control his urges, and stick to the tenets of the Christian faith that had kept him going ever since he'd killed a young man in a boxing ring, then he would have been with them that night, enjoying the simple pleasures of family life, rather than spending an evening with someone who was probably living just as much of an unfulfilling life as he was.

But of course that had all changed when she'd answered the door to him, opening it just enough so that he could see she was wearing black stockings and a black negligee.

And in that moment excitement flooded through him and he remembered exactly why he did this.

Sometimes the first kiss could be awkward – a reaction to the unnaturalness of the situation – but it hadn't been tonight. It had been warm, deep and passionate, and Dan had immediately become lost in the moment. They'd had sex (it was never 'making love' in these encounters) three times that night, breaking up their bouts by lying in bed chatting idly about small things and drinking cheap white wine. Vicky was a nice girl. Attractive, funny, with a sweet high-pitched laugh. She hailed from a town in Lancashire but had been in London for almost ten years. But there was also a deep-seated melancholy about her that Dan had seen in a number of the single women he'd met who lived alone in the big city. As if they all knew there was something deeper they were missing.

He also knew he wasn't the man to help. He was just another stop-gap, and now, as he stood up and looked at his phone, he knew it was time to go. He felt sated, and it had been fun, but he wouldn't be seeing Vicky again. He'd never seen a woman he'd met online twice, and he was sure there was an important psychological reason for this. The difficult part was extracting himself from the situation without appearing rude.

'Is everything OK?' asked Vicky.

'Yeah, all good,' he said, with fake jollity. 'Just checking my messages. I've had the phone on silent.'

'You've got a good body, you know.'

He turned round and looked at her lying there, completely naked now, the lingerie strewn round the room, a thin sheen of sweat on her shapely, pale body. A few hours ago the sight of it had driven him wild with lust, and in a month's time the memory of it would do the same, but right now, something inside him had moved on.

'So do you. You look fantastic.' He pulled on his trousers, no longer looking at her. 'I'm just going to the toilet then I'd better think about making a move.'

He was expecting some sort of protest, and was almost disappointed when none came.

'No worries,' she said. 'I could do with some sleep.'

He went back through the living room and into the bathroom, and while he was cleaning himself up he listened to Ray's message. He wondered what the urgent information Ray had for him was, but since he hadn't called a second time, Dan decided it couldn't be that urgent and could wait until tomorrow morning.

The Hanged Man

He splashed water on his face and stared at the dirty mirror, not especially pleased with the man who stared back at him. Suddenly he felt terribly depressed, standing in a stranger's flat, about to head back to a place he hated even more. 'What's happened to you?' he whispered, but of course he knew the answer to that question well enough.

With a long sigh, he turned and walked back through to the bedroom.

Straight away he knew something was wrong.

It wasn't so much the way Vicky was lying, facing away from him, her arm rolled back in an unusual position, one leg sticking right out, it was the way she was so very, very still.

'Are you OK?' he asked quietly, just in case she'd fallen asleep.

But there was no answer. The room was silent bar the barely audible sound of Dan's own breathing.

With a growing sense of foreboding he put a hand on her shoulder and slowly turned her round.

Which was when he saw the single, deep knife wound between her breasts.

He froze, immediately going into police mode and trying to compute what had happened. The knife blow had been to the heart by someone who knew what he or she was doing. Death had been very quick, as was evidenced by the lack of blood, and the bedside lamp was still in place, which meant there hadn't been much of a struggle. But how had it happened? He'd only been gone three, four minutes at most, and he hadn't seen or heard a thing.

He stood back up fast, looking round the cramped bedroom. There was a single wardrobe that didn't look big enough to hide anyone. The doors were shut. Without giving himself too much time to think, Dan flung one of the doors open and looked inside. Nothing. Just clothes. He looked under the bed. Again nothing. The window, which didn't look big enough to climb through, was still shut and locked from the inside.

Dan had no idea how the killer had got in, but he also knew enough about police investigations not to spend too much time thinking about that. The most important thing was to get out quickly.

So, keeping his fear under control, he threw on the rest of his clothes, looked around to check that he hadn't left anything, and strode out of the bedroom, shutting the door behind him, unable to look again at Vicky's corpse.

'You seem to be in a hurry, Mr Watts,' said a voice in the gloom.

Dan turned and saw the silhouette of a man sitting in one of the two living-room armchairs.

'I think it's time for us to talk.'

Forty-five

The man leaned over to switch on the lamp, and it took Dan's eyes a couple of seconds to adapt to the sudden light in the room. He blinked twice, and then took a closer look at the man who was sitting only a few feet away.

He was wearing a hat and an old-fashioned suit with no tie, his shirt buttoned to the top. Beneath the brim of the hat, Dan could see that he was an older man, in his sixties, with pale, waxy skin and vaguely Mediterranean features. He was wearing a benign smile and there was nothing threatening about him except his eyes, which were dark, cold and knowing, and the black evidence-handling gloves on his hands.

Dan had never seen this man before but he knew immediately that this was the Mr Bone he'd heard about, and that he worked for Cem Kalaman.

'Take a seat,' said Mr Bone.

Dan shook his head and pulled out his phone. He didn't want the shame of Denise and the kids finding out he was here, but he had to take control of the situation now before it slipped away.

'Stay exactly where you are,' he said. 'You're under arrest for murder.'

Mr Bone was still smiling. 'I don't think so. Look behind you.'

Dan turned and saw a second man in the shadows, much younger, with a shock of blond hair. He was dressed in black and also wearing gloves, and in his hand he had a large pistol with a suppressor attached. As he raised the gun, Dan saw a large fleck of blood on his temporarily uncovered wrist. So he was the one who'd taken Vicky's life. He was chewing gum, as if he didn't have a care in the world, and grinning at Dan.

'Give me the phone, Mr Watts, and do as you're told, or I'll order my man here to shoot you. I'd rather not have to do this. We've worked hard to get you in this position, and you are far more useful to us alive than dead, but . . .' Mr Bone shrugged. 'Your death will only be a minor inconvenience.'

Dan was sensible enough to know he had no choice. He was also certain they weren't going to kill him if he cooperated. It hurt him to have to admit it, but if they'd wanted him dead, he already would have been.

'Let me keep my phone,' he said.

'You can have it back shortly. Put it on the floor and kick it over. Then sit down and put your hands where I can see them.'

Reluctantly, Dan did as he was told, perching on the edge of the seat and wondering if it was worth trying to run.

The Hanged Man

'Let me explain how things work,' said Mr Bone, picking up the phone from the floor in front of him. 'The woman you've just slept with was an actress. We hired her to make contact with you online, knowing your habit of meeting women like this. She believed she was working on behalf of your wife and signed a strict confidentiality clause. In other words, no one knows about what she was doing except us. And now you. As I see it, you have three choices. Firstly, you can refuse to cooperate with us. In which case we will kill you. Secondly, you can pretend you're going to cooperate, then leave here and report the girl's murder to your colleagues in the police, blaming us for it. However, I can guarantee you that this won't work. The police will see that the two of you have been talking online and made arrangements to meet tonight, and that you had sex with her just before she died. They will also find your fingerprints on the murder weapon.'

Dan met his gaze. 'Except I haven't touched it.'

'No,' said Mr Bone, 'not yet.'

He nodded to his associate, who walked over to Dan's chair pointing the gun down at him.

Dan saw that the blond man had a knife in his hand. It was a stiletto with a long, thin blade covered in blood and he was holding it away from his body by the tip, so that even if Dan managed to get hold of it he wouldn't be able to stab him before getting a bullet in the head. Not that he'd be able to stab someone anyway, whoever they were. It had been hard enough punching Ugo the previous evening and his reward for that had been a restless night of tossing and turning.

As if he was reading Dan's thoughts, Mr Bone produced a

pistol of his own, complete with suppressor, from beside his chair, and pointed it at him.

'Place your right hand on the knife's handle and grip it firmly,' he said. 'But don't try to take it.'

Dan hesitated. He knew the moment he did as instructed it was all over, and they had him. But he also knew they would kill him if he didn't. What they'd done to Vicky was proof enough of that. He cursed himself for getting into this situation. If he'd just been a decent husband none of this would have happened. This was God punishing him for his weakness.

'Do it,' said Mr Bone.

Dan's hand slowly enveloped the handle. He had a vision of shoving the blade into the blond man's gut and going down in a blaze of glory, but the moment passed, and when Mr Bone told him to let go, he did so.

The blond man retreated into the shadows along with the knife, and Mr Bone continued talking.

'You of all people can now see that the evidence against you for the girl's murder is overwhelming. But it doesn't have to be this way. If you take the third option and help us, all of this will go away. The woman's body will be removed and buried where no one will find it, along with the murder weapon. This place will be cleaned and disinfected from top to bottom. Her online account, which was set up in a fake name, using fake details, will be removed. It will be as if she never existed. She'll be reported missing at some point, but without suspicious circumstances, no one will really care.'

Dan felt sick. It was the casual way this man talked about the literal erasing of a human being, someone Dan had been talking to only a few minutes ago. A woman who was someone's daughter, someone's sister, whose passing would cause pain. And in its own indirect way, it was his fault. He stared at Mr Bone with a combination of loathing and frustration. Mr Bone stared back with the blank indifference of a true psychopath. Dan had seen their kind before – you could hardly avoid doing so during a career in the police – but never had he felt so vulnerable in the presence of one.

'What do you want from me?' he asked, after a long pause.

'Your knowledge of the NCA investigation into the Bone Field killings and the hunt for Hugh Manning. You need to make sure we stay ahead of the police, so that when Manning is eventually tracked down, we get to him before he talks.'

'I'm not in that kind of position.'

'You are, and you're going to make sure you stay in it. If Manning talks, or the Bone Field investigation progresses significantly without you telling us about it in advance, your colleagues will receive an anonymous call giving them the details of where the woman you just slept with is buried. With our help, it won't take them long to trace her back to you, then you will go to prison for life. But I'm afraid that won't be the end of it.' Mr Bone leaned forward in his seat, resting the gun on his lap so that it still pointed at Dan, and his lips formed a cold, knowing smile. 'One day – it might be in a few months, perhaps a few years – one of your daughters will be out walking, and then out of nowhere someone will throw acid in her face, disfigure her for life . . . and there'll be nothing you can do about it.'

Dan clenched his fists at the mention of his beautiful daughters by this man, this *thing*, in front of him, and he began to shake as a deep rage welled up inside him.

'But, as I said, it doesn't have to be like that,' Mr Bone continued. 'All we are after is information. We protect our sources very carefully, and we won't do anything to compromise your position. Your secret will remain buried for ever. We will even pay you from time to time. Your family will remain safe. You can lead a happy life. All you have to do is help us.'

Dan let out a long breath, and tried to think straight. But it was impossible. There was no turning the clock back. This was his reality now. For the first time in his life he was a victim.

'What are you going to do, Mr Watts? You have one minute to decide.'

Forty-six

It's hard for me to quantify the shock I felt when I saw my father's photo in among those of the people who'd attended that occult party forty years ago. The last time I'd set eyes on him in real life I'd been seven years old and about to jump out of a first-floor window to escape him. After murdering my mother and brothers, he'd come rushing into the room where I'd been hiding, the long coat he was wearing already in flames, a look of utter madness in his eyes, and a bloodied knife raised high above his head as he moved in for the kill, no longer my father, no longer even a human being. In those final moments, he was a malevolent demon made flesh.

All my life I've wondered what drove him to commit such a horrendous crime, and I've never been able to come up with an answer. He wasn't a good man. Born into money, he drifted through life, not bothering to work, living off his trust fund, and when that ran dry, living off other people. My mother had been twenty years his junior and, even though I was only very young, I remember him treating her badly. He would go away for days, occasionally weeks at a time, and when he was at home he seemed to break up the family dynamic with his dark moods and angry outbursts.

The problem was that after his death no one ever talked about him, so I was never able to find out much about who he really was. Nor, in many ways, did I want to. He was responsible for all the darkness in my life, and he would always be the demon from that final night. My strategy had been to turn my back on my past and let my father rot, alone and ignored, in hell.

And yet now, suddenly, he'd been thrust right back into my life, somehow connected to the Sheridan family and the killings I'd been trying to solve these past three months.

After I told Tina that it was him in the photo, she tried to get me to sit down and talk about it. She knew my story as well as anyone, and there was no one else I could have talked to about it. But right then I needed to be alone.

I went outside and walked round the village and beyond, trying and failing to come to terms with what I'd just discovered, until at last, tired and exhausted by the stresses of the last twenty-four hours, I found my way back to Tina's in the darkness.

'I was worried about you,' she said, and kissed me.

'Don't be,' I said, and kissed her back, hard and with passion, wanting to clear my head of all that was wrong in the world, and replace it with just a few moments of peace.

Afterwards, when we were lying in each other's arms, trying to enjoy the warm silence, neither wanting to spoil the moment by bringing up the subject of my father, my phone started ringing. I was comfortable where I was and considered leaving it, but I still hadn't heard from Hugh Manning, and now more than ever I didn't want to miss his call, so I got up, found my trousers, and pulled out the phone.

Dan's number flashed up on the screen. I looked at my watch. It was 11.15, and I suddenly remembered that he wasn't living at home any more. That he'd split up with Denise a couple of months ago without telling me.

'Hey,' I said, 'how are you? First of all, I'm sorry about today. I didn't mean it to happen like that.'

'It's OK,' he said vaguely.

'Are you all right?' I said. 'You sound, I don't know . . . different.'

'Ah, I'm fine.'

'I tried to get hold of you tonight and, er, after I left my message on your mobile I phoned your home number. Denise said you two had split up. I'm sorry to hear that, I really am. You should have told me.'

'It doesn't matter. It's in the past now.'

'Where are you at the moment? It sounds like you're on speakerphone.'

'At the flat I'm renting. The phone's playing up a bit. You said you had information you wanted to share with me.'

'Yeah, I do.' I told him about how Anthea Delbarto had been having an affair with Alastair and Lola Sheridan's father and was involved with devil worship and occult parties, right from when the kids were very young. 'I'm guessing she's a big part of their opera-tion,' I told him. 'The point is we – I mean you – are going to have to put her under some sort of surveillance. Bug her place, see who she talks to. I'm worried for that girl who's staying there, Katy. It wouldn't surprise me if she's destined for the Bone Field.'

'This is good information, Ray,' Dan said, but it sounded like he wasn't that interested, even though he should have been.

'And you need to act on it,' I told him.

'I'll speak to Sheryl in the morning. Have you heard anything from Hugh Manning?'

'Nothing yet. I'm going to leave it until first thing tomorrow. If I haven't heard from him by then, I'll forward the message to you and you can bring Sheryl in.'

'OK,' he said. 'If you hear anything from him in the meantime, call me. It doesn't matter what time it is. I want to hear.' He paused. 'We can't afford to let him slip through our fingers.'

I frowned at the phone. It was almost as if he was speaking from a script.

'Seriously, are you all right, Dan? If there's anything you want to talk about – you know, personal stuff – then let's talk. Don't suffer in silence.'

He managed a laugh. 'I'm fine, Ray. Just tired, that's all.'

'Get some sleep, then,' I told him.

I wanted to say something else, something to make him feel better about life and the world, because I imagined him alone and depressed somewhere away from home, knowing he couldn't go back there, and I'd spent so long in that position I knew exactly how he felt.

But none of the right words came to me, and in the end I just said goodbye.

Forty-seven

Dan put the phone back in his pocket, feeling sick to the gut. He knew that by giving up Hugh Manning he was destroying any chance of bringing the Bone Field killers to justice. Manning was their Achilles heel. Get him out of the way and the killers were strong once again. But what choice did he have? They had him where they wanted him and, in the end, self-preservation had prevailed.

Across the room, Mr Bone gave a satisfied nod and got to his feet. 'You've done the right thing, both for yourself and your family.'

'I don't want anything to happen to Ray. Or the deal's off.'

'Your friend is a dangerous fool and he will destroy many others before he destroys himself.'

'He's no longer in the police. He can't do you any harm. Leave him alone.'

Mr Bone stood up and threw the phone into Dan's lap. 'Your priority should be closer to home. If Hugh Manning makes it into police custody your life is over, and your children will suffer horrendously. Nothing will stop that.' He looked at his watch. 'Now we're going to leave. Wait here until half past eleven, then exit through the front door, keep your head down, and go home.'

Dan looked at him. 'How do I know you're not just going to call the police?'

Mr Bone gave him a dismissive look as if he couldn't believe he'd been asked such a foolish question. 'Remember this, Mr Watts. You've never been a threat. We've watched your lack of progress against us for years now. You've never even been close. And right now, you're far more use to us inside the investigation. This is your one chance. Make sure you take it.'

In that moment, Dan knew his life was over. The Kalamans would never let him live a peaceful life. They would milk him for information, force him to betray everyone and everything he held dear, and one day, when his usefulness to them ran out, which it would, they would get rid of him, just as they'd got rid of Vicky.

Shell-shocked and beaten, he sat there for ten minutes staring into space, thinking about his wife, his children, and finally the man he'd just betrayed, and who would, he was sure, be dead very soon.

'Forgive me, Ray,' he whispered, and slowly got to his feet.

Forty-eight

'What am I going to do?' I said, looking out of the bedroom window into the warm night, still unable to make sense of what I'd found out. 'The fact that my father was directly linked to the people I'm hunting . . .' I paused, trying to find the right words. 'It throws everything on its head.'

Tina was sitting up on her bed, her body partly covered by a single sheet. 'But what does it really change, Ray? Your father's been dead more than thirty years. Robert Sheridan's dead. And his children may be monsters in their own right, but they had nothing to do with what happened to your family.'

Her words made sense on a rational level, but emotionally they hardly registered, and I paced the room relentlessly, unable to settle, wondering whether more wine might do the trick.

Tina watched me, her expression pragmatic rather than

sympathetic. 'You ask what are you going to do. I'd say take a break. Let's go somewhere for a few weeks. Forget about all this.'

'We will when it's over.'

'It *is* over, Ray. You're no longer in the force, and neither am I. So what can we do?'

I was still pondering that particular question when my phone rang again from the bedside table. It was a withheld number, and half eleven at night, so I picked up.

'Is this Ray Mason?' said the man at the other end.

I recognized the voice immediately. We'd pulled a couple of videos from Hugh Manning's Facebook account in which he'd been larking about with friends. He had a public-school Home Counties accent, delivered with a slow, confident drawl that didn't quite hide its high pitch. There was no confidence in it at the moment, though. He sounded scared.

'It is. And I assume you're Hugh Manning. I've been waiting for your call.'

'Don't try to trace this.'

'I'm not going to. The only people who know you contacted Tina on her website are her and me. But I'm not going to wait around for you. You need to come in now. If you drive here, we can give you up together.'

'No, I'd rather we meet somewhere where I know you'll be alone.'

'How do I know you're not setting me up?'

'Look, I just want to make sure I give myself up to you person-ally, because I know that you're not working for my old employers. But there are plenty of people in law enforcement who are, and if it gets out that I'm giving myself up, I won't last twenty-four hours. I need guaranteed protection. You can give me that.'

And that was the problem. I couldn't guarantee him anything. Somehow I was going to have to involve the NCA, and the only person who'd help me was Dan. He could set things up with Sheryl. But I didn't want to spook Manning.

'So, what are you proposing?' I asked him.

'I'll hand myself in to you, and only you, tomorrow night. When we're in a safe place, like the inside of your headquarters. Then you call your bosses, and get proper protection organized. I assume you're able to provide me with that.'

'We are.'

'Good. I'll call you from a different phone tomorrow to make arrangements, because I want to make sure that it's only you who turns up. And don't say a word to anyone.'

'I'm not going to be messed around, Mr Manning, or sent on a wild goose chase. Tomorrow's the cut-off point. You either hand yourself over to me then, or this is all over.'

'I'll be there,' he said. 'And you definitely want to hear what I have to say.'

'What do you know about Alastair Sheridan?' I asked, just to make sure he wasn't put up to this by the Kalamans.

He replied immediately. 'That he's a cold-blooded murderer. But if you want any more then you're going to have to give me immunity.' And with that he cut the call.

'So you're going to meet him then,' said Tina. It was a statement rather than a question.

I nodded. 'I guess so. I'll have to put Dan on standby so I can hand Manning over to him at HQ. That way I know he'll get proper protective custody.'

'And you trust Dan a hundred per cent?'

I shrugged. 'With the possible exception of you, I don't think I trust anyone a hundred per cent. But it's close enough with Dan.'

'And do you think Dan or anyone else is going to do anything about Anthea Delbarto?'

'I doubt it. There's still no evidence against her, but I know she's involved with the killers, and so do you.'

'Well, you know what, Ray? I feel like I have a personal interest in this case too. The Kalamans have tried to kill me twice now, and they came very close both times. They destroyed the life of Charlotte Curtis, a completely innocent woman who'd never done them any harm, but someone I was meant to be protecting. So I feel like I owe her.'

'What are you saying?'

'I'm going to bug Anthea Delbarto's house. I've got all the necessary equipment. That way we can find out who she's talking to and listen to her conversations.'

I sighed. 'Except if you get caught, you could end up in prison. And you'll definitely make yourself a target for the Kalamans.'

Tina looked at me coolly. 'I'll take that risk. I've done plenty more dangerous things in my time than plant a few bugs. And you know that doing this makes sense. If Delbarto's involved, she'll be spooked, and she'll be talking. If and when we find out something useful, we just feed it through to Dan. Or the press.' She shrugged. 'Or even act on it ourselves. You know, being outside the force can have its advantages.'

I knew there was no point trying to persuade her otherwise. Tina might not have been particularly stubborn, which was one of the things I liked about her, but she was strong, and rightly confident in her own abilities, and when she thought she was doing the right thing, she wasn't one to be shifted.

'OK,' I said reluctantly. 'You do what you have to do.'

'But before I do anything tomorrow, I'm going to book us a holiday. Somewhere hot, somewhere sunny, and most of all somewhere quiet. Are you up for that?'

I leaned down, put my hand on her cheek and kissed her gently on the lips. 'Definitely,' I said. And I meant it. I remember thinking at the time that a holiday would be a really good way of cementing our relationship.

But like so many things in life, it was not to be.

Forty-nine

Hugh Manning switched off the phone he'd used to call Ray Mason, removed the SIM card and threw it in a bush. He'd made the call from a hill overlooking the M27 motorway a good ten miles from Harry Pheasant's house.

He looked down at the car headlights, people just going about their business without a care in the world, and knew this would never be him again. All day long he'd been torn as to what he should do. A small part of him wanted to keep lying low, to wait for that opportunity to get off this island, into Europe, and eventually Panama, where he could at last lay his hands on the money sitting in the offshore bank account. $2.2 million would go a long way, especially as he now no longer had Diana with him. It was strange how quickly he'd got used to life without her.

But he knew he'd never make it to Panama. The forces ranged

against him were too great, and the longer he stayed on the run, the harder it would be to give himself up on his own terms, and the more he put Harry himself in danger. Manning wasn't used to worrying too much about other people's feelings but he was genuinely touched by how much Harry was risking by helping him. He also knew that Harry's idea of handing himself into a police officer who couldn't be bought or corrupted was the best one of a pretty sorry bunch.

Harry was waiting in his car with the engine running as Manning climbed into the back seat, getting into the familiar crouching position so he was out of sight.

'How did it go?' he asked from the driver's seat.

'It's all set for tomorrow, but I'm not giving him the location until the last minute.' Manning sighed. 'Do you know, if it all goes according to plan tomorrow then this will be my last ever night of real freedom. And it'll be the last time I ever see you. Once I go into this, there's no way back.'

Harry looked at him pensively in the rear-view mirror, then his face broke into a broad grin. 'Then we'd better make it a good one. I've got some decent Margaux in the cellar. Let's get back to my place tout de suite and crack it open. You know what they say. Eat, drink, and be merry. For tomorrow we die.'

'Let's not make predictions,' said Manning, who wasn't grinning.

Fifty

Given what I'd found out about my father, and the fact that he so often haunted my nightmares, I slept a surprisingly deep and dreamless sleep that night and didn't wake until gone nine. The bright morning sunlight was edging round the curtains and Tina was still asleep beside me.

I looked down at her for a long time and I felt something for her that scared me. I'd let myself go, and fallen in love with her, and this made me vulnerable. When I was on my own I was hard to intimidate because I didn't care enough about myself to be scared, but now it was different. My feelings for her could be exploited. Worse, I couldn't afford to lose her. Not now. I'd lost everyone I'd cared for over the years, and had just about been able to handle it, but I had a feeling that next time it might send me over the edge.

The Hanged Man

Careful not to wake her, I got out of bed, threw on some shorts and grabbed my phone from the bedside table. When I got downstairs, I turned off the burglar alarm and checked the front and back doors, just to make sure no one had visited in the night. It was a ritual of ours. The Kalamans knew about my involvement in the hunt for them, and wouldn't hesitate to bug us if they could. We both swept our homes and cars every day with state-of-the-art bug finders. I'd already found two trackers on my car in the past month, and Tina had found one. It wasn't foolproof – the Kalamans also possessed state-of-the-art equipment – but it was as close to safety as we were going to get.

Tina's cottage had two separate burglar alarms and no one was getting through one without setting off the other, and if they came for us in the night, we were prepared. For more than three years I'd been authorized to carry a gun at all times because of the threat to my life from Islamic terrorists, who'd already tried to kill me once. But that right (I would call it a necessity) had been taken away from me after a case the previous year. I'm not the kind of man who's comfortable being a target for my enemies, so a month earlier, after a lot of shopping around, I'd bought a brand-new Walther P99C pistol with a spare magazine and a box of nine-millimetre ammunition on the black market. It's extremely hard to get hold of illegal firearms in the UK and as a result this one had ended up costing me six grand – more than ten times what it would be if I'd been able to buy it legally. It would also cost me a long prison sentence if I was ever caught with it but, even so, I considered it a price worth paying for protection. I didn't carry it with me all the time but I had it whenever I was staying at Tina's, under her bed on my side. I'd even offered to source Tina one of her own, since she was firearms trained, but she'd declined, which was probably for the best. I could just about handle going down for five years for possession of a firearm if it came to it, but I'd find it a lot harder to lose Tina that way.

You may think I'm far too reckless to be a police officer, and I think it's fair to say you'd be right. But consider this: I have only ever wanted justice for the victims of crime and I've worked tirelessly towards that end all my adult life. I have done bad things, but only in the heat of the moment and when I was under great stress, and only to bad people. I have only ever ended the lives of killers, or would-be killers. I have always tried to be fair. I am, I genuinely believe, one of the world's good people, and that men like me are needed in the battle against the bad ones, because the bad ones are many in number, and I can tell you from bitter experience that some of them, like the Kalamans and the Sheridan children, are very, very bad.

But Sheryl Trinder was right. If every cop was like me, the whole system would collapse. And for this reason, more than any other, I didn't feel bad that morning that I was no longer in the force. It didn't mean that I wouldn't keep after the Bone Field killers. I would. But now I'd do it my way.

I made myself a cup of tea and called Dan, hoping he was feeling better this morning. I was worried about him. His family had always been such a huge part of his life and losing them had clearly hit him hard. I hoped that the news about Hugh Manning would at least cheer him up a bit.

He sounded a bit shocked when I told him that Manning had

finally called me and I gave him the details, explaining how he'd approached me because he knew I wouldn't betray him. 'He's scared of the Kalamans getting to him in custody, so do me a favour please, Dan, don't tell anyone else about this. Manning's sworn me to secrecy. He says I've got to come alone otherwise the deal's off.'

'Where are you meeting?' he asked, his voice quiet.

'I don't know yet. He's going to call today to give me instructions. By the way, why are you whispering?'

'I'm in the office. And I'm definitely not meant to be speaking to you.'

'I didn't think you were going in today.'

He sighed. 'What else have I got to do?'

'I'm sorry about how things have turned out for you and Denise,' I said.

'Forget it. It's not your problem. Does Manning know you're no longer in the force?'

'No.'

'So how are you planning to offer him protection?'

'That's why I'm calling you. My plan's to meet him, then hand him over to you at HQ. Then you can organize getting him to a secure location.'

He was silent for a few seconds, and I was just about to ask him again if everything was OK – because in truth he just didn't sound right – when he spoke. 'Call me as soon as Manning makes contact,' he said, then ended the call without even saying goodbye.

Fifty-one

Back in the office, Dan Watts was staring at his phone, caught out by this new turn of events. He'd been ordered by Mr Bone to come into HQ this Saturday morning to keep abreast of the hunt for Hugh Manning but there'd been no further developments. The search round Newton Stewart in Scotland where Manning had last been seen two days earlier had turned up nothing, and though calls were still coming in from members of the public with sightings in wildly different locations, there'd been no two sightings in the same place, and none of them had been seen as worth following up on. It was as if he'd disappeared into thin air.

And now, suddenly, there was this from Ray. Hugh Manning on a plate delivered straight to him. And Dan knew there was no way Manning could make it through the door of HQ because if that happened it was all over for him and his family.

The Hanged Man

He'd spent the night tossing and turning, unable to sleep, torn apart by the reality of his situation. At exactly three a.m. he'd received a text message from an unknown number. It contained a photo showing Vicky's naked body lying in a shallow, open grave. She looked like some kind of grotesque mummy, wrapped from head to toe in clear plastic clingfilm, the tattoo of the butterfly on her belly that he'd kissed earlier while she giggled clearly visible. Resting on her chest was the murder weapon, also wrapped in clingfilm. There was no accompanying text – nothing that could incriminate anyone else for the crime for which they were so expertly framing Dan. But the message was clear enough. They'd buried Vicky as if she was nothing more than household garbage, and as long as Dan behaved himself, there she and the murder weapon would stay.

And behaving himself meant betraying Hugh Manning and, worse still, Ray, who in spite of their differences had become a good friend.

But Dan knew he had no choice. The truth was, he no longer cared about himself. He'd behaved badly and rejected his faith by constantly succumbing to his lust and committing adultery, and it was his own fault that he'd ended up in the position he was in. But if he went to prison for the rape and murder of a woman he'd met online – and they would charge him with rape, he was sure of that – then his wife and children would have to bear that terrible shame for the rest of their lives. And in prison there would be nothing he could do to protect them against the Kalamans if the man he'd met last night carried out his threat of disfiguring one of them. And again, Dan was certain he would, if only to make a point.

He cursed the Kalamans for their power and the way they chose to use it for evil ends, and he cursed himself for being foolish enough to think he could ever stop them.

And now, after years of trying to bring them to justice, he was reduced to being their messenger boy. He'd been given a number to call as soon as there were any new developments, and this was the biggest development there was ever likely to be.

Replacing the phone in his pocket, he got to his feet and used a handkerchief to wipe sweat from his brow. He could hear his heart beating rapidly in his chest. He knew he looked a state and he was finding it hard to hold himself together. Thankfully HQ was quiet, but Sheryl Trinder was around somewhere and if she saw him she'd know immediately that something was wrong – she was that kind of person.

Ten minutes later he was walking in the park near Vauxhall Bridge. The day was sunny and warm, even though it was only just gone half nine, and people were already taking up their spots on the grass. Dan found a quiet place in the shade of a huge oak tree and looked at the phone in his hand, knowing that if he made this call there was no going back. He was sending Hugh Manning to his death.

'You don't have to do this,' he whispered aloud.

But he did. That was the problem.

Even so, he stood there for a long time, and it was only when he had a vision of his youngest daughter lying mummified in clingfilm in a shallow grave, dead and gone for ever while he rotted in prison, that he brought his breathing under control and, with shaking fingers, made the call.

Fifty-two

Cem Kalaman was sitting on the master bedroom balcony over-looking his carefully manicured half-acre garden, drinking black coffee. He'd just had word from Mr Bone via the Drafts section of the email address they communicated through that the insider they'd been cultivating had come up with some more very useful information. Hugh Manning, it seemed, was preparing to hand himself in to none other than Ray Mason, and had sworn Mason to secrecy so both men would be meeting without any back-up.

It couldn't, thought Cem, have turned out any better. Ray Mason had been a constant thorn in his side these past few months, and his investigation was getting him closer and closer to the various key members of their network. Three months earlier Cem and a few of his people had paid Mason a visit at his flat in Fulham to teach him a lesson in respect. It had backfired when Mason had ended up threatening them all with a gun and making Cem lose face in front of his men. More than anything else in the world Cem hated to lose face, and since that confrontation he'd been waiting for a chance to pay Mason back. Apparently Mason had resigned from the police the previous afternoon, making him an even easier target now that he no longer enjoyed the protection of his colleagues.

Cem had told Mr Bone that neither Manning nor Mason was to leave the meeting alive, and had instructed him to use all their resources to make sure that happened. Mr Bone had assured him that it would, although Cem wouldn't rest properly until he received news that both men were dead.

The problem was, that wasn't going to be the end of it. The years of murder for pleasure were over. He had loved the ritual of the kill, the comradeship he'd felt with his fellow killers. He had never been as interested in the occult side of it as the others. For him, it had always been about power. But now the whole thing was becoming far too risky. If they continued, eventually they would be caught, and Cem's huge business empire which he'd built up singlehandedly would be destroyed. And he couldn't have that.

One useful thing his father had taught him, back in the early days when Cem was still listening to him, was that a man should never be sentimental in business. When you identify weakness, you must ruthlessly cut it out. You have to keep moving forward, and if those around you lose their usefulness in the process, then it's time to cut them out too.

Cem put down his coffee and stared into space, knowing that that time would be coming soon.

Fifty-three

I spent a surprisingly relaxing day with Tina. We stayed in bed most of the morning doing the things that couples who've recently found each other do. We even found the time to book that holiday. Two weeks in Costa Rica, a place neither of us had been, leaving in three days' time. It was something to look forward to. I hadn't had a holiday away with someone for more than seven years, and I knew I needed the break. My behaviour had been becoming progressively more manic since I'd been involved in the Bone Field case, and it was time to take stock.

After a very early dinner in her garden, during which I gave her the low-down on what Anthea Delbarto's house was like both inside and out, it was time for us to part company. I watched as Tina got her surveillance kit together and checked her car thoroughly for bugs.

'I think I should come with you,' I told her when she was done. 'As back-up. You know, just in case.'

She gave me a withering look. 'You think the little woman needs the big man's help?'

'We all need help, Tina. It's not like you haven't got yourself into situations before.'

'Don't worry, Ray, I'm not going to do anything rash. I'll check the place out. If Anthea or the girl are in, I'll plant devices and cameras outside, and get a tracker on the car. If I can, I'll get inside, but I'm not going to do anything that blows my cover.'

'I know you won't,' I said optimistically. 'But remember, Delbarto's going to be on her guard after yesterday, and she'll already have spoken to someone from the Kalamans, so they may well have people watching the place too for exactly this sort of eventuality.'

She nodded, told me not to worry about her, reminding me that she was a pro at this sort of thing (which she was), and kissed me on the lips. I held her close to me and in the end she had to manoeuvre herself out of my grip.

As she walked out of the door, I wanted to tell her I loved her because I think I did, but something stopped me, the way it always had. But I couldn't let her go without saying something.

'I don't want to lose you,' I told her.

She turned back to me, her figure framed in the sunlight, a smile on her face. 'You won't.'

After she'd left I couldn't settle, preferring to pace the house and garden trying and failing not to worry about her, and it was a real relief when I got the call from Hugh Manning at six p.m., half an hour later.

Once again, he was calling from an unidentified number.

'Whereabouts are you?' he asked, his voice tense.

'London,' I said. 'And you?'

'Further south. I want you to drive to a place called Blashford Lakes nature reserve. It's not far from Southampton.' He gave me the postcode and I wrote it down. 'Take a turning called Ellingham Drove off the Salisbury Road. Drive two hundred metres down there and park by the entrance to the quarry. Be there for 9.30 p.m., and make sure you come alone.'

I went back in the house, opened up my laptop and put the postcode into Google Maps. It was just over a two-hour drive from where I was. 'It's an isolated spot,' I said, looking at the string of half a dozen lakes on the map surrounded by open countryside.

'That's deliberate,' he said. 'What car will you be driving?'

I had to give him his dues, Manning was a thorough operator. Although I didn't like the idea of meeting up in such an isolated area, I still couldn't see how it could be a trap. The Kalamans wouldn't be using him to set me up. If they'd found him, he'd have been dead by now. So, deciding that Manning was almost certainly serious in his intentions, I gave him the make and colour of my car.

'Be there and wait for my call,' he said, and the line went dead.

Straight away I called Dan. Manning might have been playing

it straight, and I was still prepared to keep my meeting with him a secret from the NCA, but I needed Dan in the loop.

He answered on the first ring.

'It's on tonight,' I told him without preamble. 'And I'm going to need your back-up.'

Fifty-four

Mr Bone viewed the map of Blashford Lakes nature reserve carefully. Dan Watts hadn't managed to get the exact spot for the meeting but that didn't matter. The location itself was perfect. Isolated enough so there were unlikely to be any witnesses to worry about, yet close enough to the M27 motorway for a quick getaway back to London. There was no time for planning, so it was going to have to be a rapid strike using overwhelming firepower. Mr Bone already had a team of Kalaman's best people on standby, and there were more than enough of them to ensure success tonight.

He closed Google Maps and returned to his laptop's home screen which featured the photo of a dead seventeen-year-old girl, a victim he remembered well from the farmhouse in Wales. They'd temporarily released her then hunted her down for sport.

It had been he who'd caught her within fifty metres of the main house, and it had been he who had ended her life. That was ten years ago now, when he was still swift enough on his feet, and he remembered it as one of his favourite kills. He stared at the photo for a few seconds and took himself back to that day, and the smell of the girl's fear. He felt a tingle of pleasure go through him, then locked the laptop in his strongroom drawer and stood up.

It was time to organize tonight's kill.

Seventy miles away, Hugh Manning sat in Harry Pheasant's front room, knowing that he was now enjoying the last hours of true freedom. In a way he was relieved. It meant he could stop running, and if Ray Mason could secure him some kind of deal in which he avoided prosecution, then life inside the witness protection programme could actually be OK.

The previous night had been a drunken one, as befitted a last goodbye to an old friendship. They'd sat up talking, laughing and reminiscing until four in the morning, and for most of that time Manning had temporarily forgotten his many woes – or more accurately he'd been too drunk to care. Between them he and Harry had polished off four bottles of good red wine, which was why Manning's head was still throbbing and he was on his sixth coffee of the day. For the last ten minutes Harry had been going through the plan he'd hatched for the handover to Ray Mason, using an Ordnance Survey map on the table in front of him.

'You know, Harry,' said Manning, 'you've done everything you need to do for me. Just drop me off up there and let me do the rest.'

'You need a wingman, Hugh. You don't know the area, I do. Plus you need me to make sure your man Mason does what he says he's going to do. You can't trust these coppers, even the good ones.'

'I don't trust him, but I'm giving myself up anyway. The problem is, if anything goes wrong, and you get arrested, then you could go to prison for a long time for helping me. Years, not months.'

It wasn't that Manning didn't want Harry to be there when he gave himself up; he did, desperately. But he wasn't going to be responsible for wrecking Harry's life, and so, for one of the few times in his life, he was making a difficult decision. Or at least trying to. He couldn't actually seem to get the right words out.

Harry's grin filled the room. 'Do you know what, Hughie? My life's been bloody boring these last few years. I've been single for five years because I can't seem to hold down a relationship, I rattle around in this big house with its big bloody mortgage, I've got high cholesterol and high blood pressure, and I think I've got gout. My legs are going purple anyway. And my business isn't doing well either. In fact it's doing shit.' His grin grew even wider, if that was possible. 'But right now, I'm enjoying myself. I'm having an adventure. And I'm helping a mate who's had a hard time of it. I know you'd do the same for me too.'

Sadly, Manning knew he wouldn't. He wouldn't take this sort of risk for anyone. But he felt honoured that someone would do it for him.

'OK,' he conceded. 'Just don't get yourself into any trouble, please.'

'Of course I won't,' laughed Harry, grabbing the pump-action shotgun propped up on the sofa next to him and loading a shell into the chamber. 'But as my old scoutmaster Morton used to say: be prepared.'

The sound of the intercom buzzer brought Dan out of his trance. For some time now he'd been sitting on his bed staring into space and contemplating what he was about to do. He knew that he was sending Ray Mason – a colleague, and a man with a good heart – to his death. He'd asked his blackmailer again to spare Ray's life but the only response he'd received was a simple command to do what he was told or face the consequences. Realistically they were never going to get a better chance to kill Ray, and, deep down, Dan knew that in some ways it was actually better if Ray did die tonight, because if he survived he would know that Dan was the one who betrayed him and Manning, and that would be more than he could stand.

The truth was, Dan had accepted what had to be done. The decision had been made and he would have to go with it. After this was all over, he would apply for a transfer back into the Met and try to effect some kind of reconciliation with Denise. He needed his family back badly. Only then could he adequately protect them and work to atone for his sins by being a good husband and father. He'd called the girls earlier and had managed to speak to his oldest, Florence, who was fifteen. She was hanging out with friends at the park near the old family home, enjoying the good weather, and they'd chatted for about five minutes, but Florence had been distracted, and it hadn't been much of a conversation. He hadn't even managed to get hold of thirteen-year-old Lara. He'd left a message two hours earlier and she hadn't called back. He was drifting apart from his children as they grew older and more independent and he remained outside the family home.

But that would change. It had to.

The buzzer went a second time, and Dan jumped up from the bed and spoke into the intercom.

'Delivery for Mr Watts,' said the man at the other end.

Dan told him he'd be down. He knew who the parcel was from and what it contained.

It was time to commit one last sin and then he could earn his freedom.

Fifty-five

Two hours after Manning's call, I stopped en route to Southampton, parked the car at the side of the road, and got out. It was eight p.m. and a beautiful sunny evening. To my right a freshly ploughed field stretched into the distance, while to my left a narrow copse of trees followed the line of the road. The setting sun bathed the landscape in a deep orange glow, flecked with the first shadows of dusk. It was silent here and peaceful, the only sound the singing of the birds in the trees.

I took a deep breath of the fresh country air, feeling in reflective mood. My part in the Bone Field investigation was coming to an end, so it seemed fitting that I was standing at the spot where it had all begun.

Five minutes later, I heard the sound of a car coming along the road behind me. I turned round as Dan pulled up on the verge behind my car and got out.

Dan was the kind of man who liked to take care of his appearance. He was a lean, good-looking man who always dressed with an understated style – the type who always wore decent-smelling aftershave, even when he was only out with me – but tonight he looked a mess. His eyes were red and tired, his face was covered with a thin, uneven stubble, and it looked like he'd thrown on his clothes direct from the wash basket. I knew his break-up from Denise would have hit him hard, but it was still a shock to see him like this.

'Why did you want to meet here?' he asked. 'We're still thirty miles from where you're meant to be meeting Manning.'

'I thought you might have guessed the significance.'

He looked at me blankly.

'This is the exact spot where our killers snatched their first victim, Dana Brennan. July 1989. Twenty-seven years ago.'

'Of course it is.' He looked around, as if trying to picture the scene, then back at me. 'It's a morbid choice of venue, Ray.'

I stared at the bushes where Dana's bike had been discovered a few hours after she'd disappeared. 'It reminds me of why I've broken all the laws I've broken on this case. And why I've taken the risks I have. Because one sunny afternoon in the school holidays a thirteen-year-old girl on her way from an errand to the shops for her mum was taken by those bastards, brutally murdered, and buried in an anonymous grave so she could never be found. I wonder which of them actually snatched her. Was it Cem

Kalaman? Alastair Sheridan? Lola? Whoever it was, one way or another they're going to have to pay.'

'And they will. Let's hope Manning can help us there.' Dan reached into his pocket. 'I've got a high-spec GPS tracker here, and a mike. Keep them with you so I know exactly where you are and what's happening. The best bet would be for me to follow you at a distance. I'll stay a mile or so back. That way I'm only a minute away if there are any complications. I'm assuming you're not armed.'

There was no way I was going to tell a serving police officer I was carrying an illegal gun. It wouldn't have been fair on him. 'I'm a civilian now, Dan, I've got nothing to be armed with.' I took the tracker and the mike off him. 'But I'm not expecting any trouble. Once I've got Manning with me, you can follow us back to London and we can make the switch there. But promise me you're going to make sure he gets full protection, Dan. He's the one person who can put down Alastair Sheridan. And he may be able to ruin Cem too.'

'Don't worry,' he said, 'I've got it covered.'

I watched him as he spoke. It looked like he was carrying the weight of the world on his shoulders.

'Is there any way back for you and Denise?' I asked him.

He shrugged and looked away, clearly not wanting to talk about it. 'We'll see.' He looked back at me. 'Does Tina know what you're doing?'

I shook my head, not wanting to implicate her in any way. 'No, I didn't want to get her involved.'

'Probably for the best,' he said. He looked at his watch. 'You'd better get going. It's still a fair drive. As soon as you've got him, let me know. I'll only be a minute away, remember.'

'Sure,' I said. 'See you when it's over, and don't stay too close to me. Manning likes to cover all the bases and I don't want to spook him.'

He nodded and started walking back to his car, and I noticed how much his shoulders were stooped. It was as if he'd shrunk in stature. Then, as he reached the door, he turned round and looked at me.

'You've got a good heart, Ray,' he said. 'I enjoyed working with you.'

'Yeah,' I said. 'Me too.'

I got back in the car, gave him a last wave in the rear-view mirror, and pulled away.

Fifty-six

Dusk was settling on the world as Tina walked along the edge of a wheat field towards the rear of Anthea Delbarto's house, a portable stepladder strapped to her back, trying to keep out of sight of the upper windows, and anyone else who might be out walking at this time in the evening.

She'd arrived close to an hour back now and parked in a country lane well beyond the edge of the village, having checked the property from the air on Google Maps. The house was surrounded by high hedges on all sides, and the nearest property – another residential home – was fifty metres away. The hedge itself was an impenetrable leylandii, trimmed to a height of fifteen feet, and Tina had circumnavigated it twice, trying and failing to find any gaps to crawl through. There were only two ways into the property. One was over the main gates at the front, the other was over a gate at the back. The gate at the back was solid wood and only a few feet shorter than the surrounding hedge. It was topped with wrought-iron spikes to prevent entry, but that was no impediment to someone with Tina's experience of housebreaking, and Ray had told her there were no dogs – the bane of burglars the world over.

Tina knew that coming over the front gates would leave her too exposed to discovery, so instead she crept up to the back gate, stopped, and listened. She could hear the faint sound of classical music coming from inside the house. It seemed someone was in.

She waited a few moments then slipped the stepladder from her back, set it up and climbed the three steps. From here, standing on tiptoes, she could just reach the spikes. She managed to get two of them in a three-fingered grip and, silently praising herself for all the upper-body work she did in the gym, slowly lifted herself up until she was just peering over the top.

There, only ten yards away, partially concealed by a grape-vine, was a woman in her sixties. She was sitting at an outside table on a veranda, facing sideways to the hedge as she sipped from a glass of white wine. Although she no longer looked like the nanny Brian Foxley had photographed all those years ago, Tina had already found a more recent photo of Anthea Delbarto online, and knew that this was who she was looking at.

Tina slid back down out of sight. There was no way she was getting into the house this way, and she was still pondering her next move when she heard the sound of footfalls on the veranda followed by the clatter of plates.

'Oh Katy,' said Anthea, her voice clear and sonorous. 'This looks absolutely delicious.'

'Thanks, Anthea,' replied Katy. Her voice was quieter and less confident, but there was no mistaking the pleasure in it at the compliment. 'I can never seem to get the sauce how I want it.'

'It always tastes good to me. Cheers.'

Tina heard the scrape of a chair on the concrete followed by the clink of glasses. For a few seconds she listened as the two of them spoke. She could make out most of what they were saying and was surprised by the normality of their conversation. They talked like aunt and niece, and it was clear that Katy looked up to her benefactor. It didn't make Tina doubt what she was doing, though. It was no coincidence that Tracey Burn had ended up in Anthea's home and then in the Bone Field. Anthea was still involved with the Sheridans, even after all these years, and God knows what she had planned for this poor girl.

Anthea mentioned something about the crunchiness of the runner beans and it reminded Tina that even monsters can live ordinary lives most of the time. But somewhere in their lives there's always something that gives them away, and Tina wondered if she'd find it somewhere in this big art deco house.

When it was clear that they'd both settled down to eat, Tina seized her opportunity. Picking up the stepladder, she crept quickly round to the main gates. They were just as big and imposing as the back gate, with the same line of spikes on the top, and lit by two lamps on either side. Attached to the lamp posts, and protected from tampering by spiked anti-climbing collars, were TV cameras to monitor who came in and out.

Knowing that she couldn't be heard from the other side of the house where Anthea and Katy were eating, Tina stowed the stepladder out of sight then ran at the gate, planting her foot on it and using her momentum to jump up and grab the spikes. She was banking on nobody watching the camera footage as she hauled herself up, managing to squeeze a foot between two of the spikes before springing over in one movement and jumping down on to the gravel.

It was a long drop, and she rolled as she landed, before getting to her feet. She listened for a second just to make sure she hadn't been heard, and then, confident that she hadn't been, she planted battery-operated micro GPS trackers under the wheel arches of the two cars parked in the drive – a Land Rover Freelander 2 and a Mercedes convertible, both of which she'd checked were registered to Anthea. The batteries could run for up to twenty-four hours on a moving car and remain on standby for months, so now Tina would have a record of wherever Anthea went.

She pulled a pair of plastic gloves and a set of lock picks from her backpack and checked the front door. It was locked, the lock itself a new six-pin Yale.

Most members of the public didn't realize it but housebreaking is an important part of policework, and Tina had learned to pick locks in her first plain-clothes role as a DC in Islington CID. If you want to bug a suspect, you have to get into his or her home somehow. The most important thing is to leave no trace of your presence.

Six-pin locks aren't easy to get through, and it took Tina close to three minutes of wrangling with a torsion wrench and hook pick before she heard the familiar click, and the handle turned. She was inside.

Feeling the adrenalin surge that always comes with the closeness of danger, Tina put her head slowly round the door. The hallway was empty, and she could hear the music coming from the far end of the house. Quickly, she moved inside and shut the door behind her.

The staircase was in front of her with a door built under it. As Tina approached she saw the door was both locked and bolted, which was interesting. Once again the lock was a new six-pin Yale, but she decided to leave picking it for now.

Instead she headed up the stairs, moving fast. It was obvious which of the bedrooms was Anthea's – actually a suite of opulently furnished rooms, hidden behind double doors, with a balcony directly above the veranda where Anthea and Katy continued to eat and talk. The balcony doors were open, showing a view of the wheat field Tina had approached from, and the line of trees beyond where she'd parked her car, and which was now disappearing into the shadows as darkness fell.

Tina could hear Anthea asking Katy if she'd like to stay a couple of weeks longer with her at the house, rather than hurry off to France. Tina couldn't quite hear Katy's reply but from her tone it sounded like she was happy to stay for longer. Tina had no doubt that Katy had been earmarked for death, like Tracey Burn, and that France was just a ruse to throw any interested parties off the scent. But it seemed the visit from Ray and Dan had spooked Anthea, and she was now playing for time so she and the Bone Farm killers could work out their next move.

If Tina's theory was true then Anthea Delbarto was a truly cold bitch.

There was a yucca plant in one corner of the room, and Tina secured a tiny battery-operated video camera to one of its branches with thin black wire. She then methodically went through Anthea's drawers and cupboards, looking for anything of interest. In the living room there was a desk with a locked drawer. This one was easy to pick and contained a laptop but no mobile phone. Tina checked the laptop but it was password-protected. She didn't have the necessary technical know-how to break in and plant keypad-logging software, and it would be impossible to plug in a hardware-based keypad logger without it being discovered. She thought about taking the laptop with her and paying one of her hacking contacts to break in for her but it was too risky. Instead she replaced it in the drawer and used her picks to re-lock it.

Anthea was clearly very careful not to leave around anything that might incriminate her so, after planting a second camera in the lampshade above her head, and angling it so it was pointed at the desk, Tina crept back downstairs.

Having broken into a number of homes in the past, her ears were well attuned to the sound of movement, and she could hear nothing as she crossed the hallway to the front door. But, as she opened it, she paused, looking back at the door under the stairs. If Anthea had been grooming women for murder at the farmhouse in Wales, then she was almost certainly still involved with devil worship. But Tina had seen no sign of any satanic regalia upstairs.

She knew she should simply walk out of the door now, head back to the car, and drive home to wait for Ray. This would have been the logical move. But Tina had always been a woman to take risks. If there was anything beyond that door, she wanted to see it, and now was her best chance, while the women were still outside enjoying the balmy evening.

Having made her decision, she pulled out the pick set, inserted the torsion wrench into the lock and got to work, conscious that at any moment she could be discovered.

But, of course, that was part of the excitement. And Tina had always thrived on the dangerous, more physical aspects of police-work. She loved the thrill of adrenalin that she got from chasing and capturing criminals, from facing down danger and, in truth, from winning. In her lifetime, she'd killed four men. Three had been classed as self-defence. The fourth no one knew about. But she still considered herself very much on the side of the angels, and in her professional life she'd never done anything that she later regretted. She'd ridden her luck, but so far had ridden it well, and if the time did ever come for her to settle properly and have children she knew she'd be able to look back and be proud of what she'd achieved.

The lock took two and a half minutes – thirty seconds faster than the front door. The only problem was the bolt. Once she opened that it would be obvious to anyone walking past that someone had been tampering with the door. To counter this, she moved it just enough for the door to open, then stepped inside.

It was pitch black when she shut the door behind her and switched on the torch. She was at the top of a single flight of concrete steps leading down into the gloom. The cellar smelled of damp and disinfectant and she descended the steps carefully, then ran her torch across the room.

She saw it straight away.

A huge pentacle sign with a flowing 'M' in the middle painted on the wall in front of her.

It was exactly what she'd been looking for.

Fifty-seven

The rendezvous was a single-track, tree-lined road with a gentle hill running up one side. I arrived fifteen minutes early, parked my car by the entrance to the quarry on my left, and got out, looking up towards the hill, which was mostly covered in trees with patches of grass between, and wondered if anyone was watching me. It was getting dark now so it was hard to tell, and I couldn't hear anything except the sound of birds, and the vague hum of traffic coming from the main road a few hundred metres away. I'd checked the spot on Google Maps and there were no residential buildings around for a good half mile. I wasn't sure if this was a good or a bad sign, but part of me didn't like being so far away from any help.

Before I'd made the turn on to the single-track road, I'd called Dan, just to let him know I was here, and he'd told me he would park up on the other side of the main road and wait for me there. He'd sounded tense, which surprised me, given that it was me who was exposed out here and not him, but I guessed he was just eager to get hold of Hugh Manning.

But for the moment at least there was no sign of Manning. I walked back round to the other side of the car so I couldn't be seen so easily from the hill, and leaned against it, keeping low and watching. I wasn't particularly nervous myself. There were two reasons for this. One, I thought Manning was genuine in his desire to give himself up. Two, and more importantly, I had the Walther P99C in the back of my waistband underneath my shirt, which as far as I was concerned left me ready for any eventuality. I didn't want to fire it, and couldn't envisage a situation in which I was going to have to tonight, but a gun's always a good confidence booster when you're in an unpredictable situation, especially when you know how to use it. And I did.

My phone started ringing. Once again the call was from an unknown number.

'I see you've arrived,' said Hugh Manning. He too sounded nervous.

'I have,' I said, looking up at the hill. 'And I'm alone.'

'I can see that. Thank you.'

'Where are you?' I asked him.

'Keep driving to the end of the road. Then turn right and follow the road round a large ninety-degree bend. Go very slowly after you hit the bend, five miles per hour maximum, and I'll call you then.'

I got back in the car and threw my phone on the passenger

seat, eager to get this over with. I could understand Manning's caution – there was, after all, a price on his head – but I wasn't prepared to be messed about much longer. It was getting late and I wanted to get home and see Tina. She'd texted me over an hour earlier to tell me she was near Delbarto's home but was still trying to work out the best way in, and I hadn't heard from her since. I knew better than to text her when she was on a job but I was going to be a lot happier when I learned she was safe and on her way home.

I didn't need to call Dan to tell him where I was going. He could hear everything I said through the mike he'd given me, which was attached to my shirt collar, so as I followed the road down to the end I repeated the instructions I'd been given for his benefit. I turned right on to another single-track lane with thick tree cover on either side which, I noted ruefully, was perfect for an ambush. The bend appeared and I followed it round, slowing right down and instinctively keeping my body low in the seat, comforted by the weight of the gun in my waistband.

The phone rang again – the same unknown number – and I picked up.

'In a few seconds you'll see an old building on your left. Drive down to the entrance and get out.'

'If you're not there this is off,' I told him.

There was a pause, and I thought he was going to say something, but he ended the call instead.

Again I repeated what I'd just been told into the mike for Dan's benefit, and as I finished speaking a clearing opened up in the trees to reveal what looked like an abandoned barn with a corrugated-iron roof, backing on to a lake. The best light now was provided by the moon, and I couldn't see anyone there, not even a parked car.

A potholed driveway led down to the building and I took it, still driving slowly, watching the trees on either side for any sign of movement. I wondered why on earth I was doing this at nearly half nine on a Saturday night when the rest of the world was out enjoying themselves, especially as I was no longer even a cop. But of course I knew the reason. It was etched on my heart.

Dana Brennan. I was doing it for her and, if she was somewhere up among the stars looking down, I hoped she was watching me now.

I stopped the car, whispered into the mike that I was getting out but couldn't see anyone, and pushed open the driver's door. I got out very slowly, keeping low so that I presented as small a target as possible, and looked towards the building.

The front door was open and hanging off by one hinge, and I was just about to call out when a voice I recognized came from inside. 'I'm here,' said Manning, and his head appeared round the doorway like something out of a cartoon. He was a good-looking guy with thick black hair and cupid lips, and his time as a fugitive didn't seem to have had any adverse effects physically. He still looked a lot younger than his forty-eight years.

I'd expected to feel an excitement when I finally got hold of him, but I didn't. I just felt a deep-seated weariness.

'Thank God for that,' I said, exhaling wearily. 'Now, let's go.'

'I thought I heard something,' he said, coming out of the door and looking round carefully. 'A car.'

I listened, but could hear nothing aside from the breeze, although I noted that the birds had stopped singing.

'I told you,' I said, 'I came alone, and I'm impressed that you managed to see me arrive from all the way over here.' It was clear Manning had had some help tonight, and probably for the past few days as well, but I wasn't going to press him on it. I had him now, and that was the main thing.

He walked over and shook my hand. He had a strong grip. 'Thank you for coming.'

'Sure,' I said, and started back to the car.

'Hold on,' said Manning and, as I turned round, I saw him pull a phone from his pocket and examine the screen, before looking back at me with a mix of mistrust and fear. 'Another car's just come past the spot where you first parked. A black SUV. Moving fast.'

I frowned. 'How do you know?'

'We set up a camera on one of the trees. That's how I saw you.'

'That car has nothing to do with me.'

'And it's nothing to do with me either. Who else knows about this?'

'Only one other person knows I'm meeting you tonight, and that's a colleague of mine. He's my back-up.'

'I told you to come alone,' Manning said angrily.

I ignored him, listening out for the sound of a vehicle.

'I can't hear anything,' I said.

'It could be an electric car or a hybrid,' Manning snapped, his voice tense. 'They don't make noise. But they're definitely on their way.'

We both ran to the car and got in, and I did a rapid U-turn.

'Is there a back way out of here?' I asked him.

He nodded frantically. 'Yes. Take a left. I'm not sure of the exact way but it takes us back on to the main road.'

I pulled out my phone and put in a call to Dan as I reached the single-track road. That was when I saw the SUV approaching from the right, only twenty metres away.

I turned the wheel hard left just in time to see that there was another SUV coming that way as well.

We were trapped.

'Oh Jesus,' wailed Manning. 'You lied to me!'

I hadn't of course, but one way or another I couldn't argue with this, nor was it a good time to work out how the Kalamans had found out about the meet. Instead, I threw down the phone and slammed the car into reverse, driving rapidly back towards the barn.

'Do everything I say,' I told him, pulling the Walther from my waistband and flicking the catch from Safe to Fire, the adrenalin pumping through my system as the two SUVs turned into the clearing in front of us, barely fifteen metres away. Already I could see men with scarves pulled over their faces leaning out of the windows with automatic weapons at the ready.

'As soon as I stop the car, fling open your door the whole way and run behind the barn with your head down,' I told him. I slammed on the brakes. 'Now!'

As I flung open my door, the first burst of automatic gunfire tore across the roof of the car and a bullet punctured the top of the windscreen only a few inches above my head. A second burst from the other car followed but went wide of us. They were using suppressors on their weapons so their noise couldn't easily be heard. They'd planned this ambush well.

There's nothing that heightens the senses more than being shot at, but the essential thing is not to let your natural fear overpower you, but use it to your advantage, and to move instinctively because everything happens very, very fast.

I rolled out of the car and on to my front, using the door as cover. As the first car stopped only three metres in front of me, a gunman leaped out. I shot him twice in the chest before he could get a round off. Another gunman was already getting out of the door behind him, and as the first gunman fell backwards he jumped out of the way, waving his gun wildly as he looked for a target.

He never found it. I shot him three times and, as he too went down, he sent a burst of automatic weapon fire into the air.

From my current position I could no longer see any of the other gunmen so I scrambled to my feet and ran low towards the barn, turning with the gun and firing a further three shots in the general direction of the cars. In the darkness I just had time to see that there were a total of four surviving gunmen, all of them armed with machine pistols. They ducked down as I pulled the trigger but almost immediately returned fire. Manning went down with a cry and I thought they had him but then he rolled over and jumped to his feet again.

We were still a good five metres from the side of the barn. Once beside it we could get a few seconds' cover from the gunfire while we tried to find an escape route. But even though these guys weren't the best shots in the world, I knew in that split second that Manning would never make it. I might, because I was further away from them than him, and the car kept me partially out of sight, but with the number of bullets being fired, at least one was bound to hit him and then he could be finished off at leisure.

And then, from off in the trees to my left, came a tremendous boom that I immediately recognized as a shotgun being fired, followed by the sound of shattering glass as one of the SUVs was hit. Straight away, all four gunmen turned towards where the shot had come from just as a second boom rang out, sending one of their number spinning round. By the time the third shot came the rest of them had dived for cover.

I kept running, grabbed Manning by the scruff of the neck, and propelled us towards the barn, turning round as I did so and loosing off more shots until I'd emptied out the magazine.

By this time we'd rounded the corner of the barn and were temporarily out of sight, but already I could hear shouting and sounds of pursuit. The lake was in front of us twenty yards away, a thick reed bed lining the edge of it. To our left was a high wire fence blocking the exit. To our right it was a run over forty yards of open ground to the nearest trees.

In such situations, you only have a split second to make a decision. Wait any longer and you've lost momentum. I made ours. Letting go of Manning's collar without dropping my pace, I hissed at him to follow me, at the same time pulling the spare magazine from my pocket and reloading the pistol with shaking hands.

We ran for the lake, scrambling into the reed bed for cover, and

Manning didn't resist as I forced him to his knees before turning round and diving into the water to make myself as small a target as possible, ignoring its chill as I pulled him down beside me.

The shotgun had fallen silent now, which suggested it was a legally held weapon with the maximum payload of three cartridges. I just hoped whoever was holding it was quick at reloading.

'I guess the guy with the shotgun is with you,' I whispered to Manning.

Manning nodded. He looked shell-shocked, and who could blame him? I'd been in situations like this before and was trained to deal with them, but even so, I was working hard to keep my own fear in check.

I looked back into the darkness, knowing I had ten rounds left, and at least three gunmen to kill.

They weren't good odds.

Harry Pheasant was enjoying himself for the first time in years. At boarding school he'd been mercilessly bullied by bigger kids and by the time he'd grown big enough to fight back school was over. He'd tried to join the army but failed the fitness test, and ended up becoming the person he'd definitely never wanted to be: a divorced office drone (albeit one with his own business) whose best years, which had never been that good, were resolutely behind him.

As a boy he'd loved the quote from Mussolini 'Better to live one day as a lion than a thousand years as a sheep', and he'd written it all over his text books and even on a piece of A4 paper taped to the wall above his bed at home. For years he'd been a sheep desperate to prove his worth, but now, in the hours since he'd been with Hugh Manning, at last he'd found his purpose.

And tonight, he'd truly proved himself. As soon as he'd seen the SUV appear on the camera feed on his phone he'd known that he was going to see action, and rather than feel fear he'd been ready for it. He was alive. He was a lion. And now he'd even shot one of the bad guys.

Crouched down in the trees like a World War Two commando, his ears ringing from the noise, he reloaded the last shell into the Mossberg and prepared to unload more withering gunfire on the enemy, knowing that he was probably going to be in a lot of trouble with the authorities, and not really caring.

But as he stood up and tucked the stock into his shoulder, he sensed rather than heard movement behind him. He swung round fast, saw nothing, and wondered if he'd imagined it. And then, out of the corner of his eye, a shadow came out of the darkness to his side. He just had time to see an oldish man with small dark eyes before he felt a loud pop in his ear and his head jerked to one side as if it had been yanked, then everything went black.

We were hiding with the lake behind us and the fence to our right so whichever way the gunmen approached we would see them coming, and because of the height of the reeds they wouldn't be able to see us until they were only a few yards away. And they were going to have to attack soon. They might have suppressors on their weapons, but my shots and those of Manning's friend would have alerted people, even in a place as isolated as this one, which meant they couldn't afford to hang around for ever.

The Hanged Man

We'd been betrayed. It couldn't have come from Manning's side, otherwise he'd have been dead already. That only left my side, and I knew it wasn't Tina. And yet I couldn't believe it was Dan either. He'd been chasing the Kalamans for years. Why suddenly join forces with them now? But the stark truth was that there were no other candidates, and as Sherlock Holmes once famously said, 'when you've eliminated the impossible, whatever remains, however improbable, must be the truth'. One way or another they'd got to him, which meant he could no longer be trusted.

I unclipped the mike he'd given me and let it drop into the water, then reached for my phone before realizing it was still in the car where I'd thrown it after trying to call Dan.

I was about to ask Manning for his but then I tensed, seeing movement on both sides of the building. The gunmen were coming. They were keeping low and close to the walls, making them hard to see in the darkness, but the thing about these guys was they weren't professional killers. They were thugs. Very well-armed ones, but thugs nonetheless, without obvious military training. I could see two of them, one on either side of the building, but not the third. I scanned the gloom, saw no suspicious movement, and faced down the Walther's sights at the gunman nearest to me, trying hard to ignore the coldness of the water. As the gunman reached the edge of the building, he moved his silenced machine pistol in an arc across the lake, as if by doing so he'd make us jump up in panic.

'When I start firing, roll away from me and then lie absolutely still,' I whispered out of the corner of my mouth, my finger tensing on the trigger. 'Do you understand?'

Manning managed a barely audible yes and then, as the gunman moved the arc of his machine pistol away from us, I fired off three rounds in rapid succession, their noise shattering the silence. Immediately I rolled away, seeing Manning do the same, as several wild bursts of automatic gunfire tore up the water a few yards behind me. The shooting was inaccurate. It's hard to keep machine pistols stable, and it's also hard to hit moving targets in the darkness, especially when they have good cover.

I kept rolling then stopped and peered through the reeds.

Twenty yards away, the gunman I'd fired at was lying on his back, moaning and holding his shoulder, his weapon beside him. No one else was visible. Now they were down to two, and surely they couldn't stay here much longer. I motioned for Manning to stay put, with his head down, and continued crawling through the water, away from where I'd fired the shots.

And then I heard it above the ringing in my ears. The sound of a car pulling up in front of the building. If they'd brought in reinforcements we were finished. I only had seven rounds left and we had nowhere to run.

But, as I saw the two figures emerge from the shadows, I realized it was worse than that.

Fifty-eight

Dan had been sitting in his car staring straight ahead in a near daze when the dull booms of a shotgun rang out, followed a few seconds later by rapid pistol fire. He'd taken a deep breath and his eyes had filled with tears. He'd never thought the day would come when he'd stand by knowing that he'd sent a good man to his death. The whole car, his whole body, everything about him, reeked of betrayal.

On the way down here his thirteen-year-old daughter Lara had finally found the time to call him. For the first time in his life he hadn't wanted to talk to her, but he also knew there was a possibility that the Kalamans might kill him too and so he'd taken the call.

They'd only chatted for a few minutes but for Dan it had been heartbreaking. Lara had wanted to know why he couldn't work it out with her mum. He'd tried to explain as best as he could that sometimes that was just the way things were – some relationships just weren't meant to last – but the important thing was that he would always love her and her sister with all his heart. 'You two are the most important people in my whole world,' he'd said, almost choking with emotion.

Lara had asked when she and Florence could come and stay with him, but the thing was Dan couldn't bear to have them come to his dingy one-room flat and see quite how low he'd fallen. Even so, he'd promised it would be soon, and that he'd take them out to Nando's one evening next week.

'You're the best dad in the world,' she'd told him, and as the tears had streamed down his face he'd told her he loved her one more time and ended the call before she knew he was crying.

He wasn't the best at anything. He was a fraud, an adulterer and, worst of all, a traitor.

He'd been ordered by the man he assumed was Mr Bone to stay nearby in case he was needed. He couldn't understand what they could possibly need him for but, as the shooting stopped, his phone had started ringing. It was the number Mr Bone had called him from earlier and, taking a deep breath, he'd picked up and been given a further set of instructions.

And now here he was, in the shadow of an abandoned building facing a perfectly still lake that stretched out into the darkness, with Mr Bone standing a few feet behind him, holding a pistol with a suppressor attached. Off to Dan's left, a black man in a scarf and combat gear was crouched down by a tree pointing an automatic weapon in the direction of the lake, while to his right a white man all in black lay on his back whimpering and holding on to his shoulder. Blood pooled on the ground beside him.

'Move forward so Mason can see you,' hissed Mr Bone. 'He's somewhere in those reeds. You tell him to give up Manning now. If he does, Mason lives, and you live. If he doesn't, you both die now. And your children die later tonight.'

Dan could hear the tension in Mr Bone's voice. Last night, when he'd confronted him at Vicky's flat, he'd been full of confidence. But it was obvious things had gone very badly wrong with the ambush. When Dan had parked his car just now he'd seen two bodies lying on the ground, and there was no sign of Ray or Manning. There was also no way that Bone and his surviving men could afford to stay here much longer. This had to be wrapped up very soon before the police arrived.

Dan walked past the wounded man and out of the shadow of the building. His eyes scanned the reed bed lining the lake but he could see nothing. Out of the corner of his eye he saw a third gunman crouched down on the other side of the building and, although a scarf was pulled up over his face like the others, Dan recognized him by his shock of blond hair as the man who'd handed him the knife used to kill Vicky the previous night.

'Speak,' hissed Bone from behind him. 'Fast.'

Dan took a deep breath. 'Ray, can you hear me? I'm so sorry for this. They framed me for murder, and they threatened my children.'

'Tell him to give up Manning now or I'll cut your children's eyes out myself,' Bone told him.

Dan thought of Lara and Florence, his beloved children, and

he felt the anger building in him. This man, this *creature*, behind him had to be stopped or he would always be a danger to his family. Suddenly, and very clearly, Dan realized there was no future for him. It was over. But he could do something for others, and atone for his sins. Then maybe God would forgive him.

He took another deep breath. 'There are three gunmen, Ray,' he called out. 'One to my left, one to my right, and one behind. Good luck.'

And with that, he turned and charged the man who'd tormented him these past twenty-four hours.

Almost immediately Dan felt something strike his shoulder like a punch, followed by an intense burning, but adrenalin and anger were driving him on, and he kept moving forward, head down, an angry bellow coming from his mouth. Another round struck him in the gut, a third tore through his cheek, but momentum was carrying him now and he saw the panicked expression on Bone's face. And then, for the second time in less than forty-eight hours, Dan launched the fist he'd always sworn he'd never use in anger again, and smashed Bone full in the face, just as a fourth round struck him somewhere in the chest.

I saw it all happen from my position in the water. Dan charging the man behind him, the shots being fired, and the two of them going down. The whole thing lasted no more than a couple of seconds but in that time I saw one of the gunmen, who'd been crouching out of sight behind a tree, instinctively jump up and turn towards Dan.

It was a mistake on his part. With a cold fury I turned the

Walther so he was in my sights and opened up with three shots, feeling a grim satisfaction as he cried out in pain and went down, somehow managing to land in a sitting position facing me, his gun spraying bullets wildly. I fired another shot and hit him in the face just as another spray of bullets from somewhere off to my left stitched across the water, the last one missing my position by less than a foot. Whoever had fired them was a better shot than the others, but he'd still have difficulty hitting a moving target, so I rolled over and scrambled to my feet, running low through the reeds to draw his fire away from Manning.

That was when I saw him coming towards me across the grass, his pace fast yet controlled, a shock of blond hair standing out in the gloom as he aimed his gun at me. I dived forward as he opened up, landing in the mud at the edge of the lake and rolling round to face him, cracking off a shot that went wide as he fired again, his bullets sending up clods of earth just in front of me as they rico-cheted off the bank. I fired again, a single shot, trying to throw him off guard, and saw that he'd run out of ammo. I had one shot left and I was on my feet in an instant, running at him, holding the Walther two-handed as he went for something in the back of his waistband.

Only ten metres separated us and he jumped out of the way, losing his footing and falling on to his side as I fired my final round, the shot missing him, and the slide on the Walther locked back, showing both of us that my gun was empty.

The blond man put a hand in his waistband and yanked out a pistol, but before he could take aim I threw mine at his face, hitting him on the forehead. He cried out in pain, fell back and let off another couple of shots, both of which almost hit me, and then I was on him, yanking back his gun hand so the weapon was no longer pointed at me and trying to butt him in the face.

But he was fast and strong and he moved his head to one side and thrust upwards, pushing me off. We rolled over, struggling. I lost my grip on his gun hand and then he was on top of me. Once again I grabbed his wrist, forcing the gun away from me, but he had the advantage now and, as I struggled beneath him, he pinned my other arm with his knee, and used both hands to force his gun hand free.

But before he could turn the gun on me he was grabbed from behind and yanked backwards by a screaming Hugh Manning.

'You killed my wife, you bastard!' he yelled, digging his fingers into the gunman's eyes.

The gunman grunted in pain and immediately brought the gun round to shoot Manning even though he couldn't see him properly. But at the last second I launched myself upwards, grabbed his wrist and pulled it down just at the moment he pulled the trigger. The gun went off with a deafening bang, hitting the gunman in the neck. Manning jumped backwards out of the way and the blond man let go of the gun and made a choking sound as his throat filled with blood.

Still underneath him, I fumbled round for the dropped weapon, grabbed the handle and shoved the barrel under his chin before he could move out of the way.

There was no mercy in me tonight. I pulled the trigger and blew the top of his head off, pushing him off me as he toppled on to his side, already dead.

Staying on the ground, I looked around quickly just in case there was still a threat, but there was nothing and no one I could see.

I'd been partially deafened by all the shooting, and there was a loud and incessant ringing in my ears, but even so I caught the faint muffled sound of a car starting.

'Stay there,' I called to Manning, who was sitting down staring in shock at the corpse of the man I'd just shot. 'And get right down on the ground.'

Moving slowly, as if every muscle in his body had stiffened up, he did as he was told while I jumped up, still holding the blond man's gun, and ran round the side of the building.

The gunman I'd shot in the shoulder was in the process of crawling over to his weapon. At least that's what it looked like. I was operating pretty much on autopilot now, using all my old military training to neutralize any threat, so, without even slowing, I leaned down as I passed and shot him once in the head at point-blank range. Just ahead of me I could see Dan lying on his side. He wasn't moving. Next to him was a crumpled fedora hat but no sign of the man who'd worn it.

As I rounded the corner, though, I saw one of the two SUVs the attackers had come in reversing rapidly towards the road with its lights on full beam. It swung into a turn and I took a shooting stance and opened fire as it pulled away. At least one round hit a window, but the SUV continued to accelerate and a second later it disappeared from view behind the trees. I could just about make out the path of the headlights as they rounded the big bend, moving fast, before fading into the darkness.

I cursed and ran over to my car, thinking about giving chase, but he already had a good start on me and I wouldn't know which way he'd turned once I got to the main road. Plus I didn't want to leave Manning behind. Instead, I grabbed my phone from between the front seats and ran over towards Dan, feeling a rush of hope when I saw that not only was he still alive but actually crawling along the ground in the direction of the lake.

Surprisingly, I wasn't angry with him. If, as he'd said, they'd threatened to harm his children, I could hardly blame him for doing what he'd done.

But my relief turned to shock when I saw him reach out and grab one of the discarded machine pistols before rolling on to his back and propping the barrel under his chin. His pale shirt was stained red and, as I got closer to him, I saw blood pouring out of a hole in his face. He looked weak, and almost delirious, but he still managed to keep hold of the pistol. As I approached he said something to me but I couldn't make out what it was.

'It's all right, mate, I'm here now,' I said, crouching down beside him as the hearing returned in one of my ears. 'Give me the gun.'

I started to reach out for it but something in his eyes stopped me.

'Don't, Ray,' he said, forcing out the words. 'It's over for me.'

'Don't be stupid,' I said, trying to take control of the situation. 'We can work things out.' I smiled at him. 'We've always managed it so far.'

He looked at me imploringly. 'They were blackmailing me. They killed a girl I was seeing, made it look like I'd done it . . .'

He paused and turned his head to cough, spitting out a thick trail of blood and saliva.

I thought about going for the gun but stopped myself. 'Dan, it's going to be OK,' I said, my voice cracking.

'They threatened my girls as well,' he continued. 'I couldn't have that, Ray.'

'I know. I understand.'

'You don't. You can't do unless you have them yourself.' He paused to spit out more blood. 'You've got to do something for me. When this story comes out, don't let them ruin my name. Please.' He reached out with his free hand and took my arm in a surprisingly firm grip, looking me right in the eyes. 'And protect my kids from the Kalamans. Promise me you'll do that.'

I wanted to tell him to put the gun down and let me call an ambulance, that he could still be the one to protect his kids, not me. But instead I told him what he wanted to hear. 'Of course I'll protect them. With my life.'

He squeezed my arm and tried to smile. 'Thank you. Did you get Bone?'

I shook my head. 'No. He got away.'

The smile faded. 'He said he'd kill my kids. You know where they live. Please, make sure he doesn't get to them.'

I nodded. 'I will.'

'Go,' he whispered, his voice faltering. 'Now.'

He coughed again and started to choke. Again he turned to the side, and more blood and spit came out. I saw his grip on the machine pistol loosen. I was only inches away. I could have got it away from him. But I didn't. He stopped coughing and looked at me. I got to my feet.

'Take care, Dan,' I said. 'Your family will be safe.'

I turned away, and a split second later I heard the shot.

I didn't turn back. My friend was dead, and in the distance I could just about make out the sound of approaching sirens.

Fifty-nine

The main problem Tina Boyd had was that she never knew when to stop.

As soon as she'd switched on the light in the basement and seen the stone altar with the pentacle sign behind it, she knew she'd stumbled on to something important. According to Ray, this was the sign that had been in the basement at the farmhouse in Wales, as well as on the wall of an old folly in the grounds of the boarding school where the remains of Kitty Sinn and Dana Brennan had been found in April. It was more evidence, if any were needed, that Anthea Delbarto was inextricably linked with the Bone Field killers.

Leaving the light on, Tina had gone down the steps and taken a number of photos of the altar, as well as a wicker basket next to it that contained the bones, some still with clumps of fur or feathers on them, of a number of small animals. She'd then planted a camera with a mike beside a cupboard in the corner of the room facing the altar.

And that was when she should have turned and gone straight back up the stairs and out the front door.

But she hadn't. There were two large cupboards and two filing cabinets, all of them locked, lining one wall, and because Tina was on the hunt for more evidence she'd decided to look inside them. It was too risky to do it with the light on in the basement, where it could be seen from outside in the hall, so she'd picked the locks using only her head torch for light, a process that had been long and laborious because she'd then had to use the picks to re-lock them so her presence here wouldn't be detected.

The cupboards had contained plenty of occult paraphernalia – robes, old books, jars containing pickled animal parts and strange-smelling substances, a number of razor-sharp knives that were doubtless used for animal sacrifice – but nothing that suggested any obvious criminal wrongdoing.

The filing cabinets had been even more of a waste of time: they contained nothing more than reams and reams of paperwork relating to a variety of mundane topics, from old tax returns to damp-proofing certificates.

It was a quarter to ten when Tina re-locked the last of the cabinets. She'd been down here for over half an hour and it was definitely time to go. Keeping the torch pointed directly down in front of her she climbed the steps and was almost at the top when she heard footsteps approaching outside and someone talking.

It was Anthea Delbarto, and she was on the phone. She was speaking in low tones and she sounded worried.

Tina yanked off her head torch and switched it off, plunging the basement into darkness as Anthea walked directly past the basement door. She couldn't hear what was being said but it was clear it was something serious. The footsteps faded as Anthea kept walking, and then the front door opened and she stepped outside, her voice still just audible.

Tina waited, concluding that, with the front door open, it was too risky for her to step out into the hall.

Then she heard it shut and the footfalls come back.

And stop. Just outside the basement door.

Anthea Delbarto was no longer on the phone. And she wasn't moving either.

Tina froze and held her breath.

The door opened an inch, and now it would have been obvious to Anthea that someone had broken in. Tina tensed, preparing to launch herself out of the door and make a run for it.

But then, just as quickly, the door shut and Tina heard the bolt being pulled across.

And just like that, she was trapped.

Sixty

I just had time to retrieve my empty Walther, clean the prints off the other gun I'd used, and grab hold of a very shaken but thankfully alive Hugh Manning before the first flashing blue lights appeared on the horizon from the main road.

We jumped in my car and left the nature reserve in the other direction, travelling at speed, neither of us really sure where we were going, but for me at least the top priority was to put as much distance between us and the lake as possible, because I was fairly certain that if the police brought in a helicopter they'd hone in on us immediately.

Incredibly, my car didn't look too bad considering it had just been in the middle of a firefight. There was the hole at the top of the windscreen where a bullet had passed through before exiting through the roof, and there were several more holes in the front and back passenger side doors, but at first glance in darkness the damage wasn't noticeable, which meant if we could get to another main road we were probably safe.

For the next ten minutes I drove at a fast yet controlled pace, half expecting to run into a roadblock around every corner, or hear the sound of a helicopter hovering overhead, knowing that if we were caught then there was no way on God's earth I'd be able to talk my way out of it. I'd killed a number of men tonight. I wasn't sure of the exact number because I wasn't sure how many were still alive, but it was at least two, and possibly as high as six. It didn't matter that they were all armed. I'd used an illegal gun that I was still carrying, and had left the scene of what was to all intents and purposes a massacre, with a serving police officer among the dead, and without reporting it. That meant a jail sentence, and, given my already controversial record, probably a long one.

But tonight at least, luck was on my side, and we reached a road containing traffic that my satnav identified as the B3078. I immediately turned north on it and slowed down, joining a queue of three cars backed up behind a slow-moving lorry.

'What the hell happens now?' said Manning, speaking for the first time since I'd hauled him off the grass by the lake. 'I need protection.'

'And you'll get it,' I said. 'I guarantee that.'

Manning gave me a disgusted look. His face was puffy and it looked like he'd been crying. '*You* can't guarantee anything right now. What happened back there was your fault.'

His voice had taken on a whining, child-like tone that annoyed me. 'My colleague was compromised by the Kalamans. They were blackmailing him.'

'And that's precisely why I need some bloody protection. Instead you're just taking me off into the middle of God knows where, running from the very people you're meant to be handing me over to. Why didn't we stay put, for Christ's sake?'

'Listen,' I said. 'First of all, it was your choice to get me involved. Secondly, I've just saved your life.'

'Only because you put it at risk in the first place by not keeping the meeting to yourself.'

I glared at him. 'No, Hughie boy. *You* were the one who put things at risk when you got involved with violent gangsters, just because they paid you lots of money, instead of doing a normal day's work like everyone else. And secondly, for your information, we're not on the run. I just need to get away to plan our next move.'

'Which is?'

I sighed. 'When we get close to London, you're going to call the number of the woman I reported to until yesterday. Her name's Sheryl Trinder and she's high up in the NCA. I also know she's clean.'

'How do you know? I assume you thought your colleague was clean too.'

I sighed, thinking of Dan lying dead on the ground, his life destroyed by the Bone Field killers. The shock of that still hadn't hit me, although I had a feeling it wouldn't be long until it did. 'He had a weakness which they exploited. One thing I can tell you about Sheryl is she doesn't have any. She's hard as nails, and honest with it. I'll be here while you make arrangements to meet her at HQ, then I'll drop you off nearby, and she'll take over.'

Manning shook his head angrily and stared out of the window. 'If I'd known this was how it was going to end up, I'd have stayed on the run.'

'Yeah? Well, it's too late for that now.'

He pulled a phone from his pocket. 'I need to know what happened to my friend. The one who was there tonight. I think he might be hurt.'

'The police will be there now. They'll find him.'

'They might not. He was in the woods.'

I didn't want Manning to complicate things by phoning someone at the crime scene but I didn't like the idea of leaving someone behind injured either, so I told him to go ahead and make the call.

He did. At the same time, my own phone vibrated in my pocket.

'It went to voicemail,' said Manning quietly. 'I think he might be dead. He helped me, you know. He didn't have to.'

'Then pay him back by helping put the Bone Field killers behind bars. You were there when Alastair Sheridan killed a woman, weren't you? A long time ago.'

He looked at me. 'How do you know about that?'

'The woman was a prostitute and her pimp at the time told me about it. He said it happened at Alastair's house and that you were there. For all we know you might have been involved.'

Manning shook his head vehemently. 'That had nothing to do with me.'

I met his eye. 'So you say.'

Manning sighed. 'I won't lie to you, I was there. I thought Alastair and I were just going to have a threesome with her. We did that sometimes in those days with girls. Sometimes we even got a bit rough with them. But that night, Alastair was on coke and he'd been drinking, and he was in a very belligerent mood. He knocked the girl around. She yelled at him to stop and when he didn't, she fought back. It turned out she was quite handy with her fists and she forced him off her, and cut his face as well.' Manning looked out of the window. 'He was furious. He grabbed some kind of statuette and hit her with it. She went down on her knees but instead of stopping he kept hitting her with it. I couldn't look. I felt physically sick. And I'm not proud to say it but I ran out of the room and left her in there with him.'

'Then what happened?'

'I didn't know what to do.'

'You could have called the police.'

'And I wish I had. But I didn't. I was in shock. Alastair came out of the room a little while afterwards. He was still naked and covered from head to foot in blood. He told me it had been an accident and the girl was dead. He also told me that he knew people – dangerous people, he called them – who could get rid of her, but if I said a word about what had happened to anyone, he wouldn't be able to protect me. I'd be killed too. The thing I remember most is the way he wasn't really that bothered about the fact that he'd just killed someone. It was like it was a minor inconvenience.'

'You're going to have to testify against him to have any hope of getting into witness protection,' I said.

'As long as I don't go to prison, I'll do whatever I have to do.'

'Do you have any idea what happened to the dead woman?' I asked him.

'Two men came to the house. I can't remember much about them except one was older with a foreign accent, and he was the one in charge. They said they'd take care of it. I promised not to say a word to anyone so I was allowed to go.'

'And I don't suppose you remember the girl's name?'

He didn't.

It depressed me how little worth this poor woman had had for Ugo Amelu, Hugh Manning, or any of the people who'd used her in her short life. I was fairly certain even a low-life like Manning would avoid prison, as long as what he had to say was good. It was also a pity there was no body. It meant the case against Alastair Sheridan was shaky to say the least.

I looked in the rear-view mirror and saw there was no one behind us. 'The phone you just used to call your friend. Throw it out of the window now. I don't want it being tracked.'

He did as he was told and, remembering that my own phone had just vibrated, I pulled it out of my pocket. There was a message from Tina. As I drove I read it, feeling a mounting sense of concern. The message said she was trapped in the basement at Anthea Delbarto's house and that Delbarto knew she was in there.

'Shit,' I said out loud.

Manning shot me a concerned look. 'What is it?'

I texted back to let Tina know we were on our way.

'A slight change of plan,' I told him.

Sixty-one

Tina waited in the darkness, close to the top of the steps, thinking about her next move. There was no way out of the basement other than the door, and the bolt meant that no amount of lock-picking skills was going to get through that.

She'd been trapped in here for over twenty minutes now, listening to the silence outside and wondering what Anthea Delbarto, who clearly knew she was down there, intended to do with her. Ray had texted her back to say he was coming but hadn't given her any details of how he planned to extract her, only said that he wasn't far away.

She heard low voices whispering on the other side of the door. A woman she immediately identified as Anthea, and a man. Tina tensed, then slowly descended the steps in the darkness, trying to remember the layout of the place as she hunted for a place to hide.

The Hanged Man

Behind her, Tina heard the bolt being pulled back and quickly hid in a tiny alcove just to the right of the bottom of the stairs, using the end filing cabinet as cover. At the same time she removed her backpack in case she needed to use it as a weapon, and took a small can of pepper spray from her pocket.

The key turned in the lock and the door opened, allowing in a crack of light. Shoes scraped on the concrete, and a second later the light was switched on.

Tina squinted in the sudden brightness, and as her eyes refocused she realized that her hiding place was clearly visible from the bottom half of the steps. Holding her breath and staying as still as possible, she braced herself as the person who'd come inside descended the steps one at a time, until finally he came into view. It was the strange man who'd almost killed her and Charlotte Curtis in a French forest three months earlier. The man from Brian Foxley's forty-year-old photos, the one Ray had called Mr Bone. He was no longer wearing the hat he'd had on that day in France, and his thin, wispy grey hair was caked in sweat. One side of his face was badly swollen, and his right eye was almost closed. Even so, he was holding a pistol with suppressor attached and there was still a careful, spider-like stealth in the way he moved that told Tina he might be hurt but he was nowhere near finished yet.

No more than ten feet separated them, and as he sniffed the air like some kind of animal and turned both himself and the gun slowly in Tina's direction, she shot up from her hiding place and threw the backpack at him.

It hit him in the chest, but because the pack was so light it barely knocked him off balance. However it was enough to make him turn away instinctively, and before he could steady himself and fire, Tina was on him, sending them both flying through the air and crashing on to the floor in front of the altar. Tina landed on top of him and the gun flew out of his hand and clattered across the floor. Without hesitating, she brought up the pepper spray and fired it into his face, moving her head out of the way so she didn't get its effects too.

He choked and struggled but was unable to stop her as she sat up on his arms and punched him repeatedly in his already injured face, opening up a deep cut just beneath his eye.

But then she heard movement behind her and turned to see Anthea Delbarto coming down the steps fast, waving a poker.

'You whore!' shouted Anthea. 'Get off him!'

For a woman in her sixties she was quick on her feet, but Tina was a lot quicker, and she leapt up and turned to meet Anthea as she reached the bottom of the steps and lunged at her. Tina stepped aside and dodged her, grabbing Anthea's wrist and twisting, before taking a step forward and driving the flat of her palm into her nose.

Anthea cried out in pain, threw her hands up to her face, and dropped the poker as blood poured out of her nose. The palm to the nose was always a brutal blow, causing an almost intolerable burst of pain that put most people out of action temporarily. However, just to be sure, Tina drove an elbow into the side of her head, knocking her backwards into the steps, then turned round in time to see the man who'd shot Charlotte crawling along the floor towards his gun, his arm already outstretched.

Tina took two rapid steps and kicked him in the head, the force of the kick shunting him along the floor and temporarily out of reach of the gun. She immediately stepped over him and grabbed it.

'Move and I'll kill both of you,' she said, pointing the gun from one to the other.

Anthea was still holding her face as the blood from her nose dripped down her chin, but the man, although injured and still suffering from the effects of the spray, was glaring at her malevolently through the one bloodshot eye that was still open, and Tina found herself grudgingly admiring his resilience.

'I owe you for France,' she told him, 'so feel free to give me an excuse to kill you.'

He gave no reaction at all but his eye followed her, like a predator's, as she walked round him carefully, giving him as wide a berth as possible. Tina was fully prepared to shoot him if she had to. She'd long ago ceased to be squeamish about killing.

She grabbed her backpack and hurried up the steps, watching both of them the whole way, before shutting out the light and letting herself out, feeling a burst of relief as she emerged into the coolness of the hall. She locked the door and threw the bolt across, trapping them inside, and pulled out her phone to call Ray and let him know she was OK.

Then she heard a movement behind her.

Tina turned round just as something slammed hard into her face, sending her reeling.

Sixty-two

Dazed, and with her face stinging ferociously, Tina rubbed her eyes and rolled over on to her back, keeping her knees up in a defensive posture as she tried to identify this new threat.

The young woman she'd seen talking with Anthea at dinner – Katy, Anthea had called her – was standing above her holding a frying pan in one hand and the pistol in the other. Worryingly, her hands weren't shaking as she glared down at Tina.

'Stay where you are,' she said in a small but determined voice.

'These people, Mrs Delbarto and that man, they mean you harm,' said Tina, sitting up.

'No they don't. You're the one who's trespassing.'

She unlocked the door and pulled the bolt back, still keeping the gun trained on Tina.

Tina considered jumping up and trying to wrestle the gun from her but dismissed the idea as too risky. This young woman had already shown she was perfectly capable of violence, and the gun could easily go off accidentally before Tina got to it, so she continued down the persuasion route.

'Listen to me, Katy. The man who's just arrived here is a murderer. That's why he brought a pistol with him. There's no innocent explanation for that.'

'How do you know my name?' she asked, keeping her grip on the door handle but not opening it.

'I'm a private detective. My name's Tina Boyd. I'm investigating Mrs Delbarto's part in the Bone Field murders.'

'What are you talking about?'

'Don't you remember the police coming to see Mrs Delbarto yesterday? They're investigating the murder of a girl who stayed here twelve years ago, and whose remains have been found in the Bone Field. Her name was Tracey Burn. Mrs Delbarto set her up.'

Katy's expression became confused. It was clear she now had doubts. She looked down at the gun, with its long, cigar-shaped suppressor, like something out of a movie, and Tina pressed her advantage.

'You're in great danger here, Katy. You're being groomed. Have you ever seen what's in the basement? That should give you a real clue about the kind of woman Anthea Delbarto is.'

There was a noise from inside the cellar and the door was pushed open. Anthea appeared, her face covered in blood. 'Help me, Katy,' she said, staggering out into the hall. 'This woman is trying to kill me.'

Katy immediately looked concerned. 'God, are you OK, Anthea? What's she done?' She turned and glared at Tina, her grip tightening on the gun.

At the same time, the old man known as Mr Bone appeared in the doorway and stepped out into the hall. Katy instinctively moved away from him, still keeping the gun pointed in Tina's general direction.

'It's OK, honey,' said Anthea. 'This man is my friend. He's a police officer. Please give him the gun.'

'He's not a police officer,' said Tina. 'He's too old for a start, and police officers don't carry guns like that.'

'This woman is a liar and a thief,' continued Anthea. 'She broke in here tonight. Please, Katy. Give him the gun.'

'Look in the basement, Katy,' said Tina, knowing she was arguing for her life here.

Mr Bone smiled at Katy, and took a step towards her. 'Please. May I have it? That thing is dangerous in your hands. It may go off and hurt someone.' His voice was strangely soothing, and even though his face was beaten and bloodied, it seemed to have lost its predatory air. Now he looked like a harmless old man. Even his smile seemed genuine.

Tina tensed, and pushed her palms against the floor for leverage, knowing this was going to be her last chance to fight.

But Anthea saw what she was doing. 'Watch it, she's going to try to go for the gun.'

This seemed to tip things for Katy who placed the gun in Mr Bone's hand.

Quick as a flash, the smiling-old-man act was gone.

'Thank you, my dear,' he said to Katy, his bloodshot eye gleaming with malice as he shot her once in the side of the head.

For a long second Katy simply stood where she was. A thin line of blood ran down her temple and on to her cheek like a thick tear, then she crumpled silently to the floor.

'Grab a towel and wrap it round her head to stop the bleeding,' Bone told Anthea as he pointed the gun at Tina. 'Who else knows you're here?' he asked.

Tina swallowed hard. Katy lay at her feet, her eyes closed now, blood dripping from her head wound on to the marble floor. Just one shot and Tina too would be gone, and all her dreams of love, children and domestic bliss would die along with her. She wondered how close Ray was, but however close it was, it was never going to be enough.

'Ray Mason knows,' she said, hoping this information might keep her alive a few minutes longer.

'I thought he might. I saw him earlier.' A thin smile crossed his lips. 'I have unfinished business with him, just as I have unfinished business with you. Give me your phone.'

Slowly, Tina reached into her pocket, unable to take her eyes off Katy as Anthea crouched down and wrapped a white towel round her head.

'What a terrible waste,' said Anthea as she stood back up. 'And we're going to get a lot of questions about this.'

'We'll get rid of the body as we always do,' said Bone. He gestured to Tina. 'Throw the phone to my feet.'

She leaned forward and threw the phone across to him.

Watching her carefully, he picked it up. 'What's the pass code?'

She had no choice. Every delay kept her alive a little bit longer. She told him.

He scanned the phone and smiled. 'It seems the white knight is on his way here to rescue his damsel. We must prepare. Would you bring me one of the sacrificial knives from the basement, Anthea? Pick the biggest. It's time to clip this one's wings while her boyfriend listens in.'

'With pleasure,' said Anthea, stepping away from Katy's corpse. As she came close to Tina, she spat in her face.

The key method of surviving life-or-death situations is the ability to grab your chances with the minimum of delay when they present themselves, however small they might appear. Tina had survived a number of life-or-death situations and she knew this lesson all too well. When Anthea leaned down to spit on her, she came just a little bit too close, and Tina grabbed her leg and pulled as hard as she could. The movement sent Anthea completely off balance and she fell backwards into Bone. The two of them stumbled together, and Bone went down on one knee.

This time, rather than try to disarm him, Tina scrambled to her feet and bolted down the hall towards the back of the house. A shot rang out with a loud pop and she heard something ricochet off the wall in front of her, but she kept going into a large, beautifully appointed lounge with a pair of glass doors leading out on to the terrace where earlier Anthea and Katy had been eating dinner.

Tina ran over to the doors and tried to fling them open. They were locked. She looked down. There was no key in them either. She took a step back and kicked as hard as she could. The doors rattled but held.

She took three steps back this time. She could hear footsteps coming down the hallway fast and the sound of heavy breathing. Bone was coming for her. And then he was in the doorway, crouching down to aim the gun at her, holding it in both hands, his open eye alive with rage.

Tina charged the doors, shoulder first, diving into them with all the force she could muster. This time they burst open, and she crashed through them, hitting the ground hard. She rolled over, leaped to her feet, and vaulted a small adjoining wall before taking off along the grass, moving so fast that she tripped in the darkness and fell forward into the grass. In the henhouse in front of her the chickens started clucking ferociously.

Panting, she took a look over her shoulder, and her heart plummeted. Coming across the garden towards her like some demon out of a nightmare who can't be shaken off came Bone, his battered face deathly pale in the light of the moon.

It was over.

Sixty-three

I was moving towards Anthea Delbarto's front gate carrying a portable stepladder I'd spotted in the bushes (and which I assumed belonged to Tina) when I heard the sound of doors crashing open.

Ignoring Manning's protestations, I'd driven there as fast as I could and parked the car down a lane about a hundred metres away, telling him to stay put and not move. Again he'd protested so I'd taken the keys with me just in case. My plan had been to sneak into the house, threaten anyone I came across with my empty pistol, and free Tina from the basement under the stairs.

That plan had lasted right up until the moment I saw the black SUV with the shattered window parked in the driveway, which was when I knew that Mr Bone was here, and that Tina was either dead or in great danger.

The sound of the crashing doors told me it was the latter and, propelled by a new sense of urgency, I climbed the stepladder, got a foot between two of the spikes topping the gate, grabbed hold of two other spikes with my hands and launched myself over, somehow managing to land on my feet as Tina came running into view round the side of the house. I pulled out my empty gun and ran towards her, the gravel beneath my feet turning to grass as I ate up the ground. She hadn't seen me, and just as I was about to yell out, she fell, turning back towards the house as she did so, her face a mask of fear.

Almost immediately Mr Bone appeared, marching towards her, gun outstretched. He looked dishevelled, and he wasn't entirely steady on his feet, but none of that mattered because in a few seconds he'd be close enough to Tina that he couldn't miss.

Crucially he hadn't seen me, and I kept running towards him.

He lifted the gun for a headshot, then stopped, sensing my presence.

Five yards separated us. I stopped running and pointed my empty gun at his chest. 'Drop the weapon or I'll kill you,' I told him, keeping my hands steady, surprised at the confidence in my own voice.

He kept the gun trained on Tina but looked at me with something close to amusement. 'I have nothing to live for,' he said. 'But you do. You care for her. I can see that. So why don't *you* drop the gun if you want her to live?'

I didn't move. 'You know I'll kill you.'

'Then why don't you?'

'I want answers first.'

'You won't get any. I have no desire to talk to you. Now drop the gun or I kill her.'

'Shoot him, Ray,' said Tina, and I was proud of the strength in her voice. But I doubted she'd have felt so confident if she'd known that my gun wasn't loaded. It was taking all my self-control to keep up the act and not let fear get the better of me.

'Last chance,' said Mr Bone. 'Put down the gun or I kill her.'

'Don't put down the gun, Ray. He'll kill us both.'

She was right. He would. But still I didn't move.

We stared at each other, each waiting for the other to break.

It was Tina who moved first. As Bone concentrated his gaze on me, she rolled round, leaped to her feet and sprinted into the darkness.

Bone turned round, followed her with his eyes and pulled the trigger just as I jumped into him, driving my head into his with such force that the gun flew out of his hand as he went straight down.

I stayed on my feet and grabbed the gun, turning it on Bone, who lay dazed on the ground, before looking round for Tina.

She was lying on the ground, and I felt a leaden sense of terror at the prospect that she'd been killed. But then, slowly, she got to her feet and came over to me.

'I'm OK,' she said. 'Don't worry.'

I wanted to take her in my arms and kiss her but knew I couldn't.

'It's not a time for celebration yet,' Tina said, as if she could read my thoughts. 'Katy's dead and Anthea Delbarto's still inside. And he's still alive.' She pointed towards where Mr Bone was lying on his back, his head rolling from side to side. He was in a bad way but still conscious. 'I'll guard the front in case Anthea tries to get out that way.'

The Hanged Man

Before I could say anything, Tina walked away towards the front of the house. I knew she was doing this to leave me alone with Mr Bone. She knew what was going to happen. So did I.

I ejected the magazine on his pistol and checked the number of rounds. There were four. I reloaded it and walked over, pointing the gun down at him.

He looked back at me with a defiant expression. 'I told you, I'm not giving you any answers.'

'I know,' I said. 'I'll find them while you're rotting in hell. This is for my friend. For Dan.'

For just a moment, the defiance left his eyes and I saw fear. Fear of the abyss he was staring into. The same fear that I had no doubt had been in the eyes of so many of his victims, including Dana Brennan. I thought of the picture in my wallet of the young, smiling girl who'd had her whole life ahead of her. But I was no longer angry. Instead I felt a real sense of inner peace, a sure knowledge that I was doing the right thing, as I shot him once between the eyes and watched him die.

The night was warm and silent as I walked towards the back of the house. In the last hour I'd broken a dozen laws, and now I'd killed in cold blood. I should have stopped then. Left this place with Tina, headed home, and trusted that somehow no one would link me to the trail of bloodshed I was leaving behind.

But I didn't. It was almost as if I'd reverted to the frightened little boy who'd watched his whole family die, except this time I was fighting back. Because one way or another, these people – Mr Bone, Anthea Delbarto, even Cem Kalaman and the

Sheridans – were all responsible for the loss I'd suffered all those years ago, and which I'd never managed to get over.

The doors to the living room were still wide open as I approached them across the terrace where yesterday Dan and I had sat interviewing the lady of the house as she pretended to help us.

I went in carefully, keeping a firm grip on the pistol as I looked around, conscious that she might attempt to ambush me.

The living room was empty, but as I walked into the hall I saw Anthea Delbarto standing near the body of a woman in a short summer dress with a blood-drenched towel wrapped round her head. She had a bloodied face and a phone in her hand, and she was watching me with a confidence that instantly put me on the defensive.

'I've called the police,' she told me. 'They'll be here very soon. If I were you, I would leave now while you still can.'

'That's fine,' I said, calling her bluff. 'We'll wait together. You've got some big questions to answer.'

'I don't think so,' she said. 'You came here and shot the man outside – a man I don't know. I even managed to film it on here' – she waved the phone in her hand at me – 'and, before you take the phone, it's already uploaded to the internet. You also killed Katy, a young woman who'd been living with me. In fact, your prints are all over the murder weapon. I've done absolutely nothing wrong.'

I pointed the gun at her, trying to keep the sense of defeat off my face because she'd caught me out, and she knew it. I heard movement and turned to see Tina come into the hall behind me. I saw she was bleeding from a head wound, and I felt a real urge to hold her.

'Do you think I've survived this long by being a fool, Mr Mason? The police won't believe a word of your story, or Miss Boyd's. You came here making false accusations. You then committed two murders, one on film. I'm innocent. You're the guilty one. You always have been. But you can explain all that to the police when they arrive. The operator told me they'll be here in a few minutes. They're sending armed units from Salisbury and they would be scrambling a helicopter except they've been rather busy at a nature reserve south of here. Perhaps you can explain to them what you were doing there as well.'

I didn't say anything for a moment as I tried to work out how I could salvage this situation. It didn't take me long to realize I couldn't. I was finished. It was as simple as that.

So I made a decision. 'Tina,' I said, without looking over my shoulder, 'Hugh Manning is parked in my car a hundred metres to the left of the bottom of the front drive. Take him back to your car then deliver him to whichever police officer you trust the most. No one will ever know you were here, I promise you that. Go now.'

'What the hell are you going to do, Ray?'

'Yes, what are you going to do, Ray?' said Anthea in a mocking voice. 'Of course Miss Boyd was here tonight. She broke in. Her DNA is all over the house.'

'Just go, Tina, and trust me on this.' I couldn't look at her. 'Do it. And don't say a word about tonight to anyone.'

Her voice faltered. 'I'm not going without you, Ray.'

'You are,' I said, my voice colder than I was expecting. 'Go. You need to get Manning into custody.'

'Don't do this.'

It sounded like she was going to cry, and I felt a wave of emotion that almost knocked me down.

But then I steadied myself. 'It's too late. It's done.'

Still she didn't move.

I stared into Anthea Delbarto's eyes. 'Tell me something,' I said. 'You were there, weren't you, when Dana Brennan was taken?'

She smiled. 'You'll never know, will you?'

'And my father. You knew him too?'

'Oh yes. For many years. We were lovers. It might even have been me who suggested he'd be better off without a wife and brats hanging round his neck . . . but again, you'll never know.' Her face hardened. 'But right now, you are wasting your last chance of escape. You have a head start. I hear you're a rich man. I'm sure you can outrun your colleagues and find yourself and your lover somewhere safe to hide.'

I raised the gun. 'I made a promise to Dana Brennan's parents that I'd bring her killers to justice, and that's what I intend to do.'

'Don't do it, Ray,' said Tina. 'Don't kill her. It's not worth it.'

'This is for them. And this is for Dana.'

I shot her in the belly.

Anthea went down on her knees, howling in pain, and I turned to Tina. 'Go, Tina. Now.'

She looked at me, tears filling her eyes, her face battered by defeat. 'We could have made a life,' she said. 'And I wanted to, Ray. I really did. It didn't have to end this way.'

But, of course, it did. Everything in my life eventually crumbled. Those I loved always went away in the end.

The Hanged Man

With a barely suppressed sob, Tina walked away from me down the hall and I felt my heart sink as she disappeared from view.

With a deep sigh, I went over to Anthea Delbarto and lifted her chin up with the pistol's suppressor. This time the fear and panic were coming off her in waves as she realized that, like Mr Bone, she too was staring into the abyss, a place where I hoped all her sins would return to haunt her.

'I'd like you to suffer longer,' I told her, 'but I haven't got the time. This is for my mother and brothers.'

And then I pulled the trigger a final time.

The house was already well ablaze, extinguishing any trace of Tina's DNA, when I heard the police cars pulling into the lane on the other side of the front gates, their arrival announced by the sirens and flashing blue lights.

And it was with a strange sense of relief, as if I no longer had to prove myself, to anyone, that I stood up to meet them.

FIND OUT MORE ABOUT
SIMON AND HIS BOOKS ONLINE AT

www.simonkernick.com

 /SimonKernick

@simonkernick